P9-AFH-945

SHERWOOD ANDERSON:
Short Stories

Other Books by Maxwell Geismar

AMERICAN MODERNS: From Rebellion to Conformity

The Novel in America (a series):

WRITERS IN CRISIS: The American Novel, 1925-1940
(Studies of Ring Lardner, Ernest Hemingway, John Dos Passos, William Faulkner, Thomas Wolfe, John Steinbeck)

THE LAST OF THE PROVINCIALS: The American Novel, 1915-1925
(Studies of H. L. Mencken, Sinclair Lewis, Willa Cather, Sherwood Anderson, F. Scott Fitzgerald)

REBELS AND ANCESTORS: The American Novel, 1890-1915
(Studies of Frank Norris, Stephen Crane, Jack London, Ellen Glasgow, Theodore Dreiser)

SHERWOOD ANDERSON: SHORT STORIES

Edited and with an Introduction by

MAXWELL GEISMAR

American Century Series
HILL AND WANG · NEW YORK

Library of Congress catalogue card number: 62-15213

FIRST AMERICAN CENTURY SERIES EDITION SEPTEMBER 1962

The Editor's thanks are due to Mrs. Sherwood Anderson for her generous permission to use the stories in this volume, including the group of "Last Stories" from *The Sherwood Anderson Reader,* edited by Paul Rosenfeld.

Manufactured in the United States of America by
The Colonial Press, Inc., Clinton, Massachusetts

To Eleanor

CONTENTS

Introduction

I

SOME YEARS AGO I described Sherwood Anderson as a writer who had become an ancestor before he was mature. Like most bright remarks this one also was only half true; and yet the crux of Anderson's career and of the various critical judgments about it still lies in this area.

Winesburg, Ohio—in the memorable year of 1919 of the mod ern American literary revival—was surely Anderson's most notable early work, just as it remains a classic work in the fiction of the period. Before that, he had written *Windy McPherson's Son* (1916), a raw chronicle of our primitive Western town life; and *Marching Men* (1917), a curious labor novel whose hero, filled with loathing of his fellow workers, established a type of early American fascism. (In those days Anderson was perhaps influenced by Jack London's native Nietzscheism; London was to be consumed and destroyed by it, while Anderson overcame it.) And before *that,* indeed, Anderson had made his celebrated gesture at once of renunciation and self-fulfillment. He had simply walked out of his paint factory one day; he had left his wife and family, his whole respectable middle-class life, in order to become a writer.

Well, he always called himself a "scribbler" rather than a writer, and certainly not an "artist." He was among the last of those gifted and talented "amateurs" who represented the artistic life of the older American republic; or who, at best, thought of themselves as writing men before the age of specialization or the separation of the arts from the common life of the nation—or the Jamesian epoch of inviolate aesthetics. Sherwood Anderson's whole rule of life was expressed in his phrase (and title) "No Swank," and very often indeed, when asked about his profession in strange towns or cities, he called himself a traveling salesman or whatever else seemed appropriate at the time.

In the Chicago of the 'teens, while writing the early books, he became a kind of itinerant advertising copy writer, determined never again to be chained to that new American transmission line, or conveyor belt, of "fame" or "success," or even of mere wealth and social status. "Make money! Cheat! Lie! . . . Get your name up for a modern high-class American." So Sam McPherson was told; while to be poor in this new age was only to be a fool. But like Theodore Dreiser just before him, Sherwood Anderson chose to be among the fools of life, rather than the fools of material power. Some of his best stories and "sketches"—those delicate, light sketches by our own mid-American Turgenev which convey such a density of human life, feeling and experience—were written about the Chicago years. (In the present volume, for example, there is "The Yellow Gown," as well as "Milk Bottles.") And Anderson's work as a whole constitutes a critique in depth of the primary values of contemporary American civilization.

But was *Winesburg, Ohio* the radical document of the American small town which it appeared to be when it was published, and which it is generally supposed to be, even today? Certainly it was among those magic titles—*Main Street, This Side of Paradise,* and even *Jurgen*—which had announced, by the year 1920, the advent of a new epoch in our native letters, the second great revival in our literature, a new age of "realism," freedom, emancipation in both our culture and our art. It was America's "Coming-of-Age," as Van Wyck Brooks declared and Henry Mencken declaimed; even though we now realize that the twenties were actually the climax, rather than the beginning, of the Naturalistic-Realistic literary movement which extended as far back as the 1890's, and to such forerunners as William Dean Howells. Yes, *Winesburg* was among these "radical" chronicles of the early twenties, and it was attacked savagely at times for its "sexuality," its low and morbid view of human nature, amounting to a provincial pathology, its depiction of small souls struggling against an overwhelming burden of loneliness, frustration and anxiety.

What had happened to that "smiling, cheerful, happy" view of American life so celebrated in our Victorian annals?

But we presently know, too, that *Winesburg* was a nostalgic document as well as a radical one. It was written in the heat, the dirt, the noise of that raw and violent Chicago tenement life which

Sherwood Anderson knew and despised. It was also an ode and a eulogy to the passing of our buried provincial life which Anderson knew and cherished. He was to describe this process of social change—the transformation of our nineteenth-century Western towns into the bustling, mechanized and industrialized twentieth-century business cities—in his *Poor White,* a year later; and these early Anderson stories and novels are a kind of prelude and complement to Sinclair Lewis's *Babbitt,* in 1922. Anderson's frankness about the sexual activity of our own Midwestern "deserted village" was simply part of the whole Chicago "Revolt of the Flesh" against New England's Puritanism. Like Dreiser before him, or like Whitman a little earlier, he would not separate the body from the spirit, the passions from the mind, or even the wide range of human perversity from so-called—but where is it?—"normalcy." And to the early Sherwood Anderson, sexuality itself was often, though not always successfully, another means of human contact and communication which might assuage our solitude and loneliness. What is most evident in *Winesburg* today is the encompassing sense of compassion, sympathy, pity for those brooding provincial souls who, like "the twisted apples" which were not worth picking in the town's orchards, still had their hidden sweetness.

II

But had Sherwood Anderson's career really reached its peak with this tender, nostalgic evocation—rather than any exposé—of our Western village life? That is the interpretation of his work in some critical quarters today; that is even the current view of Anderson propounded by critics, I can only say, who have not understood his career at all.

There is, to be sure, a certain kind of curious logic behind the notion that Anderson wrote one great book and then quietly faded away. It makes some sense if you follow his record through the mid-twenties—and ignore the books he wrote in the thirties. It makes sense, perhaps, if you deal only with his novels, which are generally poor, and completely ignore the fact that he was a natural-born short-story writer, completely as original in this genre as he was unsuited for the novel form. Anderson's later tales are *different* from the *Winesburg* tales and the other early volumes, but no less good—perhaps even better. More than half of the stories in the present collection are from Sherwood Anderson's later period, after 1933, the period when, according to our fashionable critics, he had presumably ceased to exist as a literary figure. Isn't it curious that an officially "dismissed"—or shall we say "excluded"—writer should still continue with those later and last stories, some of which, to my mind, are simply marvelous?

No, Mr. Lionel Trilling's commiserative essay on Sherwood Anderson's presumed literary extinction after *Winesburg,* and Mr. Irving Howe's book on the same theme, are, in Mark Twain's phrase, grossly exaggerated. The rumor was premature; it was also not true. But what is the actual record on the case? It is a fact that for a little while Sherwood Anderson was caught up by the New Freedom and the New Sophistication of the post-World War I artistic scene. *Many Marriages,* in 1923, originally written as a short piece for *Dial* magazine, was a poor if not ludicrous novel on this theme, in which a respectable American businessman (mainly nude throughout the narrative) tries endlessly to explain to his wife and daughter why he is deserting them for the sake of Self-Expression. *Dark Laughter,* in 1925, still perhaps the most famous of Anderson's popular novels, is another quite lurid chronicle of the free, Bohemian life of the twenties in which the romantic picture of the Negro is contrasted with the white man's troubled existence. But the real point of the novel—which has often been missed—was that Anderson was already renouncing that "Life of Realization" whose figurehead he had become. Self-fulfillment, self-expression, even for an artist, and particularly for this artist, were not enough.

From the very start of his career, in fact, Sherwood Anderson belonged to that older order of communal artists who *cared,* in the deepest, best way, about their own country and their society—and hence were often most deeply critical about it. This was indeed the central American tradition of writers, from Emerson, Hawthorne and Melville to Howells himself, or to the late and "dark Whitman" who witnessed, with despair, that great sea-change of the old American democracy into the new industrial-financial American empire. Anderson belonged squarely in this tradition (as did Dreiser, Ellen Glasgow, and even Henry Mencken); while Ernest Hemingway's burlesque of *Dark Laughter* signified not only a personal break between the two authors, but the break between the two generations. The post-World War I American writers belonged to the "modern world" of either international or expatriated artists, as you like; but their lack of *place* or of communal ties, or of native belief and roots, was to show up clearly in their later careers, or lack of careers. William Faulkner was to endure and survive better as an artist, perhaps, just because he clung to Mississippi, with all its faults; and even though Mississippi, unfortunately, clung to *him.*

But *Dark Laughter* was easy to parody; and Anderson's later novels *Beyond Desire* (1932) and *Kit Brandon* (1936) were hardly much better. He was simply no good in this form. And, moreover, wasn't he trying, in these popular fictions, to get back a little of that "swank," or that splash of money and success, which elsewhere he had repudiated and would repudiate? He was frank to admit (as in the biographical sketch called "A Part of Earth") that he loved all the things that money could bring. Only he could not bear the process—the loss of self, the hardening of the soul, the trickery of the spirit, the actual series of "little deaths," as in "Brother Death"—of making money for its own sake. Throughout the 1920's, too, there was that curious series of Sherwood Anderson's memoirs, notebooks, reminiscences, including *A Story Teller's Story* (1924) and *Tar, a Midwest Childhood* (1926), where he was in reality wrestling with his own spirit, trying to find out who he was, or what was his real relationship with his own family—his father in particular—or the Midwestern towns of his youth which he had both hated and loved.

His earlier heroes had had patricidal fantasies about their ne'er-do-good fathers, jolly, careless, improvident. Sherwood's own childhood was poverty-stricken, almost homeless. The silent, suffering, overburdened mother is a central figure in all of Anderson's reminiscences and memoirs of his youth. And wasn't the mature artist himself, who had also renounced his own family and children, his business, his respectable place in society—wasn't Anderson himself now repeating the same shiftless role, perhaps, as that father-figure whom he had hated and despised in his youth? In all these respects the decade of the 1920's was a difficult, a tormented period in Sherwood Anderson's career, but it was certainly not the ending of it.

It was in fact a period of intense self-searching, of self-discovery and revaluation. *Hello Towns!* (1929) marked, indeed it celebrated, the beginning of a new and later phase in Sherwood Anderson's career, which was also his most mature phase, and which included some of the best things he ever wrote.

In the curious cycles of renunciation and affirmation which

marked this career—the series of worldly renunciations which led to ever greater affirmations of life itself—Anderson had decided to abandon even the urban or cosmopolitan society of art, fame and "culture" itself: the "enfabled rock" of Thomas Wolfe's later and very similar provincial pilgrimage. He had decided to return to the small-town life whose native chronicler he had always been. "Stay small," Anderson had advised himself at the peak of his literary glory after *Winesburg*; and now he was returning also to those small country souls and small country lives he knew and understood so well. "All right, I will be a country man." This time, however, it was to be in Marion, Smyth County, Virginia, where Anderson owned and ran two newspapers (one Democratic, one Republican). As a collection of Anderson's editorials, ranging from Van Gogh to the Negro question, *Hello Towns!* is a special kind of documentary, both touching and entertaining, on our rural existence. No wonder that Sherwood Anderson was outraged, toward the close of the volume, at the suggestion that he should sell his newspapers. What an idea! "It was a good deal like asking, 'Will you sell your wife?' " For: "I have a place in this community . . . I have got an occupation here, something to do." His long circling search to discover his own identity as an American writer, his own origins and his own "place"—that search which has been so misconstrued as Anderson's "decline"—had come to an end. He knew who he was. He knew where he stood. (And without this basic self-knowledge, no artist can ever understand anything else.) Always refusing to know the "answers" (the quick answers, the smart answers, the fashionable answers), Sherwood Anderson knew enough. He knew plenty—about himself, his country, and his craft.

III

Of course, as in "The Dumb Man" in his first volume of tales, *The Triumph of the Egg,* as early as 1923, Anderson, like Dreiser, had deliberately chosen the role of the puzzled and baffled spectator standing in awe before all the mysteries of life. That was the typical role of the whole new generation of native realists who had come of age in the 1900's and the 'teens and who opened up the road for that "sophistication" which marked the literature of the twenties.

This literary role of the questioning observer with no fixed answers was, moreover, not only typical of our native Naturalists (and philosophical and psychological Pragmatists like William James) standing on the threshold of twentieth-century science, with all the established values of religion, morality, society crumbling before their eyes. Wasn't it also the appropriate literary stance for a country and a culture which, as in America's case, had certainly come of age materially and physically and was apparently faced, during these years, with the question of its moral and spiritual destiny?

In actual fact, as we now know, the decision of America as a national culture had already been made in the post–Civil War epoch of material aggrandisement and moral corruption. Among other writers, both Whitman and Howells gave eloquent testimony as to the nature of the change in our society. (The other wing of our literature, the expatriated Henry James and Edith Wharton, recognized this social development too, but hardly cared to understand it with any depth of personal involvement or concern.) But the literary generation of Anderson and Dreiser, including also Jack London and Frank Norris, was the first group of native writers to face the *consequences* of the new American empire (the U.S.A.) in the twentieth century—and still with the faith, or the illusion, that the literary conscience of the country might yet prevail over its social and economic forces.

Both of Anderson's early volumes of short stories are filled with this brooding concern as to our national life and its human products. After Winesburg, what? There are so many tales of these humble or ignorant country souls, workers, artisans, drifting or rebellious girls, who have come out of the small towns to Chicago in order to have a "career," to make a "new life"—and have found only a degraded kind of urban existence, a kind of living death. There is the murder story which fills the Chicago newspapers in "Brothers." The foreman in the bicycle factory (how quaint, even nostalgic, these early factories of Anderson's work may appear today; but the cultural impact was profound) kills his pregnant wife simply because "there was no light" in the entrance to his apartment building. The janitor had neglected to light the gas, as he says in his defense; but the story tells the real reason.

In "Milk Bottles," there is the copy writer who has written a glowing account of "the mythical Chicago" in his condensed-milk advertisement. And the voice of the burlesque actress crying: "Oh, hell! We live such damned lives, we do, and we work in such a town! A dog is better off! . . . I won't stand it! I got to smash everything!" All the milk was sour to Sherwood Anderson in the Chicago scene of those years. Wasn't the central theme of *The Triumph of the Egg* contained in the lugubrious chant of the story called "Senility"? "Have you any coughs, colds, consumption, or bleeding sickness?" The American nation itself had come down with such ailments, so Anderson believed in the early twenties. One of his literary heroines declares that "there was something essentially dirty about life"—a most un-Winesburgish and un-Andersonian comment.

In perhaps the most famous of these tales, "The Egg," we notice that even Anderson's rural hero has become infected by the American passion for "getting up in the world." Thus he cherishes "all the monstrous things" which are born on the farm in hopes that he will make his fortune by producing a five-legged hen or a two-headed rooster. The source of life itself has become deformed here; or rather, the society which advocates "success" as the primary human value will come to cherish—and to exploit—even biological deformity. This was the real message of the artist who had been so mistakenly labeled as, among other things, "the phallic Chekhov," and who always, in his agrarian stories, had sympathy for the whole range of ordinary human aberrations. "He is my brother," says Anderson's old man about the Chicago murderer; just as Whitman had linked himself with all the criminals, the sinners, and the outcasts of the New World. But even by the time of *Horses and Men,* Anderson's second volume of tales in 1923, the stories of urban life were less communal and more desperate.

Could the "last of the townsmen"—as I've called Sherwood Anderson elsewhere*—even identify himself with the typical products of modern and urban society? Were these people worth saving? "Millions of us live on the vast Chicago West Side," says the protagonist of "A Chicago Hamlet," "where all streets are equally ugly and the streets go on and on forever, out of nowhere into nothing." Now this was to become a familiar lament across the board of American literature in the 1920's, from Ring Lardner's Long Island society—where on Saturday night everybody gets dressed up "like something was going to happen. But it don't"—to

* That is, in *The Last of the Provincials* (Houghton Mifflin, 1947; Hill & Wang paperback edition, 1959). I have drawn upon my Sherwood Anderson essay in that book for some detail in the present introduction to Anderson's short stories.

Hemingway's celebrated Spanish "Nada." And it is in this context of Anderson's increasing doubts and anxiety about American society itself, that his best earlier tales of youth and adolescence take on an extra dimension.

"I Want to Know Why." "I'm a Fool." "The Man Who Became a Woman." "The Sad Horn Blowers." These are the famous tales in this vein of Anderson's talent, and they are still fine stories to reread today. In these sad and ironical masculine comings-of-age, silly, funny, and touching, there is also the nostalgic and haunting note of a disappearing mid-American agrarian culture—our backwoods life. With one exception, these are stories of "horses and men," or maybe "horses *versus* men." (It is entertaining, and illuminating, to compare these stories with J. D. Salinger's modern chronicles of middle-class and neurotic prep-school "rebels"—rebels without a cause, or a base, or a future, who are really refugees from Madison Avenue.) In what is probably the best of these tales of rural adolescents, "The Man Who Became a Woman," the underlying theme becomes explicit. Horses and horse racing (before the day of the syndicates and the mobs) were still to Anderson the symbol of the pagan and plenary state, the natural life which industrialization, science and finance capitalism had all conspired to deform or destroy.

Perhaps it was even then a kind of pagan *underworld*. These youthful heroes will have no truck with a more respectable kind of job, a career, success, or even education. Anderson's early and late love of the Negro race, romantic as it may have been, derived from this same source; just as later he would turn to "perhaps women" as another possible salvation in the machine age. "Sometimes, these late years," says the hero—or the victim?—of "The Man Who Became a Woman"

> I've thought maybe Negroes would understand what I'm trying to talk about now better than any white man ever will. I mean something about men and animals, something between them, something that can perhaps only happen to a white man when he has slipped off his base a little, as I suppose I had then. I think maybe a lot of horsey people feel it sometimes though. It's something like this maybe—do you suppose it could be that something we whites have got, and think such a lot of, and are so proud of, isn't much of any good after all?

This was the early Andersonian version of the "primitive virtue" which the later Hemingway could find only in the green hills of Africa, in the killings of the kudu, or in those tortured and dying Spanish bulls. And these were the native Midwestern prose rhythms, too, which the later writer refined into his famous high style, at the expense, sometimes, of their human content.

But suppose the white man, in America, had slipped off his base for good? In the same story one notices the slaughterhouse, near the race track, which the horses shied away from. "A race horse isn't like a human being. He won't stand for it to have to do his work in any rotten ugly kind of a dump the way a man will, and he won't stand for the smells a man will either." We notice the drab, ugly, poverty-ridden mining town near the race track also (another kind of slaughterhouse for man's primitive virtue). "The sight of it all, even the sight of the kind of hellholes men are satisfied to go on living in, gave me the fantods and shivers right down in my liver, and on that night I guess I had in me a kind of contempt for all men, including myself, that I've never had so thoroughly since. Come right down to it, I suppose, women aren't so much to blame as men. They aren't running the show."

Rather loosely written as it is, a little overplayed, or even a little hammy, "The Man Who Became a Woman" is still one of Sherwood Anderson's notable short stories—a fine tale. No doubt the orthodox Freudians, noticing the dreamlike symbolism set off against both the animal world and the slaughterhouse of civilization, will construe this as a narrative of repressed or unconscious homosexuality. Perhaps it is that, too, with its classic racial nightmare of white impotence and Negro sexuality. Sherwood Anderson might have admitted that. He was never one to deny either the depths or the abysses of the human psyche. But what he was really talking about in "The Man Who Became a Woman" was the impotence—or the deformity, again—of the human spirit itself, or of man's natural life and being, on the twentieth-century American scene.

IV

In such a story as "An Ohio Pagan" (which has had to be omitted from this collection because of its length), just as in the story here called "The Other Woman," it was clear from the start that Sherwood Anderson himself was an Ohio primitive—in a central vein which has, from Hawthorne and Melville right down to Dreiser and Anderson, always paralleled and complemented our well-known Puritanism.

"We will be two human beings. We will not have to be husband and wife," says the fiancée in "The Other Woman"—a noble creature indeed, full of sentiment, while the hero's face is radiant with the memory of the tobacconist's wife, "her faith in her own desires and her courage in seeing things through." The ambiguity in man's soul—in his flesh—is endless. And Anderson's tales in this genre are almost always wonderfully ironic parables of human weakness and conflict. They are true confessions of real life, told in a manner which nobody before or after Anderson has been quite able to duplicate. But what is interesting is that this vein of his work not only persisted and developed in his later stories, grew bolder indeed, became more important and perhaps more ironical, but that it moved away from his early anti-Puritanism, and the "grotesques" of *Winesburg,* into the realm of ordinary human relationships, or what Sherwood called "the general."

Wasn't this really the unifying theme of *Death in the Woods* (1933), Anderson's first collection of stories since his two volumes in the early twenties? In "There She Is—She Is Taking Her Bath," the little hero engages a detective agency twice: first to report on his wife's "infidelity," and the second time *not* to report. Who wants to know the truth about such things? The husband's jealousy, not morbid, just human, is wonderfully described; and here Anderson raised an episode of "domestic drama" to a fine level of tragicomedy. "Like a Queen" is another beauty—the story of an aging and melancholy woman who has nevertheless lived and loved, and through her faith in life and in love has left a mark on every man she has met. Isn't that enough? And wasn't this heroine related to the aristocratic hostess of the New Orleans fancy house ("A Meeting South") where, incidentally we get an illuminating sketch of the early William Faulkner. Again, "These Mountaineers" is a notable, Turgenev-like sketch of feminine pride among the "poor-whites" of the Southern hill country. "Perhaps Women?" Yes, Sherwood Anderson always liked the ladies—cherished, respected and admired them—in a native literature which is marked too often by a misogynic strain.

In this later phase, somewhat reminiscent of Melville's career, Anderson had descended from that earlier peak of "fame" and "art"—all the things that can ruin a writer faster than anything else, and particularly in the U.S.A.—and was back again in that provincial obscurity, those "small lives," whose special chronicler he was. "What is called a great man may just be an illusion in people's minds. Who wants to be an illusion?" This statement was in "Another Wife," which was another ironic tale of mature love; and Sherwood Anderson had chosen life, with all its materiality, all its mysteries of the commonplace, all its grace to the very end, rather than the sterile illusions of wealth, power or social status. Yes; or even the illusions of reason and the mind in human affairs; or of human control over human destiny, as established by man's vaunted intellectual power. The academic hero of "The Flood" has been searching all his life for a "theory of values" which will explain everything—until he is overcome by the feminine wiles of his dead wife's sister. And he too accepts life, because everything appears to come without reason or balance, but only in causeless surges or floods. "I was in the flood. . . . What was the use? There is no balance. . . . There are only floods, one flood following another."

This note of ironical surrender to life pervades *Death in the Woods*. With the exception of the title tale, which must be ranked among Anderson's best things, perhaps none of the other stories are as notable, in themselves, as the celebrated earlier short stories. Yet the quality of this volume as a whole is remarkable. It is a pleasure to read; and one almost has the temptation to include *all* the stories in any collection such as this one. How fortunate this writer was, in his maturity and late maturity even, still to be able to receive those "floods" of emotion, of experience, of passion and yearning, of delight and tragedy, in the average course of his existence. Sherwood Anderson was still guilty at times of sentimentality in these later stories too; but isn't it the "illusion" of life itself which makes these tales so entertaining, so touching, so wise? You may suddenly find the tears in your eyes, while reading some of them, even though you have just been laughing at them. There is something buried in these stories, which no critic can quite describe, which touches something buried in most of us even while we pursue that "cynical game," as Melville declared, which is "hardly worth the poor candle burned out in playing it."

On a quick reading, too, you may miss the skill with which Anderson was able to transmute the events of ordinary life into enduring fiction. The prose texture of the later stories is harder and flatter perhaps than that of the *Winesburg* period—also less turgid and loose, or plain verbose, than it was in Anderson's middle period. It appears simple, easy, almost conversational, and "artlessly" translucent—a beautiful style at its best, not quite appreciated by the formalist critics or the admirers of that Henry Jamesian orotund, voluminous complexity of sentence structure. Don't be deceived, also, by the apparent "formlessness" of the later stories; the sudden, shifting associations of thought and feeling which come, apparently at the writer's whim, and actually by the most meticulous use of detail. At its best the "unplotted" story by Sherwood Anderson is just as carefully planned to put across its "unplot" as is the best-plotted plot-story itself. These stories, these "sketches," just *seem* to be more casual, more natural, closer to life than to "art"—which was the whole burden, the meaning, the purpose, of Sherwood Anderson's art.

And of his own life, as a writer. During the Depression years this chronicler of the machine-change in America, this last exponent of an earlier agrarian individualism which was disappearing under the pressure of a massive new scientific-industrial—standardized—urban social complex, wandered over the American earth, wandered around the American scene again. In a series of excellent documentaries—*Perhaps Women* (1931); *No Swank* (1934), *Puzzled America* (1935)—Anderson has provided us with one of the best running accounts of those turbulent years: a native chronicle of social disaster and social regeneration, for that period at least, which is unique and invaluable.* For who could reach down into, and report on, the typical American life of that period more deftly and more accurately than Sherwood Anderson—than the writer, that is to say, who had spent his own life in the attempt to understand the infinite variety of "the general"? Why, he had done nothing else *but* try to come closer to the typical life of his own people, as Anderson reflected when a Virginia labor leader asked him if he "wanted in" to a union meeting.

> Yes, of course. I want in everywhere. To go in is my aim in life. I want into fashionable hotels and clubs, I want into banks, into people's houses, into labor meetings, into courthouses. . . . That is my business in life—to find out what I can—to go in. I did not say all of this. "Sure," I said.

What Sherwood Anderson always said to situations like this, to all of life, was "Sure."

* *Sherwood Anderson's Memoirs* (1942) was another fine book which belongs to the major tradition of native autobiography along with, say, Dreiser's *A Book About Myself* and Henry James's three volumes of personal reminiscences.

V

His death, in 1941, was consistent with his whole stress on "little things." He had swallowed a toothpick, which perforated the intestines. That is the way things happen to you—by chance and accident more than by purpose or design. You never get your just deserts, for who knows what they are?

But Anderson had left, not a fortune indeed, but a group of "last tales"—either unpublished or published only in magazines—which Paul Rosenfeld included in *The Sherwood Anderson Reader* in 1947, and which are published here for the first time in any collection of Anderson's short stories. Ranging in time from 1934 to 1940, these represent Anderson's final period of work, his most mature talent, just as they are a kind of recapitulation of the various strains in his talent. (I must confess that I have included a few sketches which were not written as fiction, simply because they are quite beautiful *as* fiction.)

Complex, confused, shifting, warm, volatile, ludicrous, these last tales have to the end the particular quality of Sherwood Anderson's literary vision. Perhaps one should simply say that he stood for life, he believed in it, and he conveyed it. Isn't that enough? And isn't it a quality rare enough not only in literature, but in life itself? "The Corn Planting," sometimes considered the best of all Anderson's stories—if not by Messrs. Trilling and Howe, who apparently stopped reading this writer in 1925—is a variation on the theme of "Death in the Woods." In the earlier tale the peasant woman who nourished life, animal and human, all her days continued to serve it after her death. In the later tale, the old farming couple's answer to the senseless extinction of their son is to plant the fields again.

"Nobody Laughed" is a Lardnerian tale, so to speak, of small-town brutality. (Both of these writers, Anderson and Ring Lardner, came out of the Western towns and never got along in the big cities. Their work presents a similar indictment of twentieth-century American society.)

But the doctor-hero in "A Walk in the Moonlight" is one of those men who do laugh, in a different sense, at the whole ironic panorama of existence. "Why?" "Why, because I laugh." Why? Because it is something to look at. What Anderson did to perfection in these last tales was a marvelous quick alternation of mood so that you are always caught halfway, as it were, between laughter and tears at this spectacle of human destiny in which all of us ultimately can be classified as failures, outcasts, victims, dupes of life, and yet some do triumph. On the other side of the coin, "Morning Roll Call" is a Rabelaisian sketch of provincial harlotry. And to the very end, as in "His Chest of Drawers," Sherwood Anderson was still concerned with "the position of small men in a civilization that . . . judged everything by size."

Well, yes, in "Not Sixteen," there is a last touching story of that earlier Midwestern agrarian and adolescent innocence, that bitter-sweet coming-of-age which Anderson himself had commemorated in such early tales as "I Want to Know Why" and "The Sad Horn Blowers." The circle is complete. And, as a Nelson Algren might say—the Algren who became the bitter-sweet poet of just those Chicago slums which Anderson had foreseen to be a typical product of modern civilization—"there you are." And there was Sherwood Anderson.

—MAXWELL GEISMAR.

Harrison, New York
December, 1961.

Stories from

The Triumph of the Egg

(1921)

The Dumb Man

THERE IS a story—I cannot tell it—I have no words.
The story is almost forgotten but sometimes I remember.
The story concerns three men in a house in a street.
If I could say the words I would sing the story.
I would whisper it into the ears of women, of mothers.
I would run through the streets saying it over and over.
My tongue would be torn loose—it would rattle against my teeth.
The three men are in a room in the house.
One is young and dandified.
He continualy laughs.
There is a second man who has a long white beard.
He is consumed with doubt but occasionally his doubt leaves him and he sleeps.
A third man there is who has wicked eyes and who moves nervously about the room rubbing his hands together.
The three men are waiting—waiting.
Upstairs in the house there is a woman standing with her back to a wall, in half darkness by a window.
That is the foundation of my story and everything I will ever know is distilled in it.
I remember that a fourth man came to the house, a white silent man.
Everything was as silent as the sea at night.
His feet on the stone floor of the room where the three men were made no sound.
The man with the wicked eyes became like a boiling liquid—he ran back and forth like a caged animal.
The old gray man was infected by his nervousness—he kept pulling at his beard.
The fourth man, the white one, went upstairs to the woman.
There she was—waiting.

How silent the house was—how loudly all the clocks in the neighborhood ticked.

The woman upstairs craved love. That must have been the story. She hungered for love with her whole being. She wanted to create in love.

When the white silent man came into her presence she sprang forward.

Her lips were parted.

There was a smile on her lips.

The white one said nothing.

In his eyes there was no rebuke, no question.

His eyes were as impersonal as stars.

Downstairs the wicked one whined and ran back and forth like a little lost hungry dog.

The gray one tried to follow him about but presently grew tired and lay down on the floor to sleep.

He never awoke again.

The dandified fellow lay on the floor too.

He laughed and played with his tiny black mustache.

I have no words to tell what happened in my story.

I canot tell the story.

The white silent one may have been Death.

The waiting eager woman may have been Life.

Both the old gray bearded man and the wicked one puzzle me.

I think and think but cannot understand them.

Most of the time however I do not think of them at all.

I keep thinking about the dandified man who laughed all through my story.

If I could understand him I could understand everything.

I could run through the world telling a wonderful story.

I would no longer be dumb.

Why was I not given words?

Why am I dumb?

I have a wonderful story to tell but know no way to tell it.

I Want to Know Why

We got up at four in the morning, that first day in the East. On the evening before, we had climbed off a freight train at the edge of town and with the true instinct of Kentucky boys had found our way across town and to the race track and the stables at once. Then we knew we were all right. Hanley Turner right away found a nigger we knew. It was Bildad Johnson, who in the winter works at Ed Becker's livery barn in our home town, Beckersville. Bildad is a good cook as almost all our niggers are and of course he, like everyone in our part of Kentucky who is anyone at all, likes the horses. In the spring Bildad begins to scratch around. A nigger from our country can flatter and wheedle anyone into letting him do most anything he wants. Bildad wheedles the stable men and the trainers from the horse farms in our country around Lexington. The trainers come into town in the evening to stand around and talk and maybe get into a poker game. Bildad gets in with them. He is always doing little favors and telling about things to eat, chicken browned in a pan, and how is the best way to cook sweet potatoes and corn bread. It makes your mouth water to hear him.

When the racing season comes on and the horses go to the races and there is all the talk on the streets in the evenings about the new colts, and everyone says when they are going over to Lexington or to the spring meeting at Churchill Downs or to Latonia, and the horsemen that have been down to New Orleans or maybe at the winter meeting at Havana in Cuba come home to spend a week before they start out again, at such a time when everything talked about in Beckersville is just horses and nothing else and the outfits start out and horse racing is in every breath of air you breathe, Bildad shows up with a job as cook for some outfit. Often when I think about it, his always going all season to the races and working in the livery barn in the winter where horses are and where men like to come and talk about horses, I wish I was a nigger. It's a foolish thing to say, but that's the way I am about being around horses, just crazy. I can't help it.

Well, I must tell you about what we did and let you in on what I'm talking about. Four of us boys from Beckersville, all whites and sons of men who live in Beckersville regular, made up our minds we were going to the races, not just to Lexington or Louisville, I don't mean, but to the big Eastern track we were always hearing our Beckersville men talk about, to Saratoga. We were all pretty young then. I was just turned fifteen and I was the oldest of the four. It was my scheme. I admit that, and I talked the others into trying it. There was Hanley Turner and Henry Rieback and Tom Tumberton and myself. I had thirty-seven dollars I had earned during the winter working nights and Saturdays in Enoch Myer's grocery. Henry Rieback had eleven dollars and the others, Hanley and Tom, had only a dollar or two each. We fixed it all up and laid low until the Kentucky spring meetings were over and some of our men, the sportiest ones, the ones we envied the most, had cut out. Then we cut out too.

I won't tell you the trouble we had beating our way on freights and all. We went through Cleveland and Buffalo and other cities and saw Niagara Falls. We bought things there, souvenirs and spoons and cards and shells with pictures of the falls on them for our sisters and mothers, but thought we had better not send any of the things home. We didn't want to put the folks on our trail and maybe be nabbed.

We got into Saratoga as I said at night and went to the track. Bildad fed us up. He showed us a place to sleep in hay over a shed and promised to keep still. Niggers are all right about things like that. They won't squeal on you. Often a white man you might meet, when you had run away from home like that, might appear to be all right and give you a quarter or a half dollar or something, and then go right and give you away. White men will do that, but not a nigger. You can trust them. They are squarer with kids. I don't know why.

At the Saratoga meeting that year there were a lot of men from home. Dave Williams and Arthur Mulford and Jerry Myers and others. Then there was a lot from Louisville and Lexington Henry Rieback knew but I didn't. They were professional gamblers and Henry Rieback's father is one too. He is what is called a sheet writer and goes away most of the year to tracks. In the winter when he is home in Beckersville he don't stay there much but goes away to cities and deals faro. He is a nice man and generous, is always sending Henry presents, a bicycle and a gold watch and a boy scout suit of clothes and things like that.

My own father is a lawyer. He's all right, but don't make much money and can't buy me things, and anyway I'm getting so old now I don't expect it. He never said nothing to me against Henry, but Hanley Turner and Tom Tumberton's fathers did. They said to their boys that money so come by is no good and they didn't want their boys brought up to hear gamblers' talk and be thinking about such things and maybe embrace them.

That's all right and I guess the men know what they are talking about, but I don't see what it's got to do with Henry or with horses either. That's what I'm writing this story about. I'm puzzled. I'm getting to be a man and want to think straight and be O. K., and there's something I saw at the race meeting at the Eastern track I can't figure out.

I can't help it, I'm crazy about thoroughbred horses. I've always been that way. When I was ten years old and saw I was growing to be big and couldn't be a rider I was so sorry I nearly died. Harry Hellinfinger in Beckersville, whose father is Postmaster, is grown up and too lazy to work, but likes to stand around in the street and get up jokes on boys like sending them to a hardware store for a gimlet to bore square holes and other jokes like that. He played one on me. He told me that if I would eat a half a cigar I would be stunted and not grow any more and maybe could be a rider. I did it. When father wasn't looking I took a cigar out of his pocket and gagged it down some way. It made me awful sick and the doctor had to be sent for, and then it did no good. I kept right on growing. It was a joke. When I told what I had done and why, most fathers would have whipped me, but mine didn't.

Well, I didn't get stunted and didn't die. It serves Harry Hellinfinger right. Then I made up my mind I would like to be a stable-boy, but had to give that up too. Mostly niggers do that work and I knew father wouldn't let me go into it. No use to ask him.

If you've never been crazy about thoroughbreds, it's because you've never been around where they are much and don't know any better. They're beautiful. There isn't anything so lovely and clean and full of spunk and honest and everything as some race horses. On the big horse farms that are all around our town Beckersville there are tracks, and the horses run in the early morning.

More than a thousand times I've got out of bed before daylight and walked two or three miles to the tracks. Mother wouldn't of let me go, but father always says, "Let him alone." So I got some bread out of the breadbox and some butter and jam, gobbled it and lit out.

At the tracks you sit on the fence with men, whites and niggers, and they chew tobacco and talk, and then the colts are brought out. It's early and the grass is covered with shiny dew and in another field a man is plowing and they are frying things in a shed where the track niggers sleep, and you know how a nigger can giggle and laugh and say things that make you laugh. A white man can't do it and some niggers can't, but a track nigger can every time.

And so the colts are brought out and some are just galloped by stableboys, but almost every morning on a big track owned by a rich man who lives maybe in New York, there are always, nearly every morning, a few colts and some of the old race horses and geldings and mares that are cut loose.

It brings a lump up into my throat when a horse runs. I don't mean all horses, but some. I can pick them nearly every time. It's in my blood like in the blood of race track niggers and trainers. Even when they just go slop-jogging along with a little nigger on their backs, I can tell a winner. If my throat hurts and it's hard for me to swallow, that's him. He'll run like Sam Hill when you let him out. If he don't win every time it'll be a wonder and because they've got him in a pocket behind another or he was pulled or got off bad at the post or something. If I wanted to be a gambler like Henry Rieback's father I could get rich. I know I could and Henry says so too. All I would have to do is to wait till that hurt comes when I see a horse and then bet every cent. That's what I would do if I wanted to be a gambler, but I don't.

When you're at the tracks in the morning—not the race tracks but the training tracks around Beckersville—you don't see a horse, the kind I've been talking about, very often, but it's nice anyway. Any thoroughbred, that is sired right and out of a good mare and trained by a man that knows how, can run. If he couldn't, what would he be there for and not pulling a plow?

Well, out of the stables they come and the boys are on their backs and it's lovely to be there. You hunch down on top of the fence and itch inside you. Over in the sheds the niggers giggle and sing. Bacon is being fried and coffee made. Everything smells lovely. Nothing smells better than coffee and manure and horses and niggers and bacon frying and pipes being smoked out of doors on a morning like that. It just gets you, that's what it does.

But about Saratoga. We was there six days and not a soul from home seen us and everything came off just as we wanted it to, fine weather and horses and races and all. We beat our way home and Bildad gave us a basket with fried chicken and bread and other eatables in, and I had eighteen dollars when we got back to Beckersville. Mother jawed and cried, but Pop didn't say much. I told everything we done, except one thing. I did and saw that alone. That's what I'm writing about. It got me upset. I think about it at night. Here it is.

At Saratoga we laid up nights in the hay in the shed Bildad had showed us and ate with the niggers early and at night when the race people had all gone away. The men from home stayed mostly in the grandstand and betting field and didn't come out around the places where the horses are kept except to the paddocks just before a race when the horses are saddled. At Saratoga they don't have paddocks under an open shed as at Lexington and Churchill Downs and other tracks down in our country, but saddle the horses right out in an open place under trees on a lawn as smooth and nice as Banker Bohon's front yard here in Beckersville. It's lovely. The horses are sweaty and nervous and shine and the men come out and smoke cigars and look at them and the trainers are there and the owners, and your heart thumps so you can hardly breathe.

Then the bugle blows for post and the boys that ride come running out with their silk clothes on and you run to get a place by the fence with the niggers.

I always am wanting to be a trainer or owner, and at the risk of being seen and caught and sent home I went to the paddocks before every race. The other boys didn't, but I did.

We got to Saratoga on a Friday, and on Wednesday the next week the big Mullford Handicap was to be run. Middlestride was in it and Sunstreak. The weather was fine and the track fast. I couldn't sleep the night before.

What had happened was that both these horses are the kind it makes my throat hurt to see. Middlestride is long and looks awkward and is a gelding. He belongs to Joe Thompson, a little owner from home who only has a half dozen horses. The Mullford Handicap is for a mile and Middlestride can't untrack fast. He goes away slow and is always 'way back at the half, then he begins to run and if the race is a mile and a quarter he'll just eat up everything and get there.

Sunstreak is different. He is a stallion and nervous and belongs on the biggest farm we've got in our country, the Van Riddle place that belongs to Mr. Van Riddle of New York. Sunstreak is like a girl you think about sometimes but never see. He is hard all over and lovely too. When you look at his head you want to kiss him. He is trained by Jerry Tillford who knows me and has been good to me lots of times, lets me walk into a horse's stall to look at him close and other things. There isn't anything as sweet as that horse. He stands at the post quiet and not letting on, but he is just burning up inside. Then when the barrier goes up he is off like his name, Sunstreak. It makes you ache to see him. It hurts you. He just lays down and runs like a bird dog. There can't anything I ever see run like him except Middlestride when he gets untracked and stretches himself.

Gee! I ached to see that race and those two horses run, ached and dreaded it too. I didn't want to see either of our horses beaten. We had never sent a pair like that to the races before. Old men in Beckersville said so and the niggers said so. It was a fact.

Before the race, I went over to the paddocks to see. I looked a last look at Middlestride, who isn't such a much standing in a paddock that way, then I went to see Sunstreak.

It was his day. I knew when I see him. I forgot all about being seen myself and walked right up. All the men from Beckersville were there and no one noticed me except Jerry Tillford. He saw me and something happened. I'll tell you about that.

I was standing looking at that horse and aching. In some way, I can't tell how, I knew just how Sunstreak felt inside. He was quiet and letting the niggers rub his legs and Mr. Van Riddle himself put the saddle on, but he was just a raging torrent inside. He was like the water in the river at Niagara Falls just before its goes plunk down. That horse wasn't thinking about running. He don't have to think about that. He was just thinking about holding himself back till the time for the running came. I knew that. I could just in a way see right inside him. He was going to do some awful running and I knew it. He wasn't bragging or letting on much or prancing or making a fuss, but just waiting. I knew it and Jerry Tillford his trainer knew. I looked up, and then that man and I looked into each other's eyes. Something happened to me. I guess I loved the man as much as I did the horse because he knew what I knew. Seemed to me there wasn't anything in the world but that man and the horse and me. I cried and Jerry Tillford had a shine in his eyes. Then I came away to the fence to wait for the race. The horse was better than me, more steadier and, now I know, better than Jerry. He was the quietest and he had to do the running.

Sunstreak ran first of course and he busted the world's record for a mile. I've seen that if I never see anything more. Everything came out just as I expected. Middlestride got left at the post and was 'way back and closed up to be second, just as I knew he would. He'll get a world's record too some day. They can't skin the Beckersville country on horses.

I watched the race calm because I knew what would happen. I was sure. Hanley Turner and Henry Rieback and Tom Tumberton were all more excited than me.

A funny thing had happened to me. I was thinking about Jerry Tillford the trainer and how happy he was all through the race. I liked him that afternoon even more than I ever liked my own father. I almost forgot the horses thinking that way about him. It was because of what I had seen in his eyes as he stood in the paddocks beside Sunstreak before the race started. I knew he had been watching and working with Sunstreak since the horse was a baby colt, had taught him to run and be patient and when to let himself out and not to quit, never. I knew that for him it was like a mother seeing her child do something brave or wonderful. It was the first time I ever felt for a man like that.

After the race that night I cut out from Tom and Hanley and Henry. I wanted to be by myself and I wanted to be near Jerry Tillford if I could work it. Here is what happened.

The track in Saratoga is near the edge of town. It is all polished up and trees around, the evergreen kind, and grass and everything painted and nice. If you go past the track you get to a hard road made of asphalt for automobiles, and if you go along this for a few miles there is a road turns off to a little rummy-looking farmhouse set in a yard.

That night after the race I went along that road because I had seen Jerry and some other men go that way in an automobile. I didn't expect to find them. I walked for a ways and then sat down by a fence to think. It was the direction they went in. I wanted to be as near Jerry as I could. I felt close to him. Pretty soon I went up the side road—I don't know why—and came to the rummy farmhouse. I was just lonesome to see Jerry, like wanting to see your father at night when you are a young kid. Just then an automobile came along and turned in. Jerry was in it and Henry Rieback's father, and Arthur Bedford from home, and Dave Williams and two other men I didn't know. They got out of the car and went into the house, all but Henry Rieback's father who quarreled with them and said he wouldn't go. It was only about nine o'clock, but they were all drunk and the rummy-looking farmhouse was a place for bad women to stay in. That's what it was. I crept up along a fence and looked through a window and saw.

It's what give me the fantods. I can't make it out. The women in the house were all ugly mean-looking women, not nice to look at or be near. They were homely too, except one who was tall and looked a little like the gelding Middlestride, but not clean like him, but with a hard ugly mouth. She had red hair. I saw everything plain. I got up by an old rosebush by an open window and looked. The women had on loose dresses and sat around in chairs. The men came in and some sat on the women's laps. The place smelled rotten and there was rotten talk, the kind a kid hears around a livery stable in a town like Beckersville in the winter but don't ever expect to hear talked when there are women around. It was rotten. A nigger wouldn't go into such a place.

I looked at Jerry Tillford. I've told you how I had been feeling about him on account of his knowing what was going on inside of Sunstreak in the minute before he went to the post for the race in which he made a world's record.

Jerry bragged in that bad woman house as I know Sunstreak wouldn't never have bragged. He said that he made that horse, that it was him that won the race and made the record. He lied and bragged like a fool. I never heard such silly talk.

And then, what do you suppose he did! He looked at the woman in there, the one that was lean and hard-mouthed and looked a little like the gelding Middlestride but not clean like him, and his eyes began to shine just as they did when he looked at me and at Sunstreak in the paddocks at the track in the afternoon. I stood there by the window—gee!—but I wished I hadn't gone away from the tracks, but had stayed with the boys and the niggers and the horses. The tall rotten-looking woman was between us just as Sunstreak was in the paddocks in the afternoon.

Then, all of a sudden, I began to hate that man. I wanted to scream and rush in the room and kill him. I never had such a feeling before. I was so mad clean through that I cried and my fists were doubled up so my fingernails cut my hands.

And Jerry's eyes kept shining and he waved back and forth, and then he went and kissed that woman and I crept away and went back to the tracks and to bed and didn't sleep hardly any, and then next day I got the other kids to start home with me and never told them anything I seen.

I been thinking about it ever since. I can't make it out. Spring has come again and I'm nearly sixteen and go to the tracks mornings same as always, and I see Sunstreak and Middlestride and a new colt named Strident I'll bet will lay them all out, but no one thinks so but me and two or three niggers.

But things are different. At the tracks the air don't taste as good or smell as good. It's because a man like Jerry Tillford, who knows what he does, could see a horse like Sunstreak run, and kiss a woman like that the same day. I can't make it out. Darn him, what did he want to do like that for? I keep thinking about it and it spoils looking at horses and smelling things and hearing niggers laugh and everything. Sometimes I'm so mad about it I want to fight someone. It gives me the fantods. What did he do it for? I want to know why.

The Other Woman

"I AM in love with my wife," he said—a superfluous remark, as I had not questioned his attachment to the woman he had married. We walked for ten minutes and then he said it again. I turned to look at him. He began to talk and told me the tale I am now about to set down.

The thing he had on his mind happened during what must have been the most eventful week of his life. He was to be married on Friday afternoon. On Friday of the week before, he got a telegram announcing his appointment to a government position. Something else happened that made him very proud and glad. In secret he was in the habit of writing verses, and during the year before, several of them had been printed in poetry magazines. One of the societies that give prizes for what they think the best poems published during the year put his name at the head of its list. The story of his triumph was printed in the newspapers of his home city and one of them also printed his picture.

As might have been expected, he was excited and in a rather highly strung nervous state all during that week. Almost every evening he went to call on his fiancée, the daughter of a judge. When he got there the house was filled with people, and many letters, telegrams and packages were being received. He stood a little to one side, and men and women kept coming up to speak to him. They congratulated him upon his success in getting the government position and on his achievement as a poet. Everyone seemed to be praising him, and when he went home and to bed he could not sleep. On Wednesday evening he went to the theatre, and it seemed to him that people all over the house recognized him. Everyone nodded and smiled. After the first act, five or six men and two women left their seats to gather about him. A little group was formed. Strangers sitting along the same row of seats stretched their necks and looked. He had never received so much attention before, and now a fever of expectancy took possession of him.

As he explained when he told me of his experience, it was for him an altogether abnormal time. He felt like one floating in air. When he got into bed after seeing so many people and hearing so many words of praise his head whirled round and round. When he closed his eyes a crowd of people invaded his room. It seemed as though the minds of all the people of his city were centered on himself. The most absurd fancies took possession of him. He imagined himself riding in a carriage through the streets of a city. Windows were thrown open and people ran out at the doors of houses. "There he is. That's him," they shouted, and at the words a glad cry arose. The carriage drove into a street blocked with people. A hundred thousand pairs of eyes looked up at him. "There you are! What a fellow you have managed to make of yourself!" the eyes seemed to be saying.

My friend could not explain whether the excitement of the people was due to the fact that he had written a new poem or whether, in his new government position, he had performed some notable act. The apartment where he lived at that time was on a street perched along the top of a cliff far out at the edge of his city, and from his bedroom window he could look down over trees and factory roofs to a river. As he could not sleep and as the fancies that kept crowding in upon him only made him more excited, he got out of bed and tried to think.

As would be natural under such circumstances, he tried to control his thoughts, but when he sat by the window and was wide-awake a most unexpected and humiliating thing happened. The night was clear and fine. There was a moon. He wanted to dream of the woman who was to be his wife, to think out lines for noble poems or make plans that would affect his career. Much to his surprise his mind refused to do anything of the sort.

At a corner of the street where he lived, there was a small cigar store and newspaper stand run by a fat man of forty and his wife, a small active woman with bright gray eyes. In the morning he stopped there to buy a paper before going down to the city. Sometimes he saw only the fat man, but often the man had disappeared and the woman waited on him. She was, as he assured me at least twenty times in telling me his tale, a very ordinary person with nothing special or notable about her, but for some reason he could not explain, being in her presence stirred him profoundly. During that week in the midst of his distraction she was the only person he knew who stood out clear and distinct in his mind. When he wanted so much to think noble thoughts, he could think only of her. Before he knew what was happening, his imagination had taken hold of the notion of having a love affair with the woman.

"I could not understand myself," he declared, in telling me the story. "At night, when the city was quiet and when I should have been asleep, I thought about her all the time. After two or three days of that sort of thing the consciousness of her got into my day-time thoughts. I was terribly muddled. When I went to see the woman who is now my wife I found that my love for her was in no way affected by my vagrant thoughts. There was but one woman in the world I wanted to live with and to be my comrade in undertaking to improve my own character and my position in the world, but for the moment, you see, I wanted this other woman to be in my arms. She had worked her way into my being. On all sides people were saying I was a big man who would do big things, and there I was. That evening when I went to the theatre I walked home because I knew I would be unable to sleep, and to satisfy the annoying impulse in myself I went and stood on the sidewalk before the tobacco shop. It was a two-story building, and I knew the woman lived upstairs with her husband. For a long time I stood in the darkness with my body pressed against the wall of the building, and then I thought of the two of them up there and no doubt in bed together. That made me furious.

"Then I grew more furious with myself. I went home and got into bed, shaken with anger. There are certain books of verse and some prose writings that have always moved me deeply, and so I put several books on a table by my bed.

"The voices in the books were like the voices of the dead. I did not hear them. The printed words would not penetrate into my consciousness. I tried to think of the woman I loved, but her figure had also become something far away, something with which I for the moment seemed to have nothing to do. I rolled and tumbled about in the bed. It was a miserable experience.

"On Thursday morning I went into the store. There stood the woman alone. I think she knew how I felt. Perhaps she had been thinking of me as I had been thinking of her. A doubtful hesitating smile played about the corners of her mouth. She had on a dress made of cheap cloth and there was a tear on the shoulder. She must have been ten years older than myself. When I tried to put my pennies on the glass counter, behind which she stood, my hand trembled so that the pennies made a sharp rattling noise. When I spoke, the voice that came out of my throat did not sound like anything that had ever belonged to me. It barely arose above a thick whisper. 'I want you,' I said. 'I want you very much. Can't you run away from your husband? Come to me at my apartment at seven tonight.'

"The woman did come to my apartment at seven. That morning she didn't say anything at all. For a minute perhaps we stood looking at each other. I had forgotten everything in the world but just her. Then she nodded her head and I went away. Now that I think of it, I cannot remember a word I ever heard her say. She came to my apartment at seven and it was dark. You must understand this was in the month of October. I had not lighted a light and I had sent my servant away.

"During that day I was no good at all. Several men came to see me at my office, but I got all muddled up in trying to talk with them. They attributed my rattleheadedness to my approaching marriage and went away laughing.

"It was on that morning, just the day before my marriage that I got a long and very beautiful letter from my fiancée. During the night before, she also had been unable to sleep and had got out of bed to write the letter. Everything she said in it was very sharp and real, but she herself, as a living thing, seemed to have receded into the distance. It seemed to me that she was like a bird, flying far away in distant skies, and that I was like a perplexed barefooted boy standing in the dusty road before a farmhouse and looking at her receding figure. I wonder if you will understand what I mean?

"In regard to the letter. In it she, the awakening woman, poured out her heart. She of course knew nothing of life, but she was a woman. She lay, I suppose, in her bed feeling nervous and wrought up as I had been doing. She realized that a great change was about to take place in her life and was glad and afraid too. There she lay thinking of it all. Then she got out of bed and began talking to me on the bit of paper. She told me how afraid she was and how glad too. Like most young women she had heard things whispered. In the letter she was very sweet and fine. 'For a long time, after we are married, we will forget we are a man and woman,' she wrote. 'We will be human beings. You must remember that I am ignorant and often I will be very stupid. You must love me and be very patient and kind. When I know more, when after a long time you have taught me the way of life, I will try to repay you. I will love you tenderly and passionately. The possibility of that is in me or I would not want to marry at all. I am afraid but I am also happy. Oh, I am so glad our marriage time is near at hand!'

"Now you see clearly enough what a mess I was in. In my office, after I had read my fiancée's letter, I became at once very resolute and strong. I remember that I got out of my chair and walked about, proud of the fact that I was to be the husband of so noble a woman. Right away I felt concerning her as I had been feeling about myself before I found out what a weak thing I was. To be sure, I took a strong resolution that I would not be weak. At nine that evening I had planned to run in to see my fiancée. 'I'm all right now,' I said to myself. 'The beauty of her character has saved me from myself. I will go home now and send the other woman away.' In the morning I had telephoned to my servant and told him that I did not want him to be at the apartment that evening and I now picked up the telephone to tell him to stay at home.

"Then a thought came to me. 'I will not want him there in any event,' I told myself. 'What will he think when he sees a woman coming in my place on the evening before the day I am to be married?' I put the telephone down and prepared to go home. 'If I want my servant out of the apartment it is because I do not want him to hear me talk with the woman. I cannot be rude to her. I will have to make some kind of an explanation,' I said to myself.

"The woman came at seven o'clock, and, as you may have guessed, I let her in and forgot the resolution I had made. It is likely I never had any intention of doing anything else. There was a bell on my door, but she did not ring, but knocked very softly. It seems to me that everything she did that evening was soft and quiet, but very determined and quick. Do I make myself clear? When she came I was standing just within the door where I had been standing and waiting for a half hour. My hands were trembling as they had trembled in the morning when her eyes looked at me and when I tried to put the pennies on the counter in the store. When I opened the door she stepped quickly in and I took her into my arms. We stood together in the darkness. My hands no longer trembled. I felt very happy and strong.

"Although I have tried to make everything clear I have not told you what the woman I married is like. I have emphasized, you see, the other woman. I make the blind statement that I love my wife, and to a man of your shrewdness that means nothing at all. To tell the truth, had I not started to speak of this matter I would feel more comfortable. It is inevitable that I give you the impression that I am in love with the tobacconist's wife. That's not true. To be sure I was very conscious of her all during the week before my marriage, but after she had come to me at my apartment she went entirely out of my mind.

"Am I telling the truth? I am trying very hard to tell what happened to me. I am saying that I have not since that evening thought of the woman who came to my apartment. Now, to tell the facts of the case, that is not true. On that evening I went to my fiancée at nine, as she had asked me to do in her letter. In a kind of way I cannot explain, the other woman went with me. This is what I mean—you see I had been thinking that if anything happened between me and the tobacconist's wife I would not be able to go through with my marriage. It is one thing or the other with me, I had said to myself.

"As a matter of fact I went to see my beloved on that evening filled with a new faith in the outcome of our life together. I am afraid I muddle this matter in trying to tell it. A moment ago I said the other woman, the tobacconist's wife, went with me. I do not mean she went in fact. What I am trying to say is that something of her faith in her own desires and her courage in seeing things through went with me. Is that clear to you? When I got to my fiancée's house there was a crowd of people standing about. Some were relatives from distant places I had not seen before. She looked up quickly when I came into the room. My face must have been radiant. I never saw her so moved. She thought her letter had affected me deeply, and of course it had. Up she jumped and ran to meet me. She was like a glad child. Right before the people who turned and looked inquiringly at us, she said the thing that was in her mind. 'Oh, I am so happy,' she cried. 'You have understood. We will be two human beings. We will not have to be husband and wife.'

"As you may suppose everyone laughed, but I did not laugh. The tears came into my eyes. I was so happy I wanted to shout. Perhaps you understand what I mean. In the office that day when I read the letter my fiancée had written I had said to myself, 'I will take care of the dear little woman.' There was something smug, you see, about that. In her house when she cried out in that way, and when everyone laughed, what I said to myself was something like this: 'We will take care of ourselves.' I whispered something of the sort into her ears. To tell you the truth I had come down off my perch. The spirit of the other woman did that to me. Before all the people gathered about I held my fiancée close and we kissed. They thought it very sweet of us to be so affected at the sight of each other. What they would have thought had they known the truth about me, God only knows!

"Twice now I have said that after that evening I never thought of the other woman at all. That is partially true but, sometimes in the evening when I am walking alone in the street or in the park as we are walking now, and when evening comes softly and quickly as it has come tonight, the feeling of her comes sharply into my body and mind. After that one meeting I never saw her again. On the next day I was married and I have never gone back into her street. Often, however, as I am walking along as I am doing now, a quick sharp earthy feeling takes possession of me. It is as though I were a seed in the ground and the warm rains of the spring had come. It is as though I were not a man but a tree.

"And now you see I am married and everything is all right. My marriage is to me a very beautiful fact. If you were to say that my marriage is not a happy one I could call you a liar and be speaking the absolute truth. I have tried to tell you about this other woman. There is a kind of relief in speaking of her. I have never done it before. I wonder why I was so silly as to be afraid that I would give you the impression I am not in love with my wife. If I did not instinctively trust your understanding I would not have spoken. As the matter stands I have a little stirred myself up. Tonight I shall think of the other woman. That sometimes occurs. It will happen after I have gone to bed. My wife sleeps in the next room to mine and the door is always left open. There will be a moon tonight, and when there is a moon long streaks of light fall on her bed. I shall awake at midnight tonight. She will be lying asleep with one arm thrown over her head.

"What is it that I am now talking about? A man does not speak of his wife lying in bed. What I am trying to say is that, because of this task, I shall think of the other woman tonight. My thoughts will not take the form they did during the week before I was married. I will wonder what has become of the woman. For a moment I will again feel myself holding her close. I will think that for an hour I was closer to her than I have ever been to anyone else. Then I will think of the time when I will be as close as that to my wife. She is still, you see, an awakening woman. For a moment I will close my eyes and the quick, shrewd, determined eyes of that other woman will look into mine. My head will swim and then I will quickly open my eyes and see again the dear woman with whom I have undertaken to live out my life. Then I will sleep and when I awake in the morning it will be as it was that evening when I walked out of my dark apartment after having had the most notable experience of my life. What I mean to say, you understand is that, for me, when I awake, the other woman will be utterly gone."

The Egg

MY FATHER was, I am sure, intended by nature to be a cheerful, kindly man. Until he was thirty-four years old he worked as a farm hand for a man named Thomas Butterworth whose place lay near the town of Bidwell, Ohio. He had then a horse of his own and on Saturday evenings drove into town to spend a few hours in social intercourse with other farm hands. In town he drank several glasses of beer and stood about in Ben Head's saloon—crowded on Saturday evenings with visiting farm hands. Songs were sung and glasses thumped on the bar. At ten o'clock Father drove home along a lonely country road, made his horse comfortable for the night and himself went to bed, quite happy in his position in life. He had at that time no notion of trying to rise in the world.

It was in the spring of his thirty-fifth year that Father married my mother, then a country schoolteacher, and in the following spring I came wriggling and crying into the world. Something happened to the two people. They became ambitious. The American passion for getting up in the world took possession of them.

It may have been that Mother was responsible. Being a schoolteacher she had no doubt read books and magazines. She had, I presume, read of how Garfield, Lincoln and other Americans rose from poverty to fame and greatness and as I lay beside her—in the days of her lying-in—she may have dreamed that I would some day rule men and cities. At any rate, she induced Father to give up his place as a farm hand, sell his horse and embark on an independent enterprise of his own. She was a tall silent woman with a long nose and troubled gray eyes. For herself she wanted nothing. For Father and myself she was incurably ambitious.

The first venture into which the two people went turned out badly. They rented ten acres of poor stony land on Griggs's Road, eight miles from Bidwell, and launched into chicken raising. I grew into boyhood on the place and got my first impressions of life there. From the beginning they were impressions of disaster and if, in my turn, I am a gloomy man inclined to see the darker side of life, I attribute it to the fact that what should have been for me the happy joyous days of childhood were spent on a chicken farm.

One unversed in such matters can have no notion of the many and tragic things that can happen to a chicken. It is born out of an egg, lives for a few weeks as a tiny fluffy thing such as you will see pictured on Easter cards, then becomes hideously naked, eats quantities of corn and meal bought by the sweat of your father's brow, gets diseases called pip, cholera and other names, stands looking with stupid eyes at the sun, becomes sick and dies. A few hens and now and then a rooster, intended to serve God's mysterious ends, struggle through to maturity. The hens lay eggs out of which come other chickens and the dreadful cycle is thus made complete. It is all unbelievably complex. Most philosophers must have been raised on chicken farms. One hopes for so much from a chicken and is so dreadfully disillusioned. Small chickens, just setting out on the journey of life, look so bright and alert and they are in fact so dreadfully stupid. They are so much like people they mix one up in one's judgments of life. If disease does not kill them they wait until your expectations are thoroughly aroused and then walk under the wheels of a wagon—to go squashed and dead back to their maker. Vermin infest their youth, and fortunes must be spent for curative powders. In later life I have seen how a literature has been built up on the subject of fortunes to be made out of the raising of chickens. It is intended to be read by the gods who have just eaten of the tree of the knowledge of good and evil. It is a hopeful literature and declares that much may be done by simple ambitious people who own a few hens. Do not be led astray by it. It was not written for you. Go hunt for gold on the frozen hills of Alaska, put your faith in the honesty of a politician, believe if you will that the world is daily growing better and that good will triumph over evil, but do not read and believe the literature that is written concerning the hen. It was not written for you.

I, however, digress. My tale does not primarily concern itself with the hen. If correctly told it will center on the egg. For ten years my father and mother struggled to make our chicken farm pay and then they gave up that struggle and began another. They moved into the town of Bidwell, Ohio, and embarked in the restaurant business. After ten years of worry with incubators that did not hatch, and with tiny—and in their own way lovely—balls of fluff that passed on into seminaked pullethood and from that into dead henhood, we threw all aside and packing our belongings on a wagon drove down Griggs's Road toward Bidwell, a tiny caravan of hope looking for a new place from which to start on our upward journey through life.

We must have been a sad-looking lot, not, I fancy, unlike refugees fleeing from a battlefield. Mother and I walked in the road. The wagon that contained our goods had been borrowed for the day from Mr. Albert Griggs, a neighbor. Out of its sides stuck the legs of cheap chairs and at the back of the pile of beds, tables, and boxes filled with kitchen utensils was a crate of live chickens, and on top of that the baby carriage in which I had been wheeled about in my infancy. Why we stuck to the baby carriage I don't know. It was unlikely other children would be born, and the wheels were broken. People who have few possessions cling tightly to those they have. That is one of the facts that make life so discouraging.

Father rode on top of the wagon. He was then a bald-headed man of forty-five, a little fat and from long association with Mother and the chickens he had become habitually silent and discouraged. All during our ten years on the chicken farm he had worked as a laborer on neighboring farms, and most of the money he had earned had been spent for remedies to cure chicken diseases, on Wilmer's White Wonder Cholera Cure or Professor Bidlow's Egg Producer or some other preparations that Mother found advertised in the poultry papers. There were two little patches of hair on Father's head just above his ears. I remember that as a child I used to sit looking at him when he had gone to sleep in a chair before the stove on Sunday afternoons in the winter. I had at that time already begun to read books and have notions of my own, and the bald path that led over the top of his head was, I fancied, something like a broad road, such a road as Caesar might have made on which to lead his legions out of Rome and into the wonders of an unknown world. The tufts of hair that grew above Father's ears were, I thought, like forests. I fell into a half-sleeping, half-waking state and dreamed I was a tiny thing going along the road into a far beautiful place where there were no chicken farms and where life was a happy eggless affair.

One might write a book concerning our flight from the chicken farm into town. Mother and I walked the entire eight miles—she to be sure that nothing fell from the wagon and I to see the wonders of the world. On the seat of the wagon beside Father was his greatest treasure. I will tell you of that.

On a chicken farm where hundreds and even thousands of chickens come out of eggs, surprising things sometimes happen. Grotesques are born out of eggs as out of people. The accident does not often occur—perhaps once in a thousand births. A chicken is, you see, born that has four legs, two pairs of wings, two heads or what not. The things do not live. They go quickly back to the hand of their maker that has for a moment trembled. The fact that the poor little things could not live was one of the tragedies of life to Father. He had some sort of notion that if he could but bring into henhood or roosterhood a five-legged hen or a two-headed rooster his fortune would be made. He dreamed of taking the wonder about to county fairs and of growing rich by exhibiting it to other farm hands.

At any rate he saved all the little monstrous things that had been born on our chicken farm. They were preserved in alcohol and put each in its own glass bottle. These he had carefully put into a box and on our journey into town it was carried on the wagon seat beside him. He drove the horses with one hand and with the other clung to the box. When we got to our destination the box was taken down at once and the bottles removed. All during our days as keepers of a restaurant in the town of Bidwell, Ohio, the grotesques in their little glass bottles sat on a shelf back of the counter. Mother sometimes protested, but Father was a rock on the subject of his treasure. The grotesques were, he declared, valuable. People, he said, liked to look at strange and wonderful things.

Did I say that we embarked in the restaurant business in the town of Bidwell, Ohio? I exaggerated a little. The town itself lay at the foot of a low hill and on the shore of a small river. The railroad did not run through the town, and the station was a mile away to the north, at a place called Pickleville. There had been a cider mill and pickle factory at the station, but before the time of our coming they had both gone out of business. In the morning and in the evening, buses came down to the station along a road called Turner's Pike from the hotel on the main street of Bidwell. Our going to the out-of-the-way place to embark in the restaurant business was Mother's idea. She talked of it for a year and then one day went off and rented an empty store building opposite the railroad station. It was her idea that the restaurant would be profitable. Traveling men, she said, would be always waiting around to take trains out of town, and town people would come to the station to await incoming trains. They would come to the restaurant to buy pieces of pie and drink coffee. Now that I am older I know that she had another motive in going. She was ambitious for me. She wanted me to rise in the world, to get into a town school and become a man of the towns.

At Pickleville Father and Mother worked hard as they always had done. At first there was the necessity of putting our place into shape to be a restaurant. That took a month. Father built a shelf on which he put tins of vegetables. He painted a sign on which he put his name in large red letters. Below his name was the sharp command, EAT HERE, that was so seldom obeyed. A showcase was bought and filled with cigars and tobacco. Mother scrubbed the floor and the walls of the room. I went to school in the town and was glad to be away from the farm and from the presence of the discouraged, sad-looking chickens. Still I was not very joyous. In the evening I walked home from school along Turner's Pike and remembered the children I had seen playing in the town school yard. A troop of little girls had gone hopping about and singing. I tried that. Down along the frozen road I went hopping solemnly on one leg. "Hippity Hop To The Barber Shop," I sang shrilly. Then I stopped and looked doubtfully about. I was afraid of being seen in my gay mood. It must have seemed to me that I was doing a thing that should not be done by one who, like myself, had been raised on a chicken farm where death was a daily visitor.

Mother decided that our restaurant should remain open at night. At ten in the evening a passenger train went north past our door followed by a local freight. The freight crew had switching to do in Pickleville, and when the work was done they came to our restaurant for hot coffee and food. Sometimes one of them ordered a fried egg. In the morning at four they returned northbound and again visited us. A little trade began to grow up. Mother slept at night and during the day tended the restaurant and fed our boarders while Father slept. He slept in the same bed Mother had occupied during the night, and I went off to the town of Bidwell and to school. During the long nights, while Mother and I slept, Father cooked meats that were to go into sandwiches for the lunch baskets of our boarders. Then an idea in regard to getting up in the world came into his head. The American spirit took hold of him. He also became ambitious.

In the long nights when there was little to do, Father had time to think. That was his undoing. He decided that he had in the past been an unsuccessful man because he had not been cheerful enough and that in the future he would adopt a cheerful outlook on life. In the early morning he came upstairs and got into bed with Mother. She woke and the two talked. From my bed in the corner I listened.

It was Father's idea that both he and Mother should try to entertain the people who came to eat at our restaurant. I cannot now remember his words, but he gave the impression of one about to become in some obscure way a kind of public entertainer. When people, particularly young people from the town of Bidwell, came into our place, as on very rare occasions they did, bright entertaining conversation was to be made. From Father's words I gathered that something of the jolly innkeeper effect was to be sought. Mother must have been doubtful from the first, but she said nothing discouraging. It was Father's notion that a passion for the company of himself and Mother would spring up in the breasts of the younger people of the town of Bidwell. In the evening bright happy groups would come singing down Turner's Pike. They would troop, shouting with joy and laughter, into our place. There would be song and festivity. I do not mean to give the impression that Father spoke so elaborately of the matter. He was, as I have said, an uncommunicative man. "They want some place to go. I tell you, they want some place to go," he said over and over. That was as far as he got. My own imagination has filled in the blanks.

For two or three weeks this notion of Father's invaded our house. We did not talk much, but in our daily lives tried earnestly to make smiles take the place of glum looks. Mother smiled at the boarders and I, catching the infection, smiled at our cat. Father became a little feverish in his anxiety to please. There was no doubt, lurking somewhere in him, a touch of the spirit of the showman. He did not waste much of his ammunition on the railroad men he served at night, but seemed to be waiting for a young man or woman from Bidwell to come in to show what he could do. On the counter in the restaurant there was a wire basket kept always filled with eggs, and it must have been before his eyes when the idea of being entertaining was born in his brain. There was something prenatal about the way eggs kept themselves connected with the development of his idea. At any rate, an egg ruined his new impulse in life.

Late one night I was awakened by a roar of anger coming from Father's throat. Both Mother and I sat upright in our beds. With trembling hands she lighted a lamp that stood on a table by her head. Downstairs the front door of our restaurant went shut with a bang and in a few minutes Father tramped up the stairs. He held an egg in his hand and his hand trembled as though he were having a chill. There was a half-insane light in his eyes. As he stood glaring at us I was sure he intended throwing the egg at either Mother or me. Then he laid it gently on the table beside the lamp and dropped on his knees beside Mother's bed. He began to cry like a boy and I, carried away by his grief, cried with him. The two of us filled the little upstairs room with our wailing voices. It is ridiculous, but of the picture we made I can remember only the fact that Mother's hand continually stroked the bald path that ran across the top of his head. I have forgotten what Mother said to him and how she induced him to tell her of what had happened downstairs. His explanation also has gone out of my mind. I remember only my own grief and fright and the shiny path over Father's head glowing in the lamp light as he knelt by the bed.

As to what happened downstairs. For some unexplainable reason I know the story as well as though I had been a witness to my father's discomfiture. One in time gets to know many unexplainable things. On that evening young Joe Kane, son of a merchant of Bidwell, came to Pickleville to meet his father, who was expected on the ten-o'clock evening train from the South. The train was three hours late and Joe came into our place to loaf about and to wait for its arrival. The local freight train came in and the freight crew were fed. Joe was left alone in the restaurant with Father.

From the moment he came into our place the Bidwell young man must have been puzzled by my father's actions. It was his notion that Father was angry at him for hanging around. He noticed that the restaurant keeper was apparently disturbed by his presence and he thought of going out. However, it began to rain and he did not fancy the long walk to town and back. He bought a five-cent cigar and ordered a cup of coffee. He had a newspaper in his pocket and took it out and began to read. "I'm waiting for the evening train. It's late," he said apologetically.

For a long time, Father, whom Joe Kane had never seen before, remained silently gazing at his visitor. He was no doubt suffering from an attack of stage fright. As so often happens in life, he had thought so much and so often of the situation that now confronted him that he was somewhat nervous in its presence.

For one thing, he did not know what to do with his hands. He thrust one of them nervously over the counter and shook hands with Joe Kane. "How-de-do," he said. Joe Kane put his newspaper down and stared at him. Father's eye lighted on the basket of eggs that sat on the counter and he began to talk. "Well," he began hesitatingly, "well, you have heard of Christopher Columbus, eh?" He seemed to be angry. "That Christopher Columbus was a cheat," he declared emphatically. "He talked of making an egg stand on its end. He talked, he did, and then he went and broke the end of the egg."

My father seemed to his visitor to be beside himself at the duplicity of Christopher Columbus. He muttered and swore. He declared it was wrong to teach children that Christopher Columbus was a great man, when, after all, he cheated at the critical moment. He had declared he would make an egg stand on end and then when his bluff had been called he had done a trick. Still grumbling at Columbus, Father took an egg from the basket on the counter and began to walk up and down. He rolled the egg between the palms of his hands. He smiled genially. He began to mumble words regarding the effect to be produced on an egg by the electricity that comes out of the human body. He declared that without breaking its shell and by virtue of rolling it back and forth in his hands he could stand the egg on its end. He explained that the warmth of his hands and the gentle rolling movement he gave the egg created a new center of gravity, and Joe Kane was mildly interested. "I have handled thousands of eggs," Father said. "No one knows more about eggs than I do."

He stood the egg on the counter and it fell on its side. He tried the trick again and again, each time rolling the egg between the palms of his hands and saying the words regarding the wonders of electricity and the laws of gravity. When after a half hour's effort he did succeed in making the egg stand for a moment he looked up to find that his visitor was no longer watching. By the time he had succeeded in calling Joe Kane's attention to the success of his effort the egg had again rolled over and lay on its side.

Afire with the showman's passion and at the same time a good deal disconcerted by the failure of his first effort, Father now took the bottles containing the poultry monstrosities down from their place on the shelf and began to show them to his visitor. "How would you like to have seven legs and two heads like this fellow?" he asked, exhibiting the most remarkable of his treasures. A cheerful smile played over his face. He reached over the counter and tried to slap Joe Kane on the shoulder as he had seen men do in Ben Head's saloon when he was a young farm hand and drove to town on Saturday evenings. His visitor was made a little ill by the sight of the body of the terribly deformed bird floating in the alcohol in the bottle and got up to go. Coming from behind the counter, Father took hold of the young man's arm and led him back to his seat. He grew a little angry and for a moment had to turn his face away and force himself to smile. Then he put the bottles back on the shelf. In an outburst of generosity he fairly compelled

Joe Kane to have a fresh cup of coffee and another cigar at his expense. Then he took a pan and, filling it with vinegar taken from a jug that sat beneath the counter, he declared himself about to do a new trick. "I will heat this egg in this pan of vinegar," he said. "Then I will put it through the neck of a bottle without breaking the shell. When the egg is inside the bottle it will resume its normal shape and the shell will become hard again. Then I will give the bottle with the egg in it to you. You can take it about with you wherever you go. People will want to know how you got the egg in the bottle. Don't tell them. Keep them guessing. That is the way to have fun with this trick."

Father grinned and winked at his visitor. Joe Kane decided that the man who confronted him was mildly insane but harmless. He drank the cup of coffee that had been given him and began to read his paper again. When the egg had been heated in vinegar, Father carried it on a spoon to the counter and, going into a back room, got an empty bottle. He was angry because his visitor did not watch him as he began to do his trick, but nevertheless went cheerfully to work. For a long time he struggled, trying to get the egg to go through the neck of the bottle. He put the pan of vinegar back on the stove, intending to reheat the egg, then picked it up and burned his fingers. After a second bath in the hot vinegar the shell of the egg had been softened a little but not enough for his purpose. He worked and worked and a spirit of desperate determination took possession of him. When he thought that at last the trick was about to be consummated, the delayed train came in at the station and Joe Kane started to go nonchalantly out the door. Father made a last desperate effort to conquer the egg and make it do the thing that would establish his reputation as one who knew how to entertain guests who came into his restaurant. He worried the egg. He attempted to be somewhat rough with it. He swore and the sweat stood out on his forehead. The egg broke under his hand. When the contents spurted over his clothes, Joe Kane, who had stopped at the door, turned and laughed.

A roar of anger rose from my father's throat. He danced and shouted a string of inarticulate words. Grabbing another egg from the basket on the counter, he threw it, just missing the head of the young man as he dodged through the door and escaped.

Father came upstairs to Mother and me with an egg in his hand. I do not know what he intended to do. I imagine he had some idea of destroying it, of destroying all eggs, and that he intended to let

Mother and me see him begin. When, however, he got into the presence of Mother something happened to him. He laid the egg gently on the table and dropped on his knees by the bed as I have already explained. He later decided to close the restaurant for the night and to come upstairs and get into bed. When he did so he blew out the light and after much muttered conversation both he and Mother went to sleep. I suppose I went to sleep also, but my sleep was troubled. I awoke at dawn and for a long time looked at the egg that lay on the table. I wondered why eggs had to be and why from the egg came the hen who again laid the egg. The question got into my blood. It has stayed there, I imagine, because I am the son of my father. At any rate, the problem remains unsolved in my mind. And that, I conclude, is but another evidence of the complete and final triumph of the egg—at least as far as my family is concerned.

The Man in the Brown Coat

> Napoleon went down into a battle riding on a horse.
> Alexander went down into a battle riding on a horse.
> General Grant got off a horse and walked in a wood.
> General Hindenburg stood on a hill.
> The moon came up out of a clump of bushes.

I AM writing a history of the things men do. I have written three such histories and I am but a young man. Already I have written three hundred, four hundred thousand words.

My wife is somewhere in this house where for hours now I have been sitting and writing. She is a tall woman with black hair, turning a little gray. Listen, she is going softly up the flight of stairs. All day she goes softly about, doing the housework in our house.

I came here to this town from another town in the state of Iowa. My father was a workman, a house painter. He did not rise in the world as I have done. I worked my way through college and became a historian. We own this house in which I sit. This is my room in which I work. Already I have written three histories of peoples. I have told how states were formed and battles fought. You may see my books standing straight up on the shelves of libraries. They stand up like sentries.

I am tall like my wife, and my shoulders are a little stooped. Although I write boldly, I am a shy man. I like being at work alone in this room with the door closed. There are many books here. Nations march back and forth in the books. It is quiet here but in the books a great thundering goes on.

> Napoleon rides down a hill and into a battle.
> General Grant walks in a wood.
> Alexander rides down a hill and into a battle.

My wife has a serious, almost stern look. Sometimes the thoughts I have concerning her frighten me. In the afternoon she leaves our house and goes for a walk. Sometimes she goes to stores, sometimes to visit a neighbor. There is a yellow house opposite our house. My wife goes out at a side door and passes along the street between our house and the yellow house.

The side door of our house bangs. There is a moment of waiting. My wife's face floats across the yellow background of a picture.

> General Pershing rode down a hill and into a battle.
> Alexander rode down a hill and into a battle.

Little things are growing big in my mind. The window before my desk makes a little framed place like a picture. Every day I sit staring. I wait with an odd sensation of something impending. My hand trembles. The face that floats through the picture does something I don't understand. The face floats, then it stops. It goes from the right-hand side to the left-hand side, then it stops.

The face comes into my mind and goes out—the face floats in my mind. The pen has fallen from my fingers. The house is silent. The eyes of the floating face are turned away from me.

My wife is a girl who came here to this town from another town in the state of Ohio. We keep a servant, but my wife often sweeps the floors and she sometimes makes the bed in which we sleep together. We sit together in the evening but I do not know her. I cannot shake myself out of myself. I wear a brown coat and I cannot come out of my coat. I cannot come out of myself. My wife is very gentle and she speaks softly but she cannot come out of herself.

My wife has gone out of the house. She does not know that I know every little thought of her life. I know what she thought when she was a child and walked in the streets of an Ohio town. I have heard the voices of her mind. I have heard the little voices. I heard the voice of fear crying when she was first overtaken with passion and crawled into my arms. Again I heard the voices of fear when her lips said words of courage to me as we sat together on the first evening after we were married and moved into this house.

It would be strange if I could sit here, as I am doing now, while my own face floated across the picture made by the yellow house and the window. It would be strange and beautiful if I could meet my wife, come into her presence.

The woman whose face floated across my picture just now knows nothing of me. I know nothing of her. She has gone off, along a street. The voices of her mind are talking. I am here in this room, as alone as ever any man God made.

It would be strange and beautiful if I could float my face across my picture. If my floating face could come into her presence, if it could come into the presence of any man or any woman—that would be a strange and beautiful thing to have happen.

> Napoleon went down into a battle riding on a horse.
> General Grant went into a wood.
> Alexander went down into a battle riding on a horse.

I'll tell you what—sometimes the whole life of this world floats in a human face in my mind. The unconscious face of the world stops and stands still before me.

Why do I not say a word out of myself to the others? Why, in all our life together, have I never been able to break through the wall to my wife? Already I have written three hundred, four hundred thousand words. Are there no words that lead into life? Some day I shall speak to myself. Some day I shall make a testament unto myself.

Brothers

I AM at my house in the country and it is late October. It rains. Back of my house is a forest and in front there is a road and beyond that open fields. The country is one of low hills, flattening suddenly into plains. Some twenty miles away, across the flat country, lies the huge city Chicago.

On this rainy day the leaves of the trees that line the road before my window are falling like rain, the yellow, red and golden leaves fall straight down heavily. The rain beats them brutally down. They are denied a last golden flash across the sky. In October, leaves should be carried away, out over the plains, in a wind. They should go dancing away.

Yesterday morning I arose at daybreak and went for a walk. There was a heavy fog and I lost myself in it. I went down into the plains and returned to the hills, and everywhere the fog was as a wall before me. Out of it trees sprang suddenly, grotesquely, as in a city street late at night people come suddenly out of the darkness into the circle of light under a street lamp. Above there was the light of day forcing itself slowly into the fog. The fog moved slowly. The tops of trees moved slowly. Under the trees the fog was dense, purple. It was like smoke lying in the streets of a factory town.

An old man came up to me in the fog. I know him well. The people here call him insane. "He is a little cracked," they say. He lives alone in a little house buried deep in the forest and has a small dog he carries always in his arms. On many mornings I have met him walking on the road and he has told me of men and women who are his brothers and sisters, his cousins, aunts, uncles, brothers-in-law. It is confusing. He cannot draw close to people near at hand so he gets hold of a name out of a newspaper and his mind plays with it. On one morning he told me he was a cousin to the man named Cox who at the time when I write is a candidate for the Presidency. On another morning he told me that Caruso the singer had married a woman who was his sister-in-law. "She is my wife's sister," he said, holding the little dog close. His gray watery eyes looked appealing up to me. He wanted me to believe. "My wife was a sweet slim girl," he declared. "We lived together in a big house and in the morning walked about arm in arm. Now her sister has married Caruso the singer. He is of my family now."

As someone had told me the old man had never married, I went away wondering. One morning in early September I came upon him sitting under a tree beside a path near his house. The dog barked at me and then ran and crept into his arms. At that time the Chicago newspapers were filled with the story of a millionaire who had got into trouble with his wife because of an intimacy with an actress. The old man told me that the actress was his sister. He is sixty years old and the actress whose story appeared in the newspapers is twenty but he spoke of their childhood together. "You would not realize it to see us now, but we were poor then," he said. "It's true. We lived in a little house on the side of a hill. Once when there was a storm, the wind nearly swept our house away. How the wind blew! Our father was a carpenter and he built strong houses for other people, but our own house he did not build very strong!" He shook his head sorrowfully. "My sister the actress has got into trouble. Our house is not built very strongly," he said as I went away along the path.

For a month, two months, the Chicago newspapers, that are delivered every morning in our village, have been filled with the story of a murder. A man there has murdered his wife and there seems no reason for the deed. The tale runs something like this—

The man, who is now on trial in the courts and will no doubt be hanged, worked in a bicycle factory, where he was a foreman, and lived with his wife and his wife's mother in an apartment in Thirty-second Street. He loved a girl who worked in the office of the factory where he was employed. She came from a town in Iowa and when she first came to the city lived with her aunt, who has since died. To the foreman, a heavy stolid-looking man with gray eyes, she seemed the most beautiful woman in the world. Her desk was by a window at an angle of the factory, a sort of wing of the building, and the foreman, down in the shop had a desk by another window. He sat at his desk making out sheets containing the record of the work done by each man in his department. When he looked up he could see the girl sitting at work at her desk. The notion got into his head that she was peculiarly lovely. He did not think of trying to draw close to her or of winning her love. He looked at her as one might look at a star or across a country of low hills in October when the leaves of the trees are all red and yellow gold. "She is a pure, virginal thing," he thought vaguely. "What can she be thinking about as she sits there by the window at work?"

In fancy the foreman took the girl from Iowa home with him to his apartment in Thirty-second Street and into the presence of his wife and his mother-in-law. All day in the shop and during the evening at home he carried her figure about with him in his mind. As he stood by a window in his apartment and looked out toward the Illinois Central railroad tracks and beyond the tracks to the lake, the girl was there beside him. Down below, women walked in the street and in every woman he saw there was something of the Iowa girl. One woman walked as she did, another made a gesture with her hand that reminded him of her. All the women he saw, except his wife and his mother-in-law, were like the girl he had taken inside himself.

The two women in his own house puzzled and confused him. They became suddenly unlovely and commonplace. His wife in particular was like some strange unlovely growth that had attached itself to his body.

In the evening after the day at the factory he went home to his own place and had dinner. He had always been a silent man and when he did not talk no one minded. After dinner he with his wife went to a picture show. There were two children and his wife expected another. They came into the apartment and sat down. The climb up two flights of stairs had wearied his wife. She sat in a chair beside her mother groaning with weariness.

The mother-in-law was the soul of goodness. She took the place of a servant in the home and got no pay. When her daughter wanted to go to a picture show she waved her hand and smiled. "Go on," she said. "I don't want to go. I'd rather sit here." She got a book and sat reading. The little boy of nine awoke and cried. He wanted to sit on the po-po. The mother-in-law attended to that.

After the man and his wife came home the three people sat in silence for an hour or two before bedtime. The man pretended to read a newspaper. He looked at his hands. Although he had washed them carefully, grease from the bicycle frames left dark stains under the nails. He thought of the Iowa girl and of her white quick hands playing over the keys of a typewriter. He felt dirty and uncomfortable.

The girl at the factory knew the foreman had fallen in love with her, and the thought excited her a little. Since her aunt's death she had gone to live in a rooming house and had nothing to do in the evening. Although the foreman meant nothing to her she could in a way use him. To her he became a symbol. Sometimes he came into the office and stood for a moment by the door. His large hands were covered with black grease. She looked at him without seeing. In his place in her imagination stood a tall slender young man. Of the foreman she saw only the gray eyes that began to burn with a strange fire. The eyes expressed eagerness, a humble and devout eagerness. In the presence of a man with such eyes she felt she need not be afraid.

She wanted a lover who would come to her with such a look in his eyes. Occasionally, perhaps once in two weeks, she stayed a little late at the office, pretending to have work that must be finished. Through the window she could see the foreman waiting. When everyone had gone she closed her desk and went into the street. At the same moment the foreman came out at the factory door.

They walked together along the street a half dozen blocks to where she got aboard her car. The factory was in a place called South Chicago and as they went along evening was coming on. The streets were lined with small unpainted frame houses and dirty-faced children ran screaming in the dusty roadway. They crossed over a bridge. Two abandoned coal barges lay rotting in the stream.

He went by her side walking heavily and striving to conceal his hands. He had scrubbed them carefully before leaving the factory but they seemed to him like heavy dirty pieces of waste matter hanging at his side. Their walking together happened but a few times and during one summer. "It's hot," he said. He never spoke to her of anything but the weather. "It's hot," he said. "I think it may rain."

She dreamed of the lover who would some time come, a tall fair young man, a rich man owning houses and lands. The workingman who walked beside her had nothing to do with her conception of love. She walked with him, stayed at the office until the others had gone, to walk unobserved with him because of his eyes, because of the eager thing in his eyes that was at the same time humble, that bowed down to her. In his presence there was no danger, could be no danger. He would never attempt to approach too closely, to touch her with his hands. She was safe with him.

In his apartment in the evening the man sat under the electric light with his wife and his mother-in-law. In the next room his two children were asleep. In a short time his wife would have another child. He had been with her to a picture show and in a short time they would get into bed together.

He would lie awake thinking, would hear the creaking of the springs of a bed where, in another room, his mother-in-law was crawling between the sheets. Life was too intimate. He would lie awake eager, expectant—expecting, what?

Nothing. Presently one of the children would cry. It wanted to get out of bed and sit on the po-po. Nothing strange or unusual or lovely would or could happen. Life was too close, intimate. Nothing that could happen in the apartment could in any way stir him; the things his wife might say, her occasional halfhearted outbursts of passion, the goodness of his mother-in-law who did the work of a servant without pay—

He sat in the apartment under the electric light pretending to read a newspaper—thinking. He looked at his hands. They were large, shapeless, a workingman's hands.

The figure of the girl from Iowa walked about the room. With her he went out of the apartment and walked in silence through miles of streets. It was not necessary to say words. He walked with her by a sea, along the crest of a mountain. The night was clear and silent and the stars shone. She also was a star. It was not necessary to say words.

Her eyes were like stars and her lips were like soft hills rising out of dim, starlit plains. "She is unattainable, she is far off like the stars," he thought. "She is unattainable like the stars but unlike the stars she breathes, she lives, like myself she has being."

One evening, some six weeks ago, the man who worked as foreman in the bicycle factory killed his wife and he is now in the courts being tried for murder. Every day the newspapers are filled with the story. On the evening of the murder he had taken his wife as usual to a picture show and they started home at nine. In Thirty-second Street, at a corner near their apartment building, the figure of a man darted suddenly out of an alleyway and then darted back again. The incident may have put the idea of killing his wife into the man's head.

They got to the entrance to the apartment building and stepped into a dark hallway. Then, quite suddenly and apparently without thought, the man took a knife out of his pocket. "Suppose that man who darted into the alleyway had intended to kill us," he thought. Opening the knife he whirled about and struck at his wife. He struck twice, a dozen times—madly. There was a scream and his wife's body fell.

The janitor had neglected to light the gas in the lower hallway. Afterward, the foreman decided, that was the reason he did it, that and the fact that the dark slinking figure of a man darted out of an alleyway and then darted back again. "Surely," he told himself, "I could never have done it had the gas been lighted."

He stood in the hallway thinking. His wife was dead and with her had died her unborn child. There was a sound of doors opening in the apartments above. For several minutes nothing happened. His wife and her unborn child were dead—that was all.

He ran upstairs thinking quickly. In the darkness on the lower stairway he had put the knife back into his pocket and, as it turned out later, there was no blood on his hands or on his clothes. The knife he later washed carefully in the bathroom, when the excitement had died down a little. He told everyone the same story. "There has been a holdup," he explained. "A man came slinking out of an alleyway and followed me and my wife home. He followed us into the hallway of the building and there was no light. The janitor has neglected to light the gas." Well—there had been a struggle and in the darkness his wife had been killed. He could not tell how it had happened. "There was no light. The janitor has neglected to light the gas," he kept saying.

For a day or two they did not question him specially and he had time to get rid of the knife. He took a long walk and threw it away into the river in South Chicago where the two abandoned coal barges lay rotting under the bridge, the bridge he had crossed when on the summer evenings he walked to the streetcar with the girl who was virginal and pure, who was far off and unattainable, like a star and yet not like a star.

And then he was arrested and right away he confessed—told everything. He said he did not know why he killed his wife and was careful to say nothing of the girl at the office. The newspapers tried to discover the motive for the crime. They are still trying. Someone had seen him on the few evenings when he walked with the girl and she was dragged into the affair and had her picture printed in the papers. That has been annoying for her, as of course she has been able to prove she had nothing to do with the man.

Yesterday morning a heavy fog lay over our village here at the edge of the city and I went for a long walk in the early morning. As I returned out of the lowlands into our hill country I met the old man whose family has so many and such strange ramifications. For a time he walked beside me holding the little dog in his arms. It was cold and the dog whined and shivered. In the fog the old man's face was indistinct. It moved slowly back and forth with the fog banks of the upper air and with the tops of trees. He spoke of the man who has killed his wife and whose name is being shouted in the pages of the city newspapers that come to our village each morning. As he walked beside me he launched into a long tale concerning a life he and his brother, who has now become a murderer, once lived together. "He is my brother," he said over and over, shaking his head. He seemed afraid I would not believe. There was a fact that must be established. "We were boys together, that man and I," he began again. "You see, we played together in a barn back of our father's house. Our father went away to sea in a ship. That is the way our names became confused. You understand that. We have different names, but we are brothers. We had the same father. We played together in a barn back of our father's house. For hours we lay together in the hay in the barn and it was warm there."

In the fog the slender body of the old man became like a little gnarled tree. Then it became a thing suspended in air. It swung back and forth like a body hanging on the gallows. The face beseeched me to believe the story the lips were trying to tell. In my mind everything concerning the relationship of men and women became confused, a muddle. The spirit of the man who had killed his wife came into the body of the little old man there by the roadside. It was striving to tell me the story it would never be able to tell in the courtroom in the city, in the presence of the judge. The whole story of mankind's loneliness, of the effort to reach out to unattainable beauty tried to get itself expressed from the lips of a mumbling old man, crazed with loneliness, who stood by the side of a country road on a foggy morning holding a little dog in his arms.

The arms of the old man held the dog so closely that it began to whine with pain. A sort of convulsion shook his body. The soul seemed striving to wrench itself out of the body, to fly away through the fog, down across the plain to the city, to the singer, the politician, the millionaire, the murderer, to its brothers, cousins, sisters, down in the city. The intensity of the old man's desire was terrible and in sympathy my body began to tremble. His arms tightened about the body of the little dog so that it cried with pain. I stepped forward and tore the arms away and the dog fell to the ground and lay whining. No doubt it had been injured. Perhaps ribs had been crushed. The old man stared at the dog lying at his feet as in the hallway of the apartment building the worker from the bicycle factory had stared at his dead wife. "We are brothers," he said again. "We have different names, but we are brothers. Our father, you understand, went off to sea."

I am sitting in my house in the country and it rains. Before my eyes the hills fall suddenly away and there are the flat plains and beyond the plains the city. An hour ago the old man of the house in the forest went past my door and the little dog was not with him. It may be that as we talked in the fog he crushed the life out of his companion. It may be that the dog like the workman's wife and her unborn child is now dead. The leaves of the trees that line the road before my window are falling like rain—the yellow, red and golden leaves fall straight down, heavily. The rain beat them brutally down. They are denied a last golden flash across the sky. In October, leaves should be carried away, out over the plains, in a wind. They should go dancing away.

Stories from *Horses and Men* (1923)

I'm a Fool

It was a hard jolt for me, one of the most bitterest I ever had to face. And it all came about through my own foolishness, too. Even yet, sometimes, when I think of it I want to cry or swear or kick myself. Perhaps, even now, after all this time, there will be a kind of satisfaction in making myself look cheap by telling of it.

It began at three o'clock one October afternoon as I sat in the grandstand at the fall trotting and pacing meet at Sandusky, Ohio.

To tell the truth, I felt a little foolish that I should be sitting in the grandstand at all. During the summer before, I had left my home town with Harry Whitehead and, with a nigger named Burt, had taken a job as swipe with one of the two horses Harry was campaigning through the fall race meets that year. Mother cried and my sister Mildred, who wanted to get a job as a schoolteacher in our town that fall, stormed and scolded about the house all during the week before I left. They both thought it something disgraceful that one of our family should take a place as a swipe with race horses. I've an idea Mildred thought my taking the place would stand in the way of her getting the job she'd been working so long for.

But after all, I had to work, and there was no other work to be got. A big lumbering fellow of nineteen couldn't just hang around the house and I had got too big to mow people's lawns and sell newspapers. Little chaps who could get next to people's sympathies by their sizes were always getting jobs away from me. There was one fellow who kept saying to everyone who wanted a lawn mowed or a cistern cleaned that he was saving money to work his way through college, and I used to lay awake nights thinking up ways to injure him without being found out. I kept thinking of wagons running over him and bricks falling on his head as he walked along the street. But never mind him.

I got the place with Harry and I liked Burt fine. We got along splendid together. He was a big nigger with a lazy sprawling body and soft, kind eyes, and when it came to a fight he could hit like Jack Johnson. He had Bucephalus, a big black pacing stallion that could do 2:09 or 2:10, if he had to, and I had a little gelding named Doctor Fritz that never lost a race all fall when Harry wanted him to win.

We set out from home late in July in a boxcar with the two horses and after that, until late November, we kept moving along to the race meets and the fairs. It was a peachy time for me, I'll say that. Sometimes now I think that boys who are raised regular in houses, and never have a fine nigger like Burt for best friend, and go to high schools and college, and never steal anything, or get drunk a little, or learn to swear from fellows who know how, or come walking up in front of a grandstand in their shirt sleeves and with dirty horsey pants on when the races are going on and the grandstand is full of people all dressed up— What's the use of talking about it? Such fellows don't know nothing at all. They've never had no opportunity.

But I did. Burt taught me how to rub down a horse and put the bandages on after a race and steam a horse out and a lot of valuable things for any man to know. He could wrap a bandage on a horse's leg so smooth that if it had been the same color you would think it was his skin, and I guess he'd have been a big driver, too, and got to the top like Murphy and Walter Cox and the others, if he hadn't been black.

Gee whizz, it was fun. You got to a county seat town, maybe say on a Saturday or Sunday, and the fair began the next Tuesday and lasted until Friday afternoon. Doctor Fritz would be, say, in the 2:25 trot on Tuesday afternoon and on Thursday afternoon Bucephalus would knock 'em cold in the free-for-all pace. It left you a lot of time to hang around and listen to horse talk, and see Burt knock some yap cold that got too gay, and you'd find out about horses and men and pick up a lot of stuff you could use all the rest of your life, if you had some sense and salted down what you heard and felt and saw.

And then at the end of the week when the race meet was over, and Harry had run home to tend up to his livery stable business, you and Burt hitched the two horses to carts and drove slow and steady across country, to the place for the next meeting, so as to not overheat the horses, etc., etc., you know.

Gee whizz, Gosh amighty, the nice hickory nut and beechnut

and oaks and other kinds of trees along the roads, all brown and red, and the good smells, and Burt singing a song that was called "Deep River," and the country girls at the windows of houses and everything. You can stick your colleges up your nose for all me. I guess I know where I got my education.

Why, one of those little burgs of towns you come to on the way, say now on a Saturday afternoon, and Burt says, "Let's lay up here." And you did.

And you took the horses to a livery stable and fed them, and you got your good clothes out of a box and put them on.

And the town was full of farmers gaping, because they could see you were race horse people, and the kids maybe never see a nigger before and was afraid and run away when the two of us walked down their main street.

And that was before Prohibition and all that foolishness, and so you went into a saloon, the two of you, and all the yaps come and stood around, and there was always someone pretended he was horsey and knew things and spoke up and began asking questions, and all you did was to lie and lie all you could about what horses you had, and I said I owned them, and then some fellow said, "Will you have a drink of whisky?" and Burt knocked his eye out the way he could say, off-hand like, "Oh well, all right, I'm agreeable to a little nip. I'll split a quart with you." Gee whizz.

But that isn't what I want to tell my story about. We got home late in November and I promised Mother I'd quit the race horses for good. There's a lot of things you've got to promise a mother, because she don't know any better.

And so, there not being any work in our town any more than when I left there to go to the races, I went off to Sandusky and got a pretty good place taking care of horses for a man who owned a teaming and delivery and storage and coal and real estate business there. It was a pretty good place with good eats, and a day off each week, and sleeping on a cot in a big barn, and mostly just shoveling in hay and oats to a lot of big good-enough skates of horses, that couldn't have trotted a race with a toad. I wasn't dissatisfied and I could send money home.

And then, as I started to tell you, the fall races come to Sandusky and I got the day off and I went. I left the job at noon and had on my good clothes and my new brown derby hat I'd just bought the Saturday before, and a stand-up collar.

First of all I went downtown and walked about with the dudes. I've always thought to myself, Put up a good front, and so I did it. I had forty dollars in my pocket and so I went into the West House, a big hotel, and walked up to the cigar stand. "Give me three twenty-five-cent cigars," I said. There was a lot of horsemen and strangers and dressed-up people from other towns standing around in the lobby and in the bar, and I mingled amongst them. In the bar there was a fellow with a cane and a Windsor tie on, that it made me sick to look at him. I like a man to be a man and dress up, but not to go put on that kind of airs. So I pushed him aside, kind of rough, and had me a drink of whisky. And then he looked at me as though he thought maybe he'd get gay, but he changed his mind and didn't say anything. And then I had another drink of whisky, just to show him something, and went out and had a hack out to the races, all to myself, and when I got there I bought myself the best seat I could get up in the grandstand, but didn't go in for any of these boxes. That's putting on too many airs.

And so there I was, sitting up in the grandstand as gay as you please and looking down on the swipes coming out with their horses, and with their dirty horsey pants on and the horse blankets swung over their shoulders, same as I had been doing all the year before. I liked one thing about the same as the other, sitting up there and feeling grand and being down there and looking up at the yaps and feeling grander and more important, too. One thing's about as good as another, if you take it just right. I've often said that.

Well, right in front of me, in the grandstand that day, there was a fellow with a couple of girls and they was about my age. The young fellow was a nice guy all right. He was the kind maybe that goes to college and then comes to be a lawyer or maybe a newspaper editor or something like that, but he wasn't stuck on himself. There are some of that kind are all right and he was one of the ones.

He had his sister with him and another girl, and the sister looked around over his shoulder, accidental at first, not intending to start anything—she wasn't that kind—and her eyes and mine happened to meet.

You know how it is. Gee, she was a peach! She had on a soft dress, kind of a blue stuff and it looked carelessly made, but was well sewed and made and everything. I knew that much. I blushed when she looked right at me and so did she. She was the nicest girl

I've ever seen in my life. She wasn't stuck on herself and she could talk proper grammar without being like a schoolteacher or something like that. What I mean is, she was O. K. I think maybe her father was well-to-do, but not rich to make her chesty because she was his daughter, as some are. Maybe he owned a drugstore or a drygoods store in their home town, or something like that. She never told me and I never asked.

My own people are all O. K. too, when you come to that. My grandfather was Welsh and over in the old country, in Wales, he was— But never mind that.

The first heat of the first race came off and the young fellow setting there with the two girls left them and went down to make a bet. I knew what he was up to, but he didn't talk big and noisy and let everyone around know he was a sport, as some do. He wasn't that kind. Well, he come back and I heard him tell the two girls what horse he'd bet on, and when the heat was trotted they all half got to their feet and acted in the excited, sweaty way people do when they've got money down on a race, and the horse they bet on is up there pretty close at the end, and they think maybe he'll come on with a rush, but he never does because he hasn't got the old juice in him, come right down to it.

And then, pretty soon, the horses came out for the 2:18 pace and there was a horse in it I knew. He was a horse Bob French had in his string but Bob didn't own him. He was a horse owned by a Mr. Mathers down at Marietta, Ohio.

This Mr. Mathers had a lot of money and owned some coal mines or something, and he had a swell place out in the country, and he was stuck on race horses, but was a Presbyterian or something, and I think more than likely his wife was one, too, maybe a stiffer one than himself. So he never raced his horses hisself, and the story round the Ohio race tracks was that when one of his horses got ready to go to the races he turned him over to Bob French and pretended to his wife he was sold.

So Bob had the horses and he did pretty much as he pleased, and you can't blame Bob, at least I never did. Sometimes he was out to win and sometimes he wasn't. I never cared much about that when I was swiping a horse. What I did want to know was that my horse had the speed and could go out in front, if you wanted him to.

And, as I'm telling you, there was Bob in this race with one of Mr. Mathers' horses, was named "About Ben Ahem" or something like that, and was fast as a streak. He was a gelding and had a mark of 2:21, but could step in :08 or :09.

Because when Burt and I were out, as I've told you, the year before, there was a nigger Burt knew, worked for Mr. Mathers, and we went out there one day when we didn't have no race on at the Marietta Fair and our boss Harry was gone home.

And so everyone was gone to the fair but just this one nigger and he took us all through Mr. Mathers' swell house and he and Burt tapped a bottle of wine Mr. Mathers had hid in his bedroom, back in a closet, without his wife knowing, and he showed us this Ahem horse. Burt was always stuck on being a driver but didn't have much chance to get to the top, being a nigger, and he and the other nigger gulped that whole bottle of wine and Burt got a little lit up.

So the nigger let Burt take this About Ben Ahem and step him a mile in a track Mr. Mathers had all to himself, right there on the farm. And Mr. Mathers had one child, a daughter, kinda sick and not very good-looking, and she came home and we had to hustle and get About Ben Ahem stuck back in the barn.

I'm only telling you to get everything straight. At Sandusky, that afternoon I was at the fair, this young fellow with the two girls was fussed, being with the girls and losing his bet. You know how a fellow is that way. One of them was his girl and the other his sister. I had figured that out.

"Gee whizz," I says to myself, "I'm going to give him the dope."

He was mighty nice when I touched him on the shoulder. He and the girls were nice to me right from the start and clear to the end. I'm not blaming them.

And so he leaned back and I give him the dope on About Ben Ahem. "Don't bet a cent on this first heat because he'll go like an oxen hitched to a plow, but when the first heat is over go right down and lay on your pile." That's what I told him.

Well, I never saw a fellow treat anyone sweller. There was a fat man sitting beside the little girl, that had looked at me twice by this time, and I at her, and both blushing, and what did he do but have the nerve to turn and ask the fat man to get up and change places with me so I could set with his crowd.

Gee whizz, craps amighty. There I was. What a chump I was to go and get gay up there in the West House bar, and just because that dude was standing there with a cane and that kind of a necktie on, to go and get all balled up and drink that whisky, just to show off.

Of course she would know, me setting right beside her and letting her smell of my breath. I could have kicked myself right down out of that grandstand and all around that race track and made a faster record than most of the skates of horses they had there that year.

Because that girl wasn't any mutt of a girl. What wouldn't I have give right then for a stick of chewing gum to chew, or a lozenger, or some liquorice, or most anything. I was glad I had those twenty-five-cent cigars in my pocket and right away I give that fellow one and lit one myself. Then that fat man got up and we changed places and there I was, plunked right down beside her.

They introduced themselves and the fellow's best girl, he had with him, was named Miss Elinor Woodbury, and her father was a manufacturer of barrels from a place called Tiffin, Ohio. And the fellow himself was named Wilbur Wessen and his sister was Miss Lucy Wessen.

I suppose it was their having such swell names got me off my trolley. A fellow, just because he has been a swipe with a race horse, and works taking care of horses for a man in the teaming, delivery and storage business, isn't any better or worse than anyone else. I've often thought that, and said it too.

But you know how a fellow is. There's something in that kind of nice clothes, and the kind of nice eyes she had, and the way she had looked at me, awhile before, over her brother's shoulder, and me looking back at her, and both of us blushing.

I couldn't show her up for a boob, could I?

I made a fool of myself, that's what I did. I said my name was Walter Mathers from Marietta, Ohio, and then I told all three of them the smashingest lie you ever heard. What I said was that my father owned the horse About Ben Ahem and that he had let him out to this Bob French for racing purposes, because our family was proud and had never gone into racing that way, in our own name, I mean. Then I had got started and they were all leaning over and listening, and Miss Lucy Wessen's eyes were shining, and I went the whole hog.

I told about our place down at Marietta, and about the big stables and the grand brick house we had on a hill, up above the Ohio River, but I knew enough not to do it in no bragging way.

What I did was to start things and then let them drag the rest out of me. I acted just as reluctant to tell as I could. Our family hasn't got any barrel factory, and, since I've known us, we've always been pretty poor, but not asking anything of any one at that, and my grandfather, over in Wales—but never mind that.

We set there talking like we had known each other for years and years, and I went and told them that my father had been expecting maybe this Bob French wasn't on the square, and had sent me up to Sandusky on the sly to find out what I could.

And I bluffed it through I had found out all about the 2:18 pace, in which About Ben Ahem was to start.

I said he would lose the first heat by pacing like a lame cow and then he would come back and skin 'em alive after that. And to back up what I said I took thirty dollars out of my pocket and handed it to Mr. Wilbur Wessen and asked him, would he mind, after the first heat, to go down and place it on About Ben Ahem for whatever odds he could get. What I said was that I didn't want Bob French to see me and none of the swipes.

Sure enough the first heat come off and About Ben Ahem went off his stride, up the back stretch, and looked like a wooden horse or a sick one, and come in to be last. Then this Wilbur Wessen went down to the betting place under the grandstand and there I was with the two girls, and when that Miss Woodbury was looking the other way once, Lucy Wessen kinda, with her shoulder you know, kinda touched me. Not just tucking down, I don't mean. You know how a woman can do. They get close, but not getting gay either. You know what they do. Gee whizz.

And then they give me a jolt. What they had done, when I didn't know, was to get together, and they had decided Wilbur Wessen would bet fifty dollars, and the two girls had gone and put in ten dollars each, of their own money, too. I was sick then, but I was sicker later.

About the gelding, About Ben Ahem, and their winning their money, I wasn't worried a lot about that. It come out O.K. Ahem stepped the next three heats like a bushel of spoiled eggs going to market before they could be found out, and Wilbur Wessen had got nine to two for the money. There was something else eating at me.

Because Wilbur come back, after he had bet the money, and

after that he spent most of his time talking to that Miss Woodbury, and Lucy Wessen and I was left alone together like on a desert island. Gee, if I'd only been on the square or if there had been any way of getting myself on the square. There ain't any Walter Mathers, like I said to her and them, and there hasn't ever been one, but if there was, I bet I'd go to Marietta, Ohio, and shoot him tomorrow.

There I was, big boob that I am. Pretty soon the race was over, and Wilbur had gone down and collected our money, and we had a hack downtown, and he stood us a swell supper at the West House, and a bottle of champagne beside.

And I was with that girl and she wasn't saying much, and I wasn't saying much either. One thing I know. She wasn't stuck on me because of the lie about my father being rich and all that. There's a way you know. . . . Craps amighty. There's a kind of girl, you see just once in your life, and if you don't get busy and make hay, then you're gone for good and all, and might as well go jump off a bridge. They give you a look from inside of them somewhere, and it ain't no vamping, and what it means is—you want that girl to be your wife, and you want nice things around her like flowers and swell clothes, and you want her to have the kids you're going to have, and you want good music played and no ragtime. Gee whizz.

There's a place over near Sandusky, across a kind of bay, and it's called Cedar Point. And after we had supper we went over to it in a launch, all by ourselves. Wilbur and Miss Lucy and that Miss Woodbury had to catch a ten-o'clock train back to Tiffin, Ohio, because, when you're out with girls like that you can't get careless and miss any trains and stay out all night, like you can with some kinds of Janes.

And Wilbur blowed himself to the launch and it cost him fifteen cold plunks, but I wouldn't never have knew if I hadn't listened. He wasn't no tinhorn kind of a sport.

Over at the Cedar Point place, we didn't stay around where there was a gang of common kind of cattle at all.

There was big dance halls and dining places for yaps, and there was a beach you could walk along and get where it was dark, and we went there.

She didn't talk hardly at all and neither did I, and I was thinking how glad I was my mother was all right, and always made us kids learn to eat with a fork at table, and not swill soup, and not be noisy and rough like a gang you see around a race track that way.

Then Wilbur and his girl went away up the beach and Lucy and I sat down in a dark place, where there was some roots of old trees, the water had washed up, and after that the time, till we had to go back in the launch and they had to catch their trains, wasn't nothing at all. It went like winking your eye.

Here's how it was. The place we were setting in was dark, like I said, and there was the roots from that old stump sticking up like arms, and there was a watery smell, and the night was like—as if you could put your hand out and feel it—so warm and soft and dark and sweet like an orange.

I most cried and I most swore and I most jumped up and danced, I was so mad and happy and sad.

When Wilbur come back from being alone with his girl, and she saw him coming, Lucy she says, "We got to go to the train now," and she was most crying too, but she never knew nothing I knew, and she couldn't be so all busted up. And then, before Wilbur and Miss Woodbury got up to where we was, she put her face up and kissed me quick and put her head up against me and she was all quivering and— Gee whizz.

Sometimes I hope I have cancer and die. I guess you know what I mean. We went in the launch across the bay to the train like that, and it was dark, too. She whispered and said it was like she and I could get out of the boat and walk on the water, and it sounded foolish, but I knew what she meant.

And then quick we were right at the depot, and there was a big gang of yaps, the kind that goes to the fairs, and crowded and milling around like cattle, and how could I tell her? "It won't be long because you'll write and I'll write to you." That's all she said.

I got a chance like a hay barn afire. A swell chance I got.

And maybe she would write me, down at Marietta that way, and the letter would come back, and stamped on the front of it by the U.S.A. "there ain't any such guy," or something like that, whatever they stamp on a letter that way.

And me trying to pass myself off for a bigbug and a swell—to her, as decent a little body as God ever made. Craps amighty—a swell chance I got!

And then the train come in, and she got on it, and Wilbur Wessen he come and shook hands with me, and that Miss Woodbury was nice too and bowed to me, and I at her, and the train went and I busted out and cried like a kid.

Gee, I could have run after that train and made Dan Patch look like a freight train after a wreck but, socks amighty, what was the use? Did you ever see such a fool?

I'll bet you what—if I had an arm broke right now or a train had run over my foot—I wouldn't go to no doctor at all. I'd go set down and let her hurt and hurt—that's what I'd do.

I'll bet you what—if I hadn't a drunk that booze I'd a never been such a boob as to go tell such a lie—that couldn't never be made straight to a lady like her.

I wish I had that fellow right here that had on a Windsor tie and carried a cane. I'd smash him for fair. Gosh darn his eyes. He's a big fool—that's what he is.

And if I'm not another, you just go find me one and I'll quit working and be a bum and give him my job. I don't care nothing for working, and earning money, and saving it for no such boob as myself.

The Triumph of a Modern or, Send for the Lawyer

INASMUCH AS I have put to myself the task of trying to tell you a curious story in which I am myself concerned—in a strictly secondary way, you must of course understand—I will begin by giving you some notion of myself.

Very well then, I am a man of thirty-two, rather small in size, with sandy hair. I wear glasses. Until two years ago I lived in Chicago, where I had a position as clerk in an office that afforded me a good enough living. I have never married, being somewhat afraid of women—in the flesh, in a way of speaking. In fancy and in my imagination I have always been very bold, but in the flesh women have always frightened me horribly. They have a way of smiling quietly as though to say— But we will not go into that now.

Since boyhood I have had an ambition to be a painter, not, I will confess, because of a desire to produce some great masterpiece of the arts, but simply and solely because I have always thought the life painters lead would appeal to me.

I have always liked the notion (let's be honest if we can) of going about, wearing a hat tipped a little to the side of my head, sporting a mustache, carrying a cane and speaking in an offhand way of such things as form, rhythm, the effects of light and masses, surfaces, et cetera, et cetera. During my life I have read a good many books concerning painters and their work, their friendships and their loves and when I was in Chicago and poor and was compelled to live in a small room alone, I assure you I carried off many a dull weary evening by imagining myself a painter of wide renown in the world.

It was afternoon and having finished my day's work I went strolling off to the studio of another painter. He was still at work and there were two models in the room, women in the nude sitting about. One of them smiled at me, I thought a little wistfully, but pshaw, I am too blasé for anything of that sort.

I go across the room to my friend's canvas and stand looking at it.

Now he is looking at me, a little anxiously. I am the greater man, you understand. That is frankly and freely acknowledged. Whatever else may be said against my friend, he never claimed to be my equal. In fact it is generally understood, wherever I go, that I am the greater man.

"Well?" says my friend. You see he is fairly hanging on my words, as the saying goes; in short, he is waiting for me to speak, with the air of one about to be hanged.

Why? The devil! Why does he put everything up to me? One gets tired carrying such responsibility upon one's shoulders. A painter should be the judge of his own work and not embarrass his fellow painters by asking questions. That is my method.

Very well then. If I speak sharply you have only yourself to blame. "The yellow you have been using is a little muddy. The arm of this woman is not felt. In painting one should feel the arm of a woman. What I advise is that you change your palette. You have scattered too much. Pull it together. A painting should stick together as a wet snowball thrown by a boy clings to a wall."

When I had reached the age of thirty, that is to say two years ago, I received from my aunt, the sister of my father to be exact, a small fortune I had long been dreaming I might possibly inherit.

My aunt I had never seen, but I had always been saying to myself, "I must go see my aunt. The old lady will be sore at me and when she dies will not leave me a cent."

And then, lucky fellow that I am, I did go to see her just before she died.

Filled with determination to put the thing through, I set out from Chicago, and it is not my fault that I did not spend the day with her. Even although my aunt is (as I am not fool enough not to know that you know) a woman, I would have spent the day with her but that it was impossible.

She lived at Madison, Wisconsin, and I went there on Saturday morning. The house was locked and the windows boarded up. Fortunately, at just that moment, a mail carrier came along and, upon my telling him that I was my aunt's nephew, gave me her address. He also gave me some news concerning her.

For years she had been a sufferer from hay fever and every summer had to have a change of climate.

That was an opportunity for me. I went at once to a hotel and wrote her a letter telling of my visit and expressing, to the utmost of my ability, my sorrow in not having found her at home. I have been a long time doing this job but now that I am at it I fancy I shall do it rather well, I said to myself.

A sort of feeling came into my hand, as it were. I can't just say what it was, but as soon as I sat down I knew very well I should be eloquent. For the moment I was positively a poet.

In the first place, and as one should in writing a letter to a lady, I spoke of the sky. "The sky is full of mottled clouds," I said. Then, and I frankly admit in a brutally casual way, I spoke of myself as one practically prostrated with grief. To tell the truth I did not just know what I was doing. I had got the fever for writing words, you see. They fairly flowed out of my pen.

I had come, I said, on a long and weary journey to the home of my only female relative, and here I threw into the letter some reference to the fact that I was an orphan. "Imagine," I wrote, "the sorrow and desolation in my heart at finding the house unoccupied and the windows boarded up."

It was there, sitting in the hotel at Madison, Wisconsin, with the pen in my hand, that I made my fortune. Something bold and heroic came into my mood and, without a moment's hesitation, I mentioned in my letter what should never be mentioned to a woman, unless she be an elderly woman of one's own family, and then only by a physician perhaps—I spoke of my aunt's breasts, using the plural.

I had hoped, I said, to lay my tired head on her breasts. To tell the truth I had become drunken with words and now, how glad I am that I did. Mr. George Moore, Clive Bell, Paul Rosenfeld, and others of the most skillful writers of our English speech, have written a great deal about painters and, as I have already explained, there was not a book or magazine article in English and concerning painters, their lives and works, procurable in Chicago, I had not read.

What I am now striving to convey to you is something of my own pride in my literary effort in the hotel at Madison, Wisconsin, and surely, if I was at the moment an artist, no other artist has ever had such quick and wholehearted recognition.

Having spoken of putting my tired head on my aunt's breasts (poor woman, she died, never having seen me) I went on to give the general impression—which by the way was quite honest and correct—of a somewhat boyish figure, rather puzzled, wandering in a confused way through life. The imaginary but correct enough figure of myself, born at the moment in my imagination, had made its way through dismal swamps of gloom, over the rough hills of adversity and through the dry deserts of loneliness, toward the one spot in all this world where it had hoped to find rest and peace—that is to say upon the bosom of its aunt. However, as I have already explained, being a thorough modern and full of the modern boldness, I did not use the word *bosom,* as an old-fashioned writer might have done. I used the word *breasts.* When I had finished writing, tears were in my eyes.

The letter I wrote on that day covered some seven sheets of hotel paper—finely written to the margins—and cost four cents to mail.

"Shall I mail it or shall I not?" I said to myself as I came out of the hotel office and stood before a mailbox. The letter was balanced between my finger and thumb.

Eeny, meeny, miny, mo,
Catch a nigger by the toe.

The forefinger of my left hand—I was holding the letter in my right hand—touched my nose, mouth, forehead, eyes, chin, neck, shoulder, arm, hand and then tapped the letter itself. No doubt I fully intended, from the first, to drop it. I had been doing the work of an artist. Well, artists are always talking of destroying their own work but few do it, and those who do are perhaps the real heroes of life.

And so down into the mailbox it went with a thud and my fortune was made. The letter was received by my aunt, who was lying abed of an illness that was to destroy her—she had, it seems, other things beside hay fever the matter with her—and she altered her will in my favor. She had intended leaving her money, a tidy sum yielding an income of five thousand a year, to a fund to be established for the study of methods for the cure of hay fever—that is to say, really you see, to her fellow sufferers—but instead left it to me. My aunt could not find her spectacles and a nurse—may the gods bring her bright days and a good husband—read the letter aloud. Both women were deeply touched and my aunt wept. I am only telling you the facts, you understand, but I would like to suggest that this whole incident might well be taken as proof of the power of modern art. From the first I have been a firm believer in the moderns. I am one who, as an art critic might word it, has been right down through the movements. At first I was an impressionist and later a cubist, a post-impressionist, and even a vorticist. Time after time, in my imaginary life, as a painter, I have been quite swept off my feet. For example I remember Picasso's blue period— But we'll not go into that.

What I am trying to say is that, having this faith in modernity, if one may use the word thus, I did find within myself a peculiar boldness as I sat in the hotel writing room at Madison, Wisconsin. I used the word *breasts* (in the plural, you understand) and everyone will admit that it is a bold and modern word to use in a letter to an aunt one has never seen. It brought my aunt and me into one family. Her modesty never could have admitted anything else.

And then, my aunt was really touched. Afterward I talked to the nurse and made her a rather handsome present for her part in the affair. When the letter had been read my aunt felt overwhelmingly drawn to me. She turned her face to the wall and her shoulders shook. Do not think that I am not also touched as I write this. "Poor lad," my aunt said to the nurse, "I will make things easier for him. Send for the lawyer."

The Man Who Became a Woman

MY FATHER was a retail druggist in our town, out in Nebraska, which was so much like a thousand other towns I've been in since that there's no use fooling around and taking up your time and mine trying to describe it.

Anyway I became a drug clerk and after Father's death the store was sold and Mother took the money and went West, to her sister in California, giving me four hundred dollars with which to make my start in the world. I was only nineteen years old then.

I came to Chicago, where I worked as a drug clerk for a time, and then, as my health suddenly went back on me, perhaps because I was so sick of my lonely life in the city and of the sight and smell of the drugstore, I decided to set out on what seemed to me then the great adventure and became for a time a tramp, working now and then, when I had no money, but spending all the time I could loafing around out of doors or riding up and down the land on freight trains and trying to see the world. I even did some stealing in lonely towns at night—once a pretty good suit of clothes that someone had left hanging out on a clothesline, and once some shoes out of a box in a freight car—but I was in constant terror of being caught and put into jail, so I realized that success as a thief was not for me.

The most delightful experience of that period of my life was when I once worked as a groom, or swipe, with race horses, and it was during that time I met a young fellow of about my own age who has since become a writer of some prominence.

The young man of whom I now speak had gone into race track work as a groom, to bring a kind of flourish, a high spot, he used to say, into his life.

He was then unmarried and had not been successful as a writer. What I mean is he was free and I guess, with him as with me, there was something he liked about the people who hang about a race track, the touts, swipes, drivers, niggers and gamblers. You know what a gaudy undependable lot they are—if you've ever been around the tracks much—about the best liars I've ever seen, and not saving money or thinking about morals, like most druggists, dry-goods merchants and the others who used to be my father's friends in our Nebraska town—and not bending the knee much either, or kowtowing to people they thought must be grander or richer or more powerful than themselves.

What I mean is, they were an independent, go-to-the-devil, come-have-a-drink-of-whisky, kind of a crew and when one of them won a bet, "knocked 'em off," we called it, his money was just dirt to him while it lasted. No king or president or soap manufacturer—gone on a trip with his family to Europe—could throw on more dog than one of them, with his big diamond rings and the diamond horseshoe stuck in his necktie and all.

I liked the whole blamed lot pretty well and he did too.

He was groom temporarily for a pacing gelding named Lumpy Joe owned by a tall black-mustached man named Alfred Kreymborg and trying the best he could to make the bluff to himself he was a real one. It happened that we were on the same circuit, doing the West Pennsylvania county fairs all that fall, and on fine evenings we spent a good deal of time walking and talking together.

Let us suppose it to be a Monday or Tuesday evening and our horses had been put away for the night. The racing didn't start until later in the week, maybe Wednesday, usually. There was always a little place called a dining hall, run mostly by the Woman's Christian Temperance Associations of the towns, and we would go there to eat where we could get a pretty good meal for twenty-five cents. At least then we thought it pretty good.

I would manage it so that I sat beside this fellow, whose name was Tom Means and when we had got through eating we would go look at our two horses again and when we got there Lumpy Joe would be eating his hay in his box stall and Alfred Kreymborg would be standing there, pulling his mustache and looking as sad as a sick crane.

But he wasn't really sad. "You two boys want to go downtown to see the girls. I'm an old duffer and way past that myself. You go on along. I'll be setting here anyway, and I'll keep an eye on both the horses for you," he would say.

So we would set off, going, not into the town to try to get in with some of the town girls, who might have taken up with us because we were strangers and race track fellows, but out into the country.

Sometimes we got into a hilly country and there was a moon. The leaves were falling off the trees and lay in the road so that we kicked them up with the dust as we went along.

To tell the truth, I suppose I got to love Tom Means, who was five years older than me, although I wouldn't have dared say so, then. Americans are shy and timid about saying things like that and a man here don't dare own up he loves another man, I've found out, and they are afraid to admit such feelings to themselves even. I guess they're afraid it may be taken to mean something it don't need to at all.

Anyway we walked along and some of the trees were already bare and looked like people standing solemnly beside the road and listening to what we had to say. Only I didn't say much. Tom Means did most of the talking.

Sometimes we came back to the race track and it was late and the moon had gone down and it was dark. Then we often walked round and round the track, sometimes a dozen times, before we crawled into the hay to go to bed.

Tom talked always on two subjects, writing and race horses, but mostly about race horses. The quiet sounds about the race tracks and the smells of horses, and the things that go with horses, seemed to get him all excited. "Oh hell, Herman Dudley," he would burst out suddenly, "don't go talking to me. I know what I think. I've been around more than you have and I've seen a world of people. There isn't any man or woman, not even a fellow's own mother, as fine as a horse, that is to say a thoroughbred horse."

Sometimes he would go on like that a long time, speaking of people he had seen and their characteristics. He wanted to be a writer later, and what he said was that when he came to be one he wanted to write the way a well-bred horse runs or trots or paces. Whether he ever did it or not I can't say. He has written a lot, but I'm not too good a judge of such things. Anyway I don't think he has.

But when he got on the subject of horses he certainly was a darby. I would never have felt the way I finally got to feel about horses or enjoyed my stay among them half so much if it hadn't been for him. Often he would go on talking for an hour maybe, speaking of horses' bodies and of their minds and wills as though they were human beings. "Lord help us, Herman," he would say, grabbing hold of my arm, "don't it get you up in the throat? I say now, when a good one, like that Lumpy Joe I'm swiping, flattens himself at the head of the stretch and he's coming, and you know he's coming, and you know his heart's sound, and he's game, and you know he isn't going to let himself get licked—don't it get you Herman, don't it get you like the old Harry?"

That's the way he would talk, and then later, sometimes, he'd talk about writing and get himself all het up about that too. He had some notions about writing I've never got myself around to thinking much about but just the same maybe his talk, working in me, has led me to want to begin to write this story myself.

There was one experience of that time on the tracks that I am forced, by some feeling inside myself, to tell.

Well, I don't know why, but I've just got to. It will be kind of like confession is, I suppose, to a good Catholic, or maybe, better yet, like cleaning up the room you live in, if you are a bachelor, like I was for so long. The room gets pretty mussy and the bed not made some days and clothes and things thrown on the closet floor and maybe under the bed. And then you clean all up and put on new sheets, and then you take off all your clothes and get down on your hands and knees, and scrub the floor so clean you could eat bread off it, and then take a walk and come home after a while and your room smells sweet and you feel sweetened-up and better inside yourself too.

What I mean is, this story has been on my chest, and I've often dreamed about the happenings in it, even after I married Jessie and was happy. Sometimes I even screamed out at night and so I said to myself, "I'll write the dang story," and here goes.

Fall had come on and in the mornings now when we crept out of our blankets, spread out on the hay in the tiny lofts above the horse stalls, and put our heads out to look around, there was a white rime of frost on the ground. When we woke, the horses woke too. You know how it is at the tracks—the little barnlike stalls with the tiny lofts above are all set along in a row and there are two doors to each stall, one coming up to a horse's breast and then a top one, that is only closed at night and in bad weather.

In the mornings the upper door is swung open and fastened back and the horses put their heads out. There is the white rime on the grass over inside the gray oval the track makes. Usually there is some outfit that has six, ten or even twelve horses, and perhaps they have a Negro cook who does his cooking at an open fire in the clear space before the row of stalls and he is at work now, and the horses with their big fine eyes are looking about and whinnying, and a stallion looks out at the door of one of the stalls and sees a sweet-eyed mare looking at him and sends up his trumpet call, and a man's voice laughs, and there are no women anywhere in sight or no sign of one anywhere, and everyone feels like laughing and usually does.

It's pretty fine, but I didn't know how fine it was until I got to know Tom Means and heard him talk about it all.

At the time the thing happened of which I am trying to tell now, Tom was no longer with me. A week before, his owner, Alfred Kreymborg, had taken his horse Lumpy Joe over into the Ohio Fair Circuit and I saw no more of Tom at the tracks.

There was a story going about the stalls that Lumpy Joe, a big rangy brown gelding, wasn't really named Lumpy Joe at all, that he was a ringer who had made a fast record out in Iowa and up through the Northwest country the year before, and that Kreymborg had picked him up and had kept him under wraps all winter and had brought him over into the Pennsylvania country under this new name and made a cleanup in the books.

I know nothing about that and never talked to Tom about it, but anyway he, Lumpy Joe and Kreymborg were all gone now.

I suppose I'll always remember those days, and Tom's talk at night, and before that, in the early September evenings, how we sat around in front of the stalls, and Kreymborg sitting on an upturned feed box and pulling at his long black mustache and some times humming a little ditty one couldn't catch the words of. It was something about a deep well and a little gray squirrel crawling up the sides of it, and he never laughed or smiled much, but there was something in his solemn gray eyes, not quite a twinkle, something more delicate than that.

The others talked in low tones, and Tom and I sat in silence. He never did his best talking except when he and I were alone.

For his sake—if he ever sees my story—I should mention that at the only big track we ever visited, at Readville, Pennsylvania, we saw old Pop Geers, the great racing driver, himself. His horses were at a place far away across the tracks from where we were stabled. I suppose a man like him was likely to get the choice of all the good places for his horses.

We went over there one evening and stood about, and there was Geers himself, sitting before one of the stalls on a box, tapping the ground with a riding whip. They called him, around the tracks, "the silent man from Tennessee," and he was silent—that night anyway. All we did was to stand and look at him for maybe a half hour and then we went away, and that night Tom talked better than I had ever heard him. He said that the ambition of his life was to wait until Pop Geers died and then write a book about him, and to show in the book that there was at least one American who never went nutty about getting rich or owning a big factory or being any other kind of a hell of a fellow. "He's satisfied, I think, to sit around like that and wait until the big moments of his life come, when he heads a fast one into the stretch and then, darn his soul, he can give all of himself to the thing right in front of him," Tom said, and then he was so worked up he began to blubber. We were walking along the fence on the inside of the tracks and it was dusk and, in some trees nearby, some birds, just sparrows maybe, were making a chirping sound, and you could hear insects singing and, where there was a little light, off to the west between some trees, motes were dancing in the air. Tom said that about Pop Geers, although I think he was thinking most about something he wanted to be himself and wasn't, and then he went and stood by the fence and sort of blubbered and I began to blubber too, although I didn't know what about.

But perhaps I did know, after all. I suppose Tom wanted to feel, when he became a writer, like he thought old Pop must feel when his horse swung around the upper turn, and there lay the stretch before him, and if he was going to get his horse home in front he had to do it right then. What Tom said was that any man had something in him that understands about a thing like that but that no woman ever did except up in her brain. He often got off things like that about women, but I notice he later married one of them just the same.

But to get back to my knitting. After Tom had left, the stable I was with kept drifting along through nice little Pennsylvania county seat towns. My owner, a strange excitable kind of a man from over in Ohio, who had lost a lot of money on horses but was always thinking he would maybe get it all back in some big killing, had been playing in pretty good luck that year. The horse I had, a tough little gelding, a five-year-old, had been getting home in front pretty regular and so he took some of his winnings and bought a three-years-old black pacing stallion named O My Man. My gelding was called Pick-it-boy, because when he was in a race and had got into the stretch my owner always got half wild with excitement and shouted so you could hear him a mile and a half. "Go, pick it boy, pick it boy, pick it boy," he kept shouting and so when he had got hold of this good little gelding he had named him that.

The gelding was a fast one, all right. As the boys at the tracks used to say, he "picked 'em up sharp and set 'em down clean," and he was what we called a natural race horse, right up to all the speed he had, and didn't require much training. "All you got to do is to drop him down on the track and he'll go," was what my owner was always saying to other men, when he was bragging about his horse.

And so, you see, after Tom left, I hadn't much to do evenings and then the new stallion, the three-year-old, came on with a Negro swipe named Burt.

I liked him fine and he liked me, but not the same as Tom and me. We got to be friends all right, and I suppose Burt would have done things for me, and maybe me for him, that Tom and me wouldn't have done for each other.

But with a Negro you couldn't be close friends like you can with another white man. There's some reason you can't understand but it's true. There's been too much talk about the difference between whites and blacks and you're both shy, and anyway no use trying, and I suppose Burt and I both knew it and so I was pretty lonesome.

Something happened to me that happened several times, when I was a young fellow, that I have never exactly understood. Sometimes now I think it was all because I had got to be almost a man and had never been with a woman. I don't know what's the matter with me. I can't ask a woman. I've tried it a good many times in my life but every time I've tried the same thing happened.

Of course, with Jessie now, it's different, but at the time of which I'm speaking Jessie was a long ways off and a good many things were to happen to me before I got to her.

Around a race track, as you may suppose, the fellows who are swipes and drivers and strangers in the towns do not go without women. They don't have to. In any town there are always some fly girls will come around a place like that. I suppose they think they are fooling with men who lead romantic lives. Such girls will come along by the front of the stalls where the race horses are and, if you look all right to them, they will stop and make a fuss over your horse. They rub their little hands over the horse's nose and then is the time for you—if you aren't a fellow like me who can't get up the nerve—then is the time for you to smile and say, "Hello, kid," and make a date with one of them for that evening uptown after supper. I couldn't do that, although the Lord knows I tried hard enough, often enough. A girl would come along alone, and she would be a little thing and give me the eye, and I would try and try but couldn't say anything. Both Tom, and Burt afterward, used to laugh at me about it sometimes but what I think is that, had I been able to speak up to one of them and had managed to make a date with her, nothing would have come of it. We would probably have walked around the town and got off together in the dark somewhere, where the town came to an end, and then she would have had to knock me over with a club before it got any further.

And so there I was, having got used to Tom and our talks together, and Burt of course had his own friends among the black men. I got lazy and mopey and had a hard time doing my work.

It was like this. Sometimes I would be sitting, perhaps under a tree in the late afternoon when the races were over for the day and the crowds had gone away. There were always a lot of other men and boys who hadn't any horses in the races that day and they would be standing or sitting about in front of the stalls and talking.

I would listen for a time to their talk and then their voices would seem to go far away. The things I was looking at would go far away too. Perhaps there would be a tree, not more than a hundred yards away, and it would just come out of the ground and float away like a thistle. It would get smaller and smaller, away off there in the sky, and then suddenly—bang, it would be back where it belonged, in the ground, and I would begin hearing the voices of the men talking again.

When Tom was with me that summer the nights were splendid. We usually walked about and talked until pretty late and then I crawled up into my hole and went to sleep. Always out of Tom's talk I got something that stayed in my mind, after I was off by myself, curled up in my blanket. I suppose he had a way of making pictures as he talked and the pictures stayed by me as Burt was always saying pork chops did by him. "Give me the old pork chops, they stick to the ribs," Burt was always saying, and with the imagination it was always that way about Tom's talks. He started something inside you that went on and on, and your mind played with it like walking about in a strange town and seeing the sights, and you slipped off to sleep and had splendid dreams and woke up in the morning feeling fine.

And then he was gone and it wasn't that way any more and I got into the fix I have described. At night I kept seeing women's bodies and women's lips and things in my dreams, and woke up in the morning feeling like the old Harry.

Burt was pretty good to me. He always helped me cool Pick-it-boy out after a race and he did the things himself that take the most skill and quickness, like getting the bandages on a horse's leg smooth, and seeing that every strap is setting just right, and every buckle drawn up to just the right hole, before your horse goes out on the track for a heat.

Burt knew there was something wrong with me and put himself out not to let the boss know. When the boss was around he was always bragging about me. "The brightest kid I've ever worked with around the tracks," he would say and grin, and that at a time when I wasn't worth my salt.

When you go out with the horses there is one job that always takes a lot of time. In the late afternoon, after your horse has been in a race and after you have washed him and rubbed him out, he has to be walked slowly, sometimes for hours and hours, so he'll cool out slowly and won't get muscle-bound. I got so I did that job for both our horses and Burt did the more important things. It left him free to go talk or shoot dice with the other niggers and I didn't mind. I rather liked it and after a hard race even the stallion O My Man was tame enough, even when there were mares about.

You walk and walk and walk, around a little circle, and your horse's head is right by your shoulder, and all around you the life of the place you are in is going on, and in a queer way you get so you aren't really a part of it at all. Perhaps no one ever gets as I was then, except boys that aren't quite men yet and who, like me, have never been with girls or women—to really be with them, up to the hilt, I mean. I used to wonder if young girls got that way too before they married or did what we used to call "go on the town."

If I remember it right though, I didn't do much thinking then. Often I would have forgotten supper if Burt hadn't shouted at me and reminded me, and sometimes he forgot and went off to town with one of the other niggers and I did forget.

There I was with the horse, going slow slow slow, around a circle that way. The people were leaving the fairgrounds now, some afoot, some driving away to the farms in wagons and Fords. Clouds of dust floated in the air and over to the west, where the town was, maybe the sun was going down, a red ball of fire through the dust. Only a few hours before, the crowd had been all filled with excitement and everyone shouting. Let us suppose my horse had been in a race that afternoon and I had stood in front of the grandstand with my horse blanket over my shoulder, alongside of Burt perhaps, and when they came into the stretch my owner began to call, in that queer high voice of his that seemed to float over the top of all the shouting up in the grandstand. And his voice was saying over and over, "Go, pick it boy, pick it boy, pick it boy," the way he always did, and my heart was thumping so I could hardly breathe, and Burt was leaning over and snapping his fingers and muttering, "Come, little sweet. Come on home. Your mama wants you. Come get your 'lasses and bread, little Pick-it-boy."

Well, all that was over now and the voices of the people left around were all low. And Pick-it-boy—I was leading him slowly around the little ring, to cool him out slowly, as I've said—he was different too. Maybe he had pretty nearly broken his heart trying to get down to the wire in front, or getting down there in front, and now everything inside him was quiet and tired, as it was nearly all the time those days in me, except in me tired but not quiet.

You remember I've told you we always walked in a circle, round and round and round. I guess something inside me got to going round and round and round too. The sun did sometimes and the trees and the clouds of dust. I had to think sometimes about putting down my feet so they went down in the right place and I didn't get to staggering like a drunken man.

And a funny feeling came that it is going to be hard to describe. It had something to do with the life in the horse and in me. Sometimes, these late years, I've thought maybe Negroes would understand what I'm trying to talk about now better than any white man ever will. I mean something about men and animals, something between them, something that can perhaps only happen to a white man when he has slipped off his base a little, as I suppose I had then. I think maybe a lot of horsey people feel it sometimes though. It's something like this, maybe—do you suppose it could be that something we whites have got, and think such a lot of, and are so proud about, isn't much of any good after all?

It's something in us that wants to be big and grand and important maybe and won't let us just be, like a horse or a dog or a bird can. Let's say Pick-it-boy had won his race that day. He did that pretty often that summer. Well, he was neither proud, like I would have been in his place, or mean in one part of the inside of him either. He was just himself, doing something with a kind of simplicity. That's what Pick-it-boy was like and I got to feeling it in him as I walked with him slowly in the gathering darkness. I got inside him in some way I can't explain and he got inside me. Often we would stop walking for no cause and he would put his nose up against my face.

I wished he was a girl sometimes or that I was a girl and he was a man. It's an odd thing to say but it's a fact. Being with him that way, so long, and in such a quiet way, cured something in me a little. Often after an evening like that I slept all right and did not have the kind of dreams I've spoken about.

But I wasn't cured for very long and couldn't get cured. My body seemed all right and just as good as ever but there wasn't no pep in me.

Then the fall got later and later and we came to the last town we were going to make before my owner laid his horses up for the winter, in his home town over across the state line in Ohio, and the track was up on a hill, or rather in a kind of high plain above the town.

It wasn't much of a place and the sheds were rather rickety and the track bad, especially at the turns. As soon as we got to the place and got stabled, it began to rain and kept it up all week so the fair had to be put off.

As the purses weren't very large a lot of the owners shipped right out but our owner stayed. The fair owners guaranteed expenses, whether the races were held the next week or not.

And all week there wasn't much of anything for Burt and me to do but clean manure out of the stalls in the morning, watch for a chance when the rain let up a little to jog the horses around the track in the mud and then clean them off, blanket them and stick them back in their stalls.

It was the hardest time of all for me. Burt wasn't so bad off as there were a dozen or two blacks around and in the evening they went off to town, got liquored up a little and came home late, singing and talking, even in the cold rain.

And then one night I got mixed up in the thing I'm trying to tell you about.

It was a Saturday evening and when I look back at it now it seems to me everyone had left the tracks but just me. In the early evening swipe after swipe came over to my stall and asked me if I was going to stick around. When I said I was he would ask me to keep an eye out for him, that nothing happened to his horse. "Just take a stroll down that way now and then, eh, kid," one of them would say, "I just want to run up to town for an hour or two."

I would say "Yes" to be sure, and so pretty soon it was dark as pitch up there in that little ruined fairground and nothing living anywhere around but the horses and me.

I stood it as long as I could, walking here and there in the mud and rain, and thinking all the time I wished I was someone else and not myself. "If I were someone else," I thought, "I wouldn't be here but down there in town with the others." I saw myself going into saloons and having drinks and later going off to a house maybe and getting myself a woman.

I got to thinking so much that, as I went stumbling around up there in the darkness, it was as though what was in my mind was actually happening.

Only I wasn't with some cheap woman, such as I would have found had I had the nerve to do what I wanted but with such a woman as I thought then I should never find in this world. She was slender and like a flower and with something in her like a race horse too, something in her like Pick-it-boy in the stretch, I guess.

And I thought about her and thought about her until I couldn't stand thinking any more. "I'll do something anyway," I said to myself.

So, although I had told all the swipes I would stay and watch their horses, I went out of the fairgrounds and down the hill a ways. I went down until I came to a little low saloon, not in the main part of the town itself but halfway up the hillside. The saloon had once been a residence, a farmhouse perhaps, but if it was ever a farmhouse I'm sure the farmer who lived there and worked the land on that hillside hadn't made out very well. The country didn't look like a farming country, such as one sees all about the other county-seat towns we had been visiting all through the late summer and fall. Everywhere you looked there were stones sticking out of the ground and the trees mostly of the stubby, stunted kind. It looked wild and untidy and ragged, that's what I mean. On the flat plain, up above, where the fairground was, there were a few fields and pastures, and there were some sheep raised and in the field right next to the tracks, on the furtherest side from town, on the back-stretch side, there had once been a slaughterhouse, the ruins of which were still standing. It hadn't been used for quite some time but there were bones of animals lying all about in the field, and there was a smell coming out of the old building that would curl your hair.

The horses hated the place, just as we swipes did, and in the morning when we were jogging them around the track in the mud, to keep them in racing condition, Pick-it-boy and O My Man both raised old Ned every time we headed them up the back stretch and got near to where the old slaughterhouse stood. They would rear and fight at the bit, and go off their stride and run until they got clear of the rotten smells, and neither Burt nor I could make them stop it. "It's a hell of a town down there and this is a hell of a track for racing," Burt kept saying. "If they ever have their danged old fair someone's going to get spilled and maybe killed back here." Whether they did or not I don't know as I didn't stay for the fair, for reasons I'll tell you pretty soon, but Burt was speaking sense all right. A race horse isn't like a human being. He won't stand for it to have to do his work in any rotten ugly kind of a dump the way a man will, and he won't stand for the smells a man will either.

But to get back to my story again. There I was, going down the hillside in the darkness and the cold soaking rain and breaking my word to all the others about staying up above and watching the horses. When I got to the little saloon I decided to stop and have a drink or two. I'd found out long before that about two drinks upset me so I was two-thirds piped and couldn't walk straight, but on that night I didn't care a tinker's dam.

So I went up a kind of path, out of the road, toward the front door of the saloon. It was in what must have been the parlor of the place when it was a farmhouse and there was a little front porch.

I stopped before I opened the door and looked about a little. From where I stood I could look right down into the main street of the town, like being in a big city, like New York or Chicago, and looking down out of the fifteenth floor of an office building into the street.

The hillside was mighty steep and the road up had to wind and wind or no one could ever have come up out of the town to their plagued old fair at all.

It wasn't much of a town I saw—a main street with a lot of saloons and a few stores, one or two dinky moving-picture places, a few Fords, hardly any women or girls in sight and a raft of men. I tried to think of the girl I had been dreaming about, as I walked around in the mud and darkness up at the fairgrounds, living in the place but I couldn't make it. It was like trying to think of Pick-it-boy getting himself worked up to the state I was in then, and going into the ugly dump I was going into. It couldn't be done.

All the same I knew the town wasn't all right there in sight. There must have been a good many of the kinds of houses Pennsylvania miners live in back in the hills, or around a turn in the valley in which the main street stood.

What I suppose is that, it being Saturday night and raining, the women and kids had all stayed at home and only the men were out, intending to get themselves liquored up. I've been in some other mining towns since and if I was a miner and had to live in one of them, or in one of the houses they live in with their women and kids, I'd get out and liquor myself up too.

So there I stood looking, and as sick as a dog inside myself, and as wet and cold as a rat in a sewer pipe. I could see the mass of dark figures moving about down below, and beyond the main street there was a river that made a sound you could hear distinctly, even up where I was, and over beyond the river were some railroad tracks with switch engines going up and down. I suppose they had something to do with the mines in which the men of the town worked. Anyway, as I stood watching and listening there was, now and then, a sound like thunder rolling down the sky, and I suppose that was a lot of coal, maybe a whole carload, being let down plunk into a coal car.

And then besides there was, on the side of a hill far away, a long row of coke ovens. They had little doors, through which the light from the fire within leaked out, and as they were set closely, side by side, they looked like the teeth of some big man-eating giant lying and waiting over there in the hills.

The sight of it all, even the sight of the kind of hellholes men are satisfied to go on living in, gave me the fantods and the shivers right down in my liver, and on that night I guess I had in me a kind of contempt for all men, including myself, that I've never had so thoroughly since. Come right down to it, I suppose women aren't so much to blame as men. They aren't running the show.

Then I pushed open the door and went into the saloon. There were about a dozen men, miners I suppose, playing cards at tables in a little long dirty room, with a bar at one side of it, and with a big red-faced man with a mustache standing back of the bar.

The place smelled, as such places do where men hang around who have worked and sweated in their clothes and perhaps slept in them too, and have never had them washed but have just kept on wearing them. I guess you know what I mean if you've ever been in a city. You smell that smell in a city, in streetcars on rainy nights when a lot of factory hands get on. I got pretty used to that smell when I was a tramp and pretty sick of it too.

And so I was in the place now, with a glass of whisky in my hand, and I thought all the miners were staring at me, which they weren't at all, but I thought they were and so I felt just the same as though they had been. And then I looked up and saw my own face in the old cracked looking glass back of the bar. If the miners had been staring, or laughing at me, I wouldn't have wondered when I saw what I looked like.

It—I mean my own face—was white and pasty-looking, and for some reason, I can't tell exactly why, it wasn't my own face at all. It's a funny business I'm trying to tell you about and I know what you may be thinking of me as well as you do, so you needn't suppose I'm innocent or ashamed. I'm only wondering. I've thought about it a lot since and I can't make it out. I know I was never that way before that night and I know I've never been that way since. Maybe it was lonesomeness, just lonesomeness, gone on in me too long. I've often wondered if women generally are lonesomer than men.

The point is that the face I saw in the looking glass back of that bar, when I looked up from my glass of whisky that evening, wasn't my own face at all but the face of a woman. It was a girl's face, that's what I mean. That's what it was. It was a girl's face, and a lonesome and scared girl too. She was just a kid at that.

When I saw that the glass of whisky came pretty near falling out of my hand but I gulped it down, put a dollar on the bar, and called for another. "I've got to be careful here—I'm up against something new," I said to myself. "If any of these men in here get on to me there's going to be trouble." When I had got the second drink in me I called for a third and I thought, "When I get this third drink down I'll get out of here and back up the hill to the fairgrounds before I make a fool of myself and begin to get drunk."

And then, while I was thinking and drinking my third glass of whisky, the men in the room began to laugh and of course I thought they were laughing at me. But they weren't. No one in the place had really paid any attention to me.

What they were laughing at was a man who had just come in at the door. I'd never seen such a fellow. He was a huge big man, with red hair that stuck straight up like bristles out of his head, and he had a red-haired kid in his arms. The kid was just like himself, big, I mean, for his age, and with the same kind of stiff red hair.

He came and set the kid up on the bar, close beside me, and called for a glass of whisky for himself, and all the men in the room began to shout and laugh at him and his kid. Only they didn't shout and laugh when he was looking so he could tell which ones did it, but did all their shouting and laughing when his head was turned the other way. They kept calling him "cracked." "The crack is getting wider in the old tin pan," someone sang and then they all laughed.

I'm puzzled you see, just how to make you feel as I felt that night. I suppose, having undertaken to write this story, that's what I'm up against, trying to do that. I'm not claiming to be able to inform you or to do you any good. I'm just trying to make you understand some things about me, as I would like to understand some things about you, or anyone, if I had the chance. Anyway the whole blamed thing, the thing that went on I mean in that little saloon on that rainy Saturday night, wasn't like anything quite real. I've already told you how I had looked into the glass back of the bar and had seen there, not my own face but the face of a scared young girl. Well, the men, the miners, sitting at the tables in the half-dark room, the red-faced bartender, the unholy-looking big man who had come in and his queer-looking kid, now sitting on the bar—all of them were like characters in some play, not like real people at all.

There was myself, that wasn't myself—and I'm not any fairy. Anyone who has ever known me knows better than that.

And then there was the man who had come in. There was a feeling came out of him that wasn't like the feeling you get from a man at all. It was more like the feeling you get maybe from a horse, only his eyes weren't like a horse's eyes. Horses' eyes have a kind of calm something in them and his hadn't. If you've ever carried a lantern through a wood at night, going along a path, and then suddenly you felt something funny in the air and stopped, and there ahead of you somewhere were the eyes of some little animal, gleaming out at you from a dead wall of darkness— The eyes shine big and quiet but there is a point right in the center of each, where there is something dancing and wavering. You aren't afraid the little animal will jump at you, you are afraid the little eyes will jump at you—that's what's the matter with you.

Only of course a horse, when you go into his stall at night, or a little animal you had disturbed in a wood that way, wouldn't be talking and the big man who had come in there with his kid was talking. He kept talking all the time, saying something under his breath, as they say, and I could only understand now and then a few words. It was his talking made him kind of terrible. His eyes said one thing and his lips another. They didn't seem to get together, as though they belonged to the same person.

For one thing, the man was too big. There was about him an unnatural bigness. It was in his hands, his arms, his shoulders, his body, his head, a bigness like you might see in trees and bushes in a tropical country perhaps. I've never been in a tropical country but I've seen pictures. Only his eyes were small. In his big head they looked like the eyes of a bird. And I remember that his lips were thick, like Negroes' lips.

He paid no attention to me or to the others in the room but kept on muttering to himself, or to the kid sitting on the bar—I couldn't tell to which.

First he had one drink and then, quick, another. I stood staring at him and thinking—a jumble of thoughts, I suppose.

What I must have been thinking was something like this. "Well he's one of the kind you are always seeing about towns," I thought. I meant he was one of the cracked kind. In almost any small town you go to you will find one, and sometimes two or three cracked people, walking around. They go through the street, muttering to themselves and people generally are cruel to them. Their own folks make a bluff at being kind, but they aren't really, and the others in the town, men and boys, like to tease them. They send such a fellow, the mild silly kind, on some fool errand after a round square or a dozen postholes or tie cards on his back saying "Kick me," or something like that, and then carry on and laugh as though they had done something funny.

And so there was this cracked one in that saloon and I could see the men in there wanted to have some fun putting up some kind of horseplay on him, but they didn't quite dare. He wasn't one of the mild kind, that was a cinch. I kept looking at the man and at his kid, and then up at that strange unreal reflection of myself in the cracked looking glass back of the bar. "Rats, rats, digging in the ground—miners are rats, little jack rabbit," I heard him say to his solemn-faced kid. I guess, after all, maybe he wasn't so cracked.

The kid sitting on the bar kept blinking at his father, like an owl caught out in the daylight, and now the father was having another glass of whisky. He drank six glasses, one right after the other, and it was cheap ten-cent stuff. He must have had cast-iron insides all right.

Of the men in the room there were two or three (maybe they were really more scared than the others so had to put up a bluff of bravery by showing off) who kept laughing and making funny cracks about the big man and his kid and there was one fellow was the worst of the bunch. I'll never forget that fellow because of his looks and what happened to him afterward.

He was one of the showing-off kind all right, and he was the one that had started the song about the crack getting bigger in the old tin pan. He sang it two or three times, and then he grew bolder and got up and began walking up and down the room singing it over and over. He was a showy kind of man with a fancy vest, on which there were brown tobacco spots, and he wore glasses. Every time he made some crack he thought was funny, he winked at the others as though to say, "You see me. I'm not afraid of this big fellow," and then the others laughed.

The proprietor of the place must have known what was going on, and the danger in it, because he kept leaning over the bar and saying, "Shush, now quit it," to the showy-off man, but it didn't do any good. The fellow kept prancing like a turkey cock and he put his hat on one side of his head and stopped right back of the big man and sang that song about the crack in the old tin pan. He was one of the kind you can't shush until they get their blocks knocked off, and it didn't take him long to come to it that time anyhow.

Because the big fellow just kept on muttering to his kid and drinking his whisky, as though he hadn't heard anything, and then suddenly he turned and his big hand flashed out and he grabbed, not the fellow who had been showing off, but me. With just a sweep of his arm he brought me up against his big body. Then he shoved me over with my breast jammed against the bar and looking right into his kid's face and he said, "Now you watch him, and if you let him fall I'll kill you," in just quiet ordinary tones as though he was saying "good morning" to some neighbor.

Then the kid leaned over and threw his arms around my head, and in spite of that I did manage to screw my head around enough to see what happened.

It was a sight I'll never forget. The big fellow had whirled around, and he had the showy-off man by the shoulder now, and the fellow's face was a sight. The big man must have had some reputation as a bad man in the town, even though he was cracked, for the man with the fancy vest had his mouth open now, and his hat had fallen off his head, and he was silent and scared. Once, when I was a tramp, I saw a kid killed by a train. The kid was walking on the rail and showing off before some other kids, by letting them see how close he could let an engine come to him before he got out of the way. And the engine was whistling and a woman, over on the porch of a house nearby, was jumping up and down and screaming, and the kid let the engine get nearer and nearer, wanting more and more to show off, and then he stumbled and fell. God, I'll never forget the look on his face, in just the second before he got hit and killed, and now, there in that saloon, was the same terrible look on another face.

I closed my eyes for a moment and was sick all through me and then, when I opened my eyes, the big man's fist was just coming down in the other man's face. The one blow knocked him cold and he fell down like a beast hit with an axe.

And then the most terrible thing of all happened. The big man had on heavy boots, and he raised one of them and brought it down on the other man's shoulder, as he lay white and groaning on the floor. I could hear the bones crunch and it made me so sick I could hardly stand up, but I had to stand up and hold on to that kid or I knew it would be my turn next.

Because the big fellow didn't seem excited or anything, but kept on muttering to himself as he had been doing when he was standing peacefully by the bar drinking his whisky, and now he had raised his foot again, and maybe this time he would bring it down in the other man's face and, "just eliminate his map for keeps," as sports and prize fighters sometimes say. I trembled, like I was having a chill, but thank God at that moment the kid, who had his arms around me and one hand clinging to my nose, so that there were the marks of his fingernails on it the next morning, at that moment the kid, thank God, began to howl, and his father didn't bother any more with the man on the floor but turned around, knocked me aside, and taking the kid in his arms tramped out of that place, muttering to himself as he had been doing ever since he came in.

I went out too but I didn't prance out with any dignity, I'll tell you that. I slunk out like a thief or a coward, which perhaps I am, partly anyhow.

And so there I was, outside there in the darkness, and it was as cold and wet and black and Godforsaken a night as any man ever saw. I was so sick at the thought of human beings that night I could have vomited to think of them at all. For a while I just stumbled along in the mud of the road, going up the hill, back to the fairgrounds, and then, almost before I knew where I was, I found myself in the stall with Pick-it-boy.

That was one of the best and sweetest feelings I've ever had in my whole life, being in that warm stall alone with that horse that night. I had told the other swipes that I would go up and down the row of stalls now and then and have an eye on the other horses, but I had altogether forgotten my promise now. I went and stood with my back against the side of the stall, thinking how mean and low and all balled up and twisted up human beings can become, and how the best of them are likely to get that way any time, just because they are human beings and not simple and clear in their minds, and inside themselves, as animals are, maybe.

Perhaps you know how a person feels at such a moment. There are things you think of, odd little things you had thought you had forgotten. Once, when you were a kid, you were with your father, and he was all dressed up, as for a funeral or Fourth of July, and was walking along a street holding your hand. And you were going past a railroad station, and there was a woman standing. She was a stranger in your town and was dressed as you had never seen a woman dressed before, and never thought you would see one looking so nice. Long afterward you knew that was because she had lovely taste in clothes, such as so few women have really, but then you thought she must be a queen. You had read about queens in fairy stories and the thoughts of them thrilled you. What lovely eyes the strange lady had and what beautiful rings she wore on her fingers.

Then your father came out, from being in the railroad station, maybe to set his watch by the station clock, and took you by the hand and he and the woman smiled at each other, in an embarrassed kind of way, and you kept looking longingly back at her, and when you were out of her hearing you asked your father if she really were a queen. And it may be that your father was one who wasn't so very hot on democracy and a free country and talked-up bunk about a free citizenry, and he said he hoped she was a queen, and maybe, for all he knew, she was.

Or maybe, when you get jammed up as I was that night, and can't get things clear about yourself or other people and why you are alive, or for that matter why anyone you can think about is alive, you think, not of people at all but of other things you have seen and felt—like walking along a road in the snow in the winter, perhaps out in Iowa, and hearing soft warm sounds in a barn close to the road, or of another time when you were on a hill and the sun was going down and the sky suddenly became a great soft-colored bowl, all glowing like a jewel-handled bowl, a great queen in some faraway mighty kingdom might have put on a vast table out under the tree, once a year, when she invited all her loyal and loving subjects to come and dine with her.

I can't, of course, figure out what you try to think about when you are as desolate as I was that night. Maybe you are like me and inclined to think of women, and maybe you are like a man I met once, on the road, who told me that when he was up against it he never thought of anything but grub and a big nice clean warm bed to sleep in. "I don't care about anything else and I don't ever let myself think of anything else," he said. "If I was like you and went to thinking about women sometime I'd find myself hooked up to some skirt, and she'd have the old double cross on me, and the rest of my life maybe I'd be working in some factory for her and her kids."

As I say, there I was anyway, up there alone with that horse in that warm stall in that dark lonesome fairground and I had that feeling about being sick at the thought of human beings and what they could be like.

Well, suddenly I got again the queer feeling I'd had about him once or twice before, I mean the feeling about our understanding each other in some way I can't explain.

So having it again I went over to where he stood and began running my hands all over his body, just because I loved the feel of him and as sometimes, to tell the plain truth, I've felt about touching with my hands the body of a woman I've seen and who I thought was lovely too. I ran my hands over his head and neck and then down over his hard firm round body and then over his flanks and down his legs. His flanks quivered a little I remember and once he turned his head and stuck his cold nose down along my neck and nipped my shoulder a little, in a soft playful way. It hurt a little but I didn't care.

So then I crawled up through a hole into the loft above thinking that night was over anyway and glad of it, but it wasn't, not by a long sight.

As my clothes were all soaking wet and as we race track swipes didn't own any such things as night-gowns or pajamas I had to go to bed naked, of course.

But we had plenty of horse blankets and so I tucked myself in between a pile of them and tried not to think any more that night. The being with Pick-it-boy and having him close right under me that way made me feel a little better.

Then I was sound asleep and dreaming and—bang, like being hit with a club by someone who has sneaked up behind you—I got another wallop.

What I suppose is that, being upset the way I was, I had forgotten to bolt the door to Pick it-boy's stall down below and two Negro men had come in there, thinking they were in their own place, and had climbed up through the hole where I was. They were half lit up but not what you might call dead drunk, and I suppose they were up against something a couple of white swipes who had some money in their pockets wouldn't have been up against.

What I mean is that a couple of white swipes, having liquored themselves up and being down there in the town on a bat, if they wanted a woman or a couple of women, would have been able to find them. There is always a few women of that kind can be found around any town I've ever seen or heard of, and of course a bartender would have given them the tip where to go.

But a Negro, up there in that country, where there aren't any, or anyway mighty few Negro women, wouldn't know what to do when he felt that way and would be up against it.

It's so always. Burt and several other Negroes I've known pretty well have talked to me about it, lots of times. You take now a young Negro man—not a race track swipe or a tramp or any other low-down kind of a fellow—but, let us say, one who has been to college, and has behaved himself and tried to be a good man, the best he could, and be clean, as they say. He isn't any better off, is he? If he has made himself some money and wants to go sit in a swell restaurant, or go to hear some good music, or see a good play at the theatre, he gets what we used to call on the tracks, "the messy end of the dung fork," doesn't he?

And even in such a low-down place as what people call a "bad house" it's the same way. The white swipes and others can go into a place where they have Negro women fast enough, and they do it too, but you let a Negro swipe try it the other way around and see how he comes out.

You see, I can think this whole thing out fairly now, sitting here in my own house and writing, and with my wife Jessie in the kitchen making a pie or something, and I can show just how the two Negro men who came into that loft, where I was asleep, were justified in what they did, and I can preach about how the Negroes are up against it in this country, like a daisy, but I tell you what, I didn't think things out that way that night.

For, you understand, what they thought, they being half liquored up, and when one of them had jerked the blankets off me, was that I was a woman. One of them carried a lantern but it was smoky and dirty and didn't give out much light. So they must have figured it out—my body being pretty white and slender then, like a young girl's body I suppose—that some white swipe had brought me up there. The kind of girls around a town that will come with a swipe to a race track on a rainy night aren't very fancy females but you'll find that kind in the towns all right. I've seen many a one in my day.

And so, I figure, these two big buck niggers, being piped that way, just made up their minds they would snatch me away from the white swipe who had brought me out there, and who had left me lying carelessly around.

"Jes' you lie still honey. We ain't gwine hurt you none," one of them said, with a little chuckling laugh that had something in it besides a laugh, too. It was the kind of laugh that gives you the shivers.

The devil of it was I couldn't say anything, not even a word. Why I couldn't yell out and say "What the hell," and just kid them a little and shoo them out of there I don't know, but I couldn't. I tried and tried so that my throat hurt but I didn't say a word. I just lay there staring at them.

It was a mixed-up night. I've never gone through another night like it.

Was I scared? Lord Almighty, I'll tell you what, I was scared.

Because the two big black faces were leaning right over me now, and I could feel their liquored-up breaths on my cheeks, and their eyes were shining in the dim light from that smoky lantern, and right in the center of their eyes was that dancing flickering light I've told you about your seeing in the eyes of wild animals, when you were carrying a lantern through the woods at night.

It was a puzzler! All my life, you see—me never having had any sisters, and at that time never having had a sweetheart either—I had been dreaming and thinking about women, and I suppose I'd always been dreaming about a pure innocent one, for myself, made for me by God, maybe. Men are that way. No matter how big they talk about "let the women go hang," they've always got that notion tucked away inside themselves, somewhere. It's a kind of chesty man's notion, I suppose, but they've got it and the kind of up-and-coming women we have nowdays who are always saying, "I'm as good as a man and will do what the men do," are on the wrong trail if they really ever want to, what you might say "hog-tie" a fellow of their own.

So I had invented a kind of princess, with black hair and a slender willowy body to dream about. And I thought of her as being shy and afraid to ever tell anything she really felt to anyone but just me. I suppose I fancied that if I ever found such a woman in the flesh I would be the strong sure one and she the timid shrinking one.

And now I was that woman, or something like her, myself.

I gave a kind of wriggle, like a fish you have just taken off the hook. What I did next wasn't a thought-out thing. I was caught and I squirmed, that's all.

The two niggers both jumped at me but somehow—the lantern having been kicked over and having gone out the first move they made—well in some way, when they both lunged at me they missed.

As good luck would have it my feet found the hole, where you put hay down to the horse in the stall below, and through which we crawled up when it was time to go to bed in our blankets up in the hay, and down I slid, not bothering to try to find the ladder with my feet but just letting myself go.

In less than a second I was out of doors in the dark and the rain and the two blacks were down the hole and out the door of the stall after me.

How long or how far they really followed me I suppose I'll never know. It was black dark and raining hard now and a roaring wind had begun to blow. Of course, my body being white, it must have made some kind of a faint streak in the darkness as I ran, and anyway I thought they could see me and I knew I couldn't see them and that made my terror ten times worse. Every minute I thought they would grab me.

You know how it is when a person is all upset and full of terror as I was. I suppose maybe the two niggers followed me for a while, running across the muddy race track and into the grove of trees that grew in the oval inside the track, but likely enough, after just a few minutes, they gave up the chase and went back, found their own place and went to sleep. They were liquored up, as I've said, and maybe partly funning too.

But I didn't know that, if they were. As I ran I kept hearing sounds, sounds made by the rain coming down through the dead old leaves left on the trees and by the wind blowing, and it may be that the sound that scared me most of all was my own bare feet stepping on a dead branch and breaking it or something like that.

There was something strange and scary, a steady sound, like a heavy man running and breathing hard, right at my shoulder. It may have been my own breath, coming quick and fast. And I thought I heard that chuckling laugh I'd heard up in the loft, the laugh that sent the shivers right down through me. Of course every tree I came close to looked like a man standing there, ready to grab me, and I kept dodging and going—bang—into other trees. My shoulders kept knocking against trees in that way and the skin was all knocked off, and every time it happened I thought a big black hand had come down and clutched at me and was tearing my flesh.

How long it went on I don't know, maybe an hour, maybe five minutes. But anyway the darkness didn't let up, and the terror didn't let up, and I couldn't, to save my life, scream or make any sound.

Just why I couldn't I don't know. Could it be because at the time I was a woman, while at the same time I wasn't a woman? It may be that I was too ashamed of having turned into a girl and being afraid of a man to make any sound. I don't know about that. It's over my head.

But anyway I couldn't make a sound. I tried and tried and my throat hurt from trying and no sound came.

And then, after a long time, or what seemed like a long time, I got out from among the trees inside the track and was on the track itself again. I thought the two black men were still after me, you understand, and I ran like a madman.

Of course, running along the track that way, it must have been up the back stretch, I came after a time to where the old slaughter-house stood, in that field, beside the track. I knew it by its ungodly smell, scared as I was. Then, in some way, I managed to get over the high old fairground fence and was in the field, where the slaughterhouse was.

All the time I was trying to yell or scream, or be sensible and tell those two black men that I was a man and not a woman, but I couldn't make it. And then I heard a sound like a board cracking or breaking in the fence and thought they were still after me.

So I kept on running like a crazy man, in the field, and just then I stumbled and fell over something. I've told you how the old slaughterhouse field was filled with bones, that had been lying there a long time and had all been washed white. There were heads of sheep and cows and all kinds of things.

And when I fell and pitched forward I fell right into the midst of something, still and cold and white.

It was probably the skeleton of a horse lying there. In small towns like that, they take an old worn-out horse, that has died, and haul him off to some field outside of town and skin him for the hide, that they can sell for a dollar or two. It doesn't make any difference what the horse has been, that's the way he usually ends up. Maybe even Pick-it-boy, or O My Man, or a lot of other good fast ones I've seen and known have ended that way by this time.

And so I think it was the bones of a horse lying there and he must have been lying on his back. The birds and wild animals had picked all his flesh away and the rain had washed his bones clean.

Anyway I fell and pitched forward and my side got cut pretty deep and my hands clutched at something. I had fallen right in between the ribs of the horse and they seemed to wrap themselves around me close. And my hands, clutching upwards, had got hold of the cheeks of that dead horse and the bones of his cheeks were cold as ice with the rain washing over them. White bones wrapped around me and white bones in my hands.

There was a new terror now that seemed to go down to the very bottom of me, to the bottom of the inside of me, I mean. It shook me like I have seen a rat in a barn shaken by a dog. It was a terror like a big wave that hits you when you are walking on a seashore, maybe. You see it coming and you try to run and get away but when you start to run inshore there is a stone cliff you can't climb. So the wave comes high as a mountain, and there it is, right in front of you and nothing in all this world can stop it. And now it had knocked you down and rolled and tumbled you over and over and washed you clean, clean, but dead maybe.

And that's the way I felt—I seemed to myself dead with blind terror. It was a feeling like the finger of God running down your back and burning you clean, I mean.

It burned all that silly nonsense about being a girl right out of me.

I screamed at last and the spell that was on me was broken. I'll bet the scream I let out of me could have been heard a mile and a half.

Right away I felt better and crawled out from among the pile of bones, and then I stood on my own feet again and I wasn't a woman, or a young girl any more but a man and my own self, and as far as I know I've been that way ever since. Even the black night seemed warm and alive now, like a mother might be to a kid in the dark.

Only I couldn't go back to the race track because I was blubbering and crying and was ashamed of myself and of what a fool I had made of myself. Someone might see me and I couldn't stand that, not at that moment.

So I went across the field, walking now, not running like a crazy man, and pretty soon I came to a fence and crawled over and got into another field, in which there was a straw stack, I just happened to find in the pitch darkness.

The straw stack had been there a long time and some sheep had nibbled away at it until they had made a pretty deep hole, like a cave, in the side of it. I found the hole and crawled in and there were some sheep in there, about a dozen of them.

When I came in, creeping on my hands and knees, they didn't make much fuss, just stirred around a little and then settled down.

So I settled down amongst them too. They were warm and gentle and kind, like Pick-it-boy, and being in there with them made me feel better than I would have felt being with any human person I knew at that time.

So I settled down and slept after a while, and when I woke up it was daylight and not very cold and the rain was over. The clouds were breaking away from the sky now and maybe there would be a fair the next week but if there was I knew I wouldn't be there to see it.

Because what I expected to happen did happen. I had to go back across the fields and the fairground to the place where my clothes were, right in the broad daylight, and me stark naked, and of course I knew someone would be up and would raise a shout, and every swipe and every driver would stick his head out and would whoop with laughter.

And there would be a thousand questions asked, and I would be too mad and too ashamed to answer, and would perhaps begin to blubber, and that would make me more ashamed than ever.

It all turned out just as I expected, except that when the noise and the shouts of laughter were going it the loudest, Burt came out of the stall where O My Man was kept, and when he saw me he didn't know what was the matter but he knew something was up that wasn't on the square and for which I wasn't to blame.

So he got so all-fired mad he couldn't speak for a minute, and then he grabbed a pitchfork and began prancing up and down before the other stalls, giving that gang of swipes and drivers such a royal old dressing-down as you never heard. You should have heard him sling language. It was grand to hear.

And while he was doing it I sneaked up into the loft, blubbering because I was so pleased and happy to hear him swear that way, and I got my wet clothes on quick and got down, and gave Pick-it-boy a good-bye kiss on the cheek and lit out.

The last I saw of all that part of my life was Burt, still going it, and yelling out for the man who had put up a trick on me to come out and get what was coming to him. He had the pitchfork in his hand and was swinging it around, and every now and then he would make a kind of lunge at a tree or something, he was so mad through, and there was no one else in sight at all. And Burt didn't even see me cutting out along the fence through a gate and down the hill and out of the race-horse and the tramp life for the rest of my days.

Milk Bottles

I LIVED, during that summer, in a large room on the top floor of an old house on the North Side in Chicago. It was August and the night was hot. Until after midnight I sat—the sweat trickling down my back—under a lamp, laboring to feel my way into the lives of the fanciful people who were trying also to live in the tale on which I was at work.

It was a hopeless affair.

I became involved in the efforts of the shadowy people and they in turn became involved in the fact of the hot uncomfortable room, in the fact that, although it was what the farmers of the Middle West call "good corn-growing weather" it was plain hell to be alive in Chicago. Hand in hand the shadowy people of my fanciful world and myself groped our way through a forest in which the leaves had all been burned off the trees. The hot ground burned the shoes off our feet. We were striving to make our way through the forest and into some cool beautiful city. The fact is, as you will clearly understand, I was a little off my head.

When I gave up the struggle and got to my feet the chairs in the room danced about. They also were running aimlessly through a burning land and striving to reach some mythical city. "I'd better get out of here and go for a walk or go jump into the lake and cool myself off," I thought.

I went down out of my room and into the street. On a lower floor of the house lived two burlesque actresses who had just come in from their evening's work and who now sat in their room talking. As I reached the street something heavy whirled past my head and broke on the stone pavement. A white liquid spurted over my clothes and the voice of one of the actresses could be heard coming from the one lighted room of the house. "Oh, hell! We live such damned lives, we do, and we work in such a town! A dog is better off! And now they are going to take booze away from us too! I come home from working in that hot theatre on a hot night like this and what do I see—a half-filled bottle of spoiled milk standing on a window sill!

"I won't stand it! I got to smash everything!" she cried.

I walked eastward from my house. From the northwestern end of the city great hordes of men, women and children had come to spend the night out of doors, by the shore of the lake. It was stifling hot there too and the air was heavy with a sense of struggle. On a few hundred acres of flat land, that had formerly been a swamp, some two million people were fighting for the peace and quiet of sleep and not getting it. Out of the half darkness, beyond the little strip of park land at the water's edge, the huge empty houses of Chicago's fashionable folk made a grayish-blue blot against the sky. "Thank the gods," I thought, "there are some people who can get out of here, who can go to the mountains or the seashore or to Europe." I stumbled in the half darkness over the legs of a woman who was lying and trying to sleep on the grass. A baby lay beside her and when she sat up it began to cry. I muttered an apology and stepped aside and as I did so my foot struck a half-filled milk bottle and I knocked it over, the milk running out on the grass. "Oh, I'm sorry. Please forgive me," I cried. "Never mind," the woman answered, "the milk is sour."

He is a tall stoop-shouldered man with prematurely grayed hair and works as a copy writer in an advertising agency in Chicago—an agency where I also have sometimes been employed—and on that night in August I met him, walking with quick eager strides along the shore of the lake and past the tired petulant people. He did not see me at first and I wondered at the evidence of life in him when everyone else seemed half dead; but a street lamp hanging over a nearby roadway threw its light down upon my face and he pounced. "Here you, come up to my place," he cried sharply. "I've got something to show you. I was on my way down to see you. That's where I was going," he lied as he hurried me along.

We went to his apartment on a street leading back from the lake and the park. German, Polish, Italian and Jewish families, equipped with soiled blankets and the ever-present half-filled bottles of milk, had come prepared to spend the night out of doors; but the American families in the crowd were giving up the struggle to find a cool spot and a little stream of them trickled along the sidewalks, going back to hot beds in the hot houses.

It was past one o'clock and my friend's apartment was disorderly as well as hot. He explained that his wife, with their two children, had gone home to visit her mother on a farm near Springfield, Illinois.

We took off our coats and sat down. My friend's thin cheeks were flushed and his eyes shone. "You know—well—you see," he began and then hesitated and laughed like an embarrassed schoolboy. "Well now," he began again, "I've long been wanting to write something real, something besides advertisements. I suppose I'm silly but that's the way I am. It's been my dream to write something stirring and big. I suppose it's the dream of a lot of advertising writers, eh? Now look here—don't you go laughing. I think I've done it."

He explained that he had written something concerning Chicago, the capital and heart, as he said, of the whole Central West. He grew angry. "People come here from the East or from farms, or from little holes of towns like I came from and they think it smart to run Chicago into the ground," he declared. "I thought I'd show 'em up," he added, jumping up and walking nervously about the room.

He handed me many sheets of paper covered with hastily scrawled words, but I protested and asked him to read it aloud. He did, standing with his face turned away from me. There was a quiver in his voice. The thing he had written concerned some mythical town I had never seen. He called it Chicago, but in the same breath spoke of great streets flaming with color, ghost-like buildings flung up into night skies and a river, running down a path of gold into the boundless West. It was the city, I told myself, I and the people of my story had been trying to find earlier on that same evening, when because of the heat I went a little off my head and could not work any more. The people of the city he had written about were a cool-headed, brave people, marching forward to some spiritual triumph, the promise of which was inherent in the physical aspects of the town.

Now I am one who, by the careful cultivation of certain traits in my character, have succeeded in building up the more brutal side of my nature, but I cannot knock women and children down in order to get aboard Chicago streetcars, nor can I tell an author to his face that I think his work is rotten.

"You're all right, Ed. You're great. You've knocked out a regular sockdolager of a masterpiece here. Why you sound as good as Henry Mencken writing about Chicago as the literary center of

America, and you've lived in Chicago and he never did. The only thing I can see you've missed is a little something about the stock-yards, and you can put that in later," I added and prepared to de-part.

"What's this?" I asked, picking up a half dozen sheets of paper that lay on the floor by my chair. I read it eagerly. And when I had finished reading it he stammered and apologized and then, step-ping across the room, jerked the sheets out of my hand and threw them out of an open window. "I wish you hadn't seen that. It's something else I wrote about Chicago," he explained. He was flustered.

"You see the night was so hot, and, down at the office, I had to write a condensed-milk advertisement, just as I was sneaking away to come home and work on this other thing, and the streetcar was so crowded and the people stank so, and when I finally got home here—the wife being gone—the place was a mess. Well, I couldn't write and I was sore. It's been my chance, you see, the wife and kids being gone and the house being quiet. I went for a walk. I think I went a little off my head. Then I came home and wrote that stuff I've just thrown out of the window."

He grew cheerful again. "Oh, well—it's all right. Writing that fool thing stirred me up and enabled me to write this other stuff, this real stuff I showed you first, about Chicago."

And so I went home and to bed, having in this odd way stum-bled upon another bit of the kind of writing that is—for better or worse—really presenting the lives of the people of these towns and cities—sometimes in prose, sometimes in stirring colorful song. It was the kind of thing Mr. Sandburg or Mr. Masters might have done after an evening's walk on a hot night in, say, West Congress Street in Chicago.

The thing I had read of Ed's centered about a half-filled bottle of spoiled milk standing dim in the moonlight on a window sill. There had been a moon earlier on that August evening, a new moon, a thin crescent golden streak in the sky. What had hap-pened to my friend the advertising writer was something like this —I figured it all out as I lay sleepless in bed after our talk.

I am sure I do not know whether or not it is true that all adver-tising writers and newspapermen want to do other kinds of writ-ing, but Ed did, all right. The August day that had preceded the hot night had been a hard one for him to get through. All day he had been wanting to be at home in his quiet apartment producing literature, rather than sitting in an office and writing advertisements. In the late afternoon, when he had thought his desk cleared for the day, the boss of the copy writers came and ordered him to write a page advertisement for the magazines on the subject of condensed milk. "We got a chance to get a new account if we can knock out some crackerjack stuff in a hurry," he said. "I'm sorry to have to put it up to you on such a rotten hot day, Ed, but we're up against it. Let's see if you've got some of the old pep in you. Get down to hardpan now and knock out something snappy and unusual before you go home."

Ed had tried. He put away the thoughts he had been having about the city beautiful—the glowing city of the plains—and got right down to business. He thought about milk, milk for little children, the Chicagoans of the future, milk that would produce a little cream to put in the coffee of advertising writers in the morning, sweet fresh milk to keep all his brother and sister Chicagoans robust and strong. What Ed really wanted was a long cool drink of something with a kick in it, but he tried to make himself think he wanted a drink of milk. He gave himself over to thoughts of milk, milk condensed and yellow, milk warm from the cows his father owned when he was a boy—his mind launched a little boat and he set out on a sea of milk.

Out of it all he got what is called an original advertisement. The sea of milk on which he sailed became a mountain of cans of condensed milk, and out of that fancy he got his idea. He made a crude sketch for a picture showing wide rolling green fields with white farmhouses. Cows grazed on the green hills and at one side of the picture a barefooted boy was driving a herd of Jersey cows out of the sweet fair land and down a lane into a kind of funnel at the small end of which was a tin of the condensed milk. Over the picture he put a heading: "The health and freshness of a whole countryside is condensed into one can of Whitney-Wells Condensed Milk." The head copy writer said it was a humdinger.

And then Ed went home. He wanted to begin writing about the city beautiful at once and so didn't go out to dinner, but fished about in the ice chest and found some cold meat out of which he made himself a sandwich. Also, he poured himself a glass of milk, but it was sour. "Oh, damn!" he said and poured it into the kitchen sink.

As Ed explained to me later, he sat down and tried to begin writing his real stuff at once, but he couldn't seem to get into it. The last hour in the office, the trip home in the hot smelly car, and the taste of the sour milk in his mouth had jangled his nerves. The truth is that Ed has a rather sensitive, finely balanced nature, and it had got mussed up.

He took a walk and tried to think, but his mind wouldn't stay where he wanted it to. Ed is now a man of nearly forty and on that night his mind ran back to his young manhood in the city—and stayed there. Like other boys who had become grown men in Chicago, he had come to the city from a farm at the edge of a prairie town, and like all such town and farm boys, he had come filled with vague dreams.

What things he had hungered to do and be in Chicago! What he had done you can fancy. For one thing he had got himself married and now lived in the apartment on the North Side. To give a real picture of his life during the twelve or fifteen years that had slipped away since he was a young man would involve writing a novel, and that is not my purpose.

Anyway, there he was in his room—come home from his walk—and it was hot and quiet and he could not manage to get into his masterpiece. How still it was in the apartment with the wife and children away! His mind stayed on the subject of his youth in the city.

He remembered a night of his young manhood when he had gone out to walk, just as he did on that August evening. Then his life wasn't complicated by the fact of the wife and children, and he lived alone in his room; but something had got on his nerves then, too. On that evening long ago he grew restless in his room and went out to walk. It was summer and first he went down by the river where ships were being loaded and then to a crowded park where girls and young fellows walked about.

He grew bold and spoke to a woman who sat alone on a park bench. She let him sit beside her and, because it was dark and she was silent, he began to talk. The night had made him sentimental. "Human beings are such hard things to get at. I wish I could get close to someone," he said. "Oh, you go on! What are you doing? You ain't trying to kid someone?" asked the woman.

Ed jumped up and walked away. He went into a long street lined with dark silent buildings and then stopped and looked about. What he wanted was to believe that in the apartment buildings were people who lived intense eager lives, who had great dreams, who were capable of great adventures. "They are really only separated from me by the brick walls," was what he told himself on that night.

It was then that the milk bottle theme first got hold of him. He went into an alleyway to look at the backs of the apartment buildings and, on that evening also, there was a moon. Its light fell upon a long row of half-filled bottles standing on window sills.

Something within him went a little sick and he hurried out of the alleyway and into the street. A man and woman walked past him and stopped before the entrance to one of the buildings. Hoping they might be lovers, he concealed himself in the entrance to another building to listen to their conversation.

The couple turned out to be a man and wife and they were quarreling. Ed heard the woman's voice saying: "You come in here. You can't put that over on me. You say you just want to take a walk, but I know you. You want to go out and blow in some money. What I'd like to know is why you don't loosen up a little for me."

That is the story of what happened to Ed, when, as a young man, he went to walk in the city in the evening, and when he had become a man of forty and went out of his house wanting to dream and to think of a city beautiful, much the same sort of thing happened again. Perhaps the writing of the condensed-milk advertisement and the taste of the sour milk he had got out of the icebox had something to do with his mood; but, anyway, milk bottles, like a refrain in a song, got into his brain. They seemed to sit and mock at him from the windows of all the buildings in all the streets, and when he turned to look at people, he met the crowds from the West and the Northwest Sides going to the park and the lake. At the head of each little group of people marched a woman who carried a milk bottle in her hand.

And so, on that August night, Ed went home angry and disturbed, and in anger wrote of his city. Like the burlesque actress in my own house he wanted to smash something, and, as milk bottles were in his mind, he wanted to smash milk bottles. "I could grasp the neck of a milk bottle. It fits the hand so neatly. I could kill a man or woman with such a thing," he thought desperately.

He wrote, you see, the five or six sheets I had read in that mood and then felt better. And after that he wrote about the ghostlike buildings flung into the sky by the hands of a brave adventurous people and about the river that runs down a path of gold, and into the boundless West.

As you have already concluded, the city he described in his masterpiece was lifeless, but the city he, in a queer way, expressed in what he wrote about the milk bottle could not be forgotten. It frightened you a little but there it was and in spite of his anger or perhaps because of it, a lovely singing quality had got into the thing. In those few scrawled pages the miracle had been worked. I was a fool not to have put the sheets into my pocket. When I went down out of his apartment that evening I did look for them in a dark alleyway, but they had become lost in a sea of rubbish that had leaked over the tops of a long row of tin ash cans that stood at the foot of a stairway leading from the back doors of the apartments above.

The Sad Horn Blowers

IT HAD been a disastrous year in Will's family. The Appletons lived on one of the outlying streets of Bidwell, and Will's father was a house painter. In early February, when there was deep snow on the ground, and a cold bitter wind blew about the houses, Will's mother suddenly died. He was seventeen years old then, and rather a big fellow for his age.

The mother's death happened abruptly, without warning, as a sleepy man kills a fly with the hand in a warm room on a summer day. On one February day there she was coming in at the kitchen door of the Appletons' house, from hanging the wash out on the line in the back yard, and warming her long hands, covered with blue veins, by holding them over the kitchen stove—and then looking about at the children with that half-hidden, shy smile of hers—there she was like that, as the three children had always known her, and then, but a week later, she was cold in death and lying in her coffin in the place vaguely spoken of in the family as "the other room."

After that, and when summer came and the family was trying hard to adjust itself to the new conditions, there came another disaster. Up to the very moment when it happened it looked as though Tom Appleton the house painter was in for a prosperous season. The two boys, Fred and Will, were to be his assistants that year.

To be sure, Fred was only fifteen, but he was one to lend a quick alert hand at almost any undertaking. For example, when there was a job of paper hanging to be done, he was the fellow to spread on the paste, helped by an occasional sharp word from his father.

Down off his stepladder Tom Appleton hopped and ran to the long board where the paper was spread out. He liked this business of having two assistants about. Well, you see, one had the feeling of being at the head of something, of managing affairs. He grabbed the paste brush out of Fred's hand. "Don't spare the paste," he shouted. "Slap her on like this. Spread her out—so. Do be sure to catch all the edges."

It was all very warm, and comfortable, and nice, working at paper-hanging jobs in the houses on the March and April days. When it was cold or rainy outside, stoves were set up in the new houses being built, and in houses already inhabited the folks moved out of the rooms to be papered, spread newspapers on the floors over the carpets and put sheets over the furniture left in the rooms. Outside it rained or snowed, but inside it was warm and cozy.

To the Appletons it seemed, at the time, as though the death of the mother had drawn them closer together. Both Will and Fred felt it, perhaps Will the more consciously. The family was rather in the hole financially—the mother's funeral had cost a good deal of money, and Fred was being allowed to stay out of school. That pleased him. When they worked in a house where there were other children, they came home from school in the late afternoon and looked in through the door to where Fred was spreading paste over the sheets of wallpaper. He made a slapping sound with the brush, but did not look at them. Ah, go on, you kids, he thought. This was a man's business he was up to. Will and his father were on the stepladders, putting the sheets carefully into place on the ceilings and walls. "Does she match down there?" the father asked sharply. "O.K., go ahead," Will replied. When the sheet was in place Fred ran and rolled out the laps with a little wooden roller. How jealous the kids of the house were. It would be a long time before any of them could stay out of school and do a man's work, as Fred was doing.

And then in the evening, walking homeward, it was nice, too. Will and Fred had been provided with suits of white overalls that were now covered with dried paste and spots of paint and looked really professional. They kept them on and drew their overcoats on over them. Their hands were stiff with paste, too. On Main Street the lights were lighted, and other men passing called to Tom Appleton. He was called Tony in the town. "Hello, Tony!" some storekeeper shouted. It was rather too bad, Will thought, that his father hadn't more dignity. He was too boyish. Young boys growing up and merging into manhood do not fancy fathers being too boyish. Tom Appleton played a cornet in the Bidwell Silver Cornet Band and didn't do the job very well—rather made a mess of it, when there was a bit of solo work to be done—but was so well liked by the other members of the band that no one said anything. And then he talked so grandly about music, and about the lip of a cornet player, that everyone thought he must be all right. "He has an education. I tell you what, Tony Appleton knows a lot. He's a smart one," the other members of the band were always saying to each other.

"Well, the devil! A man should grow up after a time, perhaps. When a man's wife had died but such a short time before, it was just as well to walk through Main Street with more dignity—for the time being, anyway."

Tom Appleton had a way of winking at men he passed in the street, as though to say, "Well, now I've got my kids with me, and we won't say anything, but didn't you and I have the very hell of a time last Wednesday night, eh? Mum's the word, old pal. Keep everything quiet. There are gay times ahead for you and me. We'll cut loose, you bet, when you and me are out together next time."

Will grew a little angry about something he couldn't exactly understand. His father stopped in front of Jake Mann's meat market. "You kids go along home. Tell Kate I am bringing a steak. I'll be right on your heels," he said.

He would get the steak and then he would go into Alf Geiger's saloon and get a good stiff drink of whisky. There would be no one now to bother about smelling it on his breath when he got home later. Not that his wife had ever said anything when he wanted a drink—but you know how a man feels when there's a woman in the house. "Why, hello, Bildad Smith, how's the old game leg? Come on, have a little nip with me. Were you on Main Street last band meeting night and did you hear us do that new gallop? It's a humdinger. Turkey White did that trombone solo simply grand."

Will and Fred had got beyond Main Street now, and Will took a small pipe with a curved stem out of his overcoat pocket and lighted it. "I'll bet I could hang a ceiling without Father there at all, if only someone would give me a chance," he said. Now that his father was no longer present to embarrass him with his lack of dignity, he felt comfortable and happy. Also, it was something to be able to smoke a pipe without discomfiture. When Mother was alive she was always kissing a fellow when he came home at night, and then one had to be mighty careful about smoking. Now it was different. One had become a man and one accepted manhood with its responsibilities. "Don't it make you sick at all?" Fred asked. "Huh, naw!" Will answered contemptuously.

The new disaster to the family came late in August, just when the fall work was all ahead, and the prospects good too. A. P. Wrigley, the jeweler, had just built a big new house and barn on a farm he had bought the year before. It was a mile out of town on the Turner Pike.

That would be a job to set the Appletons up for the winter. The house was to have three coats outside, with all the work inside, and the barn was to have two coats—and the two boys were to work with their father and were to have regular wages.

And just to think of the work to be done inside that house made Tom Appleton's mouth water. He talked of it all the time, and in the evenings liked to sit in a chair in the Appletons' front yard, get some neighbor over, and then go on about it. How he slung house-painter's lingo about! The doors and cupboards were to be grained in imitation of weathered oak, the front door was to be curly maple, and there was to be black walnut, too. Well, there wasn't another painter in the town could imitate all the various kinds of wood as Tom could. Just show him the wood, or tell him —you didn't have to show him anything. Name what you wanted— that was enough. To be sure, a man had to have the right tools, but give him the tools and then just go off and leave everything to him.

What the devil! When A. P. Wrigley gave him this new house to do, he showed he was a man who knew what he was doing.

As for the practical side of the matter, everyone in the family knew that the Wrigley job meant a safe winter. There wasn't any speculation, as when taking work on the contract plan. All work was to be paid for by the day, and the boys were to have their wages, too. It meant new suits for the boys, a new dress and maybe a hat for Kate, the house rent paid all winter, potatoes in the cellar. It meant safety—that was the truth.

In the evenings, sometimes, Tom got out his tools and looked at them. Brushes and graining tools were spread out on the kitchen table, and Kate and the boys gathered about. It was Fred's job to see that all brushes were kept clean and, one by one, Tom ran his fingers over them and then worked them back and forth over the palm of his hand. "This is a camel's hair," he said, picking a soft fine-haired brush up and handing it to Will. "I paid four dollars and eighty cents for that." Will also worked it back and forth over the palm of his hand, just as his father had done and then Kate picked it up and did the same thing. "It's as soft as the cat's back," she said. Will thought that rather silly. He looked forward to the day when he would have brushes, ladders and pots of his own, and could show them off before people, and through his mind went words he had picked up from his father's talk. One spoke of the "heel" and "toe" of a brush. The way to put on varnish was to "flow" it on. Will knew all the words of his trade now and didn't have to talk like one of the kind of muts who just does, now and then, a jack job of house painting.

On the fatal evening a surprise party was held for Mr. and Mrs. Bardshare, who lived just across the road from the Appletons on Piety Hill. That was a chance for Tom Appleton. In any such affair he liked to have a hand in the arrangements. "Come on now, we'll make her go with a bang. They'll be setting in the house after supper, and Bill Bardshare will be in his stocking feet, and Ma Bardshare washing the dishes. They won't be expecting nothing, and we'll slip up, all dressed in our Sunday clothes, and let out a whoop. I'll bring my cornet and let out a blast on that too. 'What in Sam Hill is that?' Say, I can just see Bill Bardshare jumping up and beginning to swear, thinking we're a gang of kids come to bother him, like Hallowe'en, or something like that. You just get the grub, and I'll make the coffee over to my house and bring it over hot. I'll get ahold of two big pots and make a whooping lot of it."

In the Appleton house all was in a flurry. Tom, Will and Fred were painting a barn, three miles out of town, but they knocked off work at four and Tom got the farmer's son to drive them to town. He himself had to wash up, take a bath in a tub in the woodshed, shave and everything—just like Sunday. He looked more like a boy than a man when he got all dogged up.

And then the family had to have supper, over and done with, a little after six, and Tom didn't dare go outside the house until dark. It wouldn't do to have the Bardshares see him so fixed up. It was their wedding anniversary, and they might suspect something. He kept trotting about the house, and occasionally looked out of the front window toward the Bardshare house. "You kid, you," Kate said, laughing. Sometimes she talked up to him like that, and after she said it he went upstairs, and getting out his cornet blew on it, so softly, you could hardly hear him downstairs. When he did that you couldn't tell how badly he played, as when the band was going it on Main Street and he had to carry a passage right through alone. He sat in the room upstairs thinking. When Kate laughed at him it was like having his wife back, alive. There was the same shy sarcastic gleam in her eyes.

Well, it was the first time he had been out anywhere since his wife had died, and there might be some people think it would be better if he stayed at home now—look better, that is. When he had shaved he had cut his chin, and the blood had come. After a time he went downstairs and stood before the looking glass, hung above the kitchen sink, and dabbed at the spot with the wet end of a towel.

Will and Fred stood about.

Will's mind was working—perhaps Kate's, too. "Was there—could it be?—well, at such a party—only older people invited—there were always two or three widow women thrown in for good measure, as it were."

Kate didn't want any woman fooling around her kitchen. She was twenty years old.

"And it was just as well not to have any monkeyshine talk about motherless children," such as Tom might indulge in. Even Fred thought that. There was a little wave of resentment against Tom in the house. It was a wave that didn't make much noise, just crept, as it were softly, up a low sandy beach.

"Widow women went to such places, and then of course, people were always going home in couples." Both Kate and Will had the same picture in mind. It was late at night and in fancy they were both peeking out at front upper windows of the Appleton house. There were all the people coming out at the front door of the Bardshare house, and Bill Bardshare was standing there and holding the door open. He had managed to sneak away during the evening, and got his Sunday clothes on all right.

And the couples were coming out. "There was that woman now, that widow, Mrs. Childers." She had been married twice, both husbands dead now, and she lived away over Maumee Pike way. "What makes a woman of her age want to act silly like that? It is the very devil how a woman can keep looking young and handsome after she has buried two men. There are some who say that, even when her last husband was alive—"

"But whether that's true or not, what makes her want to act and talk silly that way?" Now her face is turned to the light and she is saying to old Bill Bardshare, "Sleep light, sleep tight, sweet dreams to you tonight."

"It's only what one may expect when one's father lacks a sense of dignity. There is that old fool Tom now, hopping out of the Bardshare house like a kid, and running right up to Mrs. Childers. 'May I see you home?' he is saying, while all the others are laughing and smiling knowingly. It makes one's blood run cold to see such a thing."

"Well, fill up the pots. Let's get the old coffee pots started, Kate. The gang'll be creeping along up the street pretty soon now," Tom shouted self-consciously, skipping busily about and breaking the little circle of thoughts in the house.

What happened was that—just as darkness came and when all the people were in the front yard before the Appleton house—Tom went and got it into his head to try to carry his cornet and two big coffee pots at the same time. Why didn't he leave the coffee until later? There the people were in the dusk outside the house, and there was that kind of low whispering and tittering that always goes on at such a time—and then Tom stuck his head out at the door and shouted, "Let her go!"

And then he must have gone quite crazy, for he ran back into the kitchen and grabbed both of the big coffee pots, hanging on to his cornet at the same time. Of course he stumbled in the darkness in the road outside and fell, and of course all of that boiling hot coffee had to spill right over him.

It was terrible. The flood of boiling hot coffee made steam under his thick clothes, and there he lay screaming with the pain of it. What a confusion! He just writhed and screamed, and the people ran round and round in the half darkness like crazy things. Was it some kind of joke the crazy fellow was up to at the last minute! Tom always was such a devil to think up things. "You should see him down at Alf Geiger's, sometimes on Saturday nights, imitating the way Joe Douglas got out on a limb, and then sawed it off between himself and the tree, and the look on Joe's face when the limb began to crack. It would make you laugh until you screamed to see him imitate that."

"But what now? My God!" There was Kate Appleton trying to tear her father's clothes off, and crying and whimpering, and young Will Appleton knocking people aside. "Say, the man's hurt! What's happened? My God! Run for the doctor, someone. He's burnt, something awful!"

Early in October Will Appleton sat in the smoking car of a day train that runs between Cleveland and Buffalo. His destination was Erie, Pennsylvania, and he had got on the passenger train at Ashtabula, Ohio. Just why his destination was Erie he couldn't very easily have explained. He was going there anyway, going to get a job in a factory or on the docks there. Perhaps it was just a quirk of the mind that had made him decide upon Erie. It wasn't as big as Cleveland or Buffalo or Toledo or Chicago, or any one of a lot of other cities to which he might have gone, looking for work.

At Ashtabula he came into the car and slid into a seat beside a little old man. His own clothes were wet and wrinkled, and his hair, eyebrows and ears were black with coal dust.

At the moment, there was in him a kind of bitter dislike of his native town, Bidwell. "Sakes alive, a man couldn't get any work there—not in the winter." After the accident to his father, and the spoiling of all the family plans, he had managed to find employment during September on the farms. He worked for a time with a threshing crew, and then got work cutting corn. It was all right. "A man made a dollar a day and board, and as he wore overalls all the time, he didn't wear out no clothes. Still and all, the time when a fellow could make any money in Bidwell was past now, and the burns on his father's body had gone pretty deep, and he might be laid up for months."

Will had just made up his mind one day, after he had tramped about all morning from farm to farm without finding work, and then he had gone home and told Kate. "Dang it all," he hadn't intended lighting out right away—had thought he would stay about for a week or two, maybe. Well, he would go up town in the evening, dressed up in his best clothes, and stand around. "Hello, Harry, what you going to do this winter? I thought I would run over to Erie, Pennsylvania. I got an offer in a factory over there. Well, so long—if I don't see you again."

Kate hadn't seemed to understand, had seemed in an almighty hurry about getting him off. It was a shame she couldn't have a little more heart. Still, Kate was all right—worried a good deal no doubt. After their talk she had just said, "Yes, I think that's best, you had better go," and had gone to change the bandages on Tom's legs and back. The father was sitting among pillows in a rocking chair in the front room.

Will went upstairs and put his things, overalls and a few shirts, into a bundle. Then he went downstairs and took a walk—went out along a road that led into the country, and stopped on a bridge. It was near a place where he and other kids used to come swimming on summer afternoons. A thought had come into his head. There was a young fellow worked in Pawsey's jewelry store came to see Kate sometimes on Sunday evenings and they went off to walk together. Did Kate want to get married? If she did, his going away now might be for good. He hadn't thought about that before. On that afternoon, and quite suddenly, all the world outside of Bidwell seemed huge and terrible to him and a few secret tears came into his eyes, but he managed to choke them back. For just a moment his mouth opened and closed queerly, like the mouth of a fish, when you take it out of the water and hold it in your hand.

When he returned to the house at suppertime things were better. He had left his bundle on a chair in the kitchen and Kate had wrapped it more carefully, and had put in a number of things he had forgotten. His father called him into the front room. "It's all right, Will. Every young fellow ought to take a whirl out in the world. I did it myself, at about your age," Tom had said, a little pompously.

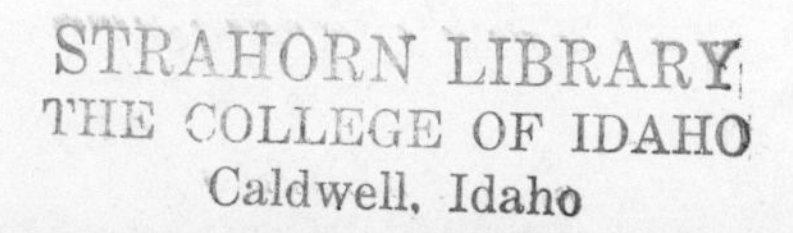

Then supper was served, and there was apple pie. That was a luxury the Appletons had perhaps better not have indulged in at that time, but Will knew Kate had baked it during the afternoon—it might be as a way of showing him how she felt. Eating two large slices had rather set him up.

And then, before he realized how the time was slipping away, ten o'clock had come, and it was time for him to go. He was going to beat his way out of town on a freight train, and there was a local going toward Cleveland at ten o'clock. Fred had gone off to bed, and his father was asleep in the rocking chair in the front room. He had picked up his bundle, and Kate had put on her hat. "I'm going to see you off," she had said.

Will and Kate had walked in silence along the streets to where he was to wait, in the shadow of Whaley's Warehouse, until the freight came along. Later when he thought back over that evening he was glad that, although she was three years older, he was taller than Kate.

How vividly everything that happened later stayed in his mind. After the train came and he had crawled into an empty coal car, he sat hunched up in a corner. Overhead he could see the sky, and when the train stopped at towns there was always the chance the car in which he was concealed would be shoved into a siding, and left. The brakemen walked along the tracks beside the car shouting to each other and their lanterns made little splashes of light in the darkness.

"How black the sky!" After a time it began to rain. His suit would be in a pretty mess. After all a fellow couldn't come right out and ask his sister if she intended to marry. If Kate married, then his father would also marry again. It was all right for a young woman like Kate, but for a man of forty to think of marriage—the devil! Why didn't Tom Appleton have more dignity? After all, Fred was only a kid, and a new woman coming in to be his mother—that might be all right for a kid.

All during that night on the freight train Will had thought a good deal about marriage—rather vague thoughts—coming and going like birds flying in and out of a bush. It was all a matter—this business of man and woman—that did not touch him very closely—not yet. The matter of having a home—that was something else. A home was something at a fellow's back. When one went off to work all week at some farm, and at night maybe went into a strange room to sleep, there was always the Appleton house

—floating, as it were, like a picture at the back of the mind—the Appleton house, and Kate moving about. She had been uptown and now had come home and was going up the stairs. Tom Appleton was fussing about in the kitchen. He liked a bite before he went off to bed for the night but presently he would go upstairs and into his own room. He liked to smoke his pipe before he slept and sometimes he got out his cornet and blew two or three soft sad notes.

At Cleveland Will had crawled off the freight train and had gone across the city in a streetcar. Workingmen were just going to the factories and he passed among them unnoticed. If his clothes were crumpled and soiled, their clothes weren't so fine. The workingmen were all silent, looking at the car floor, or out the car windows. Long rows of factories stood along the streets through which the car moved.

He had been lucky and had caught another freight out of a place called Collinswood at eight, but at Ashtabula had made up his mind it would be better to drop off the freight and take a passenger train. If he was to live in Erie it would be just as well to arrive, looking more like a gentleman and having paid his fare.

As he sat in the smoking car of the train he did not feel much like a gentleman. The coal dust had got into his hair and the rain had washed it in long dirty streaks down over his face. His clothes were badly soiled and wanted cleaning and brushing and the paper package, in which his overalls and shirts were tied, had become torn and dirty.

Outside the train window the sky was gray, and no doubt the night was going to turn cold. Perhaps there would be a cold rain.

It was an odd thing about the towns through which the train kept passing—all of the houses in all the towns looked cold and forbidding. "Dang it all." In Bidwell, before the night when his father got so badly burned being such a fool about old Bill Bardshare's party—all the houses had always seemed warm cozy places. When one was alone, one walked along the streets whistling. At night warm lights shone through the windows of the houses. "John Wyatt, the drayman, lives in that house. His wife has a wen on her neck. In that barn over there old Doctor Musgrave keeps his bony old white horse. The horse looks like the devil, but you bet he can go."

Will squirmed about on the car seat. The old man who sat beside him was small, almost as small as Fred, and he wore a queer-looking suit. The pants were brown, and the coat checked, gray and black. There was a small leather case on the floor at his feet.

Long before the man spoke Will knew what would happen. It was bound to turn out that such a fellow played a cornet. He was a man, old in years, but there was no dignity in him. Will remembered his father's marchings through the main street of Bidwell with the band. It was some great day, Fourth of July perhaps, and all the people were assembled and there was Tony Appleton, making a show of blowing his cornet at a great rate. Did all the people along the street know how badly he played, and was there a kind of conspiracy, that kept grown men from laughing at each other? In spite of the seriousness of his own situation a smile crept over Will's face.

The little man at his side smiled in return.

"Well," he began, not stopping for anything, but plunging headlong into a tale concerning some dissatisfaction he felt with life, "well, you see before you a man who is up against it, young fellow." The old man tried to laugh at his own words, but did not make much of a success of it. His lip trembled. "I got to go home like a dog, with my tail 'twixt my legs," he declared abruptly.

The old man balanced back and forth between two impulses. He had met a young man on a train, and hungered for companionship and one got oneself in with others by being jolly, a little gay perhaps. When one met a stranger on a train one told a story—"By the way, Mister, I heard a new one the other day—perhaps you haven't heard it? It's about the miner up in Alaska who hadn't seen a woman for years." One began in that way and then later perhaps spoke of oneself and one's affairs.

But the old man wanted to plunge at once into his own story. He talked, saying sad discouraged words, while his eyes kept smiling with a peculiar appealing little smile. "If the words uttered by my lips annoy or bore you, do not pay any attention to them. I am really a jolly fellow although I am an old man and not of much use any more," the eyes were saying. The eyes were pale blue and watery. How strange to see them set in the head of an old man. They belonged in the head of a lost dog. The smile was not really a smile. "Don't kick me, young fellow. If you can't give me anything to eat, scratch my head. At least show you are a fellow of good intentions. I've been kicked about quite enough." It was so very evident the eyes were speaking a language of their own.

Will found himself smiling sympathetically. It was true there was something doglike in the little old man and Will was pleased with himself for having so quickly caught the sense of him. "One who can see things with his eyes will perhaps get along all right in the world, after all," he thought. His thoughts wandered away from the old man. In Bidwell there was an old woman lived alone and owned a shepherd dog. Every summer she decided to cut away the dog's coat, and then—at the last moment and after she had in fact started the job—she changed her mind. Well, she grasped a long pair of scissors firmly in her hand and started on the dog's flanks. Her hand trembled a little. "Shall I go ahead, or shall I stop?" After two minutes she gave up the job. "It makes him look too ugly," she thought, justifying her timidity.

Later the hot days came, the dog went about with his tongue hanging out and again the old woman took the scissors in her hand. The dog stood patiently waiting but, when she had cut a long wide furrow through the thick hair of his back, she stopped again. In a sense, and to her way of looking at the matter, cutting away his splendid coat was like cutting away a part of himself. She couldn't go on. "Now there—that made him look worse than ever," she declared to herself. With a determined air she put the scissors away, and all summer the dog went about looking a little puzzled and ashamed.

Will kept smiling and thinking of the old woman's dog and then looked again at his companion of the train. The variegated suit the old man wore gave him something of the air of the half-sheared shepherd dog. Both had the same puzzled, ashamed air.

Now Will had begun using the old man for his own ends. There was something inside himself that wanted facing, he didn't want to face—not yet. Ever since he had left home, in fact ever since that day when he had come home from the country and had told Kate of his intention to set out into the world, he had been dodging something. If one thought of the little old man, and of the half-sheared dog, one did not have to think of oneself.

One thought of Bidwell on a summer afternoon. There was the old woman, who owned the dog, standing on the porch of her house, and the dog had run down to the gate. In the winter, when his coat had again fully grown, the dog would bark and make a great fuss about a boy passing in the street but now he started to bark and growl, and then stopped. "I look like the devil, and I'm attracting unnecessary attention to myself," the dog seemed to have decided suddenly. He ran furiously down to the gate, opened his mouth to bark, and then, quite abruptly, changed his mind and trotted back to the house with his tail between his legs.

Will kept smiling at his own thoughts. For the first time since he had left Bidwell he felt quite cheerful.

And now the old man was telling a story of himself and his life, but Will wasn't listening. Within the young man a crosscurrent of impulses had been set up and he was like one standing silently in the hallway of a house, and listening to two voices, talking at a distance. The voices came from two widely separated rooms of the house and one couldn't make up one's mind to which voice to listen.

To be sure, the old man was another cornet player like his father—he was a horn blower. That was his horn in the little worn leather case on the car floor.

And after he had reached middle age, and after his first wife had died, he had married again. He had a little property then and, in a foolish moment, went and made it all over to his second wife, who was fifteen years younger than himself. She took the money and bought a large house in the factory district of Erie, and then began taking in boarders.

There was the old man, feeling lost, of no account in his own house. It just came about. One had to think of the boarders—their wants had to be satisfied. His wife had two sons, almost fully grown now, both of whom worked in a factory.

Well, it was all right—everything on the square—the sons paid board all right. Their wants had to be thought of, too. He liked blowing his cornet a while in the evenings, before he went to bed, but it might disturb the others in the house. One got rather desperate going about saying nothing, keeping out of the way, and he had tried getting work in a factory himself, but they wouldn't have him. His gray hairs stood in his way, and so one night he had just got out, had gone to Cleveland, where he had hoped to get a job in a band, in a movie theatre perhaps. Anyway, it hadn't turned out, and now he was going back to Erie and to his wife. He had written and she had told him to come on home.

"They didn't turn me down back there in Cleveland because

I'm old. It's because my lip is no good any more," he explained. His shrunken old lip trembled a little.

Will kept thinking of the old woman's dog. In spite of himself, and when the old man's lip trembled, his lip also trembled.

What was the matter with him?

He stood in the hallway of a house hearing two voices. Was he trying to close his ears to one of them? Did the second voice, the one he had been trying all day, and all the night before, not to hear, did that have something to do with the end of his life in the Appleton house at Bidwell? Was the voice trying to taunt him, trying to tell him that now he was a thing swinging in air, that there was no place to put down his feet? Was he afraid? Of what was he afraid? He had wanted so much to be a man, to stand on his own feet and now what was the matter with him? Was he afraid of manhood?

He was fighting desperately now. There were tears in the old man's eyes, and Will also began crying silently, and that was the one thing he felt he must not do.

The old man talked on and on, telling the tale of his troubles, but Will could not hear his words. The struggle within was becoming more and more definite. His mind clung to the life of his boyhood, to the life in the Appleton house in Bidwell.

There was Fred, standing in the field of his fancy now, with just the triumphant look in his eyes that came when other boys saw him doing a man's work. A whole series of pictures floated up before Will's mind. He and his father and Fred were painting a barn and two farmer boys had come along a road and stood looking at Fred, who was on a ladder, putting on paint. They shouted, but Fred wouldn't answer. There was a certain air Fred had—he slapped on the paint, and then turning his head, spat on the ground. Tom Appleton's eyes looked into Will's and there was a smile playing about the corners of the father's eyes and the son's eyes too. The father and his oldest son were like two men, two workmen, having a delicious little secret between them. They were both looking lovingly at Fred. "Bless him! He thinks he's a man already."

And now Tom Appleton was standing in the kitchen of his house, and his brushes were laid out on the kitchen table. Kate was rubbing a brush back and forth over the palm of her hand. "It's as soft as the cat's back," she was saying.

Something gripped at Will's throat. As in a dream, he saw his sister Kate walking off along the street on Sunday evening with that young fellow who clerked in the jewelry store. They were going to church. Her being with him meant—well, it perhaps meant the beginning of a new home—it meant the end of the Appleton home.

Will started to climb out of the seat beside the old man in the smoking car of the train. It had grown almost dark in the car. The old man was still talking, telling his tale over and over. "I might as well not have any home at all," he was saying. Was Will about to begin crying aloud on a train, in a strange place, before many strange men? He tried to speak, to make some commonplace remark, but his mouth only opened and closed like the mouth of a fish taken out of the water.

And now the train had run into a train shed, and it was quite dark. Will's hand clutched convulsively into the darkness and alighted upon the old man's shoulder.

Then suddenly, thc train had stopped, and the two stood half embracing each other. The tears were quite evident in Will's eyes, when a brakeman lighted the overhead lamps in the car, but the luckiest thing in the world had happened. The old man, who had seen Will's tears, thought they were tears of sympathy for his own unfortunate position in life, and a look of gratitude came into his blue watery eyes. Well, this was something new in life for him, too. In one of the pauses, when he had first begun telling his tale, Will had said he was going to Erie to try to get work in some factory and now, as they got off the train, the old man clung to Will's arm. "You might as well come live at our house," he said. A look of hope flared up in the old man's eyes. If he could bring home with him, to his young wife, a new boarder, the gloom of his own home-coming would be somewhat lightened. "You come on. That's the best thing to do. You just come on with me to our house," he pleaded, clinging to Will.

Two weeks had passed and Will had, outwardly, and to the eyes of the people about him, settled into his new life as a factory hand at Erie, Pennsylvania.

Then suddenly, on a Saturday evening, the thing happened that he had unconsciously been expecting and dreading ever since the moment when he climbed aboard the freight train in the shadow of Whaley's Warehouse at Bidwell. A letter, containing great news, had come from Kate.

At the moment of their parting, and before he settled himself down out of sight in a corner of the empty coal car, on that night of his leaving, he had leaned out for a last look at his sister. She had been standing silently in the shadows of the warehouse but, just as the train was about to start, stepped toward him and a light from a distant street lamp fell on her face.

Well, the face did not jump toward Will, but remained dimly outlined in the uncertain light.

Did her lips open and close, as though in an effort to say something to him, or was that an effect produced by the distant, uncertain and wavering light? In the families of working people the dramatic and vital moments of life are passed over in silence. Even in the moments of death and birth, little is said. A child is born to a laborer's wife and he goes into the room. She is in bed with the little red bundle of new life beside her and her husband stands a moment, fumblingly, beside the bed. Neither he nor his wife can look directly into each other's eyes. "Take care of yourself, Ma. Have a good rest," he says, and hurries out of the room.

In the darkness by the warehouse at Bidwell Kate had taken two or three steps toward Will and then had stopped. There was a little strip of grass between the warehouse and the tracks, and she stood upon it. Was there a more final farewell trembling on her lips at the moment? A kind of dread had swept over Will, and no doubt Kate had felt the same thing. At the moment she had become altogether the mother, in the presence of her child, and the thing within that wanted utterance became submerged. There was a word to be said that she could not say. Her form seemed to sway a little in the darkness and, to Will's eyes, she became a slender indistinct thing. "Good-bye," he had whispered into the darkness, and perhaps her lips had formed the same words. Outwardly there had been only the silence, and in the silence she had stood as the train rumbled away.

And now, on the Saturday evening, Will had come home from the factory and had found Kate saying in the letter what she had been unable to say on the night of his departure. The factory closed at five on Saturday and he came home in his overalls and went to his room. He had found the letter on a little broken table under a spluttering oil lamp, by the front door, and had climbed the stairs carrying it in his hand. He read the letter anxiously, waiting as for a hand to come out of the blank wall of the room and strike.

His father was getting better. The deep burns that had taken such a long time to heal were really healing now and the doctor had said the danger of infection had passed. Kate had found a new and soothing remedy. One took slippery elm and let it lie in milk until it became soft. This applied to the burns enabled Tom to sleep better at night.

As for Fred, Kate and her father had decided he might as well go back to school. It was really too bad for a young boy to miss the chance to get an education, and anyway there was no work to be had. Perhaps he could get a job, helping in some store on Saturday afternoons.

A woman from the Woman's Relief Corps had had the nerve to come to the Appleton house and ask Kate if the family needed help. Well, Kate had managed to hold herself back and had been polite, but had the woman known what was in her mind her ears would have been itching for a month. The idea!

It had been fine of Will to send a postcard as soon as he had got to Erie and got a job. As for his sending money home—of course the family would be glad to have anything he could spare—but he wasn't to go depriving himself. "We've got good credit at the stores. We'll get along all right," Kate had said stoutly.

And then it was she had added the line, had said the thing she could not say that night when he was leaving. It concerned herself and her future plans. "That night when you were going away I wanted to tell you something, but I thought it was silly, talking too soon." After all though, Will might as well know she was planning to be married in the spring. What she wanted was for Fred to come and live with her and her husband. He could keep on going to school, and perhaps they could manage so that he could go to college. Someone in the family ought to have a decent education. Now that Will had made his start in life, there was no point in waiting longer before making her own.

Will sat, in his tiny room at the top of the huge frame house, owned now by the wife of the old cornet player of the train, and held the letter in his hand. The room was on the third floor, under the roof, in a wing of the house, and beside it was another small room, occupied by the old man himself. Will had taken the room because it was to be had at a low price and he could manage the room and his meals, get his washing done, send three dollars a week to Kate, and still have left a dollar a week to spend. One could get a little tobacco, and now and then see a movie.

"Ugh!" Will's lips made a little grunting noise as he read Kate's words. He was sitting in a chair, in his oily overalls, and where his fingers gripped the white sheets of the letter there was a little oily smudge. Also his hand trembled a little. He got up, poured water out of a pitcher into a white bowl, and began washing his face and hands.

When he had partly dressed, a visitor came. There was the shuffling sound of weary feet along a hallway, and the cornet player put his head timidly in at the door. The doglike appealing look Will had noted on the train was still in his eyes. Now he was planning something, a kind of gentle revolt against his wife's power in the house, and he wanted Will's moral support.

For a week he had been coming for talk to Will's room almost every evening. There were two things he wanted. In the evening sometimes, as he sat in his room, he wanted to blow upon his cornet, and he wanted a little money to jingle in his pockets.

And there was a sense in which Will, the newcomer in the house, was his property, did not belong to his wife. Often in the evenings he had talked to the weary and sleepy young workman, until Will's eyes had closed and he snored gently. The old man sat on the one chair in the room, and Will sat on the edge of the bed, while old lips told the tale of a lost youth, boasted a little. When Will's body had slumped down upon the bed the old man got to his feet and moved with catlike steps about the room. One mustn't raise the voice too loudly after all. Had Will gone to sleep? The cornet player threw his shoulders back and bold words came, in a half-whisper, from his lips. To tell the truth, he had been a fool about the money he had made over to his wife and, if his wife had taken advantage of him, it wasn't her fault. For his present position in life he had no one to blame but himself. What from the very beginning he had most lacked was boldness. It was a man's duty to be a man and, for a long time, he had been thinking—well, the boardinghouse no doubt made a profit and he should have his share. His wife was a good girl all right, but when one came right down to it, all women seemed to lack a sense of a man's position in life.

"I'll have to speak to her—yes sirree, I'm going to speak right up to her. I may have to be a little harsh, but it's my money runs this house, and I want my share of the profits. No foolishness now. Shell out, I tell you," the old man whispered, peering out of the corners of his blue, watery eyes at the sleeping form of the young man on the bed.

And now again the old man stood at the door of the room, looking anxiously in. A bell called insistently, announcing that the evening meal was ready to be served, and they went below, Will leading the way. At a long table in the dining room several men had already gathered, and there was the sound of more footsteps on the stairs.

Two long rows of young workmen eating silently. Saturday night and two long rows of young workmen eating in silence.

After the eating, and on this particular night, there would be a swift flight of all these young men down into the town, down into the lighted parts of the town.

Will sat at his place gripping the sides of his chair.

There were things men did on Saturday nights. Work was at an end for the week, and money jingled in pockets. Young workmen ate in silence and hurried away, one by one, down into the town.

Will's sister Kate was going to be married in the spring. Her walking about with the young clerk from the jewelry store, in the streets of Bidwell, had come to something.

Young workmen employed in factories in Erie, Pennsylvania, dressed themselves in their best clothes and walked about in the lighted streets of Erie on Saturday evenings. They went into parks. Some stood talking to girls, while others walked with girls through the streets. And there were still others who went into saloons and had drinks. Men stood talking together at a bar. "Dang that foreman of mine! I'll bust him in the jaw if he gives me any of his lip."

There was a young man from Bidwell, sitting at a table in a boardinghouse at Erie, Pennsylvania, and before him on a plate was a great pile of meat and potatoes. The room was not very well lighted. It was dark and gloomy, and there were black streaks on the gray wallpaper. Shadows played on the walls. On all sides of the young man sat other young men—eating silently, hurriedly.

Will got abruptly up from the table and started for the door that led into the street, but the others paid no attention to him. If he did not want to eat his meat and potatoes, it made no difference to them. The mistress of the house, the wife of the old cornet player, waited on table when the men ate, but now she had gone away to the kitchen. She was a silent grim-looking woman, dressed always in a black dress.

To the others in the room—except only the old cornet player—Will's going or staying meant nothing at all. He was a young workman, and at such places young workmen were always going and coming.

A man with broad shoulders and a black mustache, a little older than most of the others, did glance up from his business of eating. He nudged his neighbor, and then made a jerky movement with his thumb over his shoulder. "The new guy has hooked up quickly, eh?" he said, smiling. "He can't even wait to eat. Lordy, he's got an early date—some skirt waiting for him."

At his place, opposite where Will had been seated, the cornet player saw Will go, and his eyes followed, filled with alarm. He had counted on an evening of talk, of speaking to Will about his youth, boasting a little in his gentle hesitating way. Now Will had reached the door that led to the street, and in the old man's eyes tears began to gather. Again his lip trembled. Tears were always gathering in the man's eyes, and his lips trembled at the slightest provocation. It was no wonder he could no longer blow a cornet in a band.

And now Will was outside the house in the darkness and, for the cornet player, the evening was spoiled, the house a deserted, empty place. He had intended being very plain in his evening's talk with Will, and wanted particularly to speak of a new attitude he hoped to assume toward his wife in the matter of money. Talking the whole matter out with Will would give him new courage, make him bolder. Well, if his money had bought the house, that was now a boardinghouse, he should have some share in its profits. There must be profits. Why run a boardinghouse without profits? The woman he had married was no fool.

Even though a man was old, he needed a little money in his pockets. Well, an old man like himself has a friend, a young fellow, and now and then he wanted to be able to say to his friend, "Come on friend, let's have a glass of beer. I know a good place. Let's have a glass of beer and go to the movies. This is on me."

The cornet player could not eat his meat and potatoes. For a time he stared over the heads of the others, and then got up to go to his room. His wife followed into the little hallway at the foot of the stairs. "What's the matter, dearie—are you sick?" she asked.

"No," he answered, "I just didn't want any supper." He did not look at her, but tramped slowly and heavily up the stairs.

Will was walking hurriedly through streets but did not go down into the brightly lighted sections of town. The boardinghouse stood on a factory street and, turning northward, he crossed several railroad tracks and went toward the docks along the shore of Lake Erie. There was something to be settled with himself, something to be faced. Could he manage the matter?

He walked along, hurriedly at first, and then more slowly. It was getting into late October now, and there was a sharpness like frost in the air. The spaces between street lamps were long, and he plunged in and out of areas of darkness. Why was it that everything about him seemed suddenly strange and unreal? He had forgotten to bring his overcoat from Bidwell and would have to write Kate to send it.

Now he had almost reached the docks. Not only the night but his own body, the pavements under his feet and the stars far away in the sky—even the solid factory buildings he was now passing—seemed strange and unreal. It was almost as though one could thrust out an arm and push a hand through the walls, as one might push his hand into a fog or a cloud of smoke. All the people Will passed seemed strange and acted in a strange way. Dark figures surged toward him out of the darkness. By a factory wall there was a man standing—perfectly still, motionless. There was something almost unbelievable about the actions of such men and the strangeness of such hours as the one through which he was now passing. He walked within a few inches of the motionless man. Was it a man or a shadow on the wall? The life Will was now to lead alone had become a strange, a vast, terrifying thing. Perhaps all life was like that, a vastness and an emptiness.

He came out into a place where ships were made fast to a dock and stood for a time, facing the high wall-like side of a vessel. It looked dark and deserted. When he turned his head he became aware of a man and a woman passing along a roadway. Their feet made no sound in the thick dust of the roadway, and he could not see or hear them, but knew they were there. Some part of a woman's dress—something white—flashed faintly into view and the man's figure was a dark mass against the dark mass of the night.

"Oh, come on, don't be afraid," the man whispered, hoarsely. "There won't anything happen to you."

"Do shut up," a woman's voice answered, and there was a quick outburst of laughter. The figures fluttered away. "You don't know what you are talking about," the woman's voice said again.

Now that he had got Kate's letter, Will was no longer a boy. A boy is, quite naturally, and without his having anything to do with the matter, connected with something—and now that connection had been cut. He had been pushed out of the nest and that fact, the pushing of himself off the nest's rim, was something accomplished. The difficulty was that, while he was no longer a boy, he had not yet become a man. He was a thing swinging in space. There was no place to put down his feet.

He stood in the darkness under the shadow of the ship making queer little wriggling motions with his shoulders, that had become now almost the shoulders of a man. No need now to think of evenings at the Appleton house with Kate and Fred standing about, and his father, Tom Appleton, spreading his paint brushes on the kitchen table, no need of thinking of the sound of Kate's feet going up a stairway of the Appleton house, late at night when she had been out walking with her clerk. What was the good of trying to amuse oneself by thinking of a shepherd dog in an Ohio town, a dog made ridiculous by the trembling hand of a timid old woman?

One stood face to face with manhood now—one stood alone. If only one could get one's feet down upon something, could get over this feeling of falling through space, through a vast emptiness.

"Manhood"—the word had a queer sound in the head. What did it mean?

Will tried to think of himself as a man, doing a man's work in a factory. There was nothing in the factory where he was now employed upon which he could put down his feet. All day he stood at a machine and bored holes in pieces of iron. A boy brought to him the little, short, meaningless pieces of iron in a boxlike truck and, one by one, he picked them up and placed them under the point of a drill. He pulled a lever and the drill came down and bit into the piece of iron. A little, smokelike vapor arose, and then he squirted oil on the spot where the drill was working. Then the lever was thrown up again. The hole was drilled and now the meaningless pieces of iron was thrown into another boxlike truck. It had nothing to do with him. He had nothing to do with it.

At the noon hour, at the factory, one moved about a bit, stepped outside the factory door to stand for a moment in the sun. Inside, men were sitting along benches eating lunches out of dinner pails, and some had washed their hands while others had not bothered about such a trivial matter. They were eating in silence. A tall man spat on the floor and then drew his foot across the spot. Nights came, and one went home from the factory to eat, sitting with other silent men, and later a boastful old man came into one's room to talk. One lay on a bed and tried to listen, but presently fell asleep. Men were like the pieces of iron in which holes had been bored—one pitched them aside into a boxlike truck. One had nothing really to do with them. They had nothing to do with oneself. Life became a procession of days, and perhaps all life was just like that—just a procession of days.

"Manhood."

Did one go out of one place and into another? Were youth and manhood two houses in which one lived during different periods in life? It was evident something of importance must be about to happen to his sister Kate. First, she had been a young woman, having two brothers and a father, living with them in a house at Bidwell, Ohio.

And then a day was to come when she became something else. She married and went to live in another house and had a husband. Perhaps children would be born to her. It was evident that Kate had got hold of something, that her hands had reached out and had grasped something definite. Kate had swung herself off the rim of the home nest and, right away, her feet had landed on another limb of the tree of life—womanhood.

As he stood in the darkness something caught at Will's throat. He was fighting again, but what was he fighting? A fellow like himself did not move out of one house and into another. There was a house in which one lived, and then suddenly and unexpectedly, it fell apart. One stood on the rim of the nest and looked about, and a hand reached out from the warmth of the nest and pushed one off into space. There was no place for a fellow to put down his feet. He was one swinging in space.

What—a great fellow, nearly six feet tall now, and crying in the darkness, in the shadow of a ship, like a child! He walked, filled with determination, out of the darkness, along many streets of factories and came into a street of houses. He passed a store where groceries were sold and, looking in, saw by a clock on the wall that it was already ten o'clock. Two drunken men came out at the door of a house and stood on a little porch. One of them clung to a railing about the porch, and the other pulled at his arm. "Let me alone. It's settled. I want you to let me alone," grumbled the man clinging to the railing.

Will went to his boardinghouse and climbed the stairs wearily. The devil—one might face anything if one but knew what was to be faced!

He turned on a light and sat down in his room on the edge of the bed, and the old cornet player pounced upon him, pounced like a little animal lying under a bush along a path in a forest and waiting for food. He came into Will's room carrying his cornet, and there was an almost bold look in his eyes. Standing firmly on his old legs in the center of the room, he made a declaration. "I'm going to play it. I don't care what she says, I'm going to play it," he said.

He put the cornet to his lips and blew two or three notes—so softly that even Will, sitting so closely, could barely hear. Then his eyes wavered. "My lip's no good," he said. He thrust the cornet at Will. "You blow it," he said.

Will sat on the edge of the bed and smiled. There was a notion floating in his mind now. Was there something, a thought in which one could find comfort? There was now, before him, standing before him in the room, a man who was after all not a man. He was a child as Will was too, really, had always been such a child, would always be such a child. One need not be too afraid. Children were all about, everywhere. If one were a child and lost in a vast, empty space, one could at least talk to some other child. One could have conversations, understand perhaps something of the eternal childishness of oneself and others.

Will's thoughts were not very definite. He only felt suddenly warm and comfortable in the little room at the top of the boardinghouse.

And now the man was again explaining himself. He wanted to assert his manhood. "I stay up here," he explained, "and don't go down there, to sleep in the room with my wife because I don't want to. That's the only reason. I could if I wanted to. She has the bronchitis—but don't tell anyone. Women hate to have anyone told. She isn't so bad. I can do what I please."

He kept urging Will to put the cornet to his lips and blow. There was in him an intense eagerness. "You can't really make any music—you don't know how—but that don't make any difference," he said. "The thing to do is to make a noise, make a deuce of a racket, blow like the devil."

Again Will felt like crying but the sense of vastness and loneliness, that had been in him since he got aboard the train that night at Bidwell, had gone. "Well, I can't go on forever being a baby. Kate has a right to get married," he thought, putting the cornet to his lips. He blew two or three notes, softly.

"No, I tell you, no! That isn't the way! Blow on it! Don't be afraid! I tell you I want you to do it. Make a deuce of a racket! I tell you what, I own this house. We don't need to be afraid. We can do what we please. Go ahead! Make a deuce of a racket!" the old man kept pleading.

Stories from

Death in the Woods

(1933)

Death in the Woods

SHE WAS an old woman and lived on a farm near the town in which I lived. All country and small-town people have seen such old women, but no one knows much about them. Such an old woman comes into town driving an old worn-out horse or she comes afoot carrying a basket. She may own a few hens and have eggs to sell. She brings them in a basket and takes them to a grocer. There she trades them in. She gets some salt pork and some beans. Then she gets a pound or two of sugar and some flour.

Afterwards she goes to the butcher's and asks for some dog meat. She may spend ten or fifteen cents, but when she does she asks for something. Formerly the butchers gave liver to anyone who wanted to carry it away. In our family we were always having it. Once one of my brothers got a whole cow's liver at the slaughterhouse near the fairgrounds in our town. We had it until we were sick of it. It never cost a cent. I have hated the thought of it ever since.

The old farm woman got some liver and a soupbone. She never visited with anyone, and as soon as she got what she wanted she lit out for home. It made quite a load for such an old body. No one gave her a lift. People drive right down a road and never notice an old woman like that.

There was such an old woman who used to come into town past our house one summer and fall when I was a young boy and was sick with what was called inflammatory rheumatism. She went home later carrying a heavy pack on her back. Two or three large gaunt-looking dogs followed at her heels.

The old woman was nothing special. She was one of the nameless ones that hardly anyone knows, but she got into my thoughts. I have just suddenly now, after all these years, remembered her and what happened. It is a story. Her name was Grimes, and she lived with her husband and son in a small unpainted house on the bank of a small creek four miles from town.

The husband and son were a tough lot. Although the son was but twenty-one, he had already served a term in jail. It was whispered about that the woman's husband stole horses and ran them off to some other county. Now and then, when a horse turned up missing, the man had also disappeared. No one ever caught him. Once, when I was loafing at Tom Whitehead's livery barn, the man came there and sat on the bench in front. Two or three other men were there, but no one spoke to him. He sat for a few minutes and then got up and went away. When he was leaving he turned around and stared at the men. There was a look of defiance in his eyes. "Well, I have tried to be friendly. You don't want to talk to me. It has been so wherever I have gone in this town. If, some day, one of your fine horses turns up missing, well, then what?" He did not say anything actually. "I'd like to bust one of you on the jaw," was about what his eyes said. I remember how the look in his eyes made me shiver.

The old man belonged to a family that had had money once. His name was Jake Grimes. It all comes back clearly now. His father, John Grimes, had owned a sawmill when the country was new, and had made money. Then he got to drinking and running after women. When he died there wasn't much left.

Jake blew in the rest. Pretty soon there wasn't any more lumber to cut and his land was nearly all gone.

He got his wife off a German farmer, for whom he went to work one June day in the wheat harvest. She was a young thing then and scared to death. You see, the farmer was up to something with the girl—she was, I think, a bound girl and his wife had her suspicions. She took it out on the girl when the man wasn't around. Then, when the wife had to go off to town for supplies, the farmer got after her. She told young Jake that nothing really ever happened, but he didn't know whether to believe it or not.

He got her pretty easy himself, the first time he was out with her. He wouldn't have married her if the German farmer hadn't tried to tell him where to get off. He got her to go riding with him in his buggy one night when he was threshing on the place, and then he came for her the next Sunday night.

She managed to get out of the house without her employer's seeing, but when she was getting into the buggy he showed up. It was almost dark, and he just popped up suddenly at the horse's head. He grabbed the horse by the bridle and Jake got out his buggy whip.

They had it out all right! The German was a tough one. Maybe he didn't care whether his wife knew or not. Jake hit him over the face and shoulders with the buggy whip, but the horse got to acting up and he had to get out.

Then the two men went for it. The girl didn't see it. The horse started to run away and went nearly a mile down the road before the girl got him stopped. Then she managed to tie him to a tree beside the road. (I wonder how I know all this. It must have stuck in my mind from small-town tales when I was a boy.) Jake found her there after he got through with the German. She was huddled up in the buggy seat, crying, scared to death. She told Jake a lot of stuff, how the German had tried to get her, how he chased her once into the barn, how another time, when they happened to be alone in the house together, he tore her dress open clear down the front. The German, she said, might have got her that time if he hadn't heard his old woman drive in at the gate. She had been off to town for supplies. Well, she would be putting the horse in the barn. The German managed to sneak off to the fields without his wife seeing. He told the girl he would kill her if she told. What could she do? She told a lie about ripping her dress in the barn when she was feeding the stock. I remember now that she was a bound girl and did not know where her father and mother were. Maybe she did not have any father. You know what I mean.

Such bound children were often enough cruelly treated. They were children who had no parents, slaves really. There were very few orphan homes then. They were legally bound into some home. It was a matter of pure luck how it came out.

II

She married Jake and had a son and a daughter, but the daughter died.

Then she settled down to feed stock. That was her job. At the German's place she had cooked the food for the German and his wife. The wife was a strong woman with big hips and worked most of the time in the fields with her husband. She fed them and fed the cows in the barn, fed the pigs, the horses and the chickens. Every moment of every day, as a young girl, was spent feeding something.

Then she married Jake Grimes and he had to be fed. She was a slight thing, and when she had been married for three or four years, and after the two children were born, her slender shoulders became stooped.

Jake always had a lot of big dogs around the house, that stood near the unused sawmill near the creek. He was always trading horses when he wasn't stealing something and had a lot of poor bony ones about. Also he kept three or four pigs and a cow. They were all pastured in the few acres left of the Grimes place and Jake did little enough work.

He went into debt for a threshing outfit and ran it for several years, but it did not pay. People did not trust him. They were afraid he would steal the grain at night. He had to go a long way off to get work and it cost too much to get there. In the winter he hunted and cut a little firewood, to be sold in some nearby town. When the son grew up he was just like the father. They got drunk together. If there wasn't anything to eat in the house when they came home the old man gave his old woman a cut over the head. She had a few chickens of her own and had to kill one of them in a hurry. When they were all killed she wouldn't have any eggs to sell when she went to town, and then what would she do?

She had to scheme all her life about getting things fed, getting the pigs fed so they would grow fat and could be butchered in the fall. When they were butchered her husband took most of the meat off to town and sold it. If he did not do it first, the boy did. They fought sometimes and when they fought the old woman stood aside trembling.

She had got the habit of silence anyway—that was fixed. Sometimes, when she began to look old—she wasn't forty yet—and when the husband and son were both off, trading horses or drinking or hunting or stealing, she went around the house and the barnyard muttering to herself.

How was she going to get everything fed?—that was her problem. The dogs had to be fed. There wasn't enough hay in the barn for the horses and the cow. If she didn't feed the chickens how could they lay eggs? Without eggs to sell how could she get things in town, things she had to have to keep the life of the farm going? Thank heaven, she did not have to feed her husband—in a certain way. That hadn't lasted long after their marriage and after the babies came. Where he went on his long trips she did not know.

Sometimes he was gone from home for weeks, and after the boy grew up they went off together.

They left everything at home for her to manage and she had no money. She knew no one. No one ever talked to her in town. When it was winter she had to gather sticks of wood for her fire, had to try to keep the stock fed with very little grain.

The stock in the barn cried to her hungrily, the dogs followed her about. In the winter the hens laid few enough eggs. They huddled in the corners of the barn and she kept watching them. If a hen lays an egg in the barn in the winter and you do not find it, it freezes and breaks.

One day in winter the old woman went off to town with a few eggs and the dogs followed her. She did not get started until nearly three o'clock and the snow was heavy. She hadn't been feeling very well for several days and so she went muttering along, scantily clad, her shoulders stooped. She had an old grain bag in which she carried her eggs, tucked away down in the bottom. There weren't many of them, but in winter the price of eggs is up. She would get a little meat in exchange for the eggs, some salt pork, a little sugar, and some coffee perhaps. It might be the butcher would give her a piece of liver.

When she had got to town and was trading in her eggs the dogs lay by the door outside. She did pretty well, got the things she needed, more than she had hoped. Then she went to the butcher and he gave her some liver and some dog meat.

It was the first time anyone had spoken to her in a friendly way for a long time. The butcher was alone in his shop when she came in and was annoyed by the thought of such a sick-looking old woman out on such a day. It was bitter cold and the snow, that had let up during the afternoon, was falling again. The butcher said something about her husband and her son, swore at them, and the old woman stared at him, a look of mild surprise in her eyes as he talked. He said that if either the husband or the son were going to get any of the liver or the heavy bones with scraps of meat hanging to them that he had put into the grain bag, he'd see him starve first.

Starve, eh? Well, things had to be fed. Men had to be fed, and the horses that weren't any good but maybe could be traded off, and the poor thin cow that hadn't given any milk for three months.

Horses, cows, pigs, dogs, men.

III

The old woman had to get back before darkness came if she could. The dogs followed at her heels, sniffing at the heavy grain bag she had fastened on her back. When she got to the edge of town she stopped by a fence and tied the bag on her back with a piece of rope she had carried in her dress pocket for just that purpose. That was an easier way to carry it. Her arms ached. It was hard when she had to crawl over fences and once she fell over and landed in the snow. The dogs went frisking about. She had to struggle to get to her feet again, but she made it. The point of climbing over the fences was that there was a short cut over a hill and through a woods. She might have gone around by the road, but it was a mile farther that way. She was afraid she couldn't make it. And then, besides, the stock had to be fed. There was a little hay left and a little corn. Perhaps her husband and son would bring some home when they came. They had driven off in the only buggy the Grimes family had, a rickety thing, a rickety horse hitched to the buggy, two other rickety horses led by halters. They were going to trade horses, get a little money if they could. They might come home drunk. It would be well to have something in the house when they came back.

The son had an affair on with a woman at the county seat, fifteen miles away. She was a rough enough woman, a tough one. Once, in the summer, the son had brought her to the house. Both she and the son had been drinking. Jake Grimes was away and the son and his woman ordered the old woman about like a servant. She didn't mind much; she was used to it. Whatever happened she never said anything. That was her way of getting along. She had managed that way when she was a young girl at the German's and ever since she had married Jake. That time her son brought his woman to the house they stayed all night, sleeping together just as though they were married. It hadn't shocked the old woman, not much. She had got past being shocked early in life.

With the pack on her back she went painfully along across an open field, wading in the deep snow, and got into the woods.

There was a path, but it was hard to follow. Just beyond the top of the hill, where the woods was thickest, there was a small clearing. Had someone once thought of building a house there? The clearing was as large as a building lot in town, large enough for a house and a garden. The path ran along the side of the clearing, and when she got there the old woman sat down to rest at the foot of a tree.

It was a foolish thing to do. When she got herself placed, the pack against the tree's trunk, it was nice, but what about getting up again? She worried about that for a moment and then quietly closed her eyes.

She must have slept for a time. When you are about so cold you can't get any colder. The afternoon grew a little warmer and the snow came thicker than ever. Then after a time the weather cleared. The moon even came out.

There were four Grimes dogs that had followed Mrs. Grimes into town, all tall gaunt fellows. Such men as Jake Grimes and his son always keep just such dogs. They kick and abuse them, but they stay. The Grimes dogs, in order to keep from starving, had to do a lot of foraging for themselves, and they had been at it while the old woman slept with her back to the tree at the side of the clearing. They had been chasing rabbits in the woods and in adjoining fields and in their ranging had picked up three other farm dogs.

After a time all the dogs came back to the clearing. They were excited about something. Such nights, cold and clear and with a moon, do things to dogs. It may be that some old instinct, come down from the time when they were wolves and ranged the woods in packs on winter nights, comes back into them.

The dogs in the clearing, before the old woman, had caught two or three rabbits and their immediate hunger had been satisfied. They began to play, running in circles in the clearing. Round and round they ran, each dog's nose at the tail of the next dog. In the clearing, under the snow-laden trees and under the wintry moon they made a strange picture, running thus silently, in a circle their running had beaten in the soft snow. The dogs made no sound. They ran around and around in the circle.

It may have been that the old woman saw them doing that before she died. She may have awakened once or twice and looked at the strange sight with dim old eyes.

She wouldn't be very cold now, just drowsy. Life hangs on a long time. Perhaps the old woman was out of her head. She may have dreamed of her girlhood, at the German's, and before that, when she was a child and before her mother lit out and left her.

Her dreams couldn't have been very pleasant. Not many pleasant things have happened to her. Now and then one of the Grimes dogs left the running circle and came to stand before her. The dog thrust his face close to her face. His red tongue was hanging out.

The running of the dogs may have been a kind of death ceremony. It may have been that the primitive instinct of the wolf, having been aroused in the dogs by the night and the running, made them somehow afraid.

"Now we are no longer wolves. We are dogs, the servants of men. Keep alive, man! When man dies we become wolves again."

When one of the dogs came to where the old woman sat with her back against the tree and thrust his nose close to her face he seemed satisfied and went back to run with the pack. All the Grimes dogs did it at some time during the evening, before she died. I knew all about it afterward, when I grew to be a man, because once in a woods in Illinois, on another winter night, I saw a pack of dogs act just like that. The dogs were waiting for me to die as they had waited for the old woman that night when I was a child, but when it happened to me I was a young man and had no intention whatever of dying.

The old woman died softly and quietly. When she was dead and when one of the Grimes dogs had come to her and had found her dead all the dogs stopped running.

They gathered about her.

Well, she was dead now. She had fed the Grimes dogs when she was alive, what about now?

There was the pack on her back, the grain bag containing the piece of salt pork, the liver the butcher had given her, the dog meat, the soupbones. The butcher in town, having been suddenly overcome with a feeling of pity, had loaded her grain bag heavily. It had been a big haul for the old woman.

It was a big haul for the dogs now.

IV

One of the Grimes dogs sprang suddenly out from among the others and began worrying the pack on the old woman's back. Had the dogs really been wolves, that one would have been the leader of the pack. What he did, all the others did.

All of them sank their teeth into the grain bag the old woman had fastened with ropes to her back.

They dragged the old woman's body out into the open clearing. The worn-out dress was quickly torn from her shoulders.

When she was found, a day or two later, the dress had been torn from her body clear to the hips, but the dogs had not touched her body. They had got the meat out of the grain bag, that was all. Her body was frozen stiff when it was found, and the shoulders were so narrow and the body so slight that in death it looked like the body of some charming young girl.

Such things happened in towns of the Middle West, on farms near town, when I was a boy. A hunter out after rabbits found the old woman's body and did not touch it. Something, the beaten round path in the little snow-covered clearing, the silence of the place, the place where the dogs had worried the body trying to pull the grain bag away or tear it open—something startled the man and he hurried off to town.

I was in Main Street with one of my brothers who was town newsboy and who was taking the afternoon papers to the stores. It was almost night.

The hunter came into a grocery and told his story. Then he went to a hardware shop and into a drugstore. Men began to gather on the sidewalks. Then they started out along the road to the place in the woods.

My brother should have gone on about his business of distributing papers but he didn't. Everyone was going to the woods. The undertaker went and the town marshal. Several men got on a dray and rode out to where the path left the road and went into the woods, but the horses weren't very sharply shod and slid about on the slippery roads. They made no better time than those of us who walked.

The town marshal was a large man whose leg had been injured in the Civil War. He carried a heavy cane and limped rapidly along the road. My brother and I followed at his heels, and as we went other men and boys joined the crowd.

It had grown dark by the time we got to where the old woman had left the road, but the moon had come out. The marshal was thinking there might have been a murder. He kept asking the hunter questions. The hunter went along with his gun across his shoulders, a dog following at his heels. It isn't often a rabbit hunter has a chance to be so conspicuous. He was taking full advantage of it, leading the procession with the town marshal. "I didn't see any wounds. She was a beautiful young girl. Her face was buried in the snow. No, I didn't know her." As a matter of fact, the hunter had not looked closely at the body. He had been frightened. She might have been murdered and someone might spring out from behind a tree and murder him. In a woods, in the late afternoon, when the trees are all bare and there is white snow on the ground, when all is silent, something creepy steals over the mind and body. If something strange or uncanny has happened in the neighborhood all you think about is getting away from there as fast as you can.

The crowd of men and boys had got to where the old woman had crossed the field and went, following the marshal and the hunter, up the slight incline and into the woods.

My brother and I were silent. He had his bundle of papers in a bag slung across his shoulder. When he got back to town he would have to go on distributing his papers before he went home to supper. If I went along, as he had no doubt already determined I should, we would both be late. Either Mother or our older sister would have to warm our supper.

Well, we would have something to tell. A boy did not get such a chance very often. It was lucky we just happened to go into the grocery when the hunter came in. The hunter was a country fellow. Neither of us had ever seen him before.

Now the crowd of men and boys had got to the clearing. Darkness comes quickly on such winter nights, but the full moon made everything clear. My brother and I stood near the tree beneath which the old woman had died.

She did not look old, lying there in that light, frozen and still. One of the men turned her over in the snow and I saw everything. My body trembled with some strange mystical feeling and so did my brother's. It might have been the cold.

Neither of us had ever seen a woman's body before. It may have been the snow, clinging to the frozen flesh, that made it look so white and lovely, so like marble. No woman had come with the party from town; but one of the men, he was the town blacksmith, took off his overcoat and spread it over her. Then he gathered her into his arms and started off to town, all the others following silently. At that time no one knew who she was.

V

I had seen everything, had seen the oval in the snow, like a miniature race track, where the dogs had run, had seen how the men were mystified, had seen the white bare young-looking shoulders, had heard the whispered comments of the men.

The men were simply mystified. They took the body to the undertaker's, and when the blacksmith, the hunter, the marshal and several others had got inside they closed the door. If Father had been there perhaps he could have got in, but we boys couldn't.

I went with my brother to distribute the rest of his papers and when we got home it was my brother who told the story.

I kept silent and went to bed early. It may have been I was not satisfied with the way he told it.

Later, in the town, I must have heard other fragments of the old woman's story. She was recognized the next day and there was an investigation.

The husband and son were found somewhere and brought to town and there was an attempt to connect them with the woman's death, but it did not work. They had perfect enough alibis.

However, the town was against them. They had to get out. Where they went I never heard.

I remember only the picture there in the forest, the men standing about, the naked girlish-looking figure, face down in the snow, the tracks made by the running dogs and the clear cold winter sky above. White fragments of clouds were drifting across the sky. They went racing across the little open space among the trees.

The scene in the forest had become for me, without my knowing it, the foundation for the real story I am now trying to tell. The fragments, you see, had to be picked up slowly, long afterward.

Things happened. When I was a young man I worked on the farm of a German. The hired girl was afraid of her employer. The farmer's wife hated her.

I saw things at that place. Once later, I had a half-uncanny, mystical adventure with dogs in an Illinois forest on a clear, moonlit winter night. When I was a schoolboy, and on a summer day, I went with a boy friend out along a creek some miles from town and came to the house where the old woman had lived. No one had lived in the house since her death. The doors were broken from the hinges; the window lights were all broken. As the boy and I stood in the road outside, two dogs, just roving farm dogs no doubt, came running around the corner of the house. The dogs were tall, gaunt fellows and came down to the fence and glared through at us, standing in the road.

The whole thing, the story of the old woman's death, was to me as I grew older like music heard from far off. The notes had to be picked up slowly one at a time. Something had to be understood.

The woman who died was one destined to feed animal life. Anyway, that is all she ever did. She was feeding animal life before she was born, as a child, as a young woman working on the farm of the German, after she married, when she grew old, and when she died. She fed animal life in cows, in chickens, in pigs, in horses, in dogs, in men. Her daughter had died in childhood and with her one son she had no articulate relations. On the night when she died she was hurrying homeward, bearing on her body food for animal life.

She died in the clearing in the woods and even after her death continued feeding animal life.

You see, it is likely that when my brother told the story that night when we got home and my mother and sister sat listening I did not think he got the point. He was too young and so was I. A thing so complete has its own beauty.

I shall not try to emphasize the point. I am only explaining why I was dissatisfied then and have been ever since. I speak of that only that you may understand why I have been impelled to try to tell the simple story over again.

There She Is— She Is Taking Her Bath

ANOTHER DAY when I have done no work. It is maddening. I went to the office this morning as usual and tonight came home at the regular time. My wife and I live in an apartment in the Bronx, here in New York City, and we have no children. I am ten years older than she. Our apartment is on the second floor and there is a little hallway downstairs used by all the people in the building.

If I could only decide whether or not I am a fool, a man turned suddenly a little mad or a man whose honor has really been tampered with, I should be quite all right. Tonight I went home, after something most unusual had happened at the office, determined to tell everything to my wife. "I will tell her and then watch her face. If she blanches, then I will know all I suspect is true," I said to myself. Within the last two weeks everything about me has changed. I am no longer the same man. For example, I never in my life before used the word "blanched." What does it mean? How am I to tell whether my wife blanches or not when I do not know what the word means? It must be a word I saw in a book when I was a boy, perhaps a book of detective stories. But wait, I know how that happened to pop into my head.

But that is not what I started to tell you about. Tonight, as I have already said, I came home and climbed the stairs to our apartment.

When I got inside the house I spoke in a loud voice to my wife. "My dear, what are you doing?" I asked. My voice sounded strange.

"I am taking a bath," my wife answered.

And so you see she was at home taking a bath. There she was.

She is always pretending she loves me, but look at her now. Am I in her thoughts? Is there a tender look in her eyes? Is she dreaming of me as she walks along the streets?

You see she is smiling. There is a young man who has just passed her. He is a tall fellow with a little mustache and is smoking a cigarette. Now I ask you—is he one of the men who, like myself, does, in a way, keep the world going?

Once I knew a man who was president of a whist club. Well, he was something. People wanted to know how to play whist. They wrote to him. "If it turns out that after three cards are played the man to my right still has three cards while I have only two, et cetera, et cetera.

My friend, the man of whom I am now speaking, looks the matter up. "In rule four hundred and six you will see, et cetera, et cetera," he writes.

My point is that he is of some account in the world. He helps keep things going and I respect him. Often we used to have lunch together.

But I am a little off the point. The fellows of whom I am now thinking, these young squirts who go through the streets ogling women—what do they do? They twirl their mustaches. They carry canes. Some honest man is supporting them too. Some fool is their father.

And such a fellow is walking in the street. He meets a woman like my wife, an honest woman without too much experience of life. He smiles. A tender look comes into his eyes. Such deceit. Such callow nonsense.

And how are the women to know? They are children. They know nothing. There is a man, working somewhere in an office, keeping things moving, but do they think of him?

The truth is the woman is flattered. A tender look, that should be saved and bestowed only upon her husband, is thrown away. One never knows what will happen.

But pshaw, if I am to tell you the story, let me begin. There are men everywhere who talk and talk, saying nothing. I am afraid I am becoming one of that kind. As I have already told you, I have come home from the office at evening and am standing in the hallway of our apartment, just inside the door. I have asked my wife what she is doing and she has told me she is taking a bath.

Very well, I am then a fool. I shall go out for a walk in the park. There is no use my not facing everything frankly. By facing everything frankly one gets everything quite cleared up.

Aha! The very devil has got into me now. I said I would remain cool and collected, but I am not cool. The truth is I am growing angry.

I am a small man but I tell you that, once aroused, I will fight. Once when I was a boy I fought another boy in the school yard. He gave me a black eye but I loosened one of his teeth. "There, take that and that. Now I have got you against a wall. I will muss your mustache. Give me that cane. I will break it over your head. I do not intend to kill you, young man. I intend to vindicate my honor. No, I will not let you go. Take that and that. When next you see a respectable married woman on the street, going to the store, behaving herself, do not look at her with a tender light in your eyes. What you had better do is to go to work. Get a job in a bank. Work your way up. You said I was an old goat but I will show you an old goat can butt. Take that and that."

Very well, you who read also think me a fool. You laugh. You smile. Look at me. You are walking along here in the park. You are leading a dog.

Where is your wife? What is she doing?

Well, suppose she is at home taking a bath. What is she thinking? If she is dreaming as she takes her bath, of whom is she dreaming?

I will tell you what, you who go along leading that dog, you may have no reason to suspect your wife, but you are in the same position as myself.

She was at home taking a bath and all day I had been sitting at my desk and thinking such thoughts. Under the circumstances I would never have had the temerity to go calmly off and take a bath. I admire my wife. Ha, ha. If she is innocent I admire her, of course, as a husband should, and if she is guilty I admire her even more. What nerve, what insouciance. There is something noble, something almost heroic in her attitude toward me, just at this time.

With me this day is like every day now. Well, you see, I have been sitting all day with my head in my hand, thinking and thinking, and while I have been doing that she has been going about, leading her regular life.

She has got up in the morning and has had her breakfast sitting opposite her husband; that is, myself. Her husband has gone off to his office. Now she is speaking to our maid. She is going to the stores. She is sewing, perhaps making new curtains for the windows of our apartment.

There is the woman for you. Nero fiddled while Rome was burning. There was something of the woman in him.

A wife has been unfaithful to her husband. She has gone gayly off, let us say on the arm of a young blade. Who is he? He dances. He smokes cigarettes. When he is with his companions, his own kind of fellows, he laughs. "I have got me a woman," he says. "She is not very young but she is terrifically in love with me. It is very convenient." I have heard such fellows talk, in the smoking cars, on trains and in other places.

And there is the husband, a fellow like myself. Is he calm? Is he collected? Is he cool? His honor is perhaps being tampered with. He sits at his desk. He smokes a cigar. People come and go. He is thinking, thinking.

And what are his thoughts? They concern her. "Now she is still at home, in our apartment," he thinks. "Now she is walking along a street." What do you know of the secret life led by your wife? What do you know of her thoughts? Well, hello! You smoke a pipe. You put your hands in your pockets. For you, your life is all very well. You are gay and happy. "What does it matter, my wife is at home taking a bath," you are telling yourself. In your daily life you are, let us say, a useful man. You publish books, you run a store, you write advertisements. Sometimes you say to yourself, "I am lifting the burden off the shoulders of others." That makes you feel good. I sympathize with you. If you let me, or rather I should say, if we had met in the formal transactions of our regular occupations, I dare say we would be great friends. Well, we would have lunch together, not too often, but now and then. I would tell you of some real-estate deal and you would tell me what you had been doing. "I am glad we met! Call me up. Before you go away, have a cigar."

With me it is quite different. All today, for example, I have been in my office, but I have not worked. A man came in, a Mr. Albright. "Well, are you going to let that property go or are you going to hold on?" he said.

What property did he mean? What was he talking about?

You can see for yourself what a state I am in.

And now I must be going home. My wife will have finished taking her bath. We will sit down to dinner. Nothing of all this I have been speaking about will be mentioned at all. "John, what is the matter with you?" "Aha. There is nothing the matter. I am worried about business a little. A Mr. Albright came in. Shall I sell or shall I hold on?" The real thing that is on my mind shall not be mentioned at all. I will grow a little nervous. The coffee will be spilled on the tablecloth or I will upset my dessert.

"John, what is the matter with you?" What coolness. As I have already said, what insouciance.

What is the matter? Matter enough.

A week, two weeks, to be exact, just seventeen days ago, I was a happy man. I went about my affairs. In the morning I rode to my office in the subway, but, had I wished to do so, I could long ago have bought an automobile.

But no, long ago, my wife and I had agreed there should be no such silly extravagance. To tell the truth, just ten years ago I failed in business and had to put some property in my wife's name. I bring the papers home to her and she signs. That is the way it is done.

"Well, John," said my wife, "we will not get us any automobile." That was before the thing happened that so upset me. We were walking together in the park. "Mabel, shall we get us an automobile?" I asked. "No," she said, "we will not get us an automobile." "Our money," she has said, more than a thousand times, "will be a comfort to us later."

A comfort indeed. What can be a comfort now that this thing has happened?

It was just two weeks, more than that, just seventeen days ago, that I went home from the office just as I came home tonight. Well, I walked in the same streets, passed the same stores.

I am puzzled as to what that Mr. Albright meant when he asked me if I intended to sell the property or hold on to it. I answered in a noncommittal way. "We'll see," I said. To what property did he refer? We must have had some previous conversation regarding the matter. A mere acquaintance does not come into your office and speak of property in that careless, one might say, familiar way, without having previous conversation on the same subject.

As you see I am still a little confused. Even though I am facing things now, I am still, as you have guessed, somewhat confused. This morning I was in the bathroom, shaving as usual. I always shave in the morning, not in the evening, unless my wife and I are going out. I was shaving and my shaving brush dropped to the floor. I stooped to pick it up and struck my head on the bathtub. I only tell you this to show what a state I am in. It made a large bump on my head. My wife heard me groan and asked me what was the matter. "I struck my head," I said. Of course, one quite in control of his faculties does not hit his head on a bathtub when he knows it is there, and what man does not know where the bathtub stands in his own house?

But now I am thinking again of what happened, of what has upset me this way. I was going home on that evening, just seventeen days ago. Well, I walked along, thinking nothing. When I reached our apartment building I went in, and there, lying on the floor in the little hallway, in front, was a pink envelope with my wife's name, Mabel Smith, written on it. I picked it up thinking, "This is strange." It had perfume on it and there was no address, just the name Mabel Smith, written in a bold man's hand.

I quite automatically opened it and read.

Since I first met her, twelve years ago at a party at Mr. Westley's house, there have never been any secrets between me and my wife; at least, until that moment in the hallway seventeen days ago this evening, I had never thought there were any secrets between us. I have always opened her letters and she had always opened mine. I think it should be that way between a man and his wife. I know there are some who do not agree with me but what I have always argued is I am right.

I went to the party with Harry Selfridge and afterward took my wife home. I offered to get a cab. "Shall we have a cab?" I asked her. "No," she said, "let's walk." She was the daughter of a man in the furniture business and he has died since. Everyone thought he would leave her some money but he didn't. It turned out he owed almost all he was worth to a firm in Grand Rapids. Some would have been upset, but I wasn't. "I married you for love, my dear," I said to her on the night when her father died. We were walking home from his house, also in the Bronx, and it was raining a little, but we did not get very wet. "I married you for love," I said, and I meant what I said.

But to return to the note. "Dear Mabel," it said, "come to the park on Wednesday when the old goat has gone away. Wait for me on the bench near the animal cages where I met you before."

It was signed Bill. I put it in my pocket and went upstairs.

When I got into my apartment, I heard a man's voice. The voice was urging something upon my wife. Did the voice change when I came in? I walked boldly into our front room where my wife sat facing a young man who sat in another chair. He was tall and had a little mustache.

The man was pretending to be trying to sell my wife a patent carpet sweeper, but just the same, when I sat down in a chair in the corner and remained there, keeping silent, they both became self-conscious. My wife, in fact, became positively excited. She got up out of her chair and said in a loud voice, "I tell you I do not want any carpet sweeper."

The young man got up and went to the door and I followed. "Well, I had better be getting out of here," he was saying to himself. And so he had been intending to leave a note telling my wife to meet him in the park on Wednesday but at the last moment he had decided to take the risk of coming to our house. What he had probably thought was something like this: "Her husband may come and get the note out of the mailbox." Then he decided to come and see her and had quite accidentally dropped the note in the hallway. Now he was frightened. One could see that. Such men as myself are small but we will fight sometimes.

He hurried to the door and I followed him into the hallway. There was another young man coming from the floor above, also with a carpet sweeper in his hand. It is a pretty slick scheme, this carrying carpet sweepers with them, the young men of this generation have worked out, but we older men are not to have the wool pulled over our eyes. I saw through everything at once. The second young man was a confederate and had been concealed in the hallway in order to warn the first young man of my approach. When I got upstairs, of course, the first young man was pretending to sell my wife a carpet sweeper. Perhaps the second young man had tapped with the handle of the carpet sweeper on the floor above. Now that I think of that I remember there was a tapping sound.

At the time, however, I did not think everything out as I have since done. I stood in the hallway with my back against the wall and watched them go down the stairs. One of them turned and laughed at me, but I did not say anything. I suppose I might have gone down the stairs after them and challenged them both to fight but what I thought was, "I won't."

And sure enough, just as I suspected from the first, it was the young man pretending to sell carpet sweepers I had found sitting in my apartment with my wife, who had lost the note. When they got down to the hallway at the front of the house the man I had caught with my wife began to feel in his pocket. Then, as I leaned over the railing above, I saw him looking about the hallway. He laughed. "Say, Tom, I had a note to Mabel in my pocket. I intended to get a stamp at the postoffice and mail it. I had forgotten the street number. 'Oh, well,' I thought, 'I'll go see her!' I didn't want to bump into that old goat, her husband."

"You have bumped into him," I said to myself; "now we will see who will come out victorious."

I went into our apartment and closed the door.

For a long time, perhaps for ten minutes, I stood just inside the door of our apartment thinking and thinking, just as I have been doing ever since. Two or three times I tried to speak, to call out to my wife, to question her and find out the bitter truth at once, but my voice failed me.

What was I to do? Was I to go to her, seize her by the wrists, force her down into a chair, make her confess at the risk of personal violence? I asked myself that question.

"No," I said to myself, "I will not do that. I will use finesse."

For a long time I stood there thinking. My world had tumbled down about my ears. When I tried to speak, the words would not come out of my mouth.

At last I did speak, quite calmly. There is something of the man of the world about me. When I am compelled to meet a situation I do it. "What are you doing?" I said to my wife, speaking in a calm voice. "I am taking a bath," she answered.

And so I left the house and came out here to the park to think, just as I have done tonight. On that night, and just as I came out at our front door, I did something I have not done since I was a boy. I am a deeply religious man, but I swore. My wife and I have had a good many arguments as to whether or not a man in business should have dealings with those who do such things—that is to say, with men who swear. "I cannot refuse to sell a man a piece of property because he swears," I have always said. "Yes, you can," my wife says.

It only shows how little women know about business. What I have always maintained is I am right.

And I maintain too that we men must protect the integrity of our homes and our firesides. On that first night I walked about until dinnertime and then went home. I had decided not to say anything for the present but to remain quiet and use finesse, but at dinner my hand trembled and I spilled the dessert on the table cloth.

And a week later I went to see a detective.

But first something else happened. On Wednesday—I had found the note on Monday evening—I could not bear sitting in my office and thinking perhaps that that young squirt was meeting my wife in the park, so I went to the park myself.

Sure enough there was my wife sitting on a bench near the animal cages and knitting a sweater.

At first I thought I would conceal myself in some bushes but instead I went to where she was seated and sat down beside her. "How nice! What brings you here?" my wife said smiling. She looked at me with surprise in her eyes.

Was I to tell her or was I not to tell her? It was a moot question with me. "No," I said to myself. "I will not. I will go see a detective. My honor has no doubt already been tampered with and I shall find out." My naturally quick wits came to my rescue. Looking directly into my wife's eyes I said: "There was a paper to be signed and I had my own reasons for thinking you might be here, in the park."

As soon as I had spoken I could have torn out my tongue. However, she had noticed nothing and I took a paper out of my pocket and, handing her my fountain pen, asked her to sign; and when she had done so I hurried away. At first I thought perhaps I would linger about, in the distance, that is to say; but no, I decided not to do that. He will no doubt have his confederate on the watchout for me, I told myself.

And so on the next afternoon, I went to the office of the detective. He was a large man, and when I told him what I wanted he smiled. "I understand," he said, "we have many such cases. We'll track the guy down."

And so, you see, there it was. Everything was arranged. It was to cost me a pretty penny, but my house was to be watched and I was to have a report on everything. To tell the truth, when everything was arranged I felt ashamed of myself. The man in the detective place—there were several men standing about—followed me to the door and put his hand on my shoulder. For some reason I don't understand, that made me mad. He kept patting me on the shoulder as though I were a little boy. "Don't worry. We'll manage everything," was what he said. It was all right. Business is business, but for some reason I wanted to bang him in the face with my fist.

That's the way I am, you see. I can't make myself out. "Am I a fool, or am I a man among men?" I keep asking myself, and I can't get an answer.

After I had arranged with the detective I went home and didn't sleep all night long.

To tell the truth I began to wish I had never found that note. I suppose that is wrong of me. It makes me less a man, perhaps, but it's the truth.

Well, you see, I couldn't sleep. "No matter what my wife was up to, I could sleep now if I hadn't found that note," was what I said to myself. It was dreadful. I was ashamed of what I had done and at the same time ashamed of myself for being ashamed. I had done what any American man, who is a man at all, would have done, and there I was. I couldn't sleep. Every time I came home in the evening I kept thinking: "There is that man standing over there by a tree—I'll bet he is a detective." I kept thinking of the fellow who had patted me on the shoulders in the detective office, and every time I thought of him I grew madder and madder. Pretty soon I hated him more than I did the young man who had pretended to sell the carpet sweeper to Mabel.

And then I did the most foolish thing of all. One afternoon—it was just a week ago—I thought of something. When I had been in the detective office I had seen several men standing about but had not been introduced to any of them. "And so," I thought, "I'll go there pretending to get my reports. If the man I engaged is not there I'll engage someone else."

So I did it. I went to the detective office, and sure enough my man was out. There was another fellow sitting by a desk and I made a sign to him. We went into an inner office. "Look here," I whispered; you see I had made up my mind to pretend I was the man who was ruining my own fireside, wrecking my own honor. "Do I make clear what I mean?"

It was like this, you see—well, I had to have some sleep, didn't I? Only the night before, my wife had said to me, "John, I think you had better run away for a little vacation. Run away by yourself for a time and forget about business."

At another time her saying that would have been nice, you see, but now it only upset me worse than ever. "She wants me out of the way," I thought, and for just a moment I felt like jumping up and telling her everything I knew. Still I didn't. "I'll just keep quiet. I'll use finesse," I thought.

A pretty kind of finesse. There I was in that detective office again hiring a second detective. I came right out and pretended I was my wife's paramour. The man kept nodding his head and I kept whispering like a fool. Well, I told him that a man named Smith had hired a detective from that office to watch his wife. "I have my own reasons for wanting him to get a report that his wife is all right," I said, pushing some money across a table toward him. I had become utterly reckless about money. "Here is fifty dollars and when he gets such a report from your office you come to me and you may have two hundred more," I said.

I had thought everything out. I told the second man my name was Jones and that I worked in the same office with Smith. "I'm in business with him," I said, "a silent partner, you see."

Then I went out and, of course, he, like the first one, followed me to the door and patted me on the shoulder. That was the hardest thing of all to stand, but I stood it. A man has to have sleep.

And, of course, today both men had to come to my office within five minutes of each other. The first one came, of course, and told me my wife was innocent. "She is as innocent as a little lamb," he said. "I congratulate you upon having such an innocent wife."

Then I paid him, backing away so he couldn't pat me on the shoulders, and he had only just closed the door when in came the other man, asking for Jones.

And I had to see him too and give him two hundred dollars.

Then I decided to come on home, and I did, walking along the same street I have walked on every afternoon since my wife and I married. I went home and climbed the stairs to our apartment just as I described everything to you a little while ago. I could not decide whether I was a fool, a man who has gone a little mad, or a man whose honor has been tampered with, but anyway I knew there would be no detectives about.

What I thought was that I would go home and have everything out with my wife, tell her of my suspicions and then watch her face. As I have said before, I intended to watch her face and see if she blanched when I told her of the note I had found in the hallway downstairs. The word "blanched" got into my mind because I once read it in a detective story when I was a boy and I had been dealing with detectives.

And so I intended to face my wife down, force a confession from her, but you see how it turned out. When I got home the apartment was silent and at first I thought it was empty. "Has she run away with him?" I asked myself, and maybe my own face blanched a little.

"Where are you, dear, what are you doing?" I shouted in a loud voice and she told me she was taking a bath.

And so I came out here in the park.

But now I must be going home. Dinner will be waiting. I am wondering what property that Mr. Albright had in his mind. When I sit at dinner with my wife my hands will shake. I will spill the dessert. A man does not come in and speak of property in that offhand manner unless there has been conversation about it before.

The Lost Novel

He said it was all like a dream. A man like that, a writer. Well, he works for months, and perhaps years, on a book, and there is not a word put down. What I mean is that his mind is working. What is to be the book builds itself up and is destroyed.

In his fancy, figures are moving back and forth.

But there is something I neglected to say. I am talking of a certain English novelist who has got some fame, of a thing that once happened to him.

He told me about it one day in London when we were walking together. We had been together for hours. I remember that we were on the Thames Embankment when he told me about his lost novel.

He had come to see me early in the evening at my hotel. He spoke of certain stories of my own. "You almost get at something, sometimes," he said.

We agreed that no man ever quite got at—the thing.

If someone once got at it, if he really put the ball over the plate, you know, if he hit the bull's-eye.

What would be the sense of anyone trying to do anything after that?

I'll tell you what, some of the old fellows have come pretty near.

Keats, eh? And Shakespeare. And George Borrow and DeFoe.

We spent a half hour going over names.

We went off to dine together and later walked. He was a little, black, nervous man with ragged locks of hair sticking out from under his hat.

I began talking of his first book.

But here is a brief outline of his history. He came from a poor farming family in some English village. He was like all writers. From the very beginning he wanted to write.

He had no education. At twenty he got married.

She must have been a very respectable, nice girl. If I remember rightly she was the daughter of a priest of the Established English Church.

Just the kind he should not have married. But who shall say whom anyone shall love—or marry? She was above him in station. She had been to a woman's college; she was well educated.

I have no doubt she thought him an ignorant man.

"She thought me a sweet man, too. The hell with that," he said, speaking of it. "I am not sweet. I hate sweetness."

We had got to that sort of intimacy, walking in the London night, going now and then into a pub to get a drink.

I remember that we each got a bottle, fearing the pubs would close before we got through talking.

What I told him about myself and my own adventures I can't remember.

The point is he wanted to make some kind of a pagan out of his woman, and the possibilities weren't in her.

They had two kids.

Then suddenly he did begin to burst out writing—that is to say, really writing.

You know a man like that. When he writes, he writes. He had some kind of a job in his English town. I believe he was a clerk.

Because he was writing, he, of course, neglected his job, his wife, his kids.

He used to walk about the fields at night. His wife scolded. Of course, she was all broken up—would be. No woman can quite bear the absolute way in which a man who has been her lover can sometimes drop her when he is at work.

I mean an artist, of course. They can be first-class lovers. It may be they are the only lovers.

And they are absolutely ruthless about throwing direct personal love aside.

You can imagine that household. The man told me there was a little bedroom upstairs in the house where they were living at that time. This was while he was still in the English town.

The man used to come home from his job and go upstairs. Upstairs he went and locked his door. Often he did not stop to eat, and sometimes he did not even speak to his wife.

He wrote and wrote and wrote and threw away.

Then he lost his job. "The hell," he said, when he spoke of it. He didn't care, of course. What is a job?

What is a wife or child? There must be a few ruthless people in this world.

Pretty soon there was practically no food in the house.

He was upstairs in that room behind the door, writing. The house was small and the children cried. "The little brats," he said, speaking of them. He did not mean that, of course. I understand what he meant. His wife used to come and sit on the stairs outside the door, back of which he was at work. She cried audibly and the child she had in her arms cried.

"A patient soul, eh?" the English novelist said to me when he told me of it. "And a good soul, too," he said. "To hell with her," he also said.

You see, he had begun writing about her. She was what his novel was about, his first one. In time it may prove to be his best one.

Such tenderness of understanding—of her difficulties and her limitations, and such a casual, brutal way of treating her, personally.

Well, if we have a soul, that is worth something, eh?

It got so they were never together a moment without quarreling.

And then one night he struck her. He had forgotten to fasten the door of the room in which he worked. She came bursting in.

And just as he was getting at something about her, some understanding of the reality of her. Any writer will understand the difficulty of his position. In a fury he rushed at her, struck her and knocked her down.

And then, well, she quit him then. Why not? However, he finished the book. It was a real book.

But about his lost novel. He said he came up to London after his wife left him and began living alone. He thought he would write another novel.

You understand that he had got recognition, had been acclaimed.

And the second novel was just as difficult to write as the first. It may be that he was a good deal exhausted.

And, of course, he was ashamed. He was ashamed of the way in which he had treated his wife. He tried to write another novel so that he wouldn't always be thinking. He told me that for the next year or two the words he wrote on the paper were all wooden. Nothing was alive.

Months and months of that sort of thing. He withdrew from people. Well, what about his children? He sent money to his wife and went to see her once.

He said she was living with her father's people, and he went to her father's house and got her. They went to walk in the fields. "We couldn't talk," he said. "She began to cry and called me a crazy man. Then I glared at her, as I had once done that time I struck her, and she turned and ran away from me back to her father's house, and I came away."

Having written one splendid novel, he wanted, of course, to write some more. He said there were all sorts of characters and situations in his head. He used to sit at his desk for hours writing and then go out in the streets and walk as he and I walked together that night.

Nothing would come right for him.

He had got some sort of theory about himself. He said that the second novel was inside him like an unborn child. His conscience was hurting him about his wife and children. He said he loved them all right but did not want to see them again.

Sometimes he thought he hated them. One evening, he said, after he had been struggling like that, and long after he had quit seeing people he wrote his second novel. It happened like this.

All morning he had been sitting in his room. It was a small room he had rented in a poor part of London. He had got out of bed early, and without eating any breakfast had begun to write. And everything he wrote that morning was also no good.

About three o'clock in the afternoon, as he had been in the habit of doing, he went out to walk. He took a lot of writing paper with him.

"I had an idea I might begin to write at any time," he said.

He went walking in Hyde Park. He said it was a clear, bright day, and people were walking about together. He sat on a bench.

He hadn't eaten anything since the night before. As he sat there he tried a trick. Later I heard that a group of young poets in Paris took up that sort of thing and were profoundly serious about it.

The Englishman tried what is called "automatic writing."

He just put his pencil on the paper and let the pencil make what words it would.

Of course the pencil made a queer jumble of absurd words. He quit doing that.

There he sat on the bench staring at the people walking past.

He was tired, like a man who has been in love for a long time with some woman he cannot get.

Let us say there are difficulties. He is married or she is. They look at each other with promises in their eyes and nothing happens.

Wait and wait. Most people's lives are spent waiting.

And then suddenly, he said, he began writing his novel. The theme, of course, was men and women—lovers. What other theme is there for such a man? He told me that he must have been thinking a great deal of his wife and of his cruelty to her. He wrote and wrote. The evening passed, and night came. Fortunately, there was a moon. He kept on writing. He said it was the most intense writing he ever did or ever hoped to do. Hours and hours passed. He sat there on that bench writing like a crazy man.

He wrote a novel at one sitting. Then he went home to his room.

He said he never was so happy and satisfied with himself in his life.

"I thought that I had done justice to my wife and to my children, to everyone and everything," he said. If they did not know it, never would know—what difference would that make?

He said that all the love he had in his being went into the novel.

He took it home and laid it on his desk.

What a sweet feeling of satisfaction to have done—the thing.

Then he went out of his room and found an all-night place where he could get something to eat.

After he got food he walked around the town. How long he walked he didn't know.

Then he went home and slept. It was daylight by this time. He slept all through the next day.

He said that when he woke up he thought he would look at his novel. "I really knew all the time it wasn't there," he said. "On the desk, of course, there was nothing but blank empty sheets of paper.

"Anyway," he said, "this I know. I never will write such a beautiful novel as that one was."

When he said it he laughed.

I do not believe there are too many people in the world who will know exactly what he was laughing about.

But why be so arbitrary? There may be even a dozen.

Like a Queen

THERE IS a great deal of talk made about beauty but no one defines it. It clings to some people.

Among women, now— The figure is something, of course, the face, the lips, the eyes.

The way the head sits on the shoulders.

The way a woman walks across the room may mean everything.

I myself have seen beauty in the most unexpected places. What has happened to me has happened also to a great many other men.

I remember a friend I had formerly in Chicago. He had something like a nervous breakdown and went down into Missouri —to the Ozark Mountains, I think.

One day he was walking on a mountain road and passed a cabin. It was a poor place with lean dogs in the yard.

There were a great many dirty children, a slovenly woman and one young girl. The young girl had gone from the cabin to a woodpile in the yard. She had gathered an armful of wood and was walking toward the house.

There in the road was my friend. He looked up and saw her.

There must have been something—the time, the place, the mood of the man. Ten years later he was still speaking of that woman, of her extraordinary beauty.

And there was another man. He was from central Illinois and was raised on a farm. Later he went to Chicago and became a successful lawyer out there. He was the father of a large family.

The most beautiful woman he ever saw was with some horse traders that passed the farm where he lived as a boy. When he was in his cups one night he told me that all of his night dreams, the kind men have and that are concerned with women, were always concerned with her. He said he thought it was the way she walked. The odd part of it was she had a bruised eye. Perhaps, he said, she was the wife or the mistress of one of the horse traders.

It was a cold day and she was barefooted. The road was muddy. The horse traders, with their wagon, followed by a lot of bony horses, passed the field where the young man was at work. They did not speak to him. You know how such people stare.

And there she came along the road alone.

It may just have been another case of a rare moment for that man.

He had some sort of tool in his hand, a corn-cutting knife, he said. The woman looked at him. The horse traders looked back. They laughed. The corn-cutting knife dropped from his hand. Women must know when they register like that.

And thirty years later she was still registering.

All of which brings me to Alice.

Alice used to say the whole problem of life lay in getting past what she called the "times between."

I wonder where Alice is. She was a stout woman who had once been a singer. Then she lost her voice.

When I knew her she had blue veins spread over her red cheeks and short gray hair. She was the kind of woman who can never keep her stockings up. They were always falling down over her shoes.

She had stout legs and broad shoulders and had grown mannish as she grew older.

Such women can manage. Being a singer, of some fame once, she had made a great deal of money. She spent money freely.

For one thing, she knew a good many very rich men, bankers and others.

They took her advice about their daughters and sons. A son of such a man got into trouble. Well, he got mixed up with some woman, a waitress or a servant. The man sent for Alice. The son was resentful and determined.

The girl might be all right and then again . . .

Alice took the girl's part. "Now, you look here," she said to the banker. "You know nothing about people. Those who are interested in people do not get as rich as you have.

"And you do not understand your son either. This affair he has got into. His finest feelings may be involved in this matter."

Alice simply swept the banker, and perhaps his wife, out of the picture. "You people." She laughed when she said that.

Of course, the son was immature. Alice did really seem to know a lot about people. She took the boy in hand—went to see the girl.

She had been through dozens of such experiences. For one thing, the boy wasn't made to feel a fool. Sons of rich men, when they have anything worth-while in them, go through periods of desperation, like other young men. They go to college and read books.

Life in such men's houses is something pretty bad. Alice knew about all that. The rich man may go off and get himself a mistress—the boy's mother a lover. Such things happen.

Still the people are not so bad. There are all sorts of rich men, just as there are of poor and middle-class men.

After we became friends Alice used to explain a lot of things to me. At that time I was always worried about money. She laughed at me. "You take money too seriously," she said.

"Money is simply a way of expressing power," she said. "Men who get rich understand that. They get money, a lot of it, because they aren't afraid of it.

"The poor man or the middle-class man goes to a banker timidly. That will never do.

"If you have your own kind of power, show your hand. Make the man fear you in your own field. For example, you can write. Your rich man cannot do that. It is quite all right to exercise your own power. Have faith in yourself. If it is necessary to make him a little afraid, do so. The fact that you can do so, that you can express yourself, makes you seem strange to him. Suppose you uncovered his life. The average rich man has got his rotten side and his weak side.

"And for Heaven's sake do not forget that he has his good side.

"You may go at trying to understand such a one like a fool if you want to—I mean with all sorts of preconceived notions. You could show just his rottenness, a distorted picture, ruin his vanity.

"Your poor man, or your small merchant or lawyer. Such men haven't the temptations as regards women, for example, that rich men have. There are plenty of women grafters about—some of them are physically beautiful, too.

"The poor man or the middle-class man goes about condemning the rich man for the rotten side of his life, but what rottenness is there in him?

"What secret desires has he, what greeds, buried under a placid, commonplace face?"

In the matter of the rich man's son and the woman he had got involved with, Alice in some way did manage to get at the bottom of things.

I gathered that in such affairs she took it for granted people were on the whole better than others thought them or than they thought themselves. She made the idea seem more reasonable than you would ever have thought possible.

It may be that Alice really had brains. I have met few enough people I thought had.

Most people are so one-sided, so specialized. They can make money, or fight prize fights or paint pictures, or they are men who are physically attractive and can get women who are physically beautiful, women who can tie men up in knots.

Or they are just plain dubs. There are plenty of dubs everywhere.

Alice swept dubs aside; she did not bother with them. She could be as cruel as a cold wind.

She got money when she wanted it. She lived around in fine houses.

Once she got a thousand dollars for me. I was in New York and broke. One day I was walking on Fifth Avenue. You know how a writer is when he cannot write. Months of that for me. My money gone. Everything I wrote was dead.

I had grown a little shabby. My hair was long and I was thin.

Lots of times I have thought of suicide when I cannot write. Every writer has such times.

Alice took me to a man in an office building. "You give this man a thousand dollars."

"What the devil, Alice? What for?"

"Because I say so. He can write, just as you can make money. He has talent. He is discouraged now, is on his uppers. He has lost his pride in life, in himself. Look at the poor fool's lips trembling."

It was quite true. I was in a bad state.

In me a great surge of love for Alice. Such a woman! She became beautiful to me.

She was talking to the man.

"The only value I can be to you is now and then when I do something like this."

"Like what?"

"When I tell you where and how you can use a thousand dollars and use it sensibly.

"To give it to a man who is as good as yourself, who is better. When he is down—when his pride is low."

Alice came from the mountains of East Tennessee. You would not believe it. When she was twenty-four, at the height of her power as a singer, she had seemed tall. The reason I speak of it was that when I knew her she appeared short—and thick.

Once I saw a photograph of her when she was young.

She was half vulgar, half lovely.

She was a mountain woman who could sing. An older man, who had been her lover, told me that at twenty-four and until she was thirty she was like a queen.

"She walked like a queen," he said. To see her walk across a room or across the stage was something not to be forgotten.

She had lovers, a dozen of them in her time.

Then she had a bad period—for two years she drank and gambled.

Her life had apparently become useless to her and she tried to throw it away.

But people who believe in themselves make others believe. Men who had been lovers of Alice never forgot her. They never went back on her.

They said she gave them something. She was sixty when I knew her.

Once she took me up to the Adirondack Mountains. We went together in a big car with a Negro driver to a house that was half a palace. It took us two days to get there.

The whole outfit belonged to some rich man.

It was the time when Alice said she was flat. "I got you something once when you were flat, now you come with me," she had said when she saw me in New York.

She did not mean flat as regards money. She was spiritually flat.

So we went and stayed alone together in a big house. There were servants there. They had been provided for. I don't know how.

We had been there for a week and Alice had been silent. One evening we went to walk.

This was a wild country. There was a lake before the house and a mountain at the back.

It was a chilly night with a clear sky and a moon, and we walked in a country road.

Then we began to climb the mountains. I can remember Alice's thick legs and her stockings coming down.

She was short-winded too. She kept stopping to puff and blow.

We plowed on silently like that. Alice, when herself, was seldom silent.

We got clear to the top of the mountain before she spoke.

She talked about what flatness is, how it hits people—floors them. Houses gone all flat, people all flat, life flat. "You think I am courageous," she said. "The hell with that. I haven't the courage of a mouse."

We sat down on a stone and she began to tell me of her life. It was an odd, complex story, told in that way, in little jerks by an old woman.

There it was, the whole thing. She had come down out of the Tennessee mountains as a young girl to the city of Nashville, in Tennessee.

She got in with a singing master there who knew she could sing. "Well, I took him as a lover. He wasn't so bad."

The man spent money on her; he interested some Nashville rich man.

That man also may have been her lover. Alice did not say. There were plenty of others.

One of them—he must have amounted to less than any of the others—she had loved.

She said he was a young poet. There was something crooked in him. He did sneaking things.

That was when she was past thirty and he was twenty-five. She lost her head, she said, and of course lost him.

It was then she went to drinking, gambled, went broke. She declared she lost him because she loved him too much.

"But why wasn't he any good? Why did you have to love that sort?"

She did not know why. It had happened.

It must have been the experience that had tempered her.

But I was speaking of beauty in people, what an odd thing it is, how it appears, disappears and reappears.

I got a glimpse of it in Alice that night.

It was when we were coming back to the house, from the mountain, down the road.

We were on a hillside and stout Alice in front. There was a muddy stretch of road and then a woods and then an open space.

The moonlight was in the open space and I was in the woods, in the darkness of the woods, but a few steps behind.

She crossed the open space ahead of me and there it was.

The thing lasted but a fleeting second. I think that all of the rich powerful men Alice had known, who had given her money, helped her when she needed help, and who have got so much from her, must have seen what I saw then. It was what the man saw in the woman by the mountain cabin and what the other man saw in the horse trader's woman in the road.

Alice when she said she was flat wasn't flat. Alice trying to shake off the memory of an unsuccessful love.

She was walking across the open moonlit stretch of road like a queen, as that man who was once her lover said she used to walk across a room or across a stage.

The mountains out of which she came as a child must have been in her at the moment, and the moon and the night.

Myself in love with her, madly, for a moment.

Is anyone in love longer than that?

Alice shaking her head slightly. There may have been a trick of the light. Her stride lengthened and she became tall, and young. I remember stopping in the woods and staring. I was like the two other men of whom I have spoken. I had a cane in my hand and it fell to the ground. I was like the man in the road and the other man in the field.

In a Strange Town

A MORNING in a country town in a strange place. Everything is quiet. No, there are sounds. Sounds assert themselves. A boy whistles. I can hear the sound here, where I stand, at a railroad station. I have come away from home. I am in a strange place. There is no such thing as silence. Once I was in the country. I was at the house of a friend. "You see, there is not a sound here. It is absolutely silent." My friend said that because he was used to the little sounds of the place, the humming of insects, the sound of falling water—far off—the faint clattering sound of a man with a machine in the distance, cutting hay. He was accustomed to the sounds and did not hear them. Here, where I am now, I hear a beating sound. Someone has hung a carpet on a clothesline and is beating it. Another boy shouts, far off—"A-ho, a-ho."

It is good to go and come. You arrive in a strange place. There is a street facing a railroad track. You get off a train with your bags. Two porters fight for possession of you and the bags as you have seen porters do with strangers in your own town.

As you stand at the station there are things to be seen. You see the open doors of the stores on the street that faces the station. People go in and out. An old man stops and looks. "Why, there is the morning train," his mind is saying to him.

The mind is always saying such things to people. "Look, be aware," it says. The fancy wants to float free of the body. We put a stop to that.

Most of us live our lives like toads, sitting perfectly still, under a plantain leaf. We are waiting for a fly to come our way. When it comes, out darts the tongue. We nab it.

That is all. We eat it.

But how many questions to be asked that are never asked. Whence came the fly? Where was he going?

The fly might have been going to meet his sweetheart. He was stopped; a spider ate him.

The train on which I have been riding, a slow one, pauses for a time. All right, I'll go to the Empire House. As though I cared.

It is a small town—this one—to which I have come. In any event I'll be uncomfortable here. There will be the same kind of cheap brass beds as at the last place to which I went unexpectedly like this—with bugs in the bed perhaps. A traveling salesman will talk in a loud voice in the next room. He will be talking to a friend, another traveling salesman. "Trade is bad," one of them will say. "Yes, it's rotten."

There will be confidences about women picked up—some words heard, others missed. That is always annoying.

But why did I get off the train here at this particular town? I remember that I had been told there was a lake here—that there was fishing. I thought I would go fishing.

Perhaps I expected to swim. I remember now.

"Porter, where is the Empire House? Oh, the brick one. All right, go ahead. I'll be along pretty soon. You tell the clerk to save me a room, with a bath, if they have one."

I remember what I was thinking about. All my life, since that happened, I have gone off on adventures like this. A man likes to be alone sometimes.

Being alone doesn't mean being where there are no people. It means being where people are all strangers to you.

There is a woman crying there. She is getting old, that woman.

Well, I am myself no longer young. See how tired her eyes are. There is a younger woman with her. In time that younger woman will look exactly like her mother.

She will have the same patient, resigned look. The skin will sag on her cheeks that are plump now. The mother has a large nose and so has the daughter.

There is a man with them. He is fat and has red veins in his face. For some reason I think he must be a butcher.

He has that kind of hands, that kind of eyes.

I am pretty sure he is the woman's brother. Her husband is dead. They are putting a coffin on the train.

They are people of no importance. People pass them casually. No one has come to the station to be with them in their hour of trouble. I wonder if they live here. Yes, of course they do. They live somewhere, in a rather mean little house, at the edge of town, or perhaps outside the town. You see the brother is not going away with the mother and daughter. He has just come down to see them off.

They are going, with the body, to another town where the husband, who is dead, formerly lived.

The butcherlike man has taken his sister's arm. That is a gesture of tenderness. Such people make such gestures only when someone in the family is dead.

The sun shines. The conductor of the train is walking along the station platform and talking to the stationmaster. They have been laughing loudly, having their little joke.

That conductor is one of the jolly sort. His eyes twinkle, as the saying is. He has his little joke with every stationmaster, every telegraph operator, baggage man, express man, along the way. There are all kinds of conductors of passenger trains.

There, you see, they are passing the woman whose husband has died and is being taken away somewhere to be buried. They drop their jokes, their laughter. They become silent.

A little path of silence made by that woman in black and her daughter and the fat brother. The little path of silence has started with them at their house, has gone with them along streets to the railroad station, will be with them on the train and in the town to which they are going. They are people of no importance, but they have suddenly become important.

They are symbols of Death. Death is an important, a majestic thing, eh?

How easily you can comprehend a whole life, when you are in a place like this, in a strange place, among strange people. Everything is so much like other towns you have been in. Lives are made up of little series of circumstances. They repeat themselves, over and over, in towns everywhere, in cities, in all countries.

They are of infinite variety. In Paris, when I was there last year, I went into the Louvre. There were men and women there, making copies of the works of the old masters that were hung on the walls. They were professional copyists.

They worked painstakingly, were trained to do just that kind of work, very exactly.

And yet no one of them could make a copy. There were no copies made.

The little circumstances of no two lives anywhere in the world are just alike.

You see I have come over into a hotel room now, in this strange town. It is a country-town hotel. There are flies in here. A fly has just alighted on this paper on which I have been writing these impressions. I stopped writing and looked at the fly. There must be billions of flies in the world and yet, I dare say, no two of them are alike.

The circumstances of their lives are not just alike.

I think I must come away from my own place on trips, such as I am on now, for a specific reason.

At home I live in a certain house. There is my own household, the servants, the people of my household. I am a professor of philosophy in a college in my town, hold a certain definite position there, in the town life and in the college life..

Conversations in the evening, music, people coming into our house.

Myself going to a certain office, then to a classroom where I lecture, seeing people there.

I know some things about these people. That is the trouble with me perhaps. I know something but not enough.

My mind, my fancy, becomes dulled looking at them.

I know too much and not enough.

It is like a house in the street in which I live. There is a particular house in that street—in my home town—I was formerly very curious about. For some reason the people who lived in it were recluses. They seldom came out of their house and hardly ever out of the yard, into the street.

Well, what of all that?

My curiosity was aroused. That is all.

I used to walk past the house with something strangely alive in me. I had figured out this much. An old man with a beard and a white-faced woman lived there. There was a tall hedge and once I looked through. I saw the man walking nervously up and down, on a bit of lawn, under a tree. He was clasping and unclasping his hands and muttering words. The doors and shutters of the mysterious house were all closed. As I looked, the old woman with the white face opened the door a little and looked out at the man. Then the door closed again. She said nothing to him. Did she look at him with love or with fear in her eyes? How do I know? I could not see.

Another time I heard a young woman's voice, although I never saw a young woman about the place. It was evening and the woman was singing—a rather sweet young woman's voice it was.

There you are. That is all. Life is more like that than people suppose. Little odd fragmentary ends of things. That is about all we get. I used to walk past that place all alive, curious. I enjoyed it. My heart thumped a little.

I heard sounds more distinctly, felt more.

I was curious enough to ask my friends along the street about the people.

"They're queer," people said.

Well, who is not queer?

The point is that my curiosity gradually died. I accepted the queerness of the life of that house. It became a part of the life of my street. I became dulled to it.

I have become dulled to the life of my own house, or my street, to the lives of my pupils.

"Where am I? Who am I? Whence came I?" Who asks himself these questions any more?

There is that woman I saw taking her dead husband away on the train. I saw her only for a moment before I walked over to this hotel and came up to this room (an entirely commonplace hotel room it is) but here I sit, thinking of her. I reconstruct her life, go on living the rest of her life with her.

Often I do things like this, come off alone to a strange place like this. "Where are you going?" my wife says to me. "I am going to take a bath," I say.

My wife thinks I am a bit queer too, but she has grown used to me. Thank God, she is a patient and a good-natured woman. "I am going to bathe myself in the lives of people about whom I know nothing."

I will sit in this hotel until I am tired of it and then I will walk in strange streets, see strange houses, strange faces. People will see me.

Who is he?

He is a stranger.

That is nice. I like that. To be a stranger sometimes, going about in a strange place, having no business there, just walking, thinking, bathing myself.

To give others, the people here in this strange place, a little jump at the heart too—because I am something strange.

Once, when I was a young man I would have tried to pick up a girl. Being in a strange place, I would have tried to get my jump at the heart out of trying to be with her.

Now I do not do that. It is not because I am especially faithful—as the saying goes—to my wife, or that I am not interested in strange and attractive women.

It is because of something else. It may be that I am a bit dirty with life and have come here, to this strange place, to bathe myself in strange life and get clean and fresh again.

And so I walk in such a strange place. I dream. I let myself have fancies. Already I have been out into the street, into several streets of this town and have walked about. I have aroused in myself a little stream of fresh fancies, clustered about strange lives, and as I walked, being a stranger, going along slowly, carrying a cane, stopping to look into stores, stopping to look into the windows of houses and into gardens, I have, you see, aroused in others something of the same feeling that has been in me.

I have liked that. Tonight, in the houses of this town, there will be something to speak of.

"There was a strange man about. He acted queerly. I wonder who he was."

"What did he look like?"

An attempt to delve into me too, to describe me. Pictures being made in other minds. A little current of thoughts, fancies, started in others, in me too.

I sit here in this room in this strange town, in this hotel, feeling oddly refreshed. Already I have slept here. My sleep was sweet. Now it is morning and everything is still. I dare say that some time today I shall get on another train and go home.

But now I am remembering things.

Yesterday, in this town, I was in a barbershop. I got my hair cut. I hate getting my hair cut.

"I am in a strange town, with nothing to do, so I'll get my hair cut," I said to myself as I went in.

A man cut my hair. "It rained a week ago," he said. "Yes," I said. That is all the conversation there was between us.

However, there was other talk in that barbershop, plenty of it.

A man had been here in this town and had passed some bad checks. One of them was for ten dollars and was made out in the name of one of the barbers in the shop.

The man who passed the checks was a stranger, like myself. There was talk of that.

A man came in who looked like President Coolidge and had his hair cut.

Then there was another man who came for a shave. He was an old man with sunken cheeks and for some reason looked like a sailor. I dare say he was just a farmer. This town is not by the sea.

There was talk enough in there, a whirl of talk.

I came out thinking.

Well, with me it is like this. A while ago I was speaking of a habit I have formed of going suddenly off like this to some strange place. "I have been doing it ever since it happened," I said. I used the expression "it happened."

Well, what happened?

Not so very much.

A girl got killed. She was struck by an automobile. She was a girl in one of my classes.

She was nothing special to me. She was just a girl—a woman, really—in one of my classes. When she was killed I was already married.

She used to come into my room, into my office. We used to sit in there and talk.

We used to sit and talk about something I had said in my lecture.

"Did you mean this?"

"No, that is not exactly it. It is rather like this."

I suppose you know how we philosophers talk. We have almost a language of our own. Sometimes I think it is largely nonsense.

I would begin talking to that girl—that woman—and on and on I would go. She had gray eyes. There was a sweet serious look on her face.

Do you know, sometimes, when I talked to her like that (it is, I am pretty sure, all nonsense), well, I thought . . .

Her eyes seemed to me sometimes to grow a little larger as I talked to her. I had a notion she did not hear what I said.

I did not care much.

I talked so that I would have something to say.

Sometimes, when we were together that way, in my office in the college building, there would come odd times of silence.

No, it was not silence. There were sounds.

There was a man walking in a hallway, in the college building outside my door. Once when this happened I counted the man's footsteps. Twenty-six, twenty-seven, twenty-eight.

I was looking at the girl—the woman—and she was looking at me.

You see I was an older man. I was married.

I am not such an attractive man. I did, however, think she was very beautiful. There were plenty of young fellows about.

I remember now that when she had been with me like that—after she had left—I used to sit sometimes for hours alone in my office, as I have been sitting here, in this hotel room, in a strange town.

I sat thinking of nothing. Sounds came in to me. I remembered things of my boyhood.

I remembered things about my courtship and my marriage. I sat like that dumbly, a long time.

I was dumb, but I was at the same time more aware than I had ever been in my life.

It was at that time I got the reputation with my wife of being a little queer. I used to go home, after sitting dumbly like that, with that girl, that woman, and I was even more dumb and silent when I got home.

"Why don't you talk?" my wife said.

"I'm thinking," I said.

I wanted her to believe that I was thinking of my work, my studies. Perhaps I was.

Well, the girl, the woman, was killed. An automobile struck her when she was crossing a street. They said she was absent-minded —that she walked right in front of a car. I was in my office, sitting there, when a man, another professor, came in and told me. "She is quite dead, was quite dead when they picked her up," he said.

"Yes." I dare say he thought I was pretty cold and unsympathetic—a scholar, eh, having no heart.

"It was not the driver's fault. He was quite blameless."

"She walked right out in front of the car?"

"Yes."

I remember that at the moment I was fingering a pencil. I did not move. I must have been sitting like that for two or three hours.

I got out and walked. I was walking when I saw a train. So I got on.

Afterward I telephoned to my wife. I don't remember what I told her at that time.

It was all right with her. I made some excuse. She is a patient and a good-natured woman. We have four children. I dare say she is absorbed in the children.

I came to a strange town and I walked about there. I forced myself to observe the little details of life. That time I stayed three or four days and then I went home.

At intervals I have been doing the same thing ever since. It is because at home I grow dull to little things. Being in a strange place like this makes me more aware. I like it. It makes me more alive.

So you see, it is morning and I have been in a strange town, where I know no one and where no one knows me.

As it was yesterday morning, when I came here, to this hotel room, there are sounds. A boy whistles in the street. Another boy, far off, shouts "A-ho."

There are voices in the street, below my window, strange voices. Someone, somewhere in this town, is beating a carpet. I hear the sound of the arrival of a train. The sun is shining.

I may stay here in this town another day or I may go on to another town. No one knows where I am. I am taking this bath in life, as you see, and when I have had enough of it I shall go home feeling refreshed.

These Mountaineers

WHEN I had lived in the Southwest Virginia mountains for some time, people of the North, when I went up there, used to ask me many questions about the mountain people. They did it whenever I went to the city. You know how people are. They like to have everything ticketed.

The rich are so and so, the poor are so and so, the politicians, the people of the West Coast. As though you could draw one figure and say, "There it is. That's it."

The men and women of the mountains were what they were. They were people. They were poor whites. That certainly meant that they were white and poor. Also they were mountaineers.

After the factories began to come down into this country, into Virginia, Tennessee and North Carolina, a lot of them went with their families to work in the factories and to live in mill towns. For a time all was peace and quiet, and then strikes broke out. Everyone who reads newspapers knows about that. There was a lot of writing in newspapers about these mountain people. Some of it was pretty keen.

But there had been a lot of romancing about them before that. That sort of thing never did anyone much good.

So I was walking alone in the mountains and had got down into what in the mountain country is called a "hollow." I was lost. I had been fishing for trout in mountain streams and was tired and hungry. There was a road of a sort I had got into. It would have been difficult to get a car over that road. "This ought to be a good whisky-making country," I thought.

In the hollow along which the road went I came to a little town. Well, now, you would hardly call it a town. There were six or eight little unpainted frame houses and, at a crossroads, a general store.

The mountains stretched away, above the poor little houses. On both sides of the road were the magnificent hills. You understand, when you have been down there, why they are called the "Blue Ridge." They are always blue, a glorious blue. What a country it must have been before the lumbermen came! Over near my place in the mountains men were always talking of the spruce forests of former days. Many of them worked in the lumber camps. They speak of soft moss into which a man sank almost to the knees, the silence of the forest, the great trees.

The great forest is gone now, but the young trees are growing. Much of the country will grow nothing but timber.

The store before which I stood that day was closed, but an old man sat on a little porch in front. He said that the storekeeper also carried the mail and was out on his route but that he would be back and open his store in an hour or two.

I had thought I might at least get some cheese and crackers or a can of sardines.

The man on the porch was old. He was an evil-looking old man. He had gray hair and a gray beard and might have been seventy, but I could see that he was a tough-bodied old fellow.

I asked my way back over the mountain to the main road and had started to move off up the hollow when he called to me. "Are you the man who has moved in here from the North and has built a house in here?"

There is no use my trying to reproduce the mountain speech. I am not skilled at it.

The old man invited me to his house to eat. "You don't mind eating beans, do you?" he asked.

I was hungry and would be glad to have beans. I would have eaten anything at the moment. He said he hadn't any woman, that his old woman was dead. "Come on," he said, "I think I can fix you up."

We went up a path, over a half mountain and into another hollow, perhaps a mile away. It was amazing. The man was old. The skin on his face and neck was wrinkled like an old man's skin and his legs and body were thin, but he walked at such a pace that to follow him kept me panting.

It was a hot, still day in the hills. Not a breath of air stirred. That old man was the only being I saw that day in that town. If anyone else lived there he had kept out of sight.

The old man's house was on the bank of another mountain stream. That afternoon, after eating with him, I got some fine trout out of the stream.

But this isn't a fishing story. We went to his house.

It was dirty and small and seemed about to fall down. The old man was dirty. There were layers of dirt on his old hands and on his wrinkled neck. When we were in the house, which had but one room on the ground floor, he went to a small stove. "The fire is out," he said. "Do you care if the beans are cold?"

"No," I said. By this time I did not want any beans and wished I had not come. There was something evil about this old mountain man. Surely the romancers could not have made much out of him.

Unless they played on the Southern hospitality chord. He had invited me there. I had been hungry. The beans were all he had.

He put some of them on a plate and put them on a table before me. The table was a homemade one covered with a red oilcloth, now quite worn. There were large holes in it. Dirt and grease clung about the edges of the holes. He had wiped the plate, on which he had put the beans, on the sleeve of his coat.

But perhaps you have not eaten beans prepared in the mountains, in the mountain way. They are the staff of life down there. Without beans there would be no life in some of the hills. The beans are, when prepared by a mountain woman and served hot, often delicious. I do not know what they put in them or how they cook them, but they are unlike any beans you will find anywhere else in the world.

As Smithfield ham, when it is real Smithfield ham, is unlike any other ham.

But beans cold, beans dirty, beans served on a plate wiped on the sleeve of that coat . . .

I sat looking about. There was a dirty bed in the room in which we sat and an open stairway, leading up to the room above.

Someone moved up there. Someone walked barefooted across the floor. There was silence for a time and then it happened again.

You must get the picture of a very hot still place between hills. It was June. The old man had become silent. He was watching me. Perhaps he wanted to see whether or not I was going to scorn his hospitality. I began eating the beans with a dirty spoon. I was many miles away from anyplace I had ever been before.

And then there was that sound again. I had got the impression that the old man had told me his wife was dead, that he lived alone.

How did I know it was a woman upstairs? I did know.

"Have you got a woman up there?" I asked. He grinned, a toothless malicious grin, as though to say, "Oh, you're curious, eh?"

And then he laughed, a queer cackle.

"She ain't mine," he said.

We sat in silence after that and then there was the sound again. I heard bare feet walking across a plank floor.

Now the feet were descending the crude open stairs. Two legs appeared, two thin, young girl's legs.

She didn't look to be over twelve or thirteen.

She came down, almost to the foot of the stairs, and then stopped and sat down.

How dirty she was, how thin, what a wild look she had! I have never seen a wilder-looking creature. Her eyes were bright. They were like the eyes of a wild animal.

And, at that, there was something about her face. In many of these young mountain faces there is a look it is difficult to explain —it is a look of breeding, of aristocracy. I know no other word for the look.

And she had it.

And now the two were sitting there, and I was trying to eat. Suppose I rose and threw the dirty beans out at the open door. I might have said, "Thank you, I have enough." I didn't dare.

But perhaps they weren't thinking of the beans. The old man

began to speak of the girl, sitting ten feet from him, as though she were not there.

"She ain't mine," he said. "She came here. Her pop died. She ain't got anyone."

I am making a bad job of trying to reproduce his speech.

He was giggling now, a toothless old man's giggle. "Ha, she won't eat."

"She's a hellcat," he said.

He reached over and touched me on the arm. "You know what. She's a hellcat. You couldn't satisfy her. She had to have her a man.

"And she got one too."

"Is she married?" I asked, half whispering the words, not wanting her to hear.

He laughed at the idea. "Ha. Married, eh?"

He said it was a young man from farther down the hollow. "He lives here with us," the old man said laughing, and as he said it the girl rose and started back up the stairs. She had said nothing, but her young eyes had looked at us, filled with hatred. As she went up the stairs the old man kept laughing at her, his queer, high-pitched, old man's laugh. It was really a giggle. "Ha, she can't eat. When she tries to eat she can't keep it down. She thinks I don't know why. She's a hellcat. She would have a man and now she's got one.

"Now she can't eat."

I fished in the creek in the hollow during the afternoon and toward evening began to get trout. They were fine ones. I got fourteen of them and got back over a mountain and into the main road before dark.

What took me back into the hollow I don't know. The face of the girl possessed me.

And then there was good trout fishing there. That stream at least had not been fished out.

When I went back I put a twenty-dollar bill in my pocket. "Well," I thought—I hardly know what I did think. There were notions in my head, of course.

The girl was very, very young.

"She might have been kept there by that old man," I thought, "and by some young mountain rough. There might be a chance for her."

I thought I would give her the twenty dollars. "If she wants to get out perhaps she can," I thought. Twenty dollars is a lot of money in the hills.

It was just another hot day when I got in there again and the old man was not at home. At first I thought there was no one there. The house stood alone by a hardly discernible road and near the creek. The creek was clear and had a swift current. It made a chattering sound.

I stood on the bank of the creek before the house and tried to think.

"If I interfere . . ."

Well, let's admit it. I was a bit afraid. I thought I had been a fool to come back.

And then the girl suddenly came out of the house and came toward me. There was no doubt about it. She was that way. And unmarried, of course.

At least my money, if I could give it to her, would serve to buy her some clothes. The ones she had on were very ragged and dirty. Her feet and legs were bare. It would be winter by the time the child was born.

A man came out of the house. He was a tall young mountain man. He looked rough. "That's him," I thought. He said nothing.

He was dirty and unkempt as the old man had been and as the child was.

At any rate she was not afraid of me. "Hello, you are back here," she said. Her voice was clear.

Just the same I saw the hatred in her eyes. I asked about the fishing. "Are the trout biting?" I asked. She had come nearer me now, and the young man had slouched back into the house.

Again I am at a loss about how to reproduce her mountain speech. It is peculiar. So much is in the voice.

Hers was cold and clear and filled with hatred.

"How should I know? He" (indicating with a gesture of her hand the tall slouching figure who had gone into the house) "is too damn' lazy to fish.

"He's too damn' lazy for anything on earth."

She was glaring at me.

"Well," I thought, "I will at least try to give her the money." I took the bill in my hand and held it toward her. "You will need some clothes," I said. "Take it and buy yourself some clothes."

It may have been that I had touched her mountain pride. How am I to know? The look of hatred in her eyes seemed to grow more intense.

"You go to hell," she said. "You get out of here. And don't you come back in here again."

She was looking hard at me when she said this. If you have never known such people, who live like that, "on the outer fringe of life," as we writers say (you may see them sometimes in the tenement districts of cities as well as in the lonely and lovely hills) —such a queer look of maturity in the eyes of a child. . . .

It sends a shiver through you. Such a child knows too much and not enough. Before she went back into the house she turned and spoke to me again. It was about my money.

She told me to put it somewhere, I won't say where. The most modern of modern writers has to use some discretion.

Then she went into the house. That was all. I left. What was I to do? After all, a man looks after his hide. In spite of the trout I did not go fishing in that hollow again.

A Meeting South

HE TOLD me the story of his ill fortune—a crack-up in an airplane—with a very gentlemanly little smile on his very sensitive, rather thin lips. Such things happened. He might well have been speaking of another. I liked his tone and I liked him.

This happened in New Orleans, where I had gone to live. When he came, my friend Fred, for whom he was looking, had gone away, but immediately I felt a strong desire to know him better and so suggested we spend the evening together. When we went down the stairs from my apartment I noticed that he was a cripple. The slight limp, the look of pain that occasionally drifted across his face, the little laugh that was intended to be jolly, but did not quite achieve its purpose, all these things began at once to tell me the story I have now set myself to write.

"I shall take him to see Aunt Sally," I thought. One does not take every caller to Aunt Sally. However, when she is in fine feather, when she has taken a fancy to her visitor, there is no one like her. Although she has lived in New Orleans for thirty years, Aunt Sally is Middle Western, born and bred.

However I am plunging a bit too abruptly into my story.

First of all I must speak more of my guest, and for convenience's sake I shall call him David. I felt at once that he would be wanting a drink and in New Orleans—dear city of Latins and hot nights—even in Prohibition times such things can be managed. We achieved several and my own head became somewhat shaky, but I could see that what we had taken had not affected him. Evening was coming, the abrupt waning of the day and the quick smoky soft-footed coming of night, characteristic of the semitropic city, when he produced a bottle from his hip pocket. It was so large that I was amazed. How had it happened that the carrying of so large a bottle had not made him look deformed? His body was very small and delicately built. "Perhaps, like the kangaroo, his body has developed some kind of a natural pouch for taking care of supplies," I thought. Really he walked as one might fancy a kangaroo would walk when out for a quiet evening stroll. I went along thinking of Darwin and the marvels of Prohibition. "We are a wonderful people, we Americans," I thought. We were both in fine humor and had begun to like each other immensely.

He explained the bottle. The stuff, he said, was made by a Negro man on his father's plantation somewhere over in Alabama. We sat on the steps of a vacant house deep down in the old French Quarter of New Orleans—the Vieux Carré—while he explained that his father had no intention of breaking the law—that is to say, in so far as the law remained reasonable. "Our nigger just makes whisky for us," he said. "We keep him for that purpose. He doesn't have anything else to do, just makes the family whisky, that's all. If he went selling any, we'd raise hell with him. I dare say Dad would shoot him if he caught him up to any such unlawful trick, and you bet Jim, our nigger I'm telling you of, knows it too.

"He's a good whisky maker, though, don't you think?" David added. He talked of Jim in a warm friendly way. "Lord, he's been with us always, was born with us. His wife cooks for us and Jim makes our whisky. It's a race to see which is best at his job, but I think Jim will win. He's getting a little better all the time and all of our family—well, I reckon we just like and need our whisky more than we do our food."

Do you know New Orleans? Have you lived there in the summer when it is hot, in the winter when it rains, and through the glorious late fall days? Some of its own, more progressive, people scorn it now. In New Orleans there is a sense of shame because the city is not more like Chicago or Pittsburgh.

It, however, suited David and me. We walked slowly, on account of his bad leg, through many streets of the Old Town, Negro women laughing all around us in the dusk, shadows playing over old buildings, children with their shrill cries dodging in and out of old hallways. The old city was once almost altogether French, but now it is becoming more and more Italian. It, however, remains Latin. People live out of doors. Families were sitting down to dinner within full sight of the street—all doors and windows open. A man and his wife quarreled in Italian. In a patio back of an old building a Negress sang a French song.

We came out of the narrow little streets and had a drink in front of the dark cathedral and another in a little square in front. There is a statue of General Jackson, always taking off his hat to Northern tourists who in winter come down to see the city. At his horse's feet an inscription—"The Union must and will be preserved." We drank solemnly to that declaration and the general seemed to bow a bit lower. "He was sure a proud man," David said, as we went over toward the docks to sit in the darkness and look at the Mississippi. All good New Orleanians go to look at the Mississippi at least once a day. At night it is like creeping into a dark bedroom to look at a sleeping child—something of that sort—gives you the same warm nice feeling, I mean. David is a poet and so in the darkness by the river we spoke of Keats and Shelley, the two English poets all good Southern men love.

All of this, you are to understand, was before I took him to see Aunt Sally.

Both Aunt Sally and myself are Middle Westerners. We are but guests down here, but perhaps we both in some queer way belong to this city. Something of the sort is in the wind. I don't quite know how it has happened.

A great many Northern men and women come down our way and, when they go back North, write things about the South. The trick is to write nigger stories. The North likes them. They are so amusing. One of the best-known writers of nigger stories was down here recently and a man I know, a Southern man, went to call on him. The writer seemed a bit nervous. "I don't know much about the South or Southerners," he said. "But you have your reputation," my friend said. "You are so widely known as a writer about the South and about Negro life." The writer had a notion he was being made sport of. "Now look here," he said, "I don't claim to be a high-brow. I'm a businessman myself. At home, up North, I associate mostly with businessmen and when I am not at work I go out to the country club. I want you to understand I am not setting myself up as a high-brow.

"I give them what they want," he said. My friend said he appeared angry. "About what now, do you fancy?" he asked innocently.

However, I am not thinking of the Northern writer of Negro stories. I am thinking of the Southern poet, with the bottle clasped firmly in his hands, sitting in the darkness beside me on the docks facing the Mississippi.

He spoke at some length of his gift for drinking. "I didn't always have it. It is a thing built up," he said. The story of how he chanced to be a cripple came out slowly. You are to remember that my own head was a bit unsteady. In the darkness the river, very deep and very powerful off New Orleans, was creeping away to the gulf. The whole river seemed to move away from us and then to slip noiselessly into the darkness like a vast moving sidewalk.

When he had first come to me, in the late afternoon, and when we had started for our walk together I had noticed that one of his legs dragged as we went along and that he kept putting a thin hand to an equally thin cheek.

Sitting over by the river he explained as a boy would explain when he has stubbed his toe running down a hill.

When the World War broke out he went over to England and managed to get himself enrolled as an aviator, very much, I gathered, in the spirit in which a countryman, in a city for a night, might take in a show.

The English had been glad enough to take him on. He was one more man. They were glad enough to take anyone on just then. He was small and delicately built but after he got in he turned out to be a first-rate flyer, serving all through the war with a British flying squadron, but at the last got into a crash and fell.

Both legs were broken, one of them in three places, the scalp was badly torn and some of the bones of the face had been splintered.

They had put him into a field hospital and had patched him up. "It was my fault if the job was rather bungled," he said. "You see it was a field hospital, a hell of a place. Men were torn all to pieces, groaning and dying. Then they moved me back to a base hospital and it wasn't much better. The fellow who had the bed next to mine had shot himself in the foot to avoid going into a battle. A lot of them did that, but why they picked on their own feet that way is beyond me. It's a nasty place, full of small bones. If you're ever going to shoot yourself don't pick on a spot like that. Don't pick on your feet. I tell you it's a bad idea.

"Anyway, the man in the hospital was always making a fuss, and I got sick of him and the place too. When I got better I faked, said the nerves of my leg didn't hurt. It was a lie, of course. The nerves of my leg and of my face have never quit hurting. I reckon maybe, if I had told the truth, they might have fixed me up all right."

I got it. No wonder he carried his drinks so well. When I understood, I wanted to keep on drinking with him, wanted to stay with him until he got tired of me as he had of the man who lay beside him in the base hospital over there somewhere in France.

The point was that he never slept, could not sleep, except when he was a little drunk. "I'm a nut," he said smiling.

It was after we got over to Aunt Sally's that he talked most. Aunt Sally had gone to bed when we got there, but she got up when we rang the bell and we all went to sit together in the little patio back of her house. She is a large woman with great arms and rather a paunch, and she had put on nothing but a light flowered dressing gown over a thin, ridiculously girlish, nightgown. By this time the moon had come up and, outside, in the narrow street of the Vieux Carré, three drunken sailors from a ship in the river were sitting on a curb and singing a song.

I've got to get it,
You've got to get it,
We've all got to get it
In our own good time.

They had rather nice boyish voices and every time they sang a verse and had done the chorus they all laughed together heartily.

In Aunt Sally's patio there are many broad-leafed banana plants and a Chinaberry tree throwing its soft purple shadows on a brick floor.

As for Aunt Sally, she is as strange to me as he was. When we came and when we were all seated at a little table in the patio, she ran into her house and presently came back with a bottle of whisky. She, it seemed, had understood him at once, had understood without unnecessary words that the little Southern man lived always in the black house of pain, that whisky was good to him, that it quieted his throbbing nerves, temporarily at least. "Everything is temporary, when you come to that," I can fancy Aunt Sally saying.

We sat for a time in silence, David having shifted his allegiance and taken two drinks out of Aunt Sally's bottle. Presently he rose and walked up and down the patio floor, crossing and recrossing the network of delicately outlined shadows on the bricks. "It's really all right, the leg," he said, "something just presses on the nerves, that's all." In me there was a self-satisfied feeling. I had done the right thing. I had brought him to Aunt Sally. "I have brought him to a mother." She has always made me feel that way since I have known her.

And now I shall have to explain her a little. It will not be so easy. That whole neighborhood in New Orleans is alive with tales concerning her.

Aunt Sally came to New Orleans in the old days, when the town was wild, in the wide-open days. What she had been before she came no one knew, but anyway she opened a place. That was very, very long ago when I was myself but a lad, up in Ohio. As I have already said, Aunt Sally came from somewhere up in the Middle Western country. In some obscure subtle way it would flatter me to think she came from my state.

The house she had opened was one of the older places in the French Quarter down here, and when she had got her hands on it, Aunt Sally had a hunch. Instead of making the place modern, cutting it up into small rooms, all that sort of thing, she left it just as it was and spent her money rebuilding falling old walls, mending winding broad old stairways, repairing dim high-ceilinged old rooms, soft-colored old marble mantels. After all, we do seem attached to sin and there are so many people busy making sin unattractive. It is good to find someone who takes the other road. It would have been so very much to Aunt Sally's advantage to have made the place modern, that is to say, in the business she was in at that time. If a few old rooms, wide old stairways, old cooking ovens built into the walls, if all these things did not facilitate the stealing in of couples on dark nights, they at least did something else. She had opened a gambling and drinking house, but one can have no doubt about the ladies stealing in. "I was on the make all right," Aunt Sally told me once.

She ran the place and took in money, and the money she spent on the place itself. A falling wall was made to stand up straight and fine again, the banana plants were made to grow in the patio, the Chinaberry tree got started and was helped through the years of adolescence. On the wall the lovely Rose of Montana bloomed madly. The fragrant Lantana grew in a dense mass at a corner of the wall.

When the Chinaberry tree, planted at the very center of the patio, began to get up into the light it filled the whole neighborhood with fragrance in the spring.

Fifteen, twenty years of that, with Mississippi River gamblers and race-horse men sitting at tables by windows in the huge rooms upstairs in the house that had once, no doubt, been the town house of some rich planter's family—in the boom days of the forties. Women stealing in, too, in the dusk of evenings. Drinks being sold. Aunt Sally raking down the kitty from the game, raking in her share, quite ruthlessly.

At night, getting a good price too from the lovers. No questions asked, a good price for drinks. Moll Flanders might have lived with Aunt Sally. What a pair they would have made! The Chinaberry tree beginning to be lusty. The Lantana blossoming—in the fall, the Rose of Montana.

Aunt Sally getting hers. Using the money to keep the old house in fine shape. Salting some away all the time.

A motherly soul, good, sensible Middle Western woman, eh? Once a race-horse man left twenty-four thousand dollars with her and disappeared. No one knew she had it. There was a report the man was dead. He had killed a gambler in a place down by the French Market, and while they were looking for him he managed to slip in to Aunt Sally's and leave his swag. Some time later a body was found floating in the river and it was identified as the horseman but in reality he had been picked up in a wire-tapping haul in New York City and did not get out of his Northern prison for six years.

When he did get out, naturally, he skipped for New Orleans. No doubt he was somewhat shaky. She had him. If he squealed there was a murder charge to be brought up and held over his head. It was night when he arrived, and Aunt Sally went at once to an old brick oven built into the wall of the kitchen and took out a bag. "There it is," she said. The whole affair was part of the day's work for her in those days.

Gamblers at the tables in some of the rooms upstairs, lurking couples, from the old patio below the fragrance of growing things.

When she was fifty, Aunt Sally had got enough and had put them all out. She did not stay in the way of sin too long and she never went in too deep, like that Moll Flanders, and so she was all right and sitting pretty. "They wanted to gamble and drink and play with the ladies. The ladies liked it all right. I never saw none of them come in protesting too much. The worst was in the morning when they went away. They looked so sheepish and guilty. If they felt that way, what made them come? If I took a man, you bet I'd want him and no monkey business, or nothing doing.

"I got a little tired of all of them, that's the truth." Aunt Sally laughed. "But that wasn't until I had got what I went after. Oh, pshaw, they took up too much of my time, after I got enough to be safe."

Aunt Sally is now sixty-five. If you like her and she likes you, she will let you sit with her in her patio gossiping of the old times, of the old river days. Perhaps—well, you see there is still something of the French influence at work in New Orleans, a sort of matter-of-factness about life—what I started to say is that if you know Aunt Sally and she likes you, and if, by chance, your lady likes the smell of flowers growing in a patio at night—really, I am going a bit too far. I only meant to suggest that Aunt Sally at sixty-five is not harsh. She is a motherly soul.

We sat in the garden talking, the little Southern poet, Aunt Sally and myself—or rather they talked and I listened. The Southerner's great-grandfather was English, a younger son, and he came over here to make his fortune as a planter, and did it. Once he and his sons owned several great plantations with slaves, but now his father had but a few hundred acres left, about one of the old houses—somewhere over in Alabama. The land is heavily mortgaged and most of it has not been under cultivation for years. Negro labor is growing more and more expensive and unsatisfactory since so many Negroes have run off to Chicago, and the poet's father and the one brother at home are not much good at working the land. "We aren't strong enough and we don't know how," the poet said.

The Southerner had come to New Orleans to see Fred, to talk with Fred about poetry, but Fred was out of town. I could only walk about with him, help him drink his homemade whisky. Already I had taken nearly a dozen drinks. In the morning I would have a headache.

I drew within myself, listening while David and Aunt Sally talked. The Chinaberry tree had been so and so many years growing—she spoke of it as she might have spoken of a daughter. "It had a lot of different sicknesses when it was young, but it pulled through." Someone had built a high wall on one side of her patio so that the climbing plants did not get as much sunlight as they needed. The banana plants, however, did very well, and now the Chinaberry tree was big and strong enough to take care of itself. She kept giving David drinks of whisky and he talked.

He told her of the place in his leg where something, a bone perhaps, pressed on the nerve, and of the place on his left cheek. A silver plate had been set under the skin. She touched the spot with her fat old fingers. The moonlight fell softly down on the patio floor. "I can't sleep except somewhere out of doors," David said.

He explained how, at home on his father's plantation, he had to be thinking all day whether or not he would be able to sleep at night.

"I go to bed and then I get up. There is always a bottle of whisky on the table downstairs and I take three or four drinks. Then I go outdoors." Often very nice things happened.

"In the fall it's best," he said. "You see the niggers are making molasses." Every Negro cabin on the place had a little clump of ground back of it where cane grew, and in the fall the Negroes were making their 'lasses. "I take the bottle in my hand and go into the fields, unseen by the niggers. Having the bottle with me, that way, I drink a good deal and then lie down on the ground. The mosquitoes bite me some, but I don't mind much. I reckon I get drunk enough not to mind. The little pain makes a kind of rhythm for the great pain—like poetry.

"In a kind of shed the niggers are making the 'lasses, that is to say, pressing the juice out of the cane and boiling it down. They keep singing as they work. In a few years now I reckon our family won't have any land. The banks could take it now if they wanted it. They don't want it. It would be too much trouble for them to manage, I reckon.

"In the fall, at night, the niggers are pressing the cane. Our niggers live pretty much on 'lasses and grits.

"They like working at night and I'm glad they do. There is an old mule going round and round in a circle and beside the press a pile of the dry cane. Niggers come, men and women, old and young. They build a fire outside the shed. The old mule goes round and round.

"The niggers sing. They laugh and shout. Sometimes the young niggers with their gals make love on the dry cane pile. I can hear it rattle.

"I have come out of the big house, me and my bottle, and I creep along, low on the ground, 'til I get up close. There I lie. I'm a little drunk. It all makes me happy. I can sleep some, on the ground like that, when the niggers are singing, when no one knows I'm there.

"I could sleep here, on these bricks here," David said, pointing to where the shadows cast by the broad leaves of the banana plants were broadest and deepest.

He got up from his chair and went limping, dragging one foot after the other, across the patio and lay down on the bricks.

For a long time Aunt Sally and I sat looking at each other, saying nothing, and presently she made a sign with her fat finger and we crept away into the house. "I'll let you out at the front door. You let him sleep, right where he is," she said. In spite of her huge bulk and her age she walked across the patio floor as softly as a kitten. Beside her I felt awkward and uncertain. When we had got inside she whispered to me. She had some champagne left from the old days, hidden away somewhere in the old house. "I'm going to send a magnum up to his dad when he goes home," she explained.

She, it seemed, was very happy, having him there, drunk and asleep on the brick floor of the patio. "We used to have some good men come here in the old days too," she said. As we went into the house through the kitchen door I had looked back at David, asleep now in the heavy shadows at a corner of the wall. There was no doubt he also was happy, had been happy ever since I had brought him into the presence of Aunt Sally. What a small huddled figure of a man he looked, lying thus on the brick, under the night sky, in the deep shadows of the banana plants.

I went into the house and out through the front door and into a dark narrow street, thinking. Well, I was, after all, a Northern man. It was possible Aunt Sally had become completely Southern, being down here so long.

I remembered that it was the chief boast of her life that once she had shaken hands with John L. Sullivan and that she had known P. T. Barnum.

"I knew Dave Gears. You mean to tell me you don't know who Dave Gears was? Why, he was one of the biggest gamblers we ever had in this city."

As for David and his poetry—it is in the manner of Shelley. "If I could write like Shelley I would be happy. I wouldn't care what happened to me," he had said during our walk of the early part of the evening.

I went along enjoying my thoughts. The street was dark, and occasionally I laughed. A notion had come to me. It kept dancing in my head and I thought it very delicious. It had something to do with aristocrats, with such people as Aunt Sally and David. "Lordy," I thought, "maybe I do understand them a little. I'm from the Middle West myself and it seems we can produce our aristocrats too." I kept thinking of Aunt Sally and of my native state, Ohio. "Lordy, I hope she comes from up there, but I don't think I had better inquire too closely into her past," I said to myself, as I went smiling away into the soft smoky night.

Brother Death

THERE WERE the two oak stumps, knee high to a not-too-tall man and cut quite squarely across. They became to the two children objects of wonder. They had seen the two trees cut but had run away just as the trees fell. They hadn't thought of the two stumps, to be left standing there; hadn't even looked at them.

Afterward Ted said to his sister Mary, speaking of the stumps: "I wonder if they bled, like legs, when a surgeon cuts a man's leg off." He had been hearing war stories. A man came to the farm one day to visit one of the farm hands, a man who had been in the World War and had lost an arm. He stood in one of the barns talking. When Ted said that, Mary spoke up at once. She hadn't been lucky enough to be at the barn when the one-armed man was there talking, and was jealous. "Why not a woman or a girl's leg?" she said, but Ted said the idea was silly. "Women and girls don't get their legs and arms cut off," he declared. "Why not? I'd just like to know why not?" Mary kept saying.

It would have been something if they had stayed, that day the trees were cut. "We might have gone and touched the places," Ted said. He meant the stumps. Would they have been warm? Would they have bled? They did go and touch the places afterward, but it was a cold day and the stumps were cold. Ted stuck to his point that only men's arms and legs were cut off, but Mary thought of automobile accidents. "You can't think just about wars. There might be an automobile accident," she declared, but Ted wouldn't be convinced

They were both children, but something had made them both in an odd way old. Mary was fourteen and Ted eleven, but Ted wasn't strong and that rather evened things up. They were the children of a well-to-do Virginia farmer named John Grey in the Blue Ridge country in southwestern Virginia. There was a wide valley called the "Rich Valley," with a railroad and a small river running through it and high mountains in sight, to the north and south. Ted had some kind of heart disease, a lesion, something of the sort, the result of a severe attack of diphtheria when he was a child of eight. He was thin and not strong, but curiously alive. The doctor said he might die at any moment, might just drop down dead. The fact had drawn him peculiarly close to his sister Mary. It had awakened a strong and determined maternalism in her.

The whole family, the neighbors, on neighboring farms in the valley, and even the other children at the schoolhouse where they went to school recognized something as existing between the two children. "Look at them going along there," people said. "They do seem to have good times together, but they are so serious. For such young children they are too serious. Still, I suppose, under the circumstances, it's natural." Of course, everyone knew about Ted. It had done something to Mary. At fourteen she was both a child and a grown woman. The woman side of her kept popping out at unexpected moments.

She had sensed something concerning her brother Ted. It was because he was as he was, having that kind of a heart, a heart likely at any moment to stop beating, leaving him dead, cut down like a young tree. The others in the Grey family, that is to say, the older ones, the mother and father and an older brother, Don, who was eighteen now, recognized something as belonging to the two children, being, as it were, between them, but the recognition wasn't very definite. People in your own family are likely at any moment to do strange, sometimes hurtful things to you. You have to watch them. Ted and Mary had both found that out.

The brother Don was like the father, already at eighteen almost a grown man. He was that sort, the kind people speak of, saying, "He's a good man. He'll make a good solid dependable man." The father, when he was a young man, never drank, never went chasing the girls, was never wild. There had been enough wild young ones in the Rich Valley when he was a lad. Some of them had inherited big farms and had lost them, gambling, drinking, fooling with fast horses and chasing after the women. It had been almost a Virginia tradition, but John Grey was a land man. All the Greys were. There were other large cattle farms owned by Greys up and down the valley.

John Grey, everyone said, was a natural cattle man. He knew beef cattle, of the big so-called export type, how to pick and feed them to make beef. He knew how and where to get the right kind of young stock to turn into his fields. It was blue-grass country. Big beef cattle went directly off the pastures to market. The Grey farm contained over twelve hundred acres, most of it in blue grass.

The father was a land man, land hungry. He had begun, as a cattle farmer, with a small place inherited from his father, some two hundred acres, lying next to what was then the big Aspinwahl place and, after he began, he never stopped getting more land. He kept cutting in on the Aspinwahls, who were a rather horsey, fast lot. They thought of themselves as Virginia aristocrats, having, as they weren't so modest about pointing out, a family going back and back, family tradition, guests always being entertained, fast horses kept, money being bet on fast horses. John Grey getting their land, now twenty acres, then thirty, then fifty, until at last he got the old Aspinwahl house, with one of the Aspinwahl girls, not a young one, not one of the best-looking ones, as wife. The Aspinwahl place was down, by that time, to less than a hundred acres, but he went on, year after year, always being careful and shrewd, making every penny count, never wasting a cent, adding and adding to what was now the Grey place. The former Aspinwahl house was a large old brick house with fireplaces in all the rooms and was very comfortable.

People wondered why Louise Aspinwahl had married John Grey, but when they were wondering they smiled. The Aspinwahl girls were all well educated, had all been away to college, but Louise wasn't so pretty. She got nicer after marriage, suddenly almost beautiful. The Aspinwahls were, as everyone knew, naturally sensitive, really first class, but the men couldn't hang onto land and the Greys could. In all that section of Virginia, people gave John Grey credit for being what he was. They respected him. "He's on the level," they said, "as honest as a horse. He has cattle sense, that's it." He could run his big hand down over the flank of a steer and say, almost to the pound, what he would weigh on the scales or he could look at a calf or a yearling and say, "He'll do," and he would do. A steer is a steer. He isn't supposed to do anything but make beef.

There was Don, the oldest son of the Grey family. He was so evidently destined to be a Grey, to be another like his father. He had long been a star in the 4-H Club of the Virginia county and, even as a lad of nine and ten, had won prizes at steer judging. At twelve he had produced, no one helping him, doing all the work himself, more bushels of corn on an acre of land than any other boy in the state.

It was all a little amazing, even a bit queer to Mary Grey, being as she was a girl peculiarly conscious, so old and young, so aware. There was Don, the older brother, big and strong of body like the father, and there was the young brother Ted. Ordinarily, in the ordinary course of life, she being what she was—female—it would have been quite natural and right for her to have given her young-girl's admiration to Don, but she didn't. For some reason, Don barely existed for her. He was outside, not in it, while, for her, Ted, the seemingly weak one of the family, was everything.

Still there Don was, so big of body, so quiet, so apparently sure of himself. The father had begun, as a young cattle man, with the two hundred acres, and now he had the twelve hundred. What would Don Grey do when he started? Already he knew, although he didn't say anything, that he wanted to start. He wanted to run things, be his own boss. His father had offered to send him away to college, to an agricultural college, but he wouldn't go. "No. I can learn more here," he said.

Already there was a contest, always kept under the surface, between the father and son. It concerned ways of doing things, decisions to be made. As yet, the son always surrendered.

It is like that in a family, little isolated groups formed within the larger group, jealousies, concealed hatreds, silent battles secretly going on—among the Greys, Mary and Ted, Don and his father, the mother and the two younger children, Gladys, a girl child of six now, who adored her brother Don, and Harry, a boy child of two.

As for Mary and Ted, they lived within their own world, but their own world had not been established without a struggle. The point was that Ted, having the heart that might at any moment stop beating, was always being treated tenderly by the others. Only Mary understood that—how it infuriated and hurt him.

"No, Ted, I wouldn't do that."

"Now, Ted, do be careful."

Sometimes Ted went white and trembling with anger—Don, the father, the mother, all keeping at him like that. It didn't matter what he wanted to do, learn to drive one of the two family cars, climb a tree to find a bird's nest, run a race with Mary. Naturally, being on a farm, he wanted to try his hand at breaking a colt, beginning with him, getting a saddle on, having it out with him. "No, Ted. You can't." He had learned to swear, picking it up from the farm hands and from boys at the country school. "Hell! Goddam!" he said to Mary. Only Mary understood how he felt, and she had not put the matter very definitely into words, not even to herself. It was one of the things that made her old when she was so young. It made her stand aside from the others of the family, aroused in her a curious determination. "They shall not." She caught herself saying the words to herself. "They shall not.

"If he is to have but a few years of life, they shall not spoil what he is to have. Why should they make him die, over and over, day after day?" The thoughts in her did not become so definite. She had resentment against the others. She was like a soldier, standing guard over Ted.

The two children drew more and more away, into their own

world, and only once did what Mary felt come to the surface. That was with the mother.

It was on an early summer day and Ted and Mary were playing in the rain. They were on a side porch of the house, where the water came pouring down from the eaves. At a corner of the porch there was a great stream, and first Ted and then Mary dashed through it, returning to the porch with clothes soaked and water running in streams from soaked hair. There was something joyous, the feel of the cold water on the body, under clothes, and they were shrieking with laughter when the mother came to the door. She looked at Ted. There was fear and anxiety in her voice. "Oh, Ted, you know you mustn't, you mustn't." Just that. All the rest implied. Nothing said to Mary. There it was. "Oh, Ted, you mustn't. You mustn't run hard, climb trees, ride horses. The least shock to you may do it." It was the old story again, and, of course, Ted understood. He went white and trembled. Why couldn't the rest understand that was a hundred times worse for him? On that day, without answering his mother, he ran off the porch and through the rain toward the barns. He wanted to go hide himself from everyone. Mary knew how he felt.

She got suddenly very old and very angry. The mother and daughter stood looking at each other, the woman nearing fifty and the child of fourteen. It was getting everything in the family reversed. Mary felt that, but felt she had to do something. "You should have more sense, Mother," she said seriously. She also had gone white. Her lips trembled. "You mustn't do it any more. Don't you ever do it again."

"What, child?" There was astonishment and half anger in the mother's voice. "Always making him think of it," Mary said. She wanted to cry, but didn't.

The mother understood. There was a queer tense moment before Mary also walked off, toward the barns, in the rain. It wasn't all so clear. The mother wanted to fly at the child, perhaps shake her for daring to be so impudent. A child like that to decide things—to dare to reprove her mother. There was so much implied—even that Ted be allowed to die, quickly, suddenly, rather than that death, danger of sudden death, be brought again and again to his attention. There were values in life, implied by a child's words: "Life, what is it worth? Is death the most terrible thing?" The mother turned and went silently into the house, while

Mary, going to the barns, presently found Ted. He was in an empty horse stall, standing with his back to the wall, staring. There were no explanations. "Well," Ted said presently; and "Come on, Ted," Mary replied. It was necessary to do something, even perhaps more risky than playing in the rain. The rain was already passing. "Let's take off our shoes," Mary said. Going barefoot was one of the things forbidden Ted. They took their shoes off and, leaving them in the barn, went into an orchard. There was a small creek below the orchard, a creek that went down to the river and now it would be in flood. They went into it and once Mary got swept off her feet so that Ted had to pull her out. She spoke then. "I told Mother," she said, looking serious.

"What?" Ted said. "Gee, I guess maybe I saved you from drowning," he added.

"Sure you did," said Mary. "I told her to let you alone." She grew suddenly fierce. "They've all got to—they've got to let you alone," she said.

There was a bond. Ted did his share. He was imaginative and could think of plenty of risky things to do. Perhaps the mother spoke to the father and to Don, the older brother. There was a new inclination in the family to keep hands off the pair, and the fact seemed to give the two children new room in life. Something seemed to open out. There was a little inner world created, always, every day, being re-created, and in it there was a kind of new security. It seemed to the two children—they could not have put their feeling into words—that, being in their own created world, feeling a new security there, they could suddenly look out at the outside world and see, in a new way, what was going on out there in the world that belonged also to others.

It was a world to be thought about, looked at, a world of drama too, the drama of human relations, outside their own world, in a family, on a farm, in a farmhouse. . . . On a farm, calves and yearling steers arriving to be fattened, great heavy steers going off to market, colts being broken to work or to saddle, lambs born in the late winter. The human side of life was more difficult, to a child often incomprehensible, but after the speech to the mother, on the porch of the house that day when it rained, it seemed to Mary almost as though she and Ted had set up a new family. Everything about the farm, the house and the barns got nicer. There was a new freedom. The two children walked along a country road, returning to the farm from school in the late afternoon.

There were other children in the road but they managed to fall behind or they got ahead. There were plans made. "I'm going to be a nurse when I grow up," Mary said. She may have remembered dimly the woman nurse, from the county-seat town, who had come to stay in the house when Ted was so ill. Ted said that as soon as he could—it would be when he was younger yet than Don was now—he intended to leave and go out West . . . far out, he said. He wanted to be a cowboy or a broncobuster or something, and, that failing, he thought he would be a railroad engineer. The railroad that went down through the Rich Valley crossed a corner of the Grey farm, and from the road in the afternoon they could sometimes see trains, quite far away, the smoke rolling up. There was a faint rumbling noise, and, on clear days they could see the flying piston rods of the engines.

As for the two stumps in the field near the house, they were what was left of two oak trees. The children had known the trees. They were cut one day in the early fall.

There was a back porch to the Grey house—the house that had once been the seat of the Aspinwahl family—and from the porch steps a path led down to a stone spring house. A spring came out of the ground just there, and there was a tiny stream that went along the edge of a field, past two large barns and out across a meadow to a creek—called a "branch," in Virginia, and the two trees stood close together beyond the spring house and the fence.

They were lusty trees, their roots down in the rich, always damp soil, and one of them had a great limb that came down near the ground, so that Ted and Mary could climb into it and out another limb into its brother tree, and in the fall, when other trees, at the front and side of the house, had shed their leaves, blood-red leaves still clung to the two oaks. They were like dry blood on gray days, but on other days, when the sun came out, the trees flamed against distant hills. The leaves clung, whispering and talking when the wind blew, so that the trees themselves seemed carrying on a conversation.

John Grey had decided he would have the trees cut. At first it was not a very definite decision. "I think I'll have them cut," he announced.

"But why?" his wife asked. The trees meant a good deal to her. They had been planted, just in that spot, by her grandfather, she said, having in mind just a certain effect. "You see how in the fall, when you stand on the back porch, they are so nice against the hills." She spoke of the trees, already quite large, having been brought from a distant woods. Her mother had often spoken of it. The man, her grandfather, had a special feeling for trees. "An Aspinwahl would do that," John Grey said. "There is enough yard, here about the house, and enough trees. They do not shade the house or the yard. An Aspinwahl would go to all that trouble for trees and then plant them where grass might be growing." He had suddenly determined, a half-formed determination in him suddenly hardening. He had perhaps heard too much of the Aspinwahls and their ways. The conversation regarding the trees took place at the table, at the noon hour, and Mary and Ted heard it all.

It began at the table and was carried on afterward out of doors, in the yard back of the house. The wife had followed her husband out. He always left the table suddenly and silently, getting quickly up and going out heavily, shutting doors with a bang as he went. "Don't, John," the wife said, standing on the porch and calling to her husband. It was a cold day, but the sun was out and the trees were like great bonfires against gray distant fields and hills. The older son of the family, young Don, the one so physically like the father and apparently so like him in every way, had come out of the house with the mother, followed by the two children, Ted and Mary, and at first Don said nothing, but, when the father did not answer the mother's protest but started toward the barn, he also spoke. What he said was obviously the determining thing, hardening the father.

To the two other children—they had walked a little aside and stood together watching and listening—there was something. There was their own child's world. "Let us alone and we'll let you alone." It wasn't as definite as that. Most of the definite thoughts about what happened in the yard that afternoon came to Mary Grey long afterward, when she was a grown woman. At the moment, there was merely a sudden sharpening of the feeling of isolation, a wall between herself and Ted and the others. The father, even then perhaps, seen in a new light, Don and the mother seen in a new light.

There was something, a driving destructive thing in life, in all relationships between people. All of this felt dimly that day—she always believed both by herself and Ted—but only thought out long afterward, after Ted was dead. There was the farm her father had won from the Aspinwahls—greater persistence, greater shrewdness. In a family, little remarks dropped from time to time, an impression slowly built up. The father, John Grey, was a successful man. He had acquired. He owned. He was the commander, the one having power to do his will. And the power had run out and covered not only other human lives, impulses in others, wishes, hungers in others—he himself might not have, might not even understand—but it went far out beyond that. It was, curiously, the power also of life and death. Did Mary Grey think such thoughts at that moment . . . ? She couldn't have. . . . Still, there was her own peculiar situation, her relationship with her brother Ted, who was to die.

Ownership that gave curious rights, dominances—fathers over children, men and women over lands, houses, factories in cities, fields. "I will have the trees in that orchard cut. They produce apples but not of the right sort. There is no money in apples of that sort any more."

"But, sir . . . you see . . . look . . . the trees there against that hill, against the sky."

"Nonsense. Sentimentality."

Confusion.

It would have been such nonsense to think of the father of Mary Grey as a man without feeling. He had struggled hard all his life, perhaps, as a young man, gone without things wanted, deeply hungered for. Someone has to manage things in this life. Possessions mean power, the right to say, "Do this" or "Do that." If you struggle long and hard for a thing it becomes infinitely sweet to you.

Was there a kind of hatred between the father and the older son of the Grey family? "You are one also who has this thing—the impulse to power, so like my own. Now you are young and I am growing old." Admiration mixed with fear. If you would retain power it will not do to admit fear.

The young Don was so curiously like the father. There were the same lines about the jaws, the same eyes. They were both heavy men. Already the young man walked like the father, slammed doors as did the father. There was the same curious lack of delicacy of thought and touch—the heaviness that plows through, gets things done. When John Grey had married Louise Aspinwahl he was already a mature man, on his way to success.

Such men do not marry young and recklessly. Now he was nearing sixty and there was the son—so like himself, having the same kind of strength.

Both land lovers, possession lovers. "It is my farm, my house, my horses, cattle, sheep." Soon now, another ten years, fifteen at the most, and the father would be ready for death. "See, already my hand slips a little. All of this to go out of my grasp." He, John Grey, had not got all of these possessions so easily. It had taken much patience, much persistence. No one but himself would ever quite know. Five, ten, fifteen years of work and saving, getting the Aspinwahl farm piece by piece. "The fools!" They had liked to think of themselves as aristocrats, throwing the land away, now twenty acres, now thirty, now fifty.

Raising horses that could never plow an acre of land.

And they had robbed the land too, had never put anything back, doing nothing to enrich it, build it up. Such a one thinking: "I'm an Aspinwahl, a gentleman. I do not soil my hands at the plow."

"Fools who do not know the meaning of land owned, possessions, money—responsibility. It is they who are second-rate men."

He had got an Aspinwahl for a wife and, as it had turned out, she was the best, the smartest and, in the end, the best-looking one of the lot.

And now there was his son, standing at the moment near the mother. They had both come down off the porch. It would be natural and right for this one—he being what he already was, what he would become—for him, in his turn, to come into possession, to take command.

There would be, of course, the rights of the other children. If you have the stuff in you (John Grey felt that his son Don had) there is a way to manage. You buy the others out, make arrangements. There was Ted—he wouldn't be alive—and Mary and the two younger children. "The better for you if you have to struggle."

All of this, the implication of the moment of sudden struggle between father and son, coming slowly afterward to the man's daughter, as yet little more than a child. Does the drama take place when the seed is put into the ground or afterward when the plant has pushed out of the ground and the bud breaks open, or still later, when the fruit ripens? There were the Greys with their ability—slow, saving, able, determined, patient. Why had they superseded the Aspinwahls in the Rich Valley? Aspinwahl blood also in the two children, Mary and Ted.

There was an Aspinwahl man—called "Uncle Fred," a brother to Louise Grey—who came sometimes to the farm. He was a rather striking-looking, tall old man with a gray Vandyke beard and a mustache, somewhat shabbily dressed but always with an indefinable air of class. He came from the county-seat town, where he lived now with a daughter who had married a merchant, a polite, courtly old man who always froze into a queer silence in the presence of his sister's husband.

The son Don was standing near the mother on the day in the fall, and the two children, Mary and Ted, stood apart.

"Don't, John," Louise Grey said again. The father, who had started away toward the barns, stopped.

"Well, I guess I will."

"No, you won't," said young Don, speaking suddenly. There was a queer fixed look in his eyes. It had flashed into life—something that was between the two men: "I possess . . . I will possess." The father wheeled and looked sharply at the son and then ignored him.

For a moment the mother continued pleading.

"But why, why?"

"They make too much shade. The grass does not grow."

"But there is so much grass, so many acres of grass."

John Grey was answering his wife, but now again he looked at his son. There were unspoken words flying back and forth.

"I possess. I am in command here. What do you mean by telling me that I won't?"

"Ha! So! You possess now, but soon I will possess."

"I'll see you in hell first."

"You fool! Not yet! Not yet!"

None of the words, set down above, was spoken at the moment, and afterward the daughter Mary never did remember the exact words that had passed between the two men. There was a sudden quick flash of determination in Don—even perhaps sudden determination to stand by the mother—even perhaps something else—a feeling in the young Don out of the Aspinwahl blood in him—for the moment tree love superseding grass love—grass that would fatten steers. . . .

Winner of 4-H Club prizes, champion young corn-raiser, judge of steers, land lover, possession lover.

"You won't," Don said again.

"Won't what?"

"Won't cut those trees."

The father said nothing more at the moment but walked away from the little group toward the barns. The sun was still shining brightly. There was a sharp cold little wind. The two trees were like bonfires lighted against distant hills.

It was the noon hour and there were two men, both young, employees on the farm, who lived in a small tenant house beyond the barns. One of them, a man with a harelip, was married and the other a rather handsome silent young man, boarded with him. They had just come from the midday meal and were going toward one of the barns. It was the beginning of the fall corn-cutting time and they would be going together to a distant field to cut corn.

The father went to the barn and returned with the two men. They brought axes and a long crosscut saw. "I want you to cut those two trees." There was something, a blind, even stupid determination in the man, John Grey. And at that moment his wife, the mother of his children . . . There was no way any of the children could ever know how many moments of the sort she had been through. She had married John Grey. He was her man.

"If you do, Father—" Don Grey said coldly.

"Do as I tell you! Cut those two trees!" This addressed to the two workmen. The one who had a harelip laughed. His laughter was like the bray of a donkey.

"Don't," said Louise Grey, but she was not addressing her husband this time. She stepped to her son and put a hand on his arm. "Don't."

"Don't cross him. Don't cross my man." Could a child like Mary Grey comprehend? It takes time to understand things that happen in life. Life unfolds slowly to the mind. Mary was standing with Ted, whose young face was white and tense. Death at his elbow. At any moment. At any moment.

"I have been through this a hundred times. That is the way this man I married has succeeded. Nothing stops him. I married him; I have had my children by him.

"We women choose to submit.

"This is my affair, more than yours, Don, my son."

A woman hanging onto her thing—the family, created about her.

The son not seeing things with her eyes. He shook off his

mother's hand lying on his arm. Louise Grey was younger than her husband, but, if he was now nearing sixty, she was drawing near fifty. At the moment she looked very delicate and fragile. There was something, at the moment, in her bearing— Was there, after all, something in blood, the Aspinwahl blood?

In a dim way perhaps, at the moment, the child Mary did comprehend. Women and their men. For her then, at that time, there was but one male, the child Ted. Afterward she remembered how he looked at that moment, the curiously serious old look on his young face. There was even, she thought later, a kind of contempt for both the father and brother, as though he might have been saying to himself—he couldn't really have been saying it; he was too young—"Well, we'll see. This is something. These foolish ones—my father and my brother. I myself haven't long to live. I'll see what I can while I do live."

The brother Don stepped over near to where his father stood.

"If you do, Father—" he said again.

"Well?"

"I'll walk off this farm and I'll never come back."

"All right. Go then."

The father began directing the two men who had begun cutting the trees, each man taking a tree. The young man with the harelip kept laughing, the laughter like the bray of a donkey. "Stop that," the father said sharply, and the sound ceased abruptly. The son Don walked away, going rather aimlessly toward the barn. He approached one of the barns and then stopped. The mother, white now, half ran into the house.

The son returned toward the house, passing the two younger children without looking at them, but did not enter. The father did not look at him. He went hesitatingly along a path at the front of the house and through a gate and into a road. The road ran for several miles down through the valley and then, turning, went over a mountain to the county-seat town.

As it happened, only Mary saw the son Don when he returned to the farm. There were three or four tense days. Perhaps, all the time, the mother and son had been secretly in touch. There was a telephone in the house. The father stayed all day in the fields and when he was in the house was silent.

Mary was in one of the barns on the day when Don came back and when the father and son met. It was an odd meeting.

The son came, Mary always afterward thought, rather sheepishly. The father came out of a horse's stall. He had been throwing corn to work horses. Neither the father nor the son saw Mary. There was a car parked in the barn and she had crawled into the driver's seat, her hands on the steering wheel, pretending she was driving.

"Well," the father said. If he felt triumphant, he did not show his feeling.

"Well," said the son, "I have come back."

"Yes, I see," the father said. "They are cutting corn." He walked toward the barn door and then stopped. "It will be yours soon now," he said. "You can be boss then."

He said no more and both men went away, the father toward the distant fields and the son toward the house. Mary was afterwards quite sure that nothing more was ever said.

What had the father meant?

"When it is yours you can be boss." It was too much for the child. Knowledge comes slowly. It meant:

"You will be in command, and for you, in your turn, it will be necessary to assert.

"Such men as we are cannot fool with delicate stuff. Some men are meant to command and others must obey. You can make them obey in your turn.

"There is a kind of death.

"Something in you must die before you can possess and command."

There was, so obviously, more than one kind of death. For Don Grey one kind and for the younger brother Ted, soon now perhaps, another.

Mary ran out of the barn that day, wanting eagerly to get out into the light, and afterward, for a long time, she did not try to think her way through what had happened. She and her brother Ted did, however, afterward, before he died, discuss quite often the two trees. They went on a cold day and put their fingers on the stumps, but the stumps were cold. Ted kept asserting that only men got their legs and arms cut off, and she protested. They continued doing things that had been forbidden Ted to do, but no one protested, and, a year or two later, when he died, he died during the night in his bed.

But while he lived, there was always, Mary afterward thought, a curious sense of freedom, something that belonged to him that made it good, a great happiness, to be with him. It was, she finally thought, because having to die his kind of death, he never had to make the surrender his brother had made—to be sure of possessions, success, his time to command—would never have to face the more subtle and terrible death that had come to his older brother.

Stories from

The Sherwood Anderson Reader

(1947)

The Corn Planting

THE FARMERS who come to our town to trade are a part of the town life. Saturday is the big day. Often the children come to the high school in town.

It is so with Hatch Hutchenson. Although his farm, some three miles from town, is small, it is known to be one of the best-kept and best-worked places in all our section. Hatch is a little gnarled old figure of a man. His place is on the Scratch Gravel Road and there are plenty of poorly kept places out that way.

Hatch's place stands out. The little frame house is always kept painted, the trees in his orchard are whitened with lime halfway up the trunks, and the barn and sheds are in repair, and his fields are always clean-looking.

Hatch is nearly seventy. He got a rather late start in life. His father, who owned the same farm, was a Civil War man and came home badly wounded, so that, although he lived a long time after the war, he couldn't work much. Hatch was the only son and stayed at home, working the place until his father died. Then, when he was nearing fifty, he married a schoolteacher of forty, and they had a son. The schoolteacher was a small one like Hatch. After they married, they both stuck close to the land. They seemed to fit into their farm life as certain people fit into the clothes they wear. I have noticed something about people who make a go of marriage. They grow more and more alike. They even grow to look alike.

Their one son, Will Hutchenson, was a small but remarkably strong boy. He came to our high school in town and pitched on our town baseball team. He was a fellow always cheerful, bright and alert, and a great favorite with all of us.

For one thing, he began as a young boy to make amusing little drawings. It was a talent. He made drawings of fish and pigs and cows, and they looked like people you knew. I never did know, before, that people could look so much like cows and horses and pigs and fish.

When he had finished in the town high school, Will went to Chicago, where his mother had a cousin living, and he became a student in the Art Institute out there. Another young fellow from our town was also in Chicago. He really went two years before Will did. His name is Hal Weyman, and he was a student at the University of Chicago. After he graduated, he came home and got a job as principal of our high school.

Hal and Will Hutchenson hadn't been close friends before, Hal being several years older than Will, but in Chicago they got together, went together to see plays, and, as Hal later told me, they had a good many long talks.

I got it from Hal that, in Chicago, as at home here when he was a young boy, Will was immediately popular. He was good-looking, so the girls in the art school liked him, and he had a straightforwardness that made him popular with all the young fellows.

Hal told me that Will was out to some party nearly every night, and right away he began to sell some of his amusing little drawings and to make money. The drawings were used in advertisements, and he was well paid.

He even began to send some money home. You see, after Hal came back here, he used to go quite often out to the Hutchenson place to see Will's father and mother. He would walk or drive out there in the afternoon or on summer evenings and sit with them. The talk was always of Will.

Hal said it was touching how much the father and mother depended on their one son, how much they talked about him and dreamed of his future. They had never been people who went about much with the town folks or even with their neighbors. They were of the sort who work all the time, from early morning till late in the evenings, and on moonlight nights, Hal said, and after the little old wife had got the supper, they often went out into the fields and worked again.

You see, by this time old Hatch was nearing seventy and his wife would have been ten years younger. Hal said that whenever he went out to the farm they quit work and came to sit with him. They might be in one of the fields, working together, but when they saw him in the road, they came running. They had got a letter from Will. He wrote every week.

The little old mother would come running following the father.

"We got another letter, Mr. Weyman," Hatch would cry, and then his wife, quite breathless, would say the same thing, "Mr. Weyman, we got a letter."

The letter would be brought out at once and read aloud. Hal said the letters were always delicious. Will larded them with little sketches. There were humorous drawings of people he had seen or been with, rivers of automobiles on Michigan Avenue in Chicago, a policeman at a street crossing, young stenographers hurrying into office buildings. Neither of the old people had ever been to the city and they were curious and eager. They wanted the drawings explained, and Hal said they were like two children wanting to know every little detail Hal could remember about their son's life in the big city. He was always at them to come there on a visit and they would spend hours talking of that.

"Of course," Hatch said, "we couldn't go."

"How could we?" he said. He had been on that one little farm since he was a boy. When he was a young fellow, his father was an invalid and so Hatch had to run things. A farm, if you run it right, is very exacting. You have to fight weeds all the time. There are the farm animals to take care of. "Who would milk our cows?" Hatch said. The idea of anyone but him or his wife touching one of the Hutchenson cows seemed to hurt him. While he was alive, he didn't want anyone else plowing one of his fields, tending his corn, looking after things about the barn. He felt that way about his farm. It was a thing you couldn't explain, Hal said. He seemed to understand the two old people.

It was a spring night, past midnight, when Hal came to my house and told me the news. In our town we have a night telegraph operator at the railroad station and Hal got a wire. It was really addressed to Hatch Hutchenson, but the operator brought it to Hal. Will Hutchenson was dead, had been killed. It turned out later that he was at a party with some other young fellows and there might have been some drinking. Anyway, the car was wrecked, and Will Hutchenson was killed. The operator wanted Hal to go out and take the message to Hatch and his wife, and Hal wanted me to go along.

I offered to take my car, but Hal said no. "Let's walk out," he said. He wanted to put off the moment, I could see that. So we did walk. It was early spring, and I remember every moment of the silent walk we took, the little leaves just coming on the trees, the little streams we crossed, how the moonlight made the water seem alive. We loitered and loitered, not talking, hating to go on.

Then we got out there, and Hal went to the front door of the farmhouse while I stayed in the road. I heard a dog bark, away off somewhere. I heard a child crying in some distant house. I think that Hal, after he got to the front door of the house, must have stood there for ten minutes, hating to knock.

Then he did knock, and the sound his fist made on the door seemed terrible. It seemed like guns going off. Old Hatch came to the door, and I heard Hal tell him. I know what happened. Hal had been trying, all the way out from town, to think up words to tell the old couple in some gentle way, but when it came to the scratch, he couldn't. He blurted everything right out, right into old Hatch's face.

That was all. Old Hatch didn't say a word. The door was opened, he stood there in the moonlight, wearing a funny long white nightgown, Hal told him, and the door went shut again with a bang, and Hal was left standing there.

He stood for a time, and then came back out into the road to me. "Well," he said, and "Well," I said. We stood in the road looking and listening. There wasn't a sound from the house.

And then—it might have been ten minutes or it might have been a half-hour—we stood silently, listening and watching, not knowing what to do—we couldn't go away——"I guess they are trying to get so they can believe it," Hal whispered to me. I got his notion all right. The two old people must have thought of their son Will always only in terms of life, never of death.

We stood watching and listening, and then, suddenly, after a long time, Hal touched me on the arm. "Look," he whispered. There were two white-clad figures going from the house to the barn. It turned out, you see, that old Hatch had been plowing that day. He had finished plowing and harrowing a field near the barn.

The two figures went into the barn and presently came out. They went into the field, and Hal and I crept across the farmyard to the barn and got to where we could see what was going on without being seen.

It was an incredible thing. The old man had got a hand cornplanter out of the barn and his wife had got a bag of seed corn, and there, in the moonlight, that night, after they got that news, they were planting corn.

It was a thing to curl your hair—it was so ghostly. They were both in their nightgowns. They would do a row across the field, coming quite close to us as we stood in the shadow of the barn, and then, at the end of each row, they would kneel side by side by the fence and stay silent for a time. The whole thing went on in silence. It was the first time in my life I ever understood something, and I am far from sure now that I can put down what I understood and felt that night—I mean something about the connection between certain people and the earth—a kind of silent cry, down into the earth, of these two old people, putting corn down into the earth. It was as though they were putting death down into the ground that life might grow again—something like that.

They must have been asking something of the earth, too. But what's the use? What they were up to in connection with the life in their field and the lost life in their son is something you can't very well make clear in words. All I know is that Hal and I stood the sight as long as we could, and then we crept away and went back to town, but Hatch Hutchenson and his wife must have got what they were after that night, because Hal told me that when he went out in the morning to see them and to make the arrangements for bringing their dead son home, they were both curiously quiet and Hal thought in command of themselves. Hal said he thought they had got something. "They have their farm and they have still got Will's letters to read," Hal said.

Nobody Laughed

IT WASN'T, more than others of its size, a dull town. Buzz McCleary got drunk regularly, once a month, and got arrested, and for two summers there was a minor-league professional baseball team. Sol Grey managed about getting up the ball team. He went about town to the druggist, the banker, the local Standard Oil manager, and others, and got them to put up money. Some of the players were hired outright. They were college boys having a little fun during their vacation time, getting board and cigarette money, playing under assumed names, not to hurt their amateur standing. Then there were two fellows from the coal-mining country, a hundred miles to the north, in a neighboring state. The handle factory gave these men jobs. Bugs Calloway was one of them. He was a home-run hitter and afterward got into one of the big leagues. That made the town pretty proud. "It puts us on the map," Sol Grey said.

However, the baseball team couldn't carry on. It had been in a small league and the league went to pieces. Things got dull after that. In such an emergency the town had to give attention to Hallie and Pinhead Perry.

The Perrys had been in Greenhope, Tennessee, since the town was very small. Greenhope was a town of the upper South and there had always been Perrys there, ever since long before the Civil War. There were rich Perrys, well-to-do Perrys, a Perry who was a preacher, and one who had been a brigadier general in the Northern army in the Civil War. That didn't go so well with the other well-to-do Perrys. They liked to keep reminding people that the Perrys were of the Old South.

"The Perrys are one of the oldest and best families of the Old South," they said. They kept pretty quiet about Brigadier General Perry who went over to the "damned Yanks."

As for Pinhead Perry, he, to be sure, belonged to the no-account branch of the Perrys. The tree of even the best Southern family must have some such branches. Look at the Pinametters. But let's not drag in names.

Pinhead Perry was poor. He was born poor, and he was simple. He was undersized. A girl named Mag Hunter had got into trouble with a Perry named Robert, also of the no-account Perrys, and Mag's father went over to Robert's father's house one night with a shotgun. After Robert married Mag, he left Greenhope. No one knew where he went, but everyone said he went over into a neighboring state, into the coal-mining country. He was a big man with a big nose and hard fists. "What the hell'd I want a wife for? Why keep a cow when milk's so cheap?" he said before he went away.

They called his son Pinhead, began calling him that when he was a little thing. His mother worked in the kitchens of several well-to-do families in Greenhope, but it was a little hard for her to get a job, what with Negro help so low and her having Pinhead. Pinhead was a little off in the head from the first, but not so much.

His father was a big man, but the only thing big about Pinhead was his nose. It was gigantic. It was a mountain of a nose. It was very red. It looked very strange, even grotesque, sticking on Pinhead. He was such a little scrawny thing, sitting often for a half day at a time on the kitchen step, at the back of the house of some well-to-do citizen. He was a very quiet child, and his mother, in spite of the rather hard life she had, always dressed him neatly. Other kitchen help, the white kitchen help, what there was of it in Greenhope, wouldn't have much to do with Mag Perry, and all the other Perrys were indignant at the very idea of her calling herself a Perry. It was confusing, they said. The other white kitchen help whispered. "She was only married to Bob Perry a month when the Pinhead was born," they said. They avoided Mag.

There was a philosopher in the town, a sharp-tongued lawyer who hadn't much practice. He explained. "The sex morals of America are upheld by the working classes," he said. "The financial morals are in the hands of the middle classes.

"That keeps them busy," he said.

Pinhead Perry grew up and his mother Mag died and Pinhead got married. He married one of the Albright girls—her name was Hallie—from out by Albright's Creek. She was the youngest of eight children and was a cripple. She was a little pale thing and had a twisted foot. "It oughten to be allowed," people said. They said such bad blood ought not be allowed to breed. They said, "Look at them Albrights." The Albrights were always getting into jail. They were horse traders and chicken thieves. They were moon-liquor makers.

But just the same the Albrights were a proud and defiant lot. Old Will Albright, the father, had land of his own and he had money. If it came to paying a fine to get one of his boys out of jail, he could do it. He was the kind of man who, although he had less than a hundred acres of land—most of it hillside land and not much good—and a big family, mostly boys, always getting drunk, always fighting, always getting into jail for chicken stealing or liquor making—in spite, as they said in Greenhope, of hell and high water—in spite of everything, as you see, he had money. He didn't put it in a bank. He carried it. "Old Will's always got a roll," people in town said. "It's big enough to choke a cow." The town people were impressed. It gave Will Albright a kind of distinction. That family also had big noses, and old Will had a walrus mustache.

They were rather a dirty and a disorderly lot, and they were sometimes pretty defiant, but just the same, like the Perrys and other big families of that Tennessee country, they had their family pride. They stuck together. Suppose you had a few drinks in town, on a Saturday night, and you felt a little quarrelsome and not averse to a fight yourself, and you met one of the Albright boys, say down in the lower end of town, down by the Greek restaurant, and he got gay and gave you a little of his lip and you said to him, "Come on, you big stiff, let's see what you've got."

And you got ready to sock him—

Better not do that. God only knows how many other Albrights you'd have on your hands. They'd be like Stonewall Jackson at the Battle of Chancellorsville. They'd come down on you suddenly, seemingly out of nowhere, out of the woods, as it were.

"Now you take one of that crew. You can't trust 'em. One of them'll stick a knife into you. That's what he'll do."

And, think of it, little quiet Pinhead Perry marrying into that crew. He had grown up. But that's no way to put it. He was still small and rather sick-looking. Only God knows how he had lived since his mother died.

He had become a beggar. That was it. He'd stand before one of the grocery stores, when people were coming out with packages in their hands. "Hello!" He called all the other Perrys "cousin" and that was pretty bad. "Hello, Cousin John," or "Cousin Mary," or "Kate," or "Harry." He smiled in that rather nice little way he had. His mouth looked very tiny under his big nose and his teeth had got black. He was crazy about bananas. "Hello, Cousin Kate, give me a dime, please. I got to get me some bananas."

And there were men, you know, the smart alecks of the town, taking up with him too, men who should have known better, encouraging him.

That lawyer—his father was a Yank, from Ohio—the philosophic one, always making wise cracks about decent people—getting Pinhead to sweep out his office—he let him sleep up there—and Burt McHugh, the plumber, and Ed Cabe, who ran the poolroom down by the tracks . . .

"Pinhead, I think you'd better go up and see your Cousin Tom. He was asking for you. I think he'll give you a quarter."

Cousin Tom Perry was the cashier of the biggest bank in town.

One of those fellows, damn smart alecks, had seen Judge Buchanan. The Perrys and the Buchanans were the two big families of the county. They'd seen Judge Buchanan go into the bank. He was a director. There was going to be a directors' meeting. There were other men going in. You could depend on Pinhead's walking right into the directors' room where they had the big mahogany table and the mahogany chairs. The Buchanans sure liked to take down the Perrys.

"You go in there, Pinhead. Cousin Tom has been asking for you. He wants to give you a quarter."

"Lordy," said Burt McHugh, the plumber, "Cousin Tom give him a quarter, eh? Why, he'd as soon give him an automobile."

Pinhead took up with the Albrights. They liked him. He'd go out there and stay for weeks. The Albright place was three miles out of town. On a Saturday night, and sometimes all day on Sundays, there'd be a party out there.

There'd be moon-whisky, plenty of that, and sometimes there'd be some of the men from town, even sometimes men who should have known better, men like Ed Cabe and that smarty lawyer, or even maybe Willy Buchanan, the Judge's youngest son, the one who drank so hard and who, they said, had a cancer.

And all kinds of rough people too.

There were two older Albright girls, unmarried, Sally and Kath erine, and it was said they were "putting out."

Drinking, and sometimes dancing and singing and general hell raising and maybe a fight or two.

"What the hell?" old Will Albright said—his wife was dead and Sally and Katherine did the housework—"What the hell? It's my farm. It's my house. A man's king in his own house, ain't he?"

Pinhead grew fond of the little crippled Albright girl, little twisted-footed Hallie, and he'd sit out there in that house, with dancing and that kind of a jamboree going on. He'd sit in a corner of the big untidy bare room at the front of the house, two of the Albright boys playing guitars and singing rough songs at the top of their voices.

If the Albright boys were sullen and looking for a fight when they came to town, they weren't so much like that at home. They'd be singing some song like "Hand Me Down My Bottle of Moon," and that one about the warden and the prisoners in the jail, you know, on a Christmas morning, the warden trying to be Santa Claus to the boys, and what the hard-boiled prisoners said to him, and the two older Albright girls would be dancing, maybe with a couple of the men from town, and old Will Albright—he was sure boss in his own family—sitting over near the fireplace, chewing tobacco and keeping time with his feet. He'd spit clean and sharp right through his walrus mustache and never leave a trace. That lawyer said he could keep perfect time, with his feet and his jaws going together. "Look at it," he said. "There ain't another man in Tennessee can spit like old Will."

Pinhead sitting quiet, over in a corner, with his Hallie. They both smiling softly, Pinhead didn't drink. He wouldn't. "You let him alone. He's good. Don't bother him. He's got a pure heart and I understand that," Will Albright said to his boys. The couple got married one Saturday night and there was a big party, everyone howling drunk. Two of the guests wrecked a car trying to get back to town, and one of them, Henry Howard—a nice young fellow, a clerk in Williamson's dry-goods store; you wouldn't think he would want to associate with such people—got his arm broken. Will Albright gave Pinhead and Hallie ten acres of land—good enough land; not so almighty good—down by the creek at the foot of the hill, and he and the boys built them a house. It wasn't much of a house, but you could live in it if you were hardy.

Neither Pinhead nor Hallie was so very hardy.

They lived. They had children. People said there had been "ten of them children." Pinhead and Hallie were getting pretty old. It was after the Albrights were all gone. Pinhead was seventy and Hallie was even older. Women in town said, "How could she ever have had all of those children?"

"I'd like to know," they said.

The children were nearly gone. Some had died. An officer had descended on the family and four of the children had been carried off to a state institution.

There were left only Pinhead and Hallie and one daughter. They had managed to cling to her, and to the little strip of land given them by Will Albright, but the house, a mere shed in the beginning, was now in ruins. Every day the three people set out for town where now, the philosophic lawyer being dead, a new one had taken his place. There will always be at least one such smarty in every town. This one was a tall, slender young man who had inherited money and was fond of race horses.

He was also passionately fond of practical jokes.

The plumber Burt McHugh was also gone, but there were new men—Ed Hollman, the sheriff; Frank Collins, another young lawyer; Joe Walker, who owned the hotel; and Bob Cairn, who ran the weekly newspaper of Greenhope.

These were the men who with Sol Grey and others had helped organize the baseball team. They went to every game. When the team disbanded they were heartbroken.

And there was Pinhead, coming into town followed by Hallie and the one daughter. Ruby was her name. Ruby was tall and gaunt and cross-eyed. She was habitually silent and had an odd habit. Let some man or woman stop on the sidewalk and look steadily at her for a moment and she would begin to cry. When she did it, Pinhead and Hallie both ran to her. She was so tall that they had to stand on tiptoes and reach up, but they both began patting her thin cheeks, her gaunt shoulders. "There, there," they said.

It didn't turn out so badly. When someone had made Ruby cry, it usually ended by Pinhead collecting a nickel or a dime. He'd go up to the guilty one and smile softly. "Give her a little something and she'll quit," he'd say. "She wants a banana."

He had kept to his plea for bananas. It amused people, was the best way to get money. He, Hallie and Ruby always walked into town single file, Pinhead walking in front—although he was old now, he was still alive and alert—then came Hallie—her hair hanging down in strings about her little pinched face, and she had a goiter—and then Ruby, very tall, and in the summer, barelegged. Summer or winter Hallie wore the same dress.

It had been black. It had been given her by a widow. There was a little black hat that perched oddly on her head. The dress had been black but it had been patched with cloth of many colors. The colors blended. There was a good deal of discussion of the dress in town. No two people agreed on its color. Everything depended on the angle at which she approached you.

Pinhead and his family came into town every day to beg. They begged food at the back doors of houses. The town had grown and many new people had come in. Formerly the Perrys came into town along a dirt road, passing town people, who, when there had been a shower and the road was not too dusty, were out for a drive in buggies and phaetons, but now the road was paved and they passed automobiles. It was too bad for the Perrys. The family was still prosperous and had increased in numbers and standing. None of the other Perrys drove out of town by that road.

It was Sol Grey, the man who had managed about getting up the baseball team, who got up the plan that dull summer for having fun with Pinhead.

He told the others. He told the two young lawyers and Ed Hollman, the sheriff. He told Joe Walker, the hotel man, and Bob Cairn, who was editor of the newspaper.

He explained. "I was in front of Herd's grocery," he said. He had just been standing there when the three Perrys had come along. He thought that Pinhead had intended to ask him for a nickel or a dime. Anyway Pinhead had stopped before Sol, and then Hallie and Ruby had stopped. Sol said he must have been thinking of something else. Perhaps he was trying to think of some new way to break the monotony of life in Greenhope that summer. He found himself staring hard and long, not at Ruby but at Hallie Perry.

He did it unconsciously, like that, and didn't know how long he had kept it up, but suddenly there had come a queer change over Pinhead.

"Why, you all know Pinhead," Sol Grey said. They were all gathered that day before Doc Thomson's drugstore. Sol kept bending over and slapping his knees with his hands as he told of what had happened. He had been staring at Hallie that way, not thinking of what he was doing, and Pinhead had got suddenly and furiously jealous.

Up to that moment, no one in town had ever seen Pinhead angry.

"Well, did he get sore!" Sol Grey cried. He shook with laughter.

Pinhead had begun to berate him. "You let my woman alone!

"What do you mean, staring at my woman?

"I won't have any man fooling with my woman."

It was pretty rich. Pinhead had got the idea into his head that Sol—he was a lumber and coal dealer; a man who took pride in his clothes; a married man—the crazy loon had thought Sol was trying to make up to his Hallie. It was something gaudy. It was something to talk and to laugh about. It was something to work on. Sol said that Pinhead had offered to fight him. "My God!" cried Joe Walker. Pinhead Perry was past seventy by that time and there was Hallie with her lame foot and with her goiter.

And all three of the Perrys so hopelessly dirty.

"My God! Oh my Lord! He thinks she's beautiful!" Joe Walker cried.

"Swell," said Bob Cairn. The newspaperman, who was always looking for ideas, had one at once.

The plan had innumerable funny angles and all the men went to work. They began stopping Pinhead on the street. He would be coming along, followed by the two women, but the man who had stopped the little procession would draw Pinhead aside. "It's like this," he'd say. He'd declare he hated to bring the matter up, but he thought he should. "A man's a man," he'd say. "He can't have other men fooling around with his woman." It was so much fun to see the serious, baffled, hurt look in old Pinhead's eyes.

The man, who had taken Pinhead aside, spoke of an evening—a night, in fact, of the past. He said he had been out at night and had come into town past Pinhead's house. There was no road out that way and Pinhead and his two women, when they made their daily trip into town, had to follow a cowpath along Albright Creek to get into the main road, but the man did not bother to take that into account.

"I was going along the road past your house," he'd say and would suggest that no doubt Pinhead was asleep. Certain very respectable men of the town were named as having been seen creeping away from Pinhead's house. There was Hal Pawsey. He kept the jewelry store in Greenhope and was a very shy modest man.

Pinhead rushed into Pawsey's store and began to shout. The wife of the Baptist minister was in the store at the time. She was seeing about getting her watch fixed. Hallie and Ruby were outside on the sidewalk and they were both crying. Pinhead began beating with his fists on the glass show case in the store. He broke the case. He used such language that he frightened the Baptist minister's wife so that she ran out of the store.

That was one incident of the summer but there were many others. The hotel man, the newspaperman, the lawyer, Sol Grey and several others kept busily at work.

They got Pinhead to tackle a stranger in town, a traveling man, coming out of a store with bags in his hand, and Pinhead got arrested and had to serve a term in jail. It was the first time he'd ever been in a fight or in jail.

Then, when he was let out, they began again. It was swell. It was so much fun. There was a story going around town that Pinhead had begun to beat his wife and that she took it stoically. Someone had seen him doing it on the road into town. They said she just stood and took it and didn't cry much.

The men kept it going.

One evening, when the moon was shining and the corn was getting knee-high, several of the men went in a car out to Pinhead's house. They left the car in the road and crept through bushes until they got quite near to the house.

One of them had given Pinhead some money and had advised him to spend it on a small bag of flour. The men in the bushes could see into the open door of the shack. "My God," said Joe Walker. "Look!" he said. "He's got her tied to a chair!

"Ain't that rich!" he said.

Pinhead had Hallie sitting in the one chair of the one-room house—the roof was almost gone and when it rained the water poured in—and he was tying her to the chair with a piece of rope. Someone of the men had told Pinhead that another man of the town had planned to visit the house that night.

The men from town lay in the bushes and watched. The tall daughter, Ruby, was on the porch outside and she was crying. Pinhead, having got his wife tied to the chair, was scattering flour on the floor of the room and on the porch outside. He backed away from Hallie, scattering the flour. Hallie was crying. When he had got to the door and, as he was backing across the narrow rickety front porch, he scattered the flour thickly. The idea was that if any one of Hallie's lovers came, his footprints would stay in the flour.

Pinhead came out into a little yard at the front and got under a bush. He sat on the ground under the bush. In the moonlight the men from town could see him quite plainly. They said afterwards that he also began to cry. For some reason, even to the men of Greenhope, who were trying as best they could to get through a dull summer, the scene from the bushes before Pinhead's house that night had suddenly lost its fun.

They crept out from under the bushes and got back to their car and into town. Sol Grey went to the drugstore and began telling the story. There was quite a crowd of men standing about and Sol told the story with a flourish but nobody laughed. It was as though they had all suddenly begun disliking each other. They just looked at Sol. One by one they walked quietly away.

A Part of Earth

I HAD given a banker in Chicago a suggestion about a certain business in which he had money and it had worked. Although my intimate friends never will believe it, I have a head for affairs. Theodore Dreiser once laughed at the notion. "If you have a head for business, then I have one for breeding sheep," he said. But he was wrong.

The banker had a talk with me. "Why, what the hell, man, why haven't you money?" He declared he would put me in.

He had heard I was a writer. He had a son in the University of Chicago, and in one of the son's classes a professor had spoken favorably of a book of mine. "He tells me you are pretty good." The banker had a friend in New York who had large holdings in one of the movie companies. "Why not let me speak to him about getting you on? I understand there's big money in it for you writers."

The son had told him I was something of a high-brow. "I know it isn't true," he said, "but let me think so." He tried to explain an idea of his to me. He was himself interested in art. He bought paintings. He had married a woman who was somewhat of a high-brow. And he had read things about painters and poets who starved all their lives. That was all nonsense.

From the suggestion I had given him he could see I had a head for business. So if I wanted to write books that wouldn't sell, why not wait?

I could write the stuff the movies wanted for a time, get myself some dough. Then I could cut it out. I remember that when I had this conversation with the banker, we were dining. He had taken me to an expensive restaurant. The idea he was proposing to me had been held up to me by many others.

Physically he was a fine specimen of a man, and he had a passion for race horses. We had had conversations about them. "They are such clear fine creatures, not tricky as we are. A good one will give you all he's got. He likes to."

The conversation drifted back to my own situation. "There you are working in that advertising agency, in a minor place, at a piker job."

"Yes. They don't pay me much. For them my salary is a small affair. But just because my salary is comparatively small, I can occasionally get off, waste time in some town. They do not mind."

"Man, have you no ambition? Don't you want to be something? You could take on this job for a time. Then you could get out."

"Like you?" I said. He stared at me.

"I see," he said, "you mean—"

He had got it all right. I did not want to be as he was, spending my life working at something I did not care about. He owned a string of race horses, but hired a man to train them. I had been to his stables with him.

There was the fellow at the stables, the trainer, a man of the banker's own age, a solid-looking quiet man. He was a man of parts, I thought, had his feet on the ground. "Why not?" I thought. The fellow was taking the beautiful graceful young creatures, training them, watching them from day to day, picking the good ones, those that had it.

A minor man in a minor place, eh? The banker standing there. He owned the horses. For this one he had paid so and so many dollars, et cetera. The trainer seemed to be reading my thoughts. I had seen something like envy of that other fellow in the banker's eyes; the trainer of his horses, his servant. I had not been able to keep from smiling. As we walked over to a two-year-old, a young stallion, a tall yellow boy, the trainer, turned and looked hard at me. It was as though he had spoken, "Keep your thoughts to yourself!"

"But you do want money, don't you?" It was the banker speaking that noon in the restaurant.

"God, yes." How I did want it! I thought. It was that I just didn't want to earn it. I didn't even want to deserve it. I wanted what it could mean, escape from the advertising agency, from buying and selling, and other things. My glances went about the restaurant. Beautifully dressed women were sitting at the tables. I was in love at the time (I always was in love). I saw myself taking the woman I loved into an expensive shop, buying her beautiful clothes, expensive furs, elegant shoes; saw myself buying beautiful things for myself too. Whenever I saw rich fabrics, my fingers ached to touch them.

"Sure I want money. Why don't you give me some?"

A laugh. "Not me," said the banker. I understood. Spending his life as he was, doing something he didn't care about for the sake of a freedom he imagined he would get, but which really would never come to him, he wanted me to pay for my freedom.

"You won't," I said. "You couldn't set me free while you remain in prison." We sat staring at one another. There are moments when men who instinctively like one another also can hate. "Be careful. Do not get too close to the truth when talking with the rich," I was whispering to myself.

He switched the conversation. "What do you get out of it?"

"I'll tell you." And after a minute I began describing to him something which happened to me on a certain day of my life and a certain night in a Chicago rooming house following the day. I began with the morning. During all of it, I told him, I had sat at my desk by a window in a room of the advertising agency. It was a little room, quite crowded with advertising writers. The other offices of the agency occupied the entire floor of the building. They were big offices, and men sat in them, one in each office.

These were the businessmen. They brought advertisers, "clients" they were called, into the agency. They went forth, traveled up and down in fast trains, played golf with manufacturers. Once I had traveled with one of these men, grown rich now, on a train. He was taking me to see a client, a certain large manufacturer. He boasted how he had gotten the client for our house. "I got him with my little old studbook," he said, taking a little notebook out of a pocket. It was filled with the names and addresses of women. He had got the manufacturer a little drunk, introduced him to one of these women.

"And after that?"

There had been a little case of blackmail, one businessman coming into a hotel room, the other businessman in bed there with the woman. The click of a camera. "I told him I destroyed the negative, but he won't believe it. Why shouldn't his account be in our house? We have got some pretty smart advertising writers. You know that."

That morning the man who had shown me his studbook was in one of the big offices at the front of the building. There was an expensive rug on the floor. He was sitting at a big mahogany desk. But no. It had been March, and cold and rainy. He was off with some "client" playing golf in Florida. But see what muddled creatures people are! The same man who had boasted of his slickness in getting the new big client for our house only two weeks previously had called me to his office. He had heard I had published a book. "You come home some night with me," he said. "You bring a notebook. I'll tell you the story of my life. It is a wonderful story. Often I have wished I could write," he continued, and began telling me of his wife, what a fine, pure woman she was. He also had a daughter and a son. What plans he had for them. "I have had to wade through muck," he said, "but I have done it to give them all a finer way of life." He loved his wife, he declared, and had been true to her. "Of course," he said, "sometimes when I have been out with a client, you understand—he wanted a woman. Perhaps we were a little drunk. But my wife is a wonderful person."

In any case, that morning I had been given an assignment. I was to write a series of advertisements for the daily newspapers playing up a new cathartic. I was to spend the day delving in the mysteries of bowels. I had come in through wet streets, some of the other advertising writers were already there. "Hello, girls."

I explained to the banker that we in the "copy department" were making a struggle. "For God's sake, let us keep trying. It may be we can hold on." Two or three of us dreamt of some day becoming real writers. This fellow was, in secret, working on a play, that fellow on a novel. Sometimes at lunch in some little saloon we talked it over among ourselves. "We are little male harlots. We lie with these businessmen. Let us at least try keeping our minds a little clear. Don't let's fall for this dope that we are doing something worth doing, here."

"Hello, girls," I had repeated.

"Good morning, Mabel." There was a fat copy man who always addressed me as "Mabel." He had already heard of my assignment. "Mabel, they have got you a new man."

"Yes. He deals in excretions." The fat man had worked out a theory of life. He believed in heaven and hell. "It's as plain as the nose on your face," he used to say, "all the people in this life have lived before. They have been sinners in another life and are being punished for it. We might as well face the facts. We are in the advertising department of hell."

I told the banker who sat listening in silence that several people who had worked in that room with me had committed suicide. Others had become drunkards. Sitting in the little back room we could look across a street into a loft where they made cheap women's dresses. One woman sat over there by her window, never looking up. How her fingers flew! There was a kind of insanity of speed in her fingers. Sometimes at night in my dreams I saw them flying, flying thus. There were many women's fingers flying, flying, flying. Perhaps they were making some man rich.

For possibly an hour or even two hours I had worked at the series of advertisements. Thoughts of my mother came into my mind. Her life had been much like that of the woman over there in the loft across the street. Her fingers also were never quiet. They were flying, flying, trying to earn food to raise five sons. And that day was one of those on which I rebelled. These rebellions were always happening in the advertising place. Our bosses had to allow for them. "Come on, Little Eva," I called to the fat man. In recognition of our common harlotry he was "Little Eva" as I was "Mabel." He was a man who might have weighed two hundred and fifty. "Come on, let's get a drink." Formerly he had been a newspaperman, but had come into advertising because there was more money in it. He had a growing family, several sons and a daughter. "I want to give them an education, give them at least a chance at a more cultured life."

"So that, in the end, they may be ashamed of their father?"

"Yes."

We started out, went from bar to bar, made our way, not into the busy part of town, but into side streets. Some instinct led us to tough saloons. "Have another, Mabel?" "No, Little Eva. This one's on me." There were down-and-outs hanging about. They leered at us. "What have we here, a pair of fairies?" All of this was part of our satisfaction. We were getting a little drunk. "Shall we go back to the office? Maybe now while I'm drunk I can get through that series of advertisements." "No. We won't go back today. Hell is there, but it is also here. We are destined to live our lives in hell. It may even be that this place is not hell. It may be purgatory. Let us go about, seeing how other people live in purgatory."

It might have been five o'clock when I left the fat hell man to go to my hall bedroom. It was on the North Side. For a while I lingered on one of the river bridges. (This was before the great new bridges were built.) It was one of the old rickety wooden bridges that turned to let vessels pass up and down the stream, and beyond lay the crowded noisy place called South Water Street, where most of the food for the millions in the city was sold. It was a crazy hell of a place and today there was a cold rain, but the bridges were nice. The color of the river water was the apple green of semiprecious stones, and above the moving vessels sea gulls screamed and circled. A suggestion of a wide freedom, the sea's and the upper air's, both bare of men, somehow reached me. I was trying to write poetry at the time, and people with me on the turning bridge stared at me standing there and muttering words. I searched for ugly words for the ugliness of life, for beautiful words to express its beauty. Once in my room, I did not remove my wet clothes. As ever when I was drunk my imagination played madly. With head awhirl I lay on my bed, staring through my window into the rainy street, and figures began appearing before my eyes. It may be that I slept and wakened. The street lights had been lit. I sat up.

Does all of this seem trivial? I am trying to tell it again as I told it all to the banker at the lunch table.

There I was, sitting at the edge of the bed in that room. It was dark, but on the wall lay a spot of light cast by a street lamp.

"So, this is my life? This is what I am, what has become of me."

"Never mind your life. It is unimportant what has become of you. It is the disease of the world, questioning what you are or are not." Almost it seemed as though a voice in the room had spoken the words.

Faces of people kept passing in and out of the fleck of light. Dim shadows of reality, they whirled and danced, some of them parts of myself, others of other people. Again it seemed something was speaking, saying, "All of life is too much up in my head." This time I recognized the voice. It was that of one of the people, the woman in our office who had committed suicide. Of an afternoon she had gone to a department store and bought a revolver. She had sent it with cartridges to the little hotel where she roomed. This was at the lunch hour, and she went back to her desk and worked during the afternoon. She was, I thought, a rather attractive woman and that day as she was leaving the office she had spoken to me.

"Walk a little with me," she said. We went along through the hurrying crowd. I "missed" her. There was something I should have sensed, but did not. It must have been one of the days when I soaked with self-pity. We went through streets, she talking, seemingly very brightly, very cheerfully. She kept making sarcastic remarks about herself. "I'll tell you of an experience I had," she said, and told me a tale of going out one night into the street to pick up a man. She had seen prostitutes doing it and wanted to know what it must be like. "I'd been another kind so long and wanted to see what it would be like going the whole way." But she couldn't, physically or otherwise, and had to give it up. "I spoke to two or three men, but they hurried away." She thought they might have mistaken her for a detective. Her failure was due, she thought, to the fact that the whole thing was too much just up in her head. "That's the trouble with me. All my life is too much up in my head," and that evening when I left her she went home to her hotel and with the revolver blew her head out of the picture.

"And so it is also with you." This had been myself speaking to myself in the dark room. I had got up and lit the light. I had suddenly become quite sober. In all my writing, I knew, I had been using only my head. I had never let other people with their lives come into me. "This is what it is all about," said I to myself. "It's got to come down from your head and meet people."

Among the figures on the wall there had been one of a little frightened man. Perhaps it came out of some memory of my own, a face seen sometimes on the street, a story told by some man in a barroom, as well as out of the experience that very day, the fat man calling me "Mabel," me calling him "Eva," and our suspiciousness in the eyes of other men, hangers-on in the cheap barrooms. But something else was mixed in it. Out of them seemed to speak the passionate desire in all people to be understood, to have their stories told, perhaps that the terrible isolation of their lives may break. I went to my table and began writing. The story is called "Hands"; it is in *Winesburg*. In sudden almost terrible joy afterwards I had walked up and down my room. "It's there, it's solid. No matter if no one understands its implications. It's sound. For once in my life I've been a part of earth."

All writers, painters, actors, all men of the arts, have had such hours. They are something also known by workmen. Good farmers have the feeling, too. There was a piece of land, neglected, overcropped for too many years, gone to pot, scraggly weeds growing, and it had come into the hands of the good farmer. He had gone to work, was patient, a land lover. He had fed the field, slowly enriched it, gotten at last a stand of clover, plowed it under. Wait now. He has given all he has. At last a day has come.

"Look." You are leaning beside him on the fence at the field's edge. "Look," he says. His figure straightens. He is even a little embarrassed, boasting to you. "The finest stand of corn in all this section. You should have seen this field some five years ago when I got it."

Perhaps race horses have such hours, too. I remember trying to tell all of this to my banker. "I hope I've answered your question," I said, and added, "Yes, indeed, I want money. I merely do not want to have to earn it, to do what you call deserve it. Will you give it to me?"

"No," he laughed. It wasn't a very pleasant laugh. "You think," he added, "you have got now and then a thing I cannot get."

"I don't mean that at all," I said. "Everyone can have it. I mean you won't have it."

He paid the bill. "You'd better keep your money," I said. "You go to hell," he replied. Later I heard that he had sold his string of race horses.

Morning Roll Call

PEOPLE. They parade before you at night. There was Smoky Pete. He was a solidly built man, unmarried, who lived with his old mother. He had been a soldier of sorts, but could not get into the G.A.R. Father and other veterans said he had been a bounty jumper.

He was a gay, defiant man, always ready for a fight. In the spring he worked in his mother's garden, but he did no other work for the rest of the year. Perhaps his mother had a small income.

He filled a basket with vegetables and came down along the railroad track to our main street. He was intent upon trading the vegetables to some saloonkeeper for a morning drink. He shouted. He laughed loudly. He sang.

"What's the use of being poor when you can own the whole world for ten cents?" he shouted. Ten cents was the prevailing price of a drink of bar whisky.

It was Smoky Pete who started our morning roll call. He became a corrector of the morals of the town. He spread terror through the town.

His mother's house was on a street out near the edge of town and in the early morning, intent on his morning drink, he went along the street to the railroad and along the tracks toward Main Street. It was the quiet hour, a spring, summer, or fall morning. Smoky Pete swaggered along. There was a gleam in his eyes. He had a short black General Grant beard and smoked a short-stemmed clay pipe. The smoke lay like a cloud in mountain forests in his beard.

It was a day of meat-and-potato breakfasts. The wives of the town were old-fashioned friers. There was none of the modern orange-juice, toast-and-coffee addicts among the breakfasters of that day.

The women of the town bought cheap cuts of round steak at the local meat market. Somewhere near the outer edge of every Middle Western town there was a slaughterhouse filled with rats and flies and surrounded by a field piled high with bones of old cows. The women took the cheap steaks home and laid them on a board. They beat the steaks with a hammer. They pounded away. There was a drumming sound as of a hundred woodpeckers at work.

Smoky Pete was coming up the railroad track, swaggering along. Some citizen of the town had sinned. It might be a man who worked in the bank, or a merchant. It might even be a man who taught a class in the Sunday school of one of our churches.

There were in our town, as in all towns, certain women and girls. They were known as "pushovers." They were "putting out." Men met them in the evening on a side street of the town. The automobile had not come yet, but almost every man in town owned a horse and buggy.

The pushover was gotten in. Alas, often she was gathered in by some respectable married man of the town. The pushover was driven off into some quiet country lane. What ho!

But someone had slipped the word to Smoky Pete. The clerks in the stores along Main Street, having swept out the stores, were now sweeping the sidewalks before them. One of them raised his voice. The name of the man who had secretly, he had hoped, met Sally Graves in the dark street, down by the Seventh Day Adventist Church on the night before, who had got Sally into his buggy and had driven off with her into the darkness, was shouted over the roofs of the town.

"John Huntington."

Alas, poor John.

So you thought no one saw you pick up Sally, eh?

There was some clerk with a malicious streak in his make-up. "John Huntington." The name so hurled forth floated through the quiet morning streets of the town and housewives who had been busily beating breakfast steaks quit beating. They ran quickly to kitchen doors. They were waiting for Smoky Pete's answering voice from down the railroad tracks.

It came.

"S-s-s-s-l-y Graves."

There was an outburst of laughter from the clerks.

"P. T. Smith."

A fresh cry, "Mary Thompson." Poor Mary had a bad leg. She went hopping about. She hopped into dark corners with men and boys at night.

"P. T. Smith," yelled the clerks, again.

"Mary Thompson," came the echo.

It was all very cruel. It got Smoky Pete into endless fights, but he did not mind. Well, the G.A.R. wouldn't take him in. There was something wrong with his war record. He was having a good time. He was getting men. Some man of the town was always slipping him the dirt of the town.

At the county seat there was a certain house run by one Nell Hunter.

Again some respectable man's foot had slipped. He had, on a certain night, gone secretly to that place. He hoped his going would remain unknown.

He was at home now, in his own house, waiting for his breakfast, but at the sound of Smoky Pete's voice—a far-carrying one, floating thus through the quiet morning streets—he trembled.

Had someone seen him slipping into the house in the darkness?

The names of respectable men were being called off. There were twenty or thirty clerks standing now before the Main Street stores with brooms in their hands. If his name was bawled out thus by one of the clerks, it would be difficult, if not impossible, to name the culprit.

A. G. Bottomly. Bottomly had told his wife that he had to go to the county seat on business.

And now, Ye Gods, there it was!

"A. G. Bottomly." And then the answering cry from Smoky Pete.

"Nell Hunter."

It was something to drive a man mad. Late that day there would be a fight on Main Street, but what did it matter to Smoky Pete? He enjoyed fighting. He was almost always victorious in fights.

Smoky Pete advanced along the railroad track, past the railroad station, calling off names, connecting thus the names of often respectable citizens with females of ill repute. If it was spring, he carried the little basket of vegetables on his arm. He was pleased with himself and with life. He was creating trouble. He was stirring up fights. He was getting even with life. He advanced to the middle of Main Street and turned to face the clerks standing along the street before the stores. He put a hand up to his mouth, made a trumpet of his hand. His voice rolled up the street and was followed by a loud outburst of laughter. All the men of the town, whose names had not been called off in Smoky Pete's morning roll call, laughed. Women whose men were not involved giggled as they went back to their steak pounding. The old impulse in man to enjoy heartily the discomfiture of others shook the town with laughter.

Smoky Pete was standing erect, like a soldier at the foot of our Main Street. He had made a trumpet of his hand.

"Go-o-o-od Damn!" His voice rolled up the street, as it died away was followed by the outburst of laughter. The morning roll call was at an end. Three or four more citizens had been thus jerked up to stand trembling under the judgment of the town.

The Yellow Gown

I LAUGHED and stretched myself. "Work now, you slave."

"Well, what shall I do? Shall I go to work in a factory? In me there is no gift for the factories. I work and work but do not rise. You see I have read all the books. I knew that in a factory, when a man has done his work well, he is promoted. At night he takes a course in something—well, let us say in mechanical engineering —and then, some day in the factory there is a problem to solve and he solves it."

"But I cannot solve any problems. Do you not understand that figures mean nothing to me?"

"But, my dear man, you will have to work. Go then to a store. Get a job as a clerk. Be honest. There must be a way in which you can rise in the world. You should cultivate respectable people."

When I had got out of doors the sun was shining. I lived at that time in a room near a park in the city of Chicago and when I had walked in the park and had eaten my breakfast at a nearby lunch counter I stood for a moment on the street. "Shall I go look for work or shall I go call on Harold?" The trouble with me is that I cannot solve problems. As I walked along I became suddenly gloomy. "I'm in for trouble," I said to myself.

But I never had thought it would come as it did. I had not thought it would come from the woman named Mildred.

For months, I had been Harold's shadow and, I am afraid, half his servant. He was called the prize student of the Art Institute at that time and the girl students all worshiped him, but Mildred had won him. It was even said— Well, he had a studio and Mildred went there almost any time. We, who were their friends, did not use the word, but we thought, perhaps we hoped— Romance of just that sort is so hard to come at in Chicago.

She also was an art student and very quick and facile at making pleasant little drawings, but no one took her art seriously. Harold was, however, a different matter. He was a Modern. A painting of his had once been accepted and hung at a show of young moderns in New York City. I remember it now as a wild thing of red and white perpendicular lines across which went meandering a river of red and it was called, I believe, "The Red Laugh," after something Harold had read by the Russian Andreyev.

At the moment, however, and just at the time when I had become most intimate with him, Harold was up to something else. He was, in fact, in the act of showing the Chicago art world how a man of talent goes about it to win the prize in the annual fall show.

At the moment I was not working and was consequently happy and contented with life and had been so for a long time, but my money was beginning to give out. I was living in a cheap rooming house, but was living as best I could the life of leisure. In the evening I went to Harold's room or to the room of some other student and in the morning stayed in my bed. And what joy I had of life! Why get up? I had cigarettes and matches on a chair beside the bed.

Harold had a studio in what had once been a small store in the neighborhood and slept on a cot at the back. I dare say Mildred grew tired of always having me about, but Harold seemed glad of my presence in the afternoons. Perhaps I saved him from her too great ardor.

Until—well, until the great scheme had been hatched.

The great scheme was that Harold should paint a perfectly conventional picture for the fall show and win the prize. It was to be an interior. There was to be a corner of a ladies' dressing room of the old rich days, say of the fifteenth century in Italy, with a window looking out upon a rolling country, hill after hill getting smaller and smaller in the distance, such hills as Titian or Raphael liked to put into the backgrounds of their canvases.

The interior of the room would be somewhat somber, a heavily carved chair sitting before an equally heavily carved table near the window.

And across the back of the chair—ah, there was the point—across the back of the chair would be thrown— Harold was so excited about the whole matter when I went to him early that afternoon that it took him a long time to talk at all.

Across the back of the chair would be thrown a woman's heavy yellow velvet gown.

At first I could not understand Harold's excitement concerning the gown, but as he talked I began a little to understand. The folds of the gown should be made to fall in just a certain way. Harold had, in fact, got hold of such a gown as he intended painting into the picture in a secondhand store in lower State Street, Chicago, in a place where women's dresses, that had once belonged to members of the fashionable world and later perhaps been given to servants, had now been put on sale. In a place, in fact, where they were likely to catch the best trade for such wares; that is to say, in a street much frequented at that time by the women of the town.

It may have been that seeing the gown in the store window had put the notion of the painting into Harold's head and he had gone into the store and had bought it at once and now had it in the studio. Its presence there was, I could see at once, a queer sort of shock to Mildred. He kept walking across the room and throwing it across the back of a chair (not the heavily carved chair of the picture—that he would get out of a book at the institute or the public library, he explained; it would be, he thought, Spanish and very rococo—but across a kitchen chair he had bought at a nearby furniture store).

He flung the gown over the back of the chair, arranged the folds a little, picked it up again, walked across the room and again pitched it at the chair. "The thing may have to be carefully arranged, but there is a chance it may fall just right," he said, while Mildred and I looked on in wonder. The gown, he explained, was to be the central point of his painting. There it would be in the corner of the dark somber room with the dark somber landscape in the distance. Other things in the picture, the chair, the table, the hills, he could paint in quickly enough, saving all the best of himself for the painting of the gown. It was there, in the painting of the gown, he would show the old painters something. He would paint the soft rich velvet lying in folds in such a way that the committee, the men who were to hang and judge the pictures, would be fairly knocked off their feet. Did he not know such fellows? Ah, he would get them. Their feelings, their sensuality, would be worked on without their knowing. There would be brush work, color, the feel for texture. Men who had always painted in the conventional way and whose natures had become dried and half dead were always saying that men like himself, Gauguin, Cézanne, and the others, were only trying to avoid the real challenge of painting, but he would show them. I do not remember that Harold, when he called the roll of the great moderns in his studio that afternoon, put himself among them, but at least he implied something of the sort.

He would so paint the woman's dress that the power women were able to exert over all men, because of men's sensual natures, would unconsciously be felt by everyone who looked at the painting. "For the time being, for weeks perhaps, while I am doing the painting, I shall be in love, actually and physically in love with an imagined woman of old times who once wore this dress. I am sitting, you see, at the back of the room waiting for her. The dress is lying across the back of the chair, but, as I sit waiting, it, you see, represents her to me. In it I see the gentle but strong mold of her form, all she is to me, all she is to become to me when I have won her. I have not won her yet. Upon the wonder awakened in her by the way I shall paint depends whether or not I shall make her my own."

Harold had now worked himself into a state and had completely won my own admiration, but Mildred—I was not entirely sorry when I looked at Mildred's face. There had been moments when I had thought that—if Harold were not about . . .

And now Harold, having determined to begin blocking in his picture at once, that same evening, ran to prepare his canvas and easel, all the while telling us of his plans. His father was a wholesale merchant at Fort Wayne, Indiana, and had objected to his becoming an artist. It was only the mother's influence that had induced him to support Harold at the school, but after he had painted the canvas he was now about to begin, and had won the prize in the fall show, all would be changed. Money would be forthcoming and with the money got from his father and from the painting, which would be sure to sell at a large price, he would take Mildred and me with him to Paris. There we would live, Mildred and he studying painting, while I— He had stopped his preparations and, turning, had looked at me. "Well, you'll be all right whatever turns up," he had said, heartily enough, I am sure.

I had walked out of Harold's studio with Mildred and we had gone to dine at a nearby restaurant. The money that had paid for the weeks of leisure I had just been enjoying was nearly gone. Soon I would have to go to work. At the table d'hôte we spoke of Harold and what a splendid fellow he was. Mildred, I thought, was hanging between anger and tears. She had wanted a man when Harold had caught her fancy and she had got an artist. Now that he had started on his great canvas, she would, for weeks, get nothing from him. I looked at her and wondered.

She had told me, on the way to the table d'hôte, that she was nearly broke. For some time she had been holding a job as secretary to a businessman in the Loop district, but Harold was always phoning her in the afternoon and she was always running off with him, and now the man had fired her. She had intended telling Harold about it that afternoon, but had found him so absorbed in his grand plans that she had hated to disturb him. As she had talked the hope in me had flared up, and after the table d'hôte and while we were still seated at the table, I took a deep breath and unfolded my scheme.

For several weeks, I explained, Harold would be absorbed with his painting. He would not want Mildred about and she had lost her job. It might well be that she, like myself, was nearly broke. Such a painting as Harold had in hand could not be done offhand. He would be absorbed in it, thinking of nothing else. Above all he would not want a woman about. Had not Mildred heard what he had said about the feelings he would be having for some mysterious woman of old times? Such feelings, while they lasted, were often stronger than the feeling for living people. It is a part of the artist nature that this be so.

"We will have to be comrades, now, Mildred," I said, and then I unfolded my scheme.

All of this was before the days of Prohibition and Chicago had within its borders thousands of small saloons. As I had gone about the city I had noted that saloonkeepers had a penchant for pictures back of the bars and these were as a rule very stupidly done. Why not have them better done?

To the saloonkeepers I would explain how, at Barbizon and other places, paintings on the walls of little out-of-the-way cafés had become famous and had made the places where some great painter had stopped casually in his youth famous. Rich Americans took voyages out from Paris to see such places and spent money lavishly. I had no doubt that, with the tales I could invent, we could get many an order from thirty to fifty dollars. We would divide our takings and while Harold was engaged with his great work we would also be making money. "A woman wants her independence," I said, and Mildred nodded. I had been somewhat afraid she would break into tears.

And so it had been arranged, and, for me at least, the adventure with Mildred had turned out to be a great success. For weeks, and while Harold was engaged with his great masterpiece, we had tramped about the streets of Chicago, I making engagements for Mildred and she executing them. How charming she was! In the early morning we met and set out on our own mutual adventure and as she stood on a chair behind some bar, with laborers and teamsters standing about, painting on the barroom looking glass one of the several scenes we had prepared in advance, I moved among the spectators, speaking in whispers of the great future before her when she had got to Paris and had attracted the attention of the big world. "The day may come when that looking glass, because of the painting now being put on it, may be worth a thousand dollars," I said solemnly, and often some man in the crowd ordered on the spot a duplicate of the painting to be done on canvas so that it could be framed and hung up in his house.

What days for me, the presence of Mildred, the dollars rolling in, a new suit bought, an overcoat against the winter, new linen, money in my pocket! Occasionally, in the evening, Mildred went to see Harold, but he was absorbed and did not ask what she was doing and she did not tell him. "The matter may go on for months and it will surely go on until the great canvas is finished," I thought, and saw myself living for months with my books and no more compelled to go into some factory or to accept a clerkship.

And then one morning it had all come to an end, and I shall remember that morning as long as I live. It may be that I had begun to hope I would win Mildred myself.

I had gone to a place on the West Side, near Garfield Park in Chicago, where I was to meet Mildred and where our day's work was to begin, but when she appeared I knew at once something had happened. She was not wearing the gay little smock that had been a part of our stage property and there was a sad serious look on her face. At once and without words she had led the way into the park and we sat down on a bench. She was dressed in black. What a come-down! I perhaps made a mistake. I took her hand.

That may have broken the flood gates. She may have intended only to tell me she could not carry on our scheme any more. On the evening before, she had gone to Harold and the great painting was at last finished. He had wanted her back. "Where have you been and what have you been doing?" he had asked, and it was then the horror of what she had been doing had for the first time dawned upon Mildred. The thought of it had made her half ill and she had cried all night. While he, Harold, had been doing his great painting, making a real and lasting contribution to the arts, she, betrayed by me, by the baseness in my nature, had been going about to low saloons and had been painting such pictures on the looking glasses back of the bars. Now, if she had her own way, she would go about painting them all out. The common people, such people as came into small Chicago saloons, had also been betrayed. One should be engaged in lifting up, not in casting down into greater and greater vulgarities the common people.

"But, Mildred," I said. She had taken her hand from mine and was weeping. A man passing along the path had stopped and seemed about to speak. There was an angry look in his eyes. Perhaps he thought we were married and that I had been beating her. In the far distance, across a flat open green space, some golf players, tiny figures against a sea of green, were passing in and out across an opening between trees. It was early fall and in Chicago early fall days can be lovely.

To think that I had been the one who had betrayed Mildred and through her had betrayed Harold's art! "There is nothing now you can do except one thing and that you must do. Promise me that I will never see you again and that you will never see Harold again," she said, getting to her feet and preparing to leave me flat there in the park.

Without another word Mildred had left me sitting disconsolate and alone on the bench. I arose and stretched. As I have already pointed out, I am one who cannot solve problems. "Work now, you slave," I had begun saying to myself again, when another thought came. My new overcoat was warm and, as I have said, fall days in Chicago can sometimes be quite lovely. I put the paint box on the bench and stared at the man who had been staring at me. "Get out," I thought, although I said nothing to him. "Perhaps," I said to myself, "when there is a new masterpiece to be done—" I had, you see, not entirely given up the notion of Mildred.

And so I went back again to my room and my books.

As for the masterpiece, as it turned out, I did not see it at all. It was hung in the fall show and, although it did not win the prize, attracted a great deal of attention. It just happened that at that time I had gone off on my travels.

It did not win the fall prize, but that was because the jury was fixed. I had that from a friend who had it from Mildred. And had you been with us during the days of our mutual adventure, you also would have been unable to doubt what Mildred had said.

Mildred was, you see, such a masterpiece in herself.

I am very sure she must have been worthy of Harold.

Daughters

THERE WERE two Shepard girls, Kate and Wave. Wave was slender. When she walked, she thrust the upper part of her body slightly forward. She had masses of soft hair always slipping from place and falling down. "It won't stay where I put it," said Wave. Her hair was brown, touched with red, and her eyes were brown. Most of the time she wouldn't get up in the morning. She let Kate do all the work about the house, but Kate didn't care if she did.

The Shepards had come to Longville, to live in town. John Shepard got a job working as a section hand on the railroad. He had been a lumberman working in lumber camps ever since he was a boy and didn't like being in town. He came in because of his daughters. Kate, the elder of the girls, wanted to be a schoolteacher. To do that you had to go through high school. Afterwards you had to go through normal school. Kate thought she could do it.

Before moving into Longville, they had lived in a small unpainted frame house in a little valley up in the hills. The house lay six miles back in the hills beyond the Bear Creek settlement and the Bear Creek lumber camp where John Shepard had been working when his wife died. His wife was a huge fat woman with a reputation for laziness. "Look at her house," people said. Her house always was dirty. It was in disorder. It had remained that way until Kate got old enough to take a hand in the housework.

Kate was a girl who could do everything. She had kept the garden behind the house. She milked the cow. She swept and kept the house. She rose before daylight to put the house in order and be in time for school. The girls had had to walk three miles to reach the one-room country schoolhouse. Often they had to wade through snow and, in the spring, through mud. Whenever the weather was bad, when it was cold or rainy, or snow or mud lay deep on the valley road, which followed the windings of a creek, Wave didn't go.

When she did go, she always played in the boys' games. She threw a ball as if she were a boy. She could outrun the boys and sometimes tore into one of them and licked him. She swore like a boy.

"Hell, I'll not go to school, not in this weather. To hell with it," she said. Her mother could not get her to obey.

All through their childhood, the two girls saw little of their father, who often worked in lumber camps. Sometimes, coming home at the weekend after a long hard week of heavy work, and finding his wife sitting in a disordered house, dirty clothes lying about on the floor, and the bed in which he was to sleep with her unmade, and hearing her say she couldn't do anything with Wave, John Shepard, who seldom complained, had spoken almost sharply.

"What's the matter with you, Nan?" he asked. "Can't you run your house? Can't you run your children?"

"I would just like to have you try it, with that Wave," she said. "She's a little hellcat," she added. She said that if you tried to make Wave do something she didn't want to do, she'd just lay on the floor and scream.

"I got a whip and whipped her, but she just kept screaming, screaming and kicking her heels in the air. She wouldn't give in. You couldn't make her give in."

He himself, when at home and in a room with his daughter Wave, always felt a little uncomfortable. He spoke to her and, if she didn't want to, she didn't answer. She could look at you and make you feel uncomfortable. There was something a little queer. Sometimes her eyes seemed to be insulting you. "Don't bother me. Who are you that you should bother me? If I want to answer when you speak to me, I will. If I don't, I won't."

Wave sat in a chair and put her legs up. She put her feet up on the back of another chair. She left her dress all open at the front. She went about barefooted, barelegged. Her legs were dirty. She could sit for a long, long time, saying nothing, staring at you until you wanted to go and cuff her.

And then, suddenly she could grow nice. There was a soft warm look came into her eyes. You wanted to go and take her into your arms, hold her tight, cuddle her, kiss her, but you'd better not try. She might suddenly hit you with her hard, sharp little fists. Once she had done that to her father, and having taken her into his arms he put her quickly down.

"Your mother can't do anything with you, but I'll show that I can," he said. "I was as mad as I ever was in my life," he said afterward, talking with George Russell, a man who worked with him in the woods. "My wife just had two girls," he said. "I wish they had been boys." He explained to the other man how it was about girls. "They are good or they ain't. You can't make them good.

"When they're little things they're nice, but, as soon as they begin to grow up, they bother you. You get to thinking, 'Now what's going to happen to them?'

"There are always boys hanging after young girls," he said. He said that, in the country, girls, when they got to a certain age, were always going into the bushes with boys.

"You can talk to a boy, set him straight, but you can't talk about a thing like that to a girl. How can you?" he asked.

The other man, with whom John Shepard worked, didn't know how you could. He had three sons. He didn't have any girls. "I don't know how you could. I guess you can't," he said.

That time, when Wave hit her father in the face with her fists, because, just then, she didn't want to be held by him, didn't at the moment fancy being caressed by him, John went and cut a switch, a good stout one. He went to where there was a thicket beyond his farm, but, when he came back to his house, Wave wasn't there.

She was sitting astride the roof of his house. He told the man in the woods about it.

"The roof of my house is so steep a cat couldn't climb it, but she climbed it," he said.

She just sat up there, staring down at him.

"Come down," he said.

"Come down," his wife said. His wife was alive then. His wife could sit all day without moving. She took a chair out into the yard and sat in it. "I can sit down here as long as she can sit up there," John's wife said. He thought probably she could. "I never saw a woman could sit as long as my wife can," he said to the man in the woods. He said she could sit anywhere, on a chair, on the ground, even when the ground was wet, on the floor. He said that if his wife, instead of Wave, had been sitting on the roof, he'd have given up at once.

"I gave up, promised I'd never touch her if she came on down, made my wife promise, because Kate, her sister, cried so hard.

"She just sobbed and sobbed. She was so scared her sister would fall. She's such a good girl that I couldn't say no.

" 'Don't touch her, Pa. Please don't touch her. Promise you won't touch her. Make Ma promise,' she kept pleading and she kept sobbing like her heart was breaking, so I promised," he said to the man in the woods. He said he thought that his daughter Wave was just having a good time. "She was enjoying herself, the little hellcat," he said.

It was a year after his wife's death that John Shepard had moved to Longville. He hated it. He didn't want to live in town. He had saved his money and bought a little farm in a nice little valley. Working in the camps he had made plans. A stream ran through the farm, a rapid little stream that came down out of the East Tennessee hills, and he planned to build a dam and run a mill. He would grind corn for people who lived on little farms farther up the valley. A man could get his toll. He could keep enough meal to feed his family and his chickens. He could keep two or three cows, sell the calves, raise hogs. "A man can get along good," he said to another man with whom he worked—always in deep woods. "He can enjoy his family." He was a quiet, slow-speaking man who, even when a young fellow, hadn't gone off, after payday, drinking or whore-hopping like most of the young fellows in the camps.

But he had had a talk with his daughter Kate, one weekend when he was at home, after his wife had died. Kate was nearly fifteen, Wave almost thirteen. It was a Sunday morning and Kate had got his breakfast. She had been up a long time, milked the cow, fed the chickens and the two pigs. She had brought water from the spring. John had shaved. He had put on a clean shirt and a clean pair of overalls. Kate had washed them for him. The little house was all in order, everything swept, the windows washed, nothing lying about on the floor in the front room where the family ate, where they sat. There was a fireplace and, as the bright spring morning was cold, Kate had brought in wood and built a fire.

She asked him whether the coffee was good. She got him a second cup.

Wave was in bed.

"You've been doing all of the work, ain't you?" he asked, but Kate said no, she hadn't. She brought him some jelly for his bread and told him Wave had made it. Wave had baked a cake. Kate began bragging about Wave. She could make pies. She could bake the lightest cake you ever ate.

"I can't cook half as good as Wave can," Kate said. She said Wave could do anything she put her hand to. If she wanted to and when she went to school, she could be the smartest one there. Kate got a little excited when she spoke of her sister. She always did. There was a kind of shine came into her eyes. It was true, said Kate, that when there was bad weather or when she didn't want to go, she wouldn't go to school, but you give her a book, a hard one, now, any book, and she could read it right off.

She could read a book or a story and then she could tell about it, make it sound better than when you read it yourself.

And when she wanted to, she could make clothes. "You just give her some odd scraps," Kate said. She said that Wave had taken an old dress that had belonged to their mother and had cut it up. She had just slashed right into it. She had made two dresses out of the one dress, one for herself and one for Kate.

Kate came and sat at the table with her father.

"Pa, we ought to move to town," said she. Her face had got flushed. It was hard for Kate to talk as she did that morning. She wanted her father to sell the farm, to try to get a job in town, and John Shepard thought, listening to her talk, that Wave had put her up to it.

"I'll bet the little hellcat did put her up to it," he said to the man who worked with him in the woods. Kate had, however, said nothing of Wave's wishes. She had been bragging her sister up and then she stopped. She took it all on her own shoulders. She said she wanted to be a schoolteacher and had to go to high school. She said that if they lived in town, in Longville—it was twenty miles away; it was a big town—if they lived there she bet she could get a job, maybe in a store. She said she bet she could do something to help earn money. He told the man in the woods that, once she had got on the subject, she didn't let up. She talked that Sunday, and then she talked every time he went home. He said it wasn't like her. His daughter, Wave, he knew was back of it, but what could he do? He said he couldn't say no to Kate, not for long.

"She's such a good girl," he said. He said he couldn't refuse her anything. "She works so hard. She does everything. She never complains. I guess I got to give her her chance," he said, and he said he wouldn't mind, he was getting old, he didn't expect it mattered much where he worked, although he hated living in town, didn't like it at all.

He had hoped to spend his old age on his farm. That was why he had worked and saved to buy it. He expected, if he sold his farm, he'd only get enough to buy a little house in town with no ground at all, not to speak of.

"Maybe just enough for a little scrawny garden and it mighty poor soil," he said. "And I've got my place now pretty well built up. I've been buying fertilizer and putting it on. What my land needs is time," he said.

He said he knew that his youngest daughter was back of Kate's talk about moving to town and being a schoolteacher and all, but that he guessed he couldn't refuse.

It was a little yellow house. You went down a sloping, unpaved street that ended in a swamp, and the yellow house was at the end of the street. It stood on a high gravelly bank above the low swampy land and there were trees, two hickory trees and a beech, their roots reaching down into the black swampland. They stood just where the yard of the yellow house shelved off into the swamp and, just at the base of the beech—a tree with great spreading limbs, one of its great branches lying against the house wall—a spring bubbled up. People came from other houses along the short little street to get water. There had been a barrel sunk into the ground and a stream ran down from the barrel's edge, spreading out over the low black land.

The low land was covered with little grassy hills surrounded by stagnant water. There was a stream that, sometimes in the spring and fall, got out of its banks, covering the low land, but in the summer it was a mere trickle. The stream came out of the town. It went away across fields. You could stand in the yard before the yellow house and look away to long stretches of farm land. There was a big white farmhouse, standing on a low hill in the distance, and back of it was a big red barn.

John Shepard, the lumberman, had sold his little farm in the valley between high hills and bought the yellow house. He hated it, but "What's the use of complaining?" he thought. He had got a job working on the railroad that went through Longville, was a section hand. He got a dollar fifty a day. He had bought the house at the town's edge, because, he thought, "Anyway, it won't be so crowded."

There wasn't anyone to talk to in town. He was a man who went cautiously toward others—made friends slowly. He left the house early in the morning, carried his lunch pail, and was gone all day. It seemed strange and unnatural to him not to be in the deep woods, not to have the smell of the woods in his nostrils. There was that other man with whom he had worked in the woods, the fellow that had sons and no daughters. He missed him. The two men had worked together for a long time. It was a big cutting they had been on. They had kept going forward, into hills, swamping-out roads, getting the logs out. You worked with another man, felling the trees, and others came and trimmed the logs. You could get ahead of them, sit down and rest, talk with the other man who worked with you.

You didn't see much of the boss. You had your life in there, away deep in there, in the deep woods with the other man, your pardner.

John Shepard went along through busy town streets, up and out of the street at the end of which, by the swampy place, he had his house. He had to go through a street where there were big houses set in lawns. His daughter Kate had a job in one of the big houses. She prepared his breakfast, fixed his lunch pail, and then went to the big house.

She cooked there. She swept out rooms and made beds. She wasn't the first girl in the house. She was the second one. They let her go to school. The woman gave her dresses. She told her father how nice they were to her. She said they wanted her to have her chance. "I tell you, Pa, they're mighty nice to me," she said. She stayed up there at night, after school, working sometimes until eight or even nine o'clock, then she came home and got her father's supper. When there was a party or something up where she worked and she knew she'd be late, she'd slip home after school and get something cold ready for him. Regular evenings, when she had everything cleaned up, she'd sit in the kitchen, at the kitchen table, studying.

Wave wasn't there. She was off somewhere, traipsing around

with the town boys. She never seemed to want to eat much. She didn't mind missing a meal. Sometimes quite late at night, when Kate had got through studying and had gone to bed and when John Shepard was in bed, a car drove up before the house and Wave got out.

He could hear some man's voice. He could hear the car turn.

Most of the dresses Kate had given her, working up there in the rich people's house, Wave got.

She could take a dress and change it. She could make it something new. If it was out of style, she could put it back in style. She could take two dresses and make one. Wave wasn't afraid of anyone or anything. Kate, when she had time to talk to her father, maybe in the evening after the evening meal, when she was washing dishes and cleaning up and he was on the steps by the kitchen door smoking his pipe before going to bed, continued bragging Wave up.

"I wish I could cook like Wave can.

"She can do anything she sets her hand to.

"If I could fix up dresses as well as she can, I'll bet I'd have a shop."

John said nothing. It made him sore to hear Kate talk so.

"If she can cook so good, why don't she stay home and get my supper?" he thought. Sometimes he thought, "Kate is away all day and so am I. She's just bound to get herself into trouble and bring disgrace on us." Sometimes he wanted to spank Wave. He came home from work and there she was, on the front porch, sitting in a chair, her legs up on another chair. She didn't seem to mind what she showed. She'd show everything she had. She was always reading. She got books somewhere, Kate said from a free library. She didn't care if there was someone coming along the street. The people on that street were always coming down to the spring, under the trees, at the edge of the bank, right near the front of the house. There were women coming. Men came. There were some of the men who were young fellows. They worked in a factory in town.

Wave didn't care. She'd dress up, like a doll, right in the morning, when she first got up. Sometimes she didn't get up until noon. She turned night into day. She was there, like that, on the porch, reading a book, maybe just waiting for some man to come in a car and take her out, God only knew to where, when John Shepard came home.

He asked her if she had got his supper and she didn't answer. She didn't even look at him and he wanted to snatch the book out of her hands. He wanted to take her across his knees. She wasn't very big. She was slender and not very strong. He wanted to take her on his knees and spank her behind.

"I'd like to fan her little behind for her," he thought.

Sometimes when John Shepard came home from his work and Wave was there sitting maybe on the porch, not answering when he spoke to her, her feet up on another chair or on the porch rail, reading a book, and when Kate hadn't got a chance to slip home and get something ready for him and he got mad, he thought, "Kate wouldn't like it. She wouldn't stand for it," he thought. When that happened, sometimes he got a headache.

It was because he was so mad and could do nothing. It was because it was Wave who was behind Kate's wanting to come live in town. It was because Wave kept putting all the work on Kate.

"I don't know how she got to be like she is," he told himself. He hated to think about her. He didn't want to. When he thought about fanning her little behind, he got excited. It was an odd excitement. It made his head ache. It made his back ache. When he was in the woods cutting down trees, he always did heavy work, but he never had a backache or headache, but when he got mad at Wave and could do nothing because there was nothing he could do, he did.

It wasn't the work he was doing, on the railroad. He knew that. It wasn't such heavy work.

He hated being alone in the house with Wave. She could make him furious just looking at him. Sometimes, when he came home from work, and she was there and Kate wasn't—he couldn't stay. He kept opening and closing his fists. Even if it was winter and if Wave was at home and not traipsing around with some man and there was snow on the ground, he went out of the house.

He went into the back yard. There wasn't much front yard, but the back yard was long. When he had bought the place, he had thought that maybe he would raise chickens. He never had. "I don't seem to get around to begin," he said to himself. He thought maybe it was Wave's fault.

He stood about. He was waiting for Wave to go away or Kate to come home. When it was dark, he sat sometimes on the ground, under one of the hickory trees. The hickory trees were at the back of the yard, where the ground shelved off, down to the swamp.

The beech tree was in front, right by the street. He got so mad that he beat the ground with his open hand. One night he beat so hard that the gravelly soil hurt his hand. He didn't mind the hurt. He liked it, but afterwards his back ached and his head ached. It spoiled his supper.

A porch extended along one side of the little yellow house and faced the street. Through a door in the side porch you entered a small parlor, behind which lay a bedroom, where the girls slept. The kitchen was built on. The stairs to the upper story mounted out of the girls' room. There was no door at its head, and the stairs came right into the room where John Shepard had his bed. A wooden railing had been placed beside the stair pit, there, so that in case you did not light a lamp when you went to bed, or got up in the night or early in winter, you wouldn't in the darkness fall through the opening. There was a second room in the upper story, and to reach it you had to pass through John Shepard's.

He was wandering restlessly about in the back yard. It was evening. A car drove up and Wave got into it. She was "stepping out." "I'm stepping out, Kid," she would have said to her sister, fixing herself up. Wave, although younger than Kate, always called her sister "Kid." It was the assertion of a kind of superiority perhaps in worldly knowledge, which Kate didn't mind. Kate never minded anything Wave said or did. John Shepard heard a man's voice out in the road. The fellow had to turn the car and John got behind one of the hickories. He didn't want the car's headlight to search him out, find him wandering there. Anyway, he didn't want Wave to know she could worry him.

He went into the house. Kate was sitting in the kitchen by the table. She was sitting under a kerosene lamp, as the Shepards didn't have electric lights. She had a book open. It was nice and clean in there. When Kate was in the house even for just a little while, she got everything looking and smelling nice. He thought Kate was very pretty. He thought she was beautiful. Sometimes when he admired her he wondered how she had come to be as fine as she was, and was disloyal to his dead wife. "She isn't much like her Ma or me either," thought he.

"Where you been, Pa?" Kate asked, and he said he had just stepped outside. He wanted to tell her that he couldn't bear being in the house when Wave was there. He wasn't a swearing man, but he wanted to say, "Goddam Wave. I wish she'd get the hell out of my house and stay out." He wanted to say, "I don't give a goddam what happens to her. I can't bear being in the goddam house when she's here."

Sometimes he said such things aloud, when he was going to work, in the early morning, hardly anyone in the streets, even in Main Street, through which he had to pass, just maybe a few clerks, opening up and sweeping out stores. He said such things aloud, then or in the evening when he was coming home. But he knew he couldn't say them to Kate.

He said, "I guess I'll go on to bed." He didn't want to go to bed, but he didn't want to interrupt her in her studies. He thought, "Maybe I could just sit down here, near her, and smoke my pipe.

"I like to be near her," he thought.

He thought, "I never liked to be near her Ma, even when she was a young girl, before she got so fat, when I was courting her, like I like to be near Kate.

"But maybe it would bother her, me sitting about," he thought.

"And anyway," he thought, "I don't enjoy smoking when I've got a headache."

He hesitated, standing back of Kate, who was absorbed in her book.

She turned and saw him.

She had got a new lamp shade on her lamp. "Look at it, Pa," she said. "Ain't it pretty?" She said that Wave had made it. His headache got worse.

"Goddam Wave," he thought.

"She's sure got fine eyes," he thought, looking at her. He was always wondering, since he came to live in town, why it was that men and boys all seemed to be crazy to be with Wave and why so few got after Kate. He thought it showed that town men hadn't a bit of sense.

"If I was a young fellow now," he thought, "and Kate wasn't my daughter—"

He had gone to stand near the door that led into Kate's and Wave's room and to the foot of the stairs.

"I'd better not sit down," he thought. If he sat down he'd be staying. She worked hard. "She ought to get her studying done and go to bed," he thought.

Kate had been talking about the room upstairs, the one at the front of the house. She had said that sometimes she thought she'd better put an ad in the paper. "We could get something for the room and it would be a help." If, as sometimes happened, she also spoke of wanting to buy something for Wave, speaking maybe of Wave's birthday coming, or maybe Christmas, mentioning maybe a pair of silk stockings, something like that, it spoiled things. But sometimes she didn't mention Wave at all, and when she talked in her intimate way, Wave gone, it seemed to him that his back and head both were feeling better.

Kate began speaking about the roomer for the room above, giving the impression that she had given the matter a lot of thought.

"If it was a young fellow now, a quiet one."

She was attending the town high school. There were young fellows, also from the country, who came to town to school, some drove into town in cars, but others had no cars.

"If we had a young fellow like that, in the other room, upstairs, he and I could talk over our lessons."

Kate said that some of the lessons she had to take in school were mighty hard for her. She had to study a thing called Latin.

"What's that?" her father asked, and she said it was a language.

"It's the way people talked, a long time ago," she explained. She said they wrote books in a language different from the one she and her father talked. She didn't know why you had to learn to read books written in it, but you did. If she was ever going to get a chance as a schoolteacher, she had to learn it.

"Even if we got only a dollar a week," she continued. "It couldn't be a girl, up there with you, having to go back and forth through your room. If he wanted his breakfast, I could get it while I am getting yours."

She continued earnestly talking of the possible roomer. Suddenly it occurred to her father that she was describing a real person. She spoke so definitely of him.

John Shepard went upstairs and to bed. For some time a vague resentment against young men had been growing in him. Going to work and coming from it he had begun looking closely at young men he met. Now and then one of them, who came in the evening for Wave—he might be going to take her for a ride in his car—there seemed an endless stream of the men, some younger than others, big ones and little ones, men well dressed, others rather shabbily dressed—now and then one of them sat for a time on the side porch of the house.

He would himself have fled into the back yard. Wrath was rising in him. "What's she up to?" It must be, he thought, that half the town was talking about his daughter.

"I don't believe all of these men would be after her unless—"

There were thoughts he couldn't finish, didn't want to finish.

If she were going all the way with them, one after another—

Wrath boiled up in him.

But, lying in bed, it seemed to him that the young roomer was in the house. He was in the room at the front of the house, just beyond his own, behind the closed door. He was in there studying as Kate was studying below in the kitchen. . . . Now he was below with her, talking their lessons over with her. . . . He was quietly coming upstairs.

John Shepard had always wanted a son. The young man would be like Kate, not like Wave, a fellow always running around in the streets at night, crazy after girls as Wave was crazy after boys.

The resentment returned. The young fellow who had come for Wave earlier in the evening had returned with her, was sitting down on the porch with her. The two were laughing and talking together.

"Now quit that, smarty," he heard Wave say to the man.

He would have been grabbing her leg or something like that. It sounded like it.

She wasn't mad, though. She laughed when she told the fellow to quit it. She didn't sound as though she meant it. She had a curiously soft silvery laugh. She began singing.

She could do all sorts of things Kate couldn't do and that was annoying too.

For example she could sing. She had a curiously soft, clear, penetrating voice. Late at night, when she had come home, after an evening spent with some man and had got into bed with Kate and was telling Kate of her adventures and was speaking in a low voice, hardly more than a whisper, her father, in his bed upstairs could hear every word she said.

Kate had a rather husky voice. It sounded as though she were catching cold. Her father was always asking, "You ain't catching cold, are you, Kate?"

"Why, no," she said.

Wave knew a lot of songs. She'd sing songs to the men that weren't very nice. She sang a song about a girl who got pregnant by some man she wasn't married to. It was called "Careless Love." It was about a girl who got big with child so that she couldn't tie her apron strings. The strings wouldn't go around her swollen belly. The man who did it to her, after he had done it, wouldn't marry her.

It wasn't any song to sing, to just any man, especially when you weren't married to him. Wave sang it in her soft, low, clear voice, and John Shepard was sure she could be heard all along the street at the end of which they lived.

God only knew what people thought.

But, just the same, in spite of yourself, when Wave sang like that . . . you just couldn't help yourself . . . you began to like her in spite of yourself.

The singing seemed to carry John Shepard back into his young manhood. He was again a young lumberman. On Saturday night he was in a town near the lumber camp where he worked then. He had gone into town with other young lumbermen.

They were drinking and fighting. They were going whore-hopping, out to raise hell, but he wasn't. He walked about. The town was small, but he got off the main street.

There was a house, halfway up a hill, a half mile out of town. It had apple trees in the yard.

There was an old man with a gray beard, who walked with a stick. There was an old blind woman.

There was a young girl, very slender, very pretty. They had mosquito netting about the porch of their house.

On warm clear nights they brought a lamp out there and the young girl read aloud to the old white-bearded man and to the blind woman.

Her voice was like a bird singing away off somewhere in the deep woods.

The first time when John Shepard, as a young man, had gone into the town and when wandering about, not wanting to drink and raise hell with the others, not wanting to go whore-hopping—he didn't believe in it; it was against his principles—he had often said to himself, "I'll wait 'til I get honestly married . . ."

"I'm not just an animal . . ." he had said.

"I'll go clean to her. I'll be asking her to come clean to me and I ought to go clean to her. . . ."

There was deep dust in the road and when he went past that house, that was quite near the road. They didn't see him. They didn't hear him. There was a kind of hedge and he sat down under it. He hadn't ever thought that he could get a woman like the one on the porch of that house, reading aloud to the two old people, so beautiful, so evidently refined.

He thought, "I'll bet she's educated. She reads so well." He thought maybe she had just come there, to that town, maybe to visit her grandmother and grandfather.

"I'll bet, at home, she's away up in life," he thought. He imagined all sorts of things about her, creeping back to hide under the hedge, on many Saturday nights, always dreaming and thinking about her all week when he was at work in the woods. Bitterly disappointed when, having gone into town and up there, she wasn't on the porch reading to the old people, so disappointed that sometimes he cried.

Not that he had ever thought he could get such a woman.

He had never even spoken to her. How could he have gotten a chance, he told himself, and if a chance had come, what could he have said? She had been there with the two old people and then she wasn't there. He guessed she was just visiting there, in that house, in that town. He guessed they were her grandparents. It had been like spring coming after a long hard winter in the woods. Spring comes, and then after a while, it isn't spring any more.

What annoyed John Shepard, though, was that Wave, sitting singing on the porch to a man she had picked up, should rouse a funny feeling in her father. Making him think of his youth when he went creeping up a hillside road, out of a lumber town, hiding under bushes, seeing another young woman on the porch of a house, himself full of a mysterious love that made him sit by the roadside silently crying, just as if, he told himself, a man, certainly a very ordinary man, not educated, one who always had lived with rough uncouth men, drinkers, fighters and whore-hoppers, had fallen in love with an angel sitting on a star up in the sky. As if she herself, the little devil down there, were an angel sitting on a star. The singing carried you up to her. It seemed to float you. Made you as if in a dream where your feet leave the earth and you float like a bird up in the sky.

It made him angry. God knows he had seen and heard enough of his daughter Wave. In spite of himself, though, he quit wanting to fan her little behind, and went to sleep.

He awoke. Kate was up, getting his breakfast. It was lucky that, at the place where she worked, they didn't have their breakfast early like that. John guessed they stayed in bed. "How they can, when it's broad daylight, say now in the summer, I don't know," he thought.

"I like the early part of the day," he thought. He remembered how, when he was still working in the woods, he went from where he slept, in a bunk in a little shack, usually with two or three others to where they all ate their breakfast.

It would be hardly day. It would be a pinkness. You went along a creek and crossed on a log. There was good woods smells and good food smells. In the lumber camp, no one talked while they were eating. It was a rule they had. It wasn't a law. It was a rule. It was in all lumber camps. It made it nice.

You ate and got on a car, a flat one, part of a lumber train, and you went along a creek.

There were some began to talk, but John didn't. He sat silent, at the edge of a flatcar, his legs hanging down.

There was a kingfisher bird, up early and on a limb, a dead limb hanging out over the stream. There was a quiet above the talk of the men. There was a squirrel went up the trunk of a tree.

It was all nice. It was funny to think there were people in towns who wanted to stay in bed.

"I couldn't. Even if I had a million dollars, I couldn't," thought John Shepard.

He went downstairs and there was Wave in bed asleep. She had kicked the covers off again. You could see clear up her leg, all of it, and see her little behind.

He was in bed again. He had been talking with Kate again about the roomer for the room next his.

"It gets kind of real," he thought.

"I guess now he'd be down there with Kate," he thought. Sometimes, when he was in bed like that, not asleep yet, not wanting to go to sleep, not feeling like sleep, he could almost see the young man.

"He'd have to be a pretty sensible one." He thought it would be nice if the young man was good-looking, but not too good-looking. He might be smart and quick at things, like Wave was—at least like Kate was always saying Wave was—but, he thought, not too goddam smart. "Smart enough, though, not to fall for Wave," he thought.

He thought, "He'd be down there with Kate, she helping him, he helping her, but she wouldn't be showing her legs. Nothing like that," he thought.

He thought . . . "Maybe they'd both be like I was about that one on the porch that time. Like that about each other," he thought.

It got so that, having these thoughts, night after night, they got more and more real.

Sometimes he thought, when he went upstairs to bed, when he was undressing, he thought . . . "No, he ain't down there with Kate.

"He's in there. He's in his room.

"He's studying now. I got to be mighty careful.

"I can't make any noise," he thought.

He argued with himself. "The fellow can't be down there with Kate, sitting with her, studying with her, liking her, gradually getting more and more stuck on her, because I just came up from there.

"He's in there in his room, studying now," he thought.

"If he comes through the room here, going down to be with Kate, I'll pretend to be asleep." He thought of something that gave him a lot of satisfaction. "There's a lot of men that snore when they sleep, but I don't," he thought. There had been a fellow at the lumber camp where he worked. He came to bunk in the same shack. He said, "Thank God, you don't snore." He said it in the morning after the first night in the shack with John. He said, "Christ, the bedbugs are as bad here as where I was where I worked last, but thank God, you ain't no snorer." He said that, in the last camp where he had worked, he had been put in to bunk in a shack with a man who snored so that he raised the goddam roof. He said the fellow made the goddam roof flop up and down like a goddam tent that hadn't, he said, been pegged down.

"You know," he said, "like a goddam tent in a goddam storm." He meant to say that John didn't snore when he slept.

"And I'm glad I don't," John thought. He thought he'd hate to be bothering the roomer he and Kate were always speaking about. "Either," he thought, "when he's up here in his room or when he's down there sitting with Kate."

Lying there, arguing with himself in bed, upstairs in his house, John Shepard heard the sound of voices. His daughter Wave had been out with one of her men. She had come home and she and Kate were in bed.

They were talking. They were laughing. There was a fat girl who worked in the house where Kate worked.

She couldn't get any men. Kate was telling Wave a story. The fat girl, who worked at that place where Kate worked, wrote letters to herself. Kate said she had seen one of the letters.

The fat girl had let it fall on the floor. It fell out of the pocket of her apron. Her name was Evelyn. "Darling Evelyn," the letter began. The fat girl couldn't spell very well. Kate said the fat girl went down into the town. She went to a florist. She bought a box of roses and sent them to herself. She had, Kate said to Wave, gone somewhere and had some cards printed. There was a man's name on the cards.

She put one of the cards into the box of roses. She had it addressed to herself. She had it sent to the house where she worked. She left the box open. Kate saw the card lying in the box on the roses.

"When she was down in the kitchen, I went into her room. She had got a whole pack of the cards printed. They were in a little pasteboard box in there. The name printed on the cards was 'Robert Huntington.' "

There wasn't any such man. Kate and Wave were lying downstairs. They were laughing at the fat girl. Wave was telling Kate about some man.

"He wanted to kiss me.

"He put his hand on my leg."

They began talking in lowered voices. Wave was telling Kate what some man had tried to do to her. Occasionally the two girls giggled, and John Shepard silently got out of bed.

He was barefooted. He slept in the same shirt he wore during the day. At night, when he went to bed he just took off his shoes, his socks and his pants. He shivered as he went silently down the stairs. He stood there near the foot of the stairs.

Wave was telling Kate how far she thought it was safe to let the men go. She was saying that there was one man who had almost got her.

"I let him go a little too far."

"What did you let him do?"

Wave had begun to whisper. It was almost as though she knew someone was listening. Kate was living her life in Wave's life. As Wave whispered, she giggled.

Kate also giggled.

It was all strange. It was in some way terrible to hear. Kate was feeling what Wave had felt. When she giggled, it was not as it was when Wave giggled. There was something in the tone of the low laughter that came from Kate that made her father shiver again.

He got suddenly angry. He wanted to run and choke Wave. He wanted to drag her out of the bed. He wanted to fan her behind, fan it hard.

He went silently back up the stairs and got into the bed.

There was the fat girl who wrote letters to herself. She sent herself flowers. Kate was living her life in Wave's life. Something not nice, he felt, was going on in his house. It seemed to him that Wave, coming into the silent house at night and talking with Kate, had brought something in that spoiled things.

The conversation between his daughters went on. John Shepard was very angry. He was so angry that little beads of sweat stood out on his forehead. He was as he sometimes was in the darkness in the back yard. In the back yard he pounded the ground with his hand. Now he pounded the bedclothes. His head ached and his back hurt.

John Shepard and his daughter Kate got their young man. Kate had put an ad in the paper. The young man had taken the room upstairs in the Shepard house. He was in the house. He was in and out. His feet were on the stairs. He was doing exactly as John Shepard had dreamed he would do.

He was a student in the town high school and, apparently, a very studious, earnest young man. He had his breakfast in the house. Like Kate and John Shepard himself, he got up early in the morning. His name was Ben Hurd and, like John himself, he had come to town from a lumber camp. He was a tall, slender young fellow. He had black hair and dark eyes.

He had got a job in town. He was at a store. He went there in the early morning, opened the store and swept out. Then he hurried off to school and after school, in the late afternoon, he returned to the store.

He stayed at the store until ten o'clock at night and then he came to the Shepard house.

John Shepard waited for his coming. Kate waited. John wondered if he was going to study with her. John would be upstairs in his room. He would be in bed with his light out.

John had become neat. When he went to bed at night, he had always just let his clothes lie on the floor, but now he folded his pants. There was a small chest of drawers and he put socks in a drawer and his shoes under the bed. "There isn't any light, but a man might as well learn to be neat," he thought. Kate had got him some pajamas to wear. She said, "Pa, you'd better put these on at night." She said that men in town wore them. He said he'd never heard of any such thing.

"It's what the man does where I work," she said.

"All right," he said.

And Kate had got so she wished she didn't have to work as a servant. She told her father about that. "It isn't such hard work, but it's being a servant. They look down on you," she said.

She said she wished she could get some other work. "Of course," she said, "if I was working, say now in a store, I wouldn't be having clothes and things given to me." She said she was glad Wave didn't have to be a servant. She said she was determined Wave shouldn't be one. When she got to be a schoolteacher, she was going to save her money. She had a plan. She and Wave would have a shop. She thought sometimes it would be a millinery shop and at other times she thought it would be a dressmaking shop.

She thought it would be better even than being a schoolteacher. She and Wave could be together. "You wouldn't have to work so hard, Pa," she said.

John Shepard said nothing. When she talked like that, dragging Wave in, he kept still. "To hell with Wave," he thought, but he didn't say it.

He had to stand and listen to Kate talk. It was Wave this and Wave that. Kate was worried because she thought that, because she had to work as a servant, people would look down on them.

When Wave didn't do a damn thing, just loafed about the house, didn't go to school to improve herself, spent all her time fussing with her clothes and her hair, Kate didn't complain.

"Ain't she got nice hair! Ain't it soft! Ain't it pretty!" Kate said.

When she went on about Wave sometimes John Shepard could hardly stand it. He had to clinch his fist. He had to stand and listen. When, in the evening, after the young fellow came to room in the house and Wave wasn't at home—she had a date, she wasn't there—and John was standing by the door, talking to Kate, who was by the kitchen table, sitting there, her schoolbooks on the table, her lamp on the table, and John was having a little talk with Kate and it got on Wave, he just waited, saying nothing until she got through. Then he said, "Good night.

"I guess you want to study. I guess I'll say good night," he said.

He went upstairs. He got into bed. He didn't sleep.

He wondered if Ben Hurd, when he came, would stop and talk maybe with Kate. He thought, "I'll bet Wave don't get him.

"I'll bet he's got more sense than to fool with her," he thought.

"He looks to me like a sensible young fellow," he thought.

"They'd make a nice couple," he thought. Sometimes when Ben Hurd came after ten, and Wave wasn't at home and Kate was down there waiting up—no matter how late it was she always stayed up until Wave came—she and Ben Hurd would talk a little.

They didn't much at first because the young fellow was shy and Kate was shy, but then they did, more and more.

A little more and a little more. Not studying together as John Shepard had thought maybe they would, but just talking

Like, "How do you like it here in town?" or, "How do you like it working in a store?"

It was a dry-goods store. It was a kind of general store. It was owned by a Jew. He didn't have just the one store. He had different stores in different towns.

He came and he went away. Ben Hurd told Kate about the store. He stood by the door downstairs, just as John did himself when he talked to Kate.

"Won't you sit down?" Kate said. She offered him things.

"Won't you have a cup of coffee? I'll make you some.

"Won't you have a glass of milk?"

She offered him a piece of pie. "I'll bet you're hungry." She bragged about the pie. She said Wave made it. She'd begin telling him about Wave, what good pies she could make, what good cake, what good fudge.

There'd be some of her fudge, in a dish on the table downstairs. "Won't you have some?" Kate would say to young Ben Hurd. "I don't care if I do," he'd say. He'd go over to where she was and get a piece, but he wouldn't sit down.

"I got to get upstairs," the young fellow would say to Kate and, instead of sitting awhile, down there with her, he'd come on up. He'd go through John Shepard's room and into his own room.

He'd light his lamp in there. He'd study awhile and then he'd write.

"What the hell's he writing?" John Shepard wondered. The young fellow, Ben Hurd, would write and write. He'd be leaning over his desk. Maybe Wave would come home and she and Kate would go to bed. They'd laugh and talk. Wave would be telling Kate about some man. "He got pretty gay," she'd say. She'd swear sometimes.

Sometimes the young fellow, in the room up there, had left his door a little open. Wave called some man she had been out with a son-of-a-bitch.

"The son-of-a-bitch thought he could get me." She laughed when she said it. It made John Shepard furious. "I'll bet he can hear," thought he. It made him mad that, when Wave spoke in this way, Kate didn't mind. "He'll think Kate's like Wave is," thought he.

He was glad the young fellow had a job, had to work. If he was around the house when Wave was at home, very likely she'd get him. She'd rope him in. She'd do it just to show she could. Once twice, after the young man came to room in the house and when he had come upstairs and was in his room—but not in bed—sitting in there and writing like he did—the door into John's room maybe a little open—no door downstairs, at the foot of the stairs—Wave coming home, talking down there— Sometimes she'd ask—

"What's this young fellow like?" she asked.

"Is he a live wire or is he dead on his feet?" she asked.

She'd say he looked to her like a goody-goody.

"Why don't you find out about him?" she'd ask Kate.

She'd go on like that, maybe saying that if Kate didn't want him maybe she'd take a whirl at him herself.

"Hush. Be careful. He's up there. He'll hear," Kate would say, but Wave didn't seem to care. She'd go right on.

"He's yours. You saw him first. I don't want to cut in on you," Wave would say, and then she'd laugh and Kate would laugh, and if the door to the young man's room was even a little open and a streak of light from his lamp falling into John's room, John Shepard would silently get out of bed and shut the door.

He went up into the main street of the town. It was after dark and Wave was at home. He had run out of tobacco for his pipe and wasn't in a very good mood. He had been sitting at the supper table alone. Kate had got his supper and had put it on the back of the stove. She had set the table. He had to get his own supper off the stove and put it on the table.

It had made him sore because Wave was right there. She was in the girls' bedroom.

"I suppose she's dolling up," he had thought. There would be some man coming for her. "It gets so that my food doesn't do me any good. I get so I can't digest it," he thought.

He hadn't anyone to say such things to. "If a man can talk things over with another man he don't mind so much," he thought. He had thought that a lot of times since he had been living in town. . . .

He had been remembering when he used to work in the woods, most of the time with just that one other man, George Russell.

A man likes to talk about his work. On the section, where John worked after he came to town, there were two Italians. There was a Negro. There was a German.

The foreman was a silent man. On lots of days, except to tell the men what to do, he never said a word. He was a man who didn't believe in getting too friendly with men working for him. You were out in the open. You were on the railroad. You didn't hear nice sounds, far off, like in the woods.

In the woods it was almost like in church. There was a something solemn. There was a close feeling you had with your pardner. When you got ahead of the knot bumpers, you could sit down, have a pipe with him. You spoke about other times, when you were a young fellow, what you did, things you felt.

You talked about your wives and your families. You told about how it was in another camp where you had worked, before you worked with George. . . .

On the main street he went into the drugstore that kept his brand of tobacco. Some young town boys and girls were sitting in the store, in some little booths, open at the side. There was a girl with her legs crossed, her dress, he thought, pulled pretty far up. There was a man sitting with her and they were having some kind of a drink.

The girl had made him think again of Wave. She probably came into that place with men, sat in there showing herself off as she did sitting on the porch at home. He went out of the drugstore—and ran into George Russell coming along the street.

There was a gladness. There was a jumping of the heart.

"Why, hello!"

"Well, I'm damned. It's you. Hello, John."

They went walking along together. George Russell was in town to see his oldest boy off on a train.

"He just left, ten minutes ago."

He was proud. Right away he began telling John about his son. "Yep," he said, "he's going to go to college. He's been a good boy. He's saved up his money."

He was boy crazy about books. He was smart. He hadn't enough money to pay his way through college, but he was going to start. He figured maybe he could work his way through, when he got a start.

He wanted to be a lawyer.

"I'll bet he makes it too. I'll just bet he does," George said.

The two men walked along.

"How do you like it in town, John?"

"I don't like it. I did it on account of my girls. Where you staying, George?"

George was staying in a little hotel on a side street and the two went there.

John was ashamed. "Hell, I'd like to have you at the house, but we ain't got no bed."

George said he had intended looking John up. "I didn't rightly know where you live. I was going to ask," he said.

John thought, "Ain't it hell I can't ask him to come? I ought to ask him to come stay at my house. But hell, who'd cook for him?" he thought. "Not Wave. She'd let him starve," he thought. "Or sit him down maybe to a cold picked-up supper while she went hell-catting around, riding with men in automobiles, sitting in drugstores with men."

The two sat in some chairs on the porch before the hotel where George was staying, right across from the station of the railroad on which John worked. George said he knew the young fellow who was rooming in John's house. He was a good boy. He was all right. He thought maybe John knew his mother, but John said he didn't. He hadn't lived near the mill, he had lived on his farm. "That's right," George said. He talked about his boys. Two of them were all right and good steady boys, but the youngest one he thought wasn't much good. He said the boy was lazy. "And he's a damn little liar." He couldn't account for the boy. He wasn't like George himself and he wasn't like his mother.

The two men talked until quite late, and when George had got through bragging about his son who had gone away to college, John Shepard bragged up his Kate. He wasn't going to say anything about Wave, but then suddenly he did. He told everything, how she was everlasting chasing around with men, how she wouldn't do any work about the house, how she put it all on Kate.

"I'd like to fan her behind. I would, too, if it wasn't for Kate. I don't understand why Kate's like she is about Wave. She takes everything from her. I don't understand it," he said.

He was thinking how much better it must be to have boys than just girls. "You just can't understand a girl," he thought. But he thought, anyway, that George had one boy who wasn't much good. But George was talking about the woods. He was going back to his job in the early morning. There had been a big boundary he and George had worked on together, but now, George said, it was almost cleaned up. George had said he reckoned, pretty soon, he'd be in another camp. "There isn't much big timber left," George had said. "Pretty soon," George said, "there'd only be little pickerwood mills." George had said he wasn't worried. He reckoned his oldest son would get to be a lawyer. He was a good boy. He'd take care of George.

"I don't mean I'd want to go and live with him, not after he gets married." What George meant was that his son, when he had got to be a lawyer, would maybe, every month, send his father some money.

John didn't start home till nearly eleven. He was a little excited, felt it had done him good to have the talk with his friend. He didn't go right home. Ever since he had come to live in town he had been pretty lonely, but now he felt as he used to feel, when as a young fellow he went off to town with other young lumbermen on a Saturday night. He walked around. He was in quiet residential streets. He was down by the railroad. He was by a dark warehouse. There was a man in there, in his shirt sleeves, under a light, leaning over a desk. He seemed to be writing. Lots of nights Ben Hurd in his room in the Shepard house also wrote that way under the lighted lamp. Some people worked like that over books, in a warehouse, one studying to be a schoolteacher, another to be a lawyer like George Russell's boy. Some of them got rich. They lived in big houses. He thought maybe Ben Hurd and his Kate would get married and be like that.

"I wouldn't want to be like that myself," he thought. "I'd rather be a workingman in a lumber camp, or anyway just go on until I get too old, just working."

"But a man does get old," he thought that night as he walked through streets and past houses. Once he found himself again in front of the little hotel where he had sat and talked with George Russell.

"He don't want to live with them when he's old," he thought, his mind running on George Russell's boy, grown to be a lawyer and married, George grown old, not able to work any longer, and then on young Ben Hurd, married to his Kate, gotten to be a businessman, maybe, owning a warehouse, or a store, or maybe being a lawyer, like George's boy.

He supposed maybe his Wave might get married too. "If she does, I pity the man. I pity him," he thought.

He decided he'd better be home. He went through dark streets. "It must be past midnight," he thought.

He went along his own street. There was a light in his house, in the kitchen of his house.

He got off the sidewalk. He got into the road. He didn't know afterward why he did it.

He could see there was a light in the kitchen of his house. He went past in the dusty road. The street ended in the black swamp, but it was summer and the swamp was almost dried up. He went through it. He got into his own gravelly back yard.

He could hear voices.

"It's Wave," he thought.

He thought, "She's sitting on the porch. She's got a man out there. Goddam her," he thought.

He went silently up to the kitchen window and looked in. Kate was sitting in there. She had her book open, but she wasn't studying.

She was crying. She was crying silently, as he once had done, lying under a hedge by a road, near a house where there was a young girl sitting with two old people on a porch.

There was a man's voice on the porch. Wave was out there. John went into the shed that was back of his house. When he was in the shed he could see through a crack.

There was light come out from Kate's lamp onto the porch. Young Ben Hurd was there. He was sitting there with Wave. They were sitting close. He had his arm around Wave.

He must have done something with his hand.

"Now you quit," she said.

She called him a "smarty."

"You quit it, smarty," she said, and then she laughed.

She moved a little away from him. She put her legs up. The way she was sitting, the light coming out from the kitchen, through an open door, and the way young Ben Hurd was sitting, he could see plenty, all right.

"Goddam! She's showing him all she's got," her father thought.

He felt frozen. He felt cold. He just stood.

And then she began to sing. Her voice was like that of the girl on the porch of another house when he was young. There was the same clearness, the same strange sweetness.

There was tenderness. There was something like a bird singing.

It was something he couldn't stand, that had always made him furious.

She sang, and then she stopped. Ben Hurd tried to kiss her, but she wouldn't let him. She stood by a post. Her soft mass of hair had slipped down. They talked in low tones. "Good night," she said. She made him go away. She kept saying, "Good night."

She pushed him away, made him go away.

He went upstairs. John Shepard heard him go up the stairs.

Wave just sat on the porch. She put her legs up again. She sang again and John Shepard rushed out of the shed.

He ran to where she was. He got his hand on her throat. He choked her.

She struggled, but he had her down on the floor of the porch. She scratched his face. She kicked him, but he fanned her behind.

He fanned her behind with his open hand. He had her dress up. His palm struck her flesh. He fanned it hard. He kept fanning it. His hand pressed hard on her throat. He had her, she could not make a sound.

"By God, I'd 'a' killed her, I guess I'd 'a' choked her to death, if it hadn't been for Kate."

Kate had come running out. She had begun hitting him with her fist. She kept pleading. She didn't plead loud. She didn't want Ben Hurd to hear.

Ben was upstairs. He remained silent.

Kate's voice was far off. It was like in a dream. It was far off and then it got a little nearer.

It came in to him. His mind was a house and the door of the house was closed. It came open. Kate's voice pleading and pleading made it come open. He let go of Wave's throat. He quit fanning her flesh. She was very white, lying on the porch, in the light from Kate's lamp.

"Maybe she's dead," he thought, and he went away. He went into the gravelly back yard. He sat down out there. His head ached and his back hurt.

He could see through a window into the kitchen. He didn't know how long it was, but he saw Kate in there.

He saw Wave. She wasn't dead.

"I didn't kill her, goddam it. I didn't kill her," he thought. He sat a long time, his head aching and his back hurting.

"I guess they're going to bed," he thought.

"I'll bet they ain't laughing or talking now," he thought.

He sat and sat and then he went to bed himself. He went upstairs through their room.

"I got to be quiet," he thought. That young Ben Hurd was in his room. "I'm glad I don't snore when I sleep," he thought. Ben Hurd's door was a little open and he went softly and silently and closed it. He got into bed. He saw the sky through a window in his room. He saw the stars. He wanted to cry, but he didn't. He just stayed still, looking at the stars and wishing his head would quit aching and his back quit hurting, until presently he heard his two daughters in their room downstairs.

They were laughing and talking. They talked in low tones and then they laughed. There was something incomprehensible. His head didn't quit aching and his back didn't quit hurting. They ached and they hurt worse than ever. He thought he wouldn't get any sleep.

"I'll bet I don't," he thought. "I'll be tired tomorrow." He thought of the men in the woods. He wished he was like George Russell, who'd had boys. Girls were something you couldn't understand.

The sound of the whispering continued. Girls were something you couldn't understand. There was something—it was hidden from you. How strange it was!

White Spot

I AM quite sure that some of the women I had during this period never became real to me. I do not even remember the names. They exist for me as a kind of fragrance as Ruth, Prudence, Genevieve, Nelly, et cetera, et cetera. There were the very brutal-looking, very sensual women seen one night in a low dive in Chicago. I would have been with certain businessmen on a spree. The businessmen were better when drunk. The shrewdness was gone. They became sometimes terrible, sometimes rather sweet children.

For example, there was Albert, short, fat, baby-faced. He was the president of a certain manufacturing company for which I wrote advertisements. We got drunk together.

He had a wife who was rather literary, and already I had published a few stories. Albert had bragged to her about me and once he took me to his house, in an Illinois town, to dine.

She would have talked only of books—as such women do talk. They can never by any chance be right about anything in the world of the arts. Better if they would keep still. They never do.

Albert being much pleased. "The little wife—you see, Sherwood. In our house also we have a high-brow." He was proud of her, wanted to be loyal. As woman, in bed with her man, she wouldn't have been much.

Albert knowing that and wanting in the flesh. He had got himself a little warm thing, bought her fur coats, sent her money. He could never go to her except when he had been drinking.

He explained to me, when we were drunk together. "I am faithful to my wife, Sherwood." He had his code. "To be sure, I sleep with my Mabel, but I have been faithful. I never kissed her on the lips." His reserving that as his own rock on which to stand. I thought it as good as most rocks upon which men stand.

But I was speaking of women—certain women, who touched me vitally in the flesh, left something with me. It's all very strange sometimes. I have just thought of that rather big, thick-lipped woman seen in a cheap restaurant, half dive, in South State Street. There was a little burlesque show a few doors up the street.

Businessmen, perhaps clients of the firm for which I worked, explaining to me. The president of our company would have been deacon in some suburban church.

"Take these men out and entertain them. You do not need to make an itemized account of expenses.

"I would not want company money spent for anything evil."

Oh, thou fraud!

I would have been blowing money. The burlesque women came down along a dirty alleyway from the stage door of the cheap show and into the restaurant, half dive. They may have got a percentage on the cost of the drinks bought for them.

And there was that big one, with the thick lips, sitting and staring at me. "I want you"—and myself wanting her. Now! Now!

The evil smell of the terrible little place. Street-women's pimps sitting about, the businessmen with me. One of them made a remark. "God, look at that one." She had one eye gone, torn out perhaps in a fight with some other woman over some man, and there was the scar from a cut on her low forehead.

Above the cut her shining blue-black hair, very thick, very beautiful. I wanted my hands in it.

She knew. She felt as I felt, but I was ashamed. I didn't want the businessmen with me to know.

What?

That I was a brute. That I was also gentle, modest, that I possessed also a subtle mind.

The women would have been going and coming in at a back door of the place, as the act they did, a kind of weird, almost naked dance before yokels, was due to be repeated. I went out into the alleyway and waited, and she came.

There were no preliminaries. Now or never. There were some boxes piled up and we got in behind them. What evil smells back in there. I got my two hands buried deep in her beautiful hair.

And afterward, her saying, when I asked her the question—Do you want money?—"A little," she said. Her voice was soft. There were drunken men going up and down. There was the loud rasping sound from a phonograph, playing over and over some dance tune in the burlesque place.

Can a man retain something? I had no feeling of anything unclean. She laughed softly—"Give me something, fifty cents. I don't like the foolish feeling of giving it away."

"O.K."

Myself hurrying back to the businessmen, not wanting them to suspect.

"You were a long time."

"Yes." I would have made up some quick lie.

That other one, met on a train, when the train was delayed because something went wrong with the engine. Is there a sense in which the rational man loves all women? The train stopping by a wood and that woman and I going into the wood to gather flowers.

Again. "Now. Now." "You will be gone." We may never meet again.

And then our coming back to the train. She going to sit with an older woman, perhaps her mother, taking her the flowers we had got.

It was Sally, the quiet one, who saw the white spot. It was in a room in a hotel in Chicago, one of that sort. You go in without baggage. You register . . . Mr. and Mrs. John Jones . . . Buffalo, New York. I remember a friend, who was a woman's man, telling me that he always used my name.

We were lying in there in the dark at night, in that rabbit warren of a place. For all I knew, the place was full of other such couples. We were in the half sleep that follows, lying in black darkness, a moment ago so close, now so far apart.

Sound of trains rattling along a nearby elevated railroad. This may have been on an election night. There was the sound of men cheering and a band played.

We are human, a male and a female. How lonely we are!

It may be that we only come close in art.

No. Wait.

There is something grown evil in men's minds about contacts.

How we want, want, want! How little we dare take!

It is very silent, here in the darkness. The sounds of the city, of life going on, city life, out there in the street.

A woman cry of animal gratification from a neighboring room.

We exist in infinite dirt, in infinite cleanliness.

Waters of life wash us.

The mind and fancy reaching out.

Now, for an hour, two, three hours, the puzzling lust of the flesh is gone. The mind, the fancy, is free.

It may have been that fancy, the always busy imagination of the artist-man, she wanted.

She began to talk softly of the white spot. "It floats in the darkness," she said softly, and I think I did understand, almost at once, her need . . .

After the flesh the spirit. Minds, fancy, draw close now.

It was a wavering white spot, like a tiny snow-white cloud in the darkness of a close little room in a Chicago bed-house.

You not wanting what our civilization has made of us.

It is you men, males, always making the world ugly.

You have made the dirt. It is you. It is you.

Yes. I understand.

But do you see the white spot?

Yes. It floats there, under the ceiling. Now it descends and floats along the floor.

It is the thing lost. It eludes us.

It belongs to us. It is our whiteness.

A moment of real closeness, with that strange thing to the male —a woman.

I had a thought I remember. It was a game I played with my brother Earl when I was a lad and he not much more than a babe. We slept together for a time and I invented a game. With our minds we stripped the walls of a room in a little yellow house quite away. We swept the ceiling of our room and the floors away. Our bed floated in space. Perhaps I had picked up a line from some poem. "We are between worlds. Earth is far, far beneath us. We float over Earth."

All this on a hot August night, but we could feel the coolness of outer space. I explained the game to the woman in the room and we played it, following on our floating bed the white drifting spot her fancy had found in that space.

How strange afterward, going down into the street. It might have been midnight, but the street was still crowded with people.

"And so we did float. We did see and follow the white spot and we are here. You make your living writing advertisements and I have a job in an office where they sell patent medicine.

"I am a woman of twenty-eight and unmarried. I live with my sister who is married."

The cheap little hotel run for such couples as we were had its office on the second floor. There was a little desk with a hotel register. What rows of Jones, Smiths, and, yes—Andersons. That friend of mine might have been in that place. He might have put my real name down there.

I would have gone down the stairs first, looked up and down the street. "O.K.," the pair of us dodging out. "You'd better take a taxi home. Let me pay."

"But can you? It is such a long way out. It will cost so much."

"Yes. Here."

Who was it invented money? There it lies, the dirty green bill in her hand. The taxi man looking, perhaps listening.

"But, but—does anything of beauty cling to me? Is it to be remembered?"

"Yes. You are very beautiful. Good night."

A lie. There was no beauty. The night, the street, the city, was the night, the street, the city.

A Walk in the Moonlight

THE DOCTOR told the story. He got very quiet, very serious, in speaking of it. I knew him well, knew his wife, his sons and his daughter. He said that I must know, of course, that in his practice he came into intimate contact with a good many women. We had been speaking of the relations of men and women. He had been living through an experience that must come to a great many men.

In the first place, I should say, in speaking of the doctor, that he is a rather large, very strong and very handsome man. He had always lived in the country where I knew him. He was a doctor, and his father had been a doctor in that country before him. I spent only one summer there, but we became great friends. I went with him in his car to visit his patients, living here and there over a wide countryside—valleys, hills, and plains. We were both fond of fishing, and there were good trout streams in that country.

And then, besides, there was something else we had in common. The doctor was a great reader, and, as with all true book-lovers, there were certain books, certain tales, he read over and over.

"Do you know," he said, laughing, "I one time thought seriously of trying to become a writer. I knew that Chekhov, the Russian, was a doctor; but I couldn't make it; found that when I took pen in hand I became dumb and self-conscious." He looked at me, smiling. He had steady gray eyes and a big head on which grew thick, curly hair, now turning a little gray.

"You see, we doctors find out a good many things." That, I of course knew. What writer does not envy these country doctors the opportunity they have to enter houses, hear stories, stand with people in times of trouble? Oh, the stories buried away in lonely farmhouses, in the houses of town people, of the rich, the well-to-do, the poor; tales of love, of sacrifice and of envy, hatred, too. There is, however, this consolation: The problem is never to find and know a little the people whose stories are interesting. There are too many stories. The great difficulty is to tell the stories.

"When I get my pen in hand, I become dumb." How foolish! After I had left, the country doctor used to write me long letters. He still does sometimes, but not often enough. The letters are wonderful, little stories of the doctor's moods on certain days as he drives about in the country, descriptions of days, of fall days and spring days— How full of true feeling the man is, what a deep and true culture he has—little tales of people, his patients. He has forgotten he is writing. The letters are like his talk.

But I must say something of the doctor's wife and of his daughter The daughter was a cripple, a victim of infantile paralysis, moving about with great difficulty. She would have been, but for this misfortune, very beautiful. She died some four years after the summer when her father and I were so much together. And there was the wife. Her name was, I remember, Martha.

I did not know well either the wife or the daughter. Sometimes there are such friendships formed between men. "Now you look here—I have a certain life, inside my own house. I have, let me say, a certain loyalty to that life, but it is not the whole of my life. It isn't that I don't want to share that intimate life with you, but—I am sure you will understand—we have chanced upon each other . . . You are in one field of work, and I in another."

There is a life that goes on between men, too—something almost like love can be born and grow steadily . . . (What an absurd word that—love!—it does not at all describe what I mean.)

Common experience, feelings a man sometimes has, his own kind of male flights of fancy, as it were—we men, you see . . . I wonder if it is peculiarly true of Americans . . . I often think so. We men here, I often think, depend too much upon women. It is due to our intense hunger, half shy, for each other.

I wonder if two men, in the whole history of man, were ever much together that they did not begin to speak presently of their experiences with women. I dare say that the same thing goes on between woman and woman. Not that the doctor ever spoke much of his wife. She was rather small and dark, a woman very beautiful in her own way—the way, I should say, of a good deal of suffering.

In the first place, the doctor, that man, so very male, virile, naturally quick and even affectionate in all his relation with people, and particularly with women, was a man needing more than one outlet for his feelings. He needed dozens. If he had let himself go in that direction, he could have had his office always full of women patients of the neurotic sort. There are that sort, plenty of them, on farms and in country towns as well as in the cities. He could not stand them. "I won't have it. I will not be that sort of doctor." They were the only sort of people he ever treated rudely. "Now you get out of here, and don't come back. There is nothing wrong with you that I can cure."

I knew, from little tales he told, of what a struggle it had been. Some of the women were very persistent, were determined not to be put off. It happened that his practice was in a hill country to which in the summer a good many city people came. There would be wives without husbands, the husbands coming from a distant city for the weekend or for a short vacation in the hot months. . . . Women with money, with husbands who had money. There was one such woman with a husband who was an insurance man in a city some two hundred miles away. I think he was president of the company, a small rather mouselike man, but with eyes that were like the eyes of a ferret, sharp, quick-moving little eyes, missing nothing. The woman, his wife, had money, plenty of it from him, and she had inherited money.

She wanted the doctor to come to the city. "You could be a great success. You could get rich." When he would not see her in his office, she wrote him letters and every day sent flowers for his office, to the office of a country doctor. "I don't mind selling her out to you," he said. "There are women and women." There were roses ordered for him from the city. They came in big boxes, and he used to throw them out of his office window and into an alleyway. "The whole town, including my wife, knew of it. You can't conceal anything of this sort in a small town. At any rate, my wife has a head. She knew well enough I was not to be caught by one of that sort."

He showed me a letter she had written him. It may sound fantastic, but she actually offered, in the letter, to place at his disposal a hundred thousand dollars. She said she did not feel disloyal to her husband in making the offer. It was her own money. She said she was sure he had in him the making of a great doctor. Her husband need know nothing at all of the transaction. She did not ask him to give himself to her, to be her lover. There was but one string to the offer, intended to give him the great opportunity, to move, let us say, to the city, set up offices in a fashionable quarter, become a doctor to rich women. He was to take her as a patient, see her daily.

"The hell!" he said. "I am in no way a student and never have been. By much practice I have become a fairly good country doctor. It is what I am."

"There is but one other thing I ask. If you are not to be my lover, you must promise that you will not become the lover of some other woman." He was, I gathered, to keep himself, as she said, "pure."

The doctor had very little money. His daughter was the only living child of his marriage. Two sons had been born, but they had both died in the outbreak of infantile paralysis that had crippled the daughter.

The daughter, then a young woman of seventeen, had to spend most of her life in a wheel chair. It was possible that, with plenty of money to send her off to some famous physician, perhaps to Europe—the woman in her letter suggested something of the sort—she might be cured.

"Oho!" The doctor was one of the men who throw money about, cannot save it, cannot accumulate. He was very careless about sending bills. His wife had undertaken that job, but there were many calls he did not report to her. He forgot them, often purposely.

"My husband need know nothing of all this."

"Is that so? What, that little ferret-eyed man? Why, he has never missed a money bet in his life."

The doctor took the letter to his wife, who read it and smiled. I have already said that his wife was in her own way beautiful. Her beauty was certainly not very obvious. She had been through too much, had been too badly hurt in the loss of her sons. She had grown thin and, in repose, there was a seeming hardness about her mouth and about her eyes, which were of a curious greenish gray. The great beauty of the doctor's wife only came to life when she smiled. There was then a curious, a quite wonderful transformation. "By this woman, hard or soft, hurt or unhurt, I will stand until I die. . . .

"It is not always, however, so easy," said the doctor. He spoke of something. We had gone for an afternoon's fishing and were sitting and resting on a flat rock under a small tree by a mountain brook. We had brought some beer packed in ice in a hamper. "It is not a story you may care to use." I have already said that the doctor is a great reader. "Nowadays, it seems that there is not much interest in human relations. Human relations are out of style. You must write now of the capitalists and of the proletariat. You must give things an economic slant. Hurrah for economics! Economics forever!"

I have spoken of his wife's smile. The doctor seldom smiled. He laughed heartily, with a great roar of laughter that could frighten the trout for a mile along a stream. His big body and his big head shook. He enjoyed his own laughter.

"And so it shall be an old-fashioned story of love, eh what?"

Another woman had come to him. It had all happened some two or three years before the summer when I knew him and when I spent so much time in his company. There was a well-to-do family, he said, that came into that country for the summer, and they had an only child, a daughter, crippled as was his own daughter. They were not, he said, extremely rich, but they had money enough, or at first he thought they had. He said that the father, the head of that family, was some sort of manufacturer.

"I never saw him but twice, and then we did not have much talk, although I think we liked each other. He let me know that he was very busy and I saw that he was a little worried. It was because things at his factory were not going so well.

"There was the man's wife and daughter and a servant, and

they had brought for the daughter a nurse. She was a very strong woman, a Pole. They engaged me to come on my regular rounds to their house. They had taken a house in the country, some three miles out of town. There were certain instructions from their city doctor. There was the wish to have within call a doctor, to be at hand in case of an emergency.

"And so I went there."

I have already spoken of sitting with the doctor at the end of an afternoon's fishing. Certain men and also women a man meets leave a deep impression. Moments and hours with such people as the doctor are always afterward remembered. There is something —shall I call it inner laughter? or, to speak in the terms of fighters, they can "take it." They have something; it may be knowledge, or better yet, maturity—surely a rare enough quality, that last, that maturity. You get the feeling from all sorts of people.

There is a little farmer who has worked for years. For no fault of his own—as everyone knows. Nature can be very whimsical and cruel—long droughts coming, corn withering, hail in the young crops, or sudden pests of insects coming, suddenly destroying all. And so everything goes. You imagine such a one struggling on into late middle life, trying to get money to educate his children, to give them a chance he did not have; a man not afraid of work, an upstanding, straight-going man.

And so all is gone. Let us think of him thus, say on a fall day. His little place, fields he has learned to love, as all real workers love the materials in which they work, to be sold over his head. You imagine him, the sun shining. He takes a walk alone over the fields.

His old wife, who has also worked as he has, with rough hands and careworn face—she is in the house, has been trying to brace him up. "Never mind, John. We'll make it yet." The children with solemn faces. The wife would really like to go alone into a room and cry. "We'll make it yet, eh?"

"The hell we will! Not us."

He says nothing of the sort. He walks across his fields, goes into a wood. He stands for a while there, perhaps at the edge of the wood, looking over the fields.

And then the laughter, down inside him—laughter not bitter. "It has happened to others. I am not alone in this. All over the world men are getting it in the neck as I am now—men are being forced into wars in which they do not believe. . . . There is a Jew, an upright man, cultured, a man of fine feeling, suddenly insulted in a hotel or in the street—the bitter necessity of standing and taking it . . . A Negro scholar spat upon by some ignorant white.

"Well, men, here we are. Life is like this.

"But I do not go back on life. I have learned to laugh, not loudly, boisterously, bitterly, because it happens that I, by some strange chance, have been picked upon by Fate. I laugh quietly.

"Why?

"Why, because I laugh."

There must be thousands of men and women—they may be the finest flowers of humanity—who will understand. It is the secret of America's veneration for Abraham Lincoln. He was that sort of man.

"And so," the doctor said, "I went to that house. There was the woman, the mother of the crippled girl, a very gentle-looking woman, in some odd way like my wife.

"There was the crippled girl herself, destined perhaps to spend her life in bed, or going laboriously about in a wheel chair. Would it not be wonderful to have some of these cocksure people explain the mystery of such things in the world? There is a job for your thinker, eh what?

"And then there was the woman, the Polish woman."

The doctor, with a queer smile, began to speak of something that often happens suddenly to men and women. He was a man at that time forty-seven years old, and the Polish woman—he never told me her name—might have been thirty. I have already said that the doctor was physically very strong, have tried to give the suggestion of a fine animal. There are men like that who are sometimes subject to very direct and powerful calls from women. The calls descend on them as storms descend on peaceful fields. It happened to him with the Polish woman the moment he saw her, and as it turned out, it also happened to her.

He said that she was in the room with the crippled girl when he went in. She was sitting in a chair near the bed. She arose and they faced each other. It all happened, I gather, at once.

"I am the doctor."

"Yes," she said. There was something slightly foreign in her pronunciation of even the one simple English word, a slight shade of something he thought colored the word, made it extraordinarily nice.

For a moment he just stood, looking at her as she did at him.

She was a rather large woman, strong in the shoulders, big-breasted, in every way, he said, physically full and rich. She had, he said, something very full and strong about her head. He spoke particularly of the upper part of her face, the way the eyes were set in the head, the broad white forehead, the shape of the head. "It is odd," he said, "now that she is gone, that I do not remember the lower part of her face." He began to speak of woman's beauty. "All this nonsense you writers write concerning beauty in women," he said. "You know yourself that the extraordinary beauty of my own wife is not in the color of her eyes, the shape of her mouth. . . . This rosebud-mouth business, Cupid's bow, eyes of blue, or, damn it, man, of red or pink or lavender for that matter!" I remember thinking, as the man talked, that he might have made a fine sculptor. He was emphasizing form, what he felt in the Polish woman as great beauty of line. "In my wife beauty comes at rare intervals, but then how glorious it is! It comes, as I think you may have noted, with her rare and significant smile."

He was standing in that room, with the little crippled girl and the Polish woman.

"For a time, I do not know how long, I couldn't move, could not take my eyes from her—

"My God, how crazy it now seems!" the doctor said.

"There she was. Voices I had never heard before were calling in me, and, as I later found out, in her also. The strangeness of it. 'Why, there you are. At last, at last, there you are.'

"You have to keep it all in mind," said the doctor, "my love of my wife, our suffering together over the loss of our two sons, our one child, one daughter, a cripple as you know.

"And there I was, you see, suddenly stricken like that—by love, ha! What does any sensible man know of this love?

"I did not know that woman, had never seen her until that moment, did not know her name. As it was with me, so, it turned out, it was with her. In some way I knew that. Afterward she told me, and I believed her, that as the Bible puts it, she had never known man.

"I stood there, you understand, looking at her and she at me." He spoke of all this happening, as he presently realized when with an effort he got himself in hand, in the presence of the little crippled girl in the bed. "It seemed to me that the woman was something I had all of my life been wanting with a kind of terrible force, you understand, with my entire being."

The doctor's mind went off at a tangent. The reader is not to think that he told me all this in a high, excited voice. Quite the contrary. His voice was very low and quiet, and I remember the scene before us as we sat on the flat rock above the mountain stream—we had driven a hundred miles to get to that stream—the soft hills in the distance beyond the stream, which just there went dashing down over the rocks, the deepening light over distant hills and distant forests. Later we got some very nice trout out of a pool below the rapids above which we sat.

It may have been the stream that sent him off into a side tale of a fishing trip, taken alone, on a moonlight night, in a very wild mountain stream, on the night after he had buried his second son; the strangeness of that night, himself wading in a rushing stream, feeling his way sometimes in half darkness, touches of moonlight on occasional pools, the casts made into such pools, often dark forests coming down to the stream's edge, the cast, and now and then the strike, himself standing in the swift running water.

Himself fighting, all that night, not to be overcome by the loss of the second and last of his sons, the utter strangeness of what seemed to him that night a perfectly primitive world. "As though," he said, "I had stepped off into a world never before known to man, untouched by any man."

And then the strike, perhaps of a fine big trout—the sudden sharp feeling of life out there at the end of a slender cord, running between it and him—the fight for life out there, and at the other end of the cord, in him.

The fight to save himself from despair.

Was it the same thing between him and the Polish woman? He said he did manage at last to free himself from the immediate thing.

He had a terrible week, a time of intense jealousy. "Would you believe it, it did not seem possible to me that any man could resist that woman," he said. He suspected the child's father. "That man, that manufacturer—he is her lover. It cannot be otherwise." The doctor laughed. "As for my wife, she was, for the time, utterly out of my life. I do not mean to say I did not respect her. What a word, eh, that respect! I told myself that I loved her. For the rest of the week I was in a muddle, could not remember what patients needed my services. I kept missing calls; and of course my wife, who, as I have told you, attends to all the details of my life, was disturbed.

"And, at that, she may well have been deeply aware. I do not think that people ever successfully lie to each other."

It was during that week he saw and talked briefly to the manufacturer from the city, the father of the crippled child, going there to that house, he said, hoping again to see the woman. He did not see her; and as for the man—"I had been having such silly suspicions. I wonder yet whether or not, at the time, I knew how silly they were.

"The manufacturer was a man in terrible trouble. Afterward I learned that at just that time his affairs were going to pieces. He stood to lose all he had gained by a lifetime of work. He was thinking of his wife and of his crippled daughter. He might have to begin life again, perhaps as a workman, with a workman's pay. His daughter would, perhaps, all her life be needing the care of physicians."

I gathered that the city man had tried to take the country doctor into his confidence. They had gone into the yard of the country house and had stood together, the doctor's heart beating heavily. "I am near her. She is there in the house. If I were a real man, I would go to her at once, tell her how I feel. In some way I know that this terrible hunger in me is in her also." The man, the manufacturer, was trying to tell him.

"Yes, yes, of course, it is all right."

There were certain words said. The man in trouble was trying to explain.

"Doctor, I shall be very grateful if you can feel that you can come here, that we can depend upon you. I am a stranger to you. It may be you will get no pay for your trouble."

"Aha! What, in God's name, could keep me away?"

He did not say the words. "It is all right. I understand. It is all right."

The doctor waited a few days; then he went again. He said he was asleep in his own house, or rather was lying in his bed. Of a sudden, he arose. To leave the house, he had to pass through his wife's room. "It is," he said, "a great mistake for a man and wife to give up sleeping together. There is something in the perfectly natural and healthy fact of being nightly so close physically to the other. It should not be given up." The doctor and his wife had, however, I gathered, given it up. He went through her room, and she was awake.

"It is you, Harry?" she asked.

Yes, it was he.

"And you are going out? I have not heard any call. I have been wide-awake."

It was a white moonlight night, just such a night as the one when he went in his desperation over the loss of his second son to wade in the mountain stream.

It was a moonlight night, and the moonlight was streaming into his wife's room and fell upon her face. It was one of the times when she was, for some perverse reason, most beautiful to him.

"And I had got out of bed to go to that woman, had thought out a plan."

He would go to that house, would arouse and speak to the mistress of the house. "There has been an accident. I need a nurse for the night. There is no one available."

He would get the Polish woman into his car.

"I was sure—I don't know why—that she felt as I did. As I had been lying so profoundly disturbed in my bed, so she in her bed had been lying."

She was almost a stranger to him. "She wants me. I know she does."

He had got into his wife's room. "Well, you see, when at night I had to go out to answer a call, it was my custom to go to my wife, to kiss her before I left. It was a simple enough thing. I could not do it.

"I knew that the Polish woman was waiting for me. I will take her into my car. We will turn into a wood, and there, in the moonlight . . .

"A man cannot help what he is. After this one time, it may be that things will get clear."

He was hurrying thus through his wife's room.

"No, my dear, I have had no call.

"A feeling has come to me," he said. "It is that girl, the crippled one, crippled as is Katie, our daughter. I have told you of her. It is, my dear, as though a voice has been calling me.

"(And what a lie, what a terrible lie!)

"All right. I accepted that. There was a voice calling to me. It was the voice of that strange woman, the woman I scarcely knew, who had never spoken but the one word to me."

The doctor was hurrying through his wife's room. There was a stairway that led directly down out of the room. His crippled daughter slept in another room on the same floor; and a servant, a colored woman who had been in the household for years, slept in the daughter's room on a cot. The doctor had got through his wife's room and was on the stairs when his wife spoke to him.

"But Harry!" she said. "You have forgotten something. you have not kissed me."

"Why, of course," he said. His feet were on the stairs, but he came back up into her room. She was lying there, wide-awake. "I am going to that woman. I do not know what will happen. I must, I must.

"It may all end in some sort of scandal, I do not know, but I cannot help doing what I am about to do. There are times when a man is in the grip of forces stronger than himself.

"What is this thing about women, about men? Why does all of this thing, this force, so powerful, so little understood, why with the male does it all become suddenly directed upon one woman and not upon another?

"There is this force, so powerful. I have suddenly, at forty-seven, a man established in life, fallen into its grip. I am powerless.

"There is this woman, my wife, in bed here, in this room. The moonlight is falling upon her upturned face. How beautiful she is! I do not want her, do not want to kiss her. She is looking up expectantly at me." The doctor was by his wife's bed. He leaned over her.

"I am going to this woman. I am going. I am going."

He was leaning over his wife, about to kiss her, but suddenly he turned away. His wife's name is Martha.

"Martha," he said, "I cannot explain. This is a strange night for me. I will, perhaps, explain it all later."

"Wait. Wait."

He was hurrying away from her down the stairs. He got into his car. He went to that house. He got the woman, the Polish woman. "When I explained to her, she was quite willing." He thought afterward that she had been on the whole rather fine, telling him quite plainly that as he had felt when he saw her, so she also had felt.

She was definite enough. "I am not a weak woman. Although I am thirty, I am still a virgin. However, I am in no way virginal."

She had been, the doctor said, half a mystic, saying that she had always known that the man who would answer some powerful call in her would some day come. "He has come. It is you."

They went to walk. She told him that since she had first seen him, she had made some inquiries. She had found out about the loss of his two sons, about his crippled daughter, about his wife.

All this, the doctor explained, as, having left his car by the roadside, they walked in country roads. It was a very beautiful night, and they had got into a road lined with trees. There were splashes of moonlight falling down through the leaves in the road before them as they walked, not, as it turned out, ever touching each other. Sometimes they stopped and stood silent for a long time. He said that, several times, he put out his hand to touch her, but each time he drew it back.

"Why?"

It was the doctor himself who asked the question. He tried to explain. "There she was. She was mine to possess." He said that he thought she was to him the most beautiful woman he had ever known or ever would know.

"But that is not true," he said. "It is both true and untrue.

"It may be that if I had touched her, even with my finger-ends, there would have been quite a different story to tell. She was beautiful, with her own beauty, so appealing, so very appealing to me; but there was also, at home—lying as I knew, awake in her bed—my wife."

He said that in the end, after he had been with the Polish woman for perhaps an hour, she understood. He thought she must have been extremely intelligent. They had stopped in the road and she turned to him; and again, as in the room with the cripple, there was a long silence. "You are not going to make love to me," she said. "I have never wanted love until I saw you. I am a woman of thirty, and it may be that now I never shall have love."

The doctor said he did not answer. "I couldn't," he explained. What was to be said? He thought that it was the great moment of his life. He used the word I have also used in speaking of him. "I think, a little, I have been, since that moment, a mature man."

The doctor had stopped talking, but I could not resist questioning him.

"And you ended by not touching her?" I asked.

"Yes. I took her back to her place, and when I next went there to see the crippled girl, she was gone and another woman had taken her place."

There was another time of silence. "After all," I thought, "this man has, from his own impulse, told me this tale. I have not asked for it."

"There is a question I think now that I may dare ask," I ventured. "Your wife?"

There was that laugh that I so liked. It is my theory that it can come only from the men and women who have got their maturity.

"I returned to her. I gave her the kiss I had denied earlier that night."

I was, of course, not satisfied.

"But—" I said.

Again the laugh.

"If I had not wanted to tell you, I should not have begun this tale," he said. We got up from the flat stone on which we had been sitting and prepared for the great moment of trout fishing, as every trout fisherman knows the quivering time, so short a time between the last of the day and the beginning of the night. The doctor preceded me down across a flat sloping rock to the pool, where we each got two fine trout. "I was in love with my wife as I had never really been with the Polish woman, and in the same way. Not the troubles we had shared, all we had gone through together, not scruples of conscience—I was in love with my wife in a way that I never had been until after that walk in the moonlight with another woman."

The doctor stopped talking, but did not look at me. He was selecting a fly.

"When I returned to her that night and when I kissed her, she, for a moment, held my face in her hands. She said something.'We have been through it again, haven't we?' she said. She took her hands away and turned her face from me. 'I have been thinking for the last week or two that we had lost each other,' she said. 'I do not know why,' she added, and then she laughed. It was the nicest laugh I ever heard from her lips. It seemed to come from so far down inside. I guess all men and women who have got something know that it might be easily lost," the doctor said, as he finished his tale. He had hooked a trout, and was absorbed in playing his fish.

His Chest of Drawers

We worked in the same advertising office for several years, both copy men, our desks beside each other, and from time to time he confided in me, telling me many little secrets of his life. He was a small, very slender and delicately built man who couldn't have weighed over a hundred and twenty pounds, and he had very small hands and feet, a little black mustache, a mass of blue-black hair, and a narrow chest. That was one of his difficulties and he frequently spoke of it.

"Look at me," he said. "How can I ever get on in business? How can I ever rise?"

Saying this, he arose and walked over to my desk. He slapped himself on the chest.

"I want space and spread there," he said. "The world is full of stuffed shirts, and what chance have I? I have no place to wear a shirt front."

Although he was a man of Spanish descent, with much of the sensitivity and the pride of the Spaniard, my friend's name was Bill. When I first knew him, he had been married for several years and he was the father of four children, all girls. He spoke of this occasionally. "It's a little tough," he said. He was a devout Catholic and once confided to me it had been his ambition to be a priest. "I wanted to be a Jesuit priest," he said, "but I got married."

"Not," he added, "that I would have you think I have anything against my wife." He thought that we men should honor women.

"You look at me now. I know well enough that I am insignificant-looking. A woman marries such a man as myself. She bestows her favors upon him. He would be an ungrateful man if he complained, but, you take the life of a priest now, he cannot marry, you see. He can be small or he can be large. He is respected by his people."

With Bill it was as it was with all of us who were writers of advertising copy. There were other men, also employed by the advertising agency which employed us, who were called "solicitors." Nowadays I believe they are called "contact men." These men, having to bring in clients, keep them satisfied, convince them that we who wrote their copy were men of talent, quite extraordinary men, had, of course, to put up a front. They were provided with private offices, often expensively furnished; they arrived and departed, seemingly at will, did not have to ring time clocks, went off for long afternoons of golf with some client, while we copy men, herded together as we were in one room, away at the back, a room that looked out upon a lofty building through the windows of which we could see rows of women sewing busily away, making men's pants, felt all the time that we were the ones who kept the whole institution going. We kept speaking of it to each other.

"We furnish the brains, don't we? If we don't, who does?"

"Surely it isn't these other guys, these stuffed shirts, out there in front," we said.

In our agency, as in all such institutions, there was an occasional flurry. One or another of us in the copy department had prepared for some advertiser a series of advertisements that were taken by one of the salesmen to the client. He dismissed them with a wave of his hand.

"They are no good," he said, and when this happened, we copy men burned with inner anger.

"I guess the guy's got indigestion," we said. As for our own work, or the work of others in our department, we never spoke ill of that. The man, the client, simply didn't know good work when he saw it.

Or it was the fault of the salesman, the contact man. It was his business to sell our work. If he couldn't do that, what good was he? Why was he provided with a private office, why permitted to lead a life of leisure, while we, poor slaves that we were, had to do all the work?

We used to get ourselves all heated up over these things, and occasionally, when we thought that it had got too thick, one or another of us went off on a binge. It was a thing to be expected and for the most part it was overlooked; but once, when it had happened to Bill, at a time when a client whose work he had long been doing had suddenly appeared in the city and it was felt that he was badly needed, I was sent to look for him and if possible to straighten him out. It was understood that the client could be stalled overnight.

"You find him and sober him up. You get him in here," they said to me.

And so I went to find Bill, and knowing something of his habits, I did find him. He was in a certain saloon, run by a brother Spaniard, and when I found him he was leaning against a bar, a group of men for whom he was buying drinks gathered around, and he was delivering a talk on the position of small men in a civilization that, as he said, judged everything by size.

I had got Bill out of the place and we were in a Turkish bath and he was in a solemn mood.

"You think you know the reason why I got drunk, but you don't," he said. He began to explain. He said that this time his getting drunk had nothing to do with affairs at the office.

"There is a greater tragedy in my life," he said. We were in the hot room in the bath and as the sweat ran in streams from our bodies he explained that, while his size—his inability, as he had often said, to wear a big shirt front—had, as I well knew, been a handicap to his business; I had perhaps not known that the same handicap had operated against him in his home.

"It's true," he said, shaking his head solemnly. "You see, my house is overrun with females." He explained that, being unable because of his handicaps to make a big salary, he was compelled to live in a small house in a certain suburb.

"You know," he said, "that I have a wife and four daughters." His daughters were rapidly growing up. "I have given up having a son," he said, and went into a long explanation of how, his house being small and the closet space therefore somewhat limited, he had been compelled—he had thought it the only decent thing to do—to cut down on his wardrobe.

"What's the use of buying clothes to put on a little runt like me?" he asked, and added that, as his daughters were growing up, he had needed all the money he could spare to buy clothes for them. "I guess they've got to get husbands. I've got to give them a break."

He explained that in following out this policy, he had gradually given up using any closet space in his house, and that for two or three years he had confined himself, in this matter of space in which to put his clothes, to a certain chest of drawers, and as he talked on, becoming all the time more earnest, I came to understand that the chest of drawers had become a kind of symbol to him.

It had come to the point where the chest of drawers had begun to mean everything in the world to him. He was sure I couldn't understand and said that no man, not put in the position he was in, living as he did in a house with five females—all of whom he declared he profoundly respected—could ever understand.

It had gone on so in his house for several years, but some several weeks before, his eldest daughter had become engaged. She had been getting a wardrobe together and one day, when he came home, he had found the top drawer to his chest of drawers gone.

He had stood for that. "I guess the girl has to have clothes," he said. He hadn't even complained.

And then, two days before, his wife's mother had come on a visit and he had lost the second drawer in his chest.

"It was a hard dose to swallow, but I swallowed it," he said.

His wife, who he kept declaring was a good woman ("I don't want you to think I am criticizing her," he said) had been, he presumed, doing the best she could. She had taken his things—his shirts, underwear, except what he needed from day to day—and had put them in a box. "She put it under the bed," he said, and added that, on the evening when he had gone home and had found the second drawer to the chest gone, he hadn't said a word.

"I didn't say a word, but when we were at dinner that evening and I was trying to take a boiled potato out of a dish, to put it on my wife's mother's plate, I was so wrought up and my hand trembled so that, when I had it nicely balanced on a fork and was just going to put it on her plate, it fell off into a bowl of gravy."

He had gone home and to his chest of drawers, to the last drawer of new dresses.

It made his wife sore because she thought he had been drinking when he hadn't at all.

And then it had come to the evening before. A sister of his wife had come. He thought the women had become excited because his eldest daughter had become engaged. They were gathering in—"I guess to look at the guy," he said.

He had gone home and to his chest of drawers, to the last drawer of his chest of drawers, and it was gone.

"But no," he said; "I want to be fair. It wasn't all gone."

His wife had left him half of the last drawer. He thought his wife had done the best she could; she should, he thought, have married a salesman, not a little runt of a copy man, such as he was.

"I think we ought to treat our women with respect," he said.

"After all," he said, "they do bestow their favors upon us.

"I just looked at the drawer a moment and then I came away. I took a train back to town, I got drunk. Why not?" he asked.

He thought that sometimes, when a man was drunk, he could get temporarily the illusion that he cut some figure in life.

Not Sixteen

SHE KEPT insisting on it. She whispered it in the barn at night, after the day in the cornfield. Her father was milking a cow. John could hear the milk strike against the side of the pail. When the sound stopped, they had to dodge into an empty horse stall.

He was pressing her body against a board wall. She was limp, relaxed in his arms. Was he in love? He didn't know. He thought he was.

There had been moments during the weeks he was there on her father's farm, working there—he was helping with the fall corn cutting—when he had wanted her to marry him. He spoke of it.

"Shall we get married?" he asked.

"No," she said. "I am not sixteen."

"Well," he said.

"No, and not that either," she said. "Not yet," she said. "I am not sixteen."

He thought about it at night in bed.

"It would be too stupid to get married now," he thought. He had no money and he didn't want to go on, perhaps all of his life, being a farmhand.

She had a baffling attitude about it all. They had spoken of it, John pressing the question.

"Let's," he said.

"There won't nobody know," he said.

"Let's! Just once! Let's!" he pleaded.

He talked and talked, exaggerated his suffering, his pain, his sleeplessness. He threatened to go away.

"Please don't," she said. "You stay here. It won't be long. I'll be sixteen in a year."

She kept insisting. She was slender, with bright red spots on her pale cheeks. Her mouth was inviting, her eyes were inviting.

She was curiously frank, had not been shocked by John's words, when he began to plead with her. She knew what he meant.

She came down into the field to work with John and her father.

John had got the job on the farm. It was in the fall, after the spring when he came home from the First World War.

"I'll work," he had thought. "I'll take any job I can get, for say another year. I'll save my money." He had brought some money home from the war—had hidden it away. It wasn't much.

The war, the traveling about, the seeing strange places, mountains, the sea, the being in a foreign land—all of these things had made him restless. He didn't know what he wanted.

"I want her, but I don't want to settle down, not yet."

He had come home to his Michigan town with other soldiers, and there had been parades. There had been a banquet in the town hall. He and the other soldiers had been called heroes again. He thought it was the bunk. He had been lucky, hadn't been in any battles. He was only nineteen, and that girl Lillian, on the farm, was only fifteen. When he came home from the war and was called a hero, he spoke to other men who had been soldiers.

"All this talk. It's bushwa," he said.

"They are handing us the lousy bunk," he said.

There was no work to be had. When he had gone off to war, he had chucked a job. That was in Detroit in an automobile plant. He didn't want to go back. He had been on the line in the plant.

The job had got his goat. He said so. "This here bunk," he said. "I didn't go to be no hero. The job had got me. I didn't sleep good at night.

"All right," he said. "I'll go take a look." He thought he would go on the bum for a time. There was an old man in the Michigan town who had a deformed hip. The Michigan town was near the larger town, Kalamazoo, where grand-circuit trotting meetings are held and the old man had been a race-horse driver. Now he owned a garage, but he still kept two or three good ones. He had been thrown from a sulky during a race and his hip had been broken. It had never been properly mended. He walked in a curious way, swinging his body from side to side.

He stopped John in a street. Before the war and before John

went away to Detroit, he had worked for the man, whose name was Yardley. It was when John was sixteen. He had been a swipe. He had got the race-horse bug.

"If you want to work for me again, you can," the man said.

He said that he already had two men in his barn.

"I don't need another one, not now, not till the races begin, but if you want to come, you can.

"I can't pay you anything. You can take care of What Chance," he said.

What Chance was a trotter. He was a bay gelding, a three-year-old. He was fast.

"You take care of him this winter and jog him on the roads. It won't be much work. I can't pay you anything, but you can come up and live at my house. You can sleep there, get your meals there."

The man Yardley said he was making John the offer because he admired the boys who had the guts to go out and fight for their country. They walked over to the barn, the man Yardley swaying along behind John. He was chewing tobacco. He kept spitting. They went into the box stall to the horse.

It had been a temptation to John. He went to caress the horse. He ran his hand along his back and down his legs. "He's a good one," he thought.

He thought of the drifting from town to town. In time he might become a driver. It was an old dream come back. Yardley would be doing the half-mile tracks. With a good one like What Chance they might clean up.

John had a little money. He'd be on the inside. He could lay some bets.

He thought of nights in strange towns with the other swipes. There'd be drinking, there'd be some whoring done. He stood looking at the horse.

"Naw," he thought, "I got to cut that out."

"These race-horse men," he thought, "where do they ever get?"

"I'll see. I'll let you know," he said to Yardley. He took a walk.

"I can't," he told himself. He had brought a little money home from the war. When he had been a kid around the tracks, he had learned to juggle dice. He had got into crap games in the camp, in France, on the boats, going and coming.

He wanted to go with Yardley, but he felt guilty. There was his sister. John's mother was dead and his sister was running the house.

His father was out of work, and John's sister, three years older than John, was wanting to get John's two younger brothers through school.

"I ought to tell her about the money, give it to her," he thought.

"I can't," he thought.

It seemed to him that if he gave up the money he had won at craps, he would be sunk.

"If I could go to school now, just for two or three years," he thought.

He could maybe get into business, become a prosperous man. John had a picture in mind, of himself, a man risen in the world, money in pocket, good clothes to wear.

"If I can pull it off I can do ten times as much for the kids," he thought.

It seemed to him that everything depended upon his getting an education. "If I don't do it now I'm gone." If he did not get an education he would remain as he was—sunk, a worker, a man going through life with his feet in the mud.

There was a ladder up which you climbed. Education was the thing that did it.

"O.K.," John had said to himself. "But I'll give up going to school this year. I'll give up what I want to be, a horseman." John had been through grade school. He had an idea that presently he would take the money put secretly away, and would go somewhere, perhaps to a business college.

There was a young man he knew who was going to dental college. John thought he might do that. There was another who was away from home at a school where you learned to fix watches.

"That might be better," he thought.

You begin by repairing watches. You save your money. Then presently you own a store where jewelry is sold. You sell rings and watches. You dress well. Very likely you marry—say now, a rich girl.

It might be that her father would be the one that would set you up in your own business. When you had such a business of your own, you could, if you chose, own some horses of your own.

So you get a clerk to take care of your store. You go away to the races. You drive your own horses.

John had got on a freight train at night and had begun beating his way from town to town, looking for work. He thought he would earn some money and send it home. Pretty soon what little money he had in his pockets was gone, and he had to take what he could get. He had got down into Ohio, was in a town in Ohio. He had hired out to the farmer. He was cutting corn. It was a new kind of work for John. He thought it was a pretty hard job, but he could stand it all right.

Her name was Lillian, and her father and mother were old. They seemed old to John. The man, her father, was a renter. Once he had owned a farm of his own, but, he told John, he had had hard luck and had lost it.

His wife was a small woman, with bright eyes, like Lillian's, John thought.

The mother had a curiously bent back. "They must have been married a long time," he thought. He was always doing things like that, wondering about people, thinking of them. "I wonder if, when you get old and live with your wife, you have any fun," he thought. There had been four children, three of them grown now, and all married except Lillian. The others were gone. Lillian told John about it all when she came down into the field where he was cutting corn.

She got him at once. "Oh, Lord, she's got me," he thought. She was small, but she could cut corn like a man. She was shy, and at the same time bold. She looked weak, but she was strong. The work was new to John and she kept showing him how. There was a certain swing you got. You learned to ease yourself.

You have to cut the tall corn and carry it to the shock. You hold it in one arm and swing the knife with the other. There is a way you handle your body, easing it to the load. When you know how, it's twice as easy. She showed John how.

They talked and talked. When her father was with them, working with them, they worked in silence, he continually looking at her and she at him, but when her father had gone, to the barn or the house, they talked. It was was something new to John. He talked and talked. He looked at her. "I wonder whether she will," he thought.

"She doesn't seem so young," he thought. Right away he knew she liked to be with him.

They talked at night. There were moonlight nights.

"Come. Let's go and work awhile," she said. It wasn't in the agreement that John was to work at night, but he went. He was glad to go.

Her father, the farmer, did not come at night. He said he was tired. He said he was getting too old. She told John of a sister who was married and lived with her husband, a railroad brakeman in another town. The sister had been fifteen years old before Lillian was born. "She got married when she was fifteen, but I am not going to," she said. John wanted to ask whether it was a shot-gun marriage. He didn't.

"How do you reckon I came to come so late?" she asked. She asked John that and laughed.

"I'd 'a' thought they'd got so old they couldn't," she said.

She kept saying bold things to John.

When they were working together thus, in the evening, in the cornfield, in the moonlight, they kept talking. She didn't seem young to John. "It may be because she came so late," he thought. He thought she had a figure, nice, like a woman's. She seemed curiously old for her years.

They were at work in a big field and there was the part of the field where the corn was already cut. They could look across the open place. There were the shocks of corn they had cut, standing out there. There were yellow pumpkins on the ground. Beyond the open place where the corn shocks stood, there was a wood. There was a strange feeling, John had, as though he were alone with her in a place where no man had ever been before. "Like maybe in the Garden of Eden," he thought. Out there in the field with her, like that, at night, quite far from the farmhouse, there were always strange sounds and sometimes there was a wind. The leaves were turning on the trees in the wood. They were falling. The wind made them race across the open place. They seemed like little living things, running along. "I wonder why they let her come," he thought. He thought maybe they wanted to get her married. "Then maybe I'd have to stay here and work for them, for nothing, like with Yardley," he thought. She had told him about her sister. "I'll bet that's the way she got that brakeman," he thought.

He talked to her of the leaves, running along the ground. "Look," he said. The shocked corn standing in the open place made him think of his life in the army. They could look off across the open place, where the corn was cut, to other fields on other farms. It was a flat country. They could see other corn already cut and in its shocks in other fields.

John kept talking to her. He never talked so before. He spoke of the shocks standing in the moonlight. They were like armies of soldiers standing, he said. He grew bolder as he talked. He couldn't touch her, until he began to talk and then he could.

They didn't cut much corn that night. He went to her and put an arm about her shoulders. He was quite tall and she was short. Standing thus, he could say things about the dry leaves running along the ground and the little sounds they made. He could pretend there was another world, besides the one they lived in, a world of little living things, men and women like themselves, but small, he said. "No bigger than that," he said. He put his thumb at the first joint of a finger. He began inventing. He told her that the little people lived, in the daytime, in the wood, that they hid there.

"Now see, they've come out to play," he said.

"They are men and women like us," he said, "but they don't get married." Two dry leaves went skipping along. "Look," he said. They stood in silence.

They quit working and went to stand by the fence. He had an arm about her. He made her put her head down on his shoulder. It could just reach. Their corn knives fell on the ground.

He talked and talked. He told her about his life in the army, about things he'd seen.

Then he told her about a girl he'd been with once. "It was when I was younger than you are," he said. He said it was a little town girl. "It was when I was at the races. A man older than me, who worked with our outfit, got me a girl." He said that she with another one had come at night to a fairground where they were. The man had given one of the girls to John to go with him into an empty horse stall.

He told of it and how he felt, how he couldn't speak to the girl, how excited he was. 'It was my first,' he said. A quiver ran through her body and he held her close.

He went on talking, holding her, not feeling at all as he had with the girl in the horse stall.

"I was afraid of her, but I'm not of you," he said.

"Was it nice?" she asked, and he said it was.

She was like that. She seemed to come right up to him, with her mind, with all of herself, not afraid or ashamed.

"I'm going to when I'm sixteen," she said.

"I won't wait any longer," she said.

It had begun between them and it went on. It was in the moonlight, when they were in the cornfield at night. It was in the barn.

It was upstairs, in the house, at night. He went up to her. He went up in his bare feet. Her father snored and her mother snored. He waited until he heard it, and then he went up to her.

She had a room up there.

Her father and mother were asleep downstairs. She said it would be all right for him to come. He had been given a room downstairs. "You come up. I want you to," she said.

It seemed to John that he was near to being insane. He was very strong. Now the work didn't tire him at all.

"I'll ask her to marry me," he thought.

Then he thought, "No. I won't," but he did, and she laughed. "No. We won't do that," she said. He was glad, because her people were poor. They were too much like his own people, he thought. He kept thinking that, if they got married, he couldn't ever go to school and rise in the world.

He did not speak to her of that. When he wasn't with her, alone with her, he got half frantic, but when he was with her, in the barn —while her father was milking—holding her tight, or in the field, or when he went up to her at night, he got strangely quiet.

She had fixed a blanket on the floor by her bed. She said he could lie there for a time. "There's no harm in that," she said. She said that if there was, she didn't care. She would be lying on the edge of her bed. The bed was low. She leaned down. She had hard little hands.

"You talk," she said, and sometimes he did.

"Like out there, with the leaves running like that," she said.

He would lie thus and whisper to her and sometimes she would lean down and they'd kiss. He wanted to pull her down, make her come to him, struggle with her until she surrendered, but for some obscure reason he didn't.

He talked and talked. He had never talked so before. When he was talking, he could not tell what, of all he told her, was real and what invented.

Sometimes he'd beg her, growing a little frantic, but she could quiet him.

"I can't. I'm not sixteen," she said.

She said it would be almost a year before she could. She laughed softly.

"You can stay and wait or you can go away and come back," she said.

"If you go away and you're not here on time—" She laughed.

She had a laugh that made him grow quiet. There was something in her, he thought, like a wall. "There's no use pounding against a wall," he thought. At times, on some nights when he had crept up there and had talked for a long time, he grew suddenly sad. Tears came to his eyes.

"Please, please," he said.

"Be quiet," she said.

"When I am sixteen," she said.

She kept saying it. It was like a song in his head. He had to give it up. He stood it as long as he could, and then he ran away. He had come down from her room. It was on one of the moonlight nights and cold. He'd been lying up there on the blanket by her bed.

"When I'm sixteen.

"When I'm sixteen."

He was a young man and a year seemed infinitely long. If he could have been with her all the time, day and night, near her, he thought he could have stood it.

He came down to his own room at night and suddenly knew.

"It's because I'm not like her," he thought.

"She can wait and I can't."

He dressed and slipped silently out of the house. He walked a moonlit road.

There was something in her as strong as iron, but it wasn't in him. Her father owed him some money he never got, but he didn't care. When he had got into the road, he was suddenly proud. "I have controlled myself," he thought. He began to walk proudly along.

"After all, she is not sixteen," he thought.

Partial Bibliography

SHERWOOD ANDERSON: 1876-1941

Windy McPherson's Son	1916
Marching Men	1917
Mid-American Chants	1918
Winesburg, Ohio	1919
Poor White	1920
The Triumph of the Egg	1921
Many Marriages	1923
Horses and Men	1923
A Story Teller's Story	1924
Dark Laughter	1925
Tar, a Midwest Childhood	1926
Sherwood Anderson's Notebook	1926
A New Testament	1927
Hello Towns!	1929
Alice, and the Lost Novel	1929
The American County Fair	1930
Perhaps Women	1931
Beyond Desire	1932
Death in the Woods	1933
No Swank	1934
Puzzled America	1935
Kit Brandon, A Portrait	1936
Home Town	1940
Sherwood Anderson's Memoirs	1942
The Sherwood Anderson Reader edited by Paul Rosenfeld	1947
Letters of Sherwood Anderson edited by Howard Mumford Jones with Walter B. Rideout	1953

AMERICAN CENTURY SERIES

Distinguished paperback books in the fields of literature and history, covering the entire span of American culture.

AC 1 *The Hoosier School-Master* by Edward Eggleston
S 2 *The Magnificent Ambersons* by Booth Tarkington
S 3 *The Harbor* by Ernest Poole
S 4 *Sister Carrie* by Theodore Dreiser
S 5 *The Flush Times of Alabama and Mississippi* by Joseph Baldwin
S 6 *Ivory, Apes, and Peacocks* by James Gibbons Huneker
S 7 *The Higher Learning in America* by Thorstein Veblen
AC 8 *The Shame of the Cities* by Lincoln Steffens
S 9 *Company K* by William March
AC 10 *The Influence of Seapower upon History* by Alfred T. Mahan
S 11 *A Daughter of the Middle Border* by Hamlin Garland
S 12 *How the Other Half Lives* by Jacob Riis
S 13 *His Fifty Years of Exile (Israel Potter)* by Herman Melville
AC 14 *Barren Ground* by Ellen Glasgow
S 15 *Hospital Sketches* by Louisa May Alcott
S 16 *A Traveler from Altruria* by William Dean Howells
AC 17 *The Devil's Dictionary* by Ambrose Bierce
S 18 *Moon-Calf* by Floyd Dell
S 19 *The Big Rock Candy Mountain* by Wallace Stegner
S 20 *The Octopus* by Frank Norris
AC 21 *Life on the Mississippi* by Mark Twain
S 22 *Troubadour* by Alfred Kreymborg
S 23 *The Iron Heel* by Jack London
S 24 *Georgia Scenes* by A. B. Longstreet
S 25 *The Grandissimes* by George W. Cable
S 26 *The Autocrat of the Breakfast Table* by Oliver Wendell Holmes
AC 27 *The Neon Wilderness* by Nelson Algren
AC 28 *The Jeffersonian Tradition in American Democracy* by Charles Wiltse
AC 29 *The Narrative of Arthur Gordon Pym* by Edgar Allan Poe
AC 30 *A Connecticut Yankee in King Arthur's Court* by Mark Twain
AC 31 *Theodore Roosevelt and the Progressive Movement* by George E. Mowry

AC 32 *The Autobiography of an Ex-Coloured Man* by James Weldon Johnson

AC 33 *Jack London: Short Stories*

AC 34 *Jefferson* by Albert Jay Nock

AC 35 *America Goes to War* by Bruce Catton

AC 36 *Hemingway and His Critics: An International Anthology* edited and with an introduction by Carlos Baker

AC 37 *Stars Fell on Alabama* by Carl Carmer

AC 38 *Writers in Crisis: The American Novel, 1925-1940* by Maxwell Geismar

AC 39 *The Best of Simple* by Langston Hughes

AC 40 *American Social Thought* edited by Ray Ginger

ACW 41 *William Dean Howells* edited by Rudolf and Clara Marburg Kirk

ACW 42 *Walt Whitman* edited by Floyd Stovall

ACW 43 *Thomas Paine* edited by Harry Hayden Clark

AC 44 *The Last of the Provincials: The American Novel, 1915-1925* by Maxwell Geismar

AC 45 *American Moderns: From Rebellion to Conformity* by Maxwell Geismar

ACW 46 *Edgar Allan Poe* edited by Hardin Craig and Margaret Alterton

ACW 47 *Jonathan Edwards* edited by Clarence H. Faust and Thomas H. Johnson

ACW 48 *Benjamin Franklin* edited by Frank Luther Mott and Chester E. Jorgenson

AC 49 *Indian Tales* by Jaime de Angulo

AC 50 *A Time of Harvest* edited by Robert E. Spiller

AC 51 *The Limits of Language* edited by Walker Gibson

AC 52 *Sherwood Anderson: Short Stories* edited and with an Introduction by Maxwell Geismar

AC 53 *The World of Lincoln Steffens* edited by Ella Winter and Herbert Shapiro, with an Introduction by Barrows Dunham

AC 54 *Mark Twain and the Damned Human Race* edited and with an Introduction by Janet Smith

AC 55 *The Happy Critic and Other Essays* by Mark Van Doren

AC 56 *Man Against Myth* by Barrows Dunham

H 13 *Mark Twain and the Russians: An Exchange of Views* by Charles Neider